Karolinum Press

Ján Rozner (1922–2006) was a leading Slovak literary, theatre and film critic, journalist and translator from German and English. Following the Soviet-led invasion of Czechoslovakia in August 1968 Rozner and his wife Zora Jesenská (1909–1972), an eminent translator of Russian literature, both active proponents of the Prague Spring, were blacklisted and lost their jobs. When Jesenská died of cancer, her funeral turned into a political event and everyone attending it faced recriminations. *Seven Days to the Funeral*, Rozner's lightly fictionalised account of the days leading up to his wife's funeral, is both a significant chronicle of Slovak history under communism and a writer's deeply personal coming to terms with himself. His two other books, *Noc po fronte* (The Night after the Front, 2010) and *Výlet na Devín* (An Outing to Devín Castle, 2011) explore a similar intertwining of the personal and historical while closely scrutinising the nature of memory. In 1976 Ján Rozner emigrated to Germany with his second wife Sláva, a doctor. They lived first in Stuttgart and then in Munich, where he died in 2006 and is buried at Munich's Nordfriedhof cemetery. All of his books were published posthumously, sensitively edited by his widow, who died in 2014 and is buried beside him.

MODERN SLOVAK CLASSICS

Ján Rozner
Seven Days
to the Funeral

Translated from the Slovak
by Julia and Peter Sherwood

Afterword by Ivana Taranenková

KAROLINUM PRESS 2024

KAROLINUM PRESS
Karolinum Press is a publishing department
of Charles University
Ovocný trh 560/5, 116 36 Prague 1
Czech Republic
www.karolinum.cz

The translation and publication of this work was supported using public
funding by the Slovak Arts Council and by Slovak Literature Abroad
(SLOLIA).

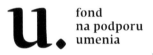

Cover and graphic design by Zdeněk Ziegler
Set and printed in the Czech Republic by Karolinum Press
First English edition

Cataloging-in Publication Data is available
from the National Library of the Czech Republic

ISBN 978-80-246-5633-5 (pbk)
ISBN 978-80-246-5634-2 (pdf)
ISBN 978-80-246-5635-9 (epub)

CONTENTS

Zora Jesenská died in Bratislava on 21 December 1972 and was buried a week later, on 28 December 1972. This book recounts what her husband went through in the course of those seven days.

It was around seven o'clock by the time he got home, some-what later than on the previous few days, his head empty from hours of the intense strain of keeping alert, but he was also feeling hungry and, as a result, angry and irritable. He decided that this time he wouldn't just cut a few slices of bread, put some butter and cheese on them, and proceed to chew them in the same way he'd been stuffing himself at breakfast and dinner for over a week now. On his last trip to the shops he'd bought some canned meat; it said on the can that all you had to do was put it into boiling water, unopened, for five minutes or so.

He filled a pot with water and put it on the gas stove. He laid out a plate and cutlery, and removed the empty bottles of mineral water and fruit juice, as well as the two thick books from the bag he had brought home. Tomorrow he would re-turn the books to the library and choose two different ones. He left the bottles in the corner of the kitchen, carried the books into the living room and by the time he returned to the kitchen the water was already bubbling away in the pot, so he placed the can in the water and it was only then that he remembered he hadn't checked how long it had to be left for. But he didn't take it out. He sat down on the bench at the kitchen table, and when he thought he'd waited long enough he turned off the gas, quickly took the can out of the hot wa-ter, opened it, tipped half the contents onto a plate and cut himself a slice of bread, even though he saw small pieces of potato floating among the pieces of meat in the unappetizing looking sauce.

The canned meat was lukewarm. It tasted disgusting and sticky like industrial rubber but that made sense, being of a piece with everything else that had conspired against him.

Lately he'd taken to talking to himself, though only brief sentences, mainly expletives directed at himself, and questions (so what else was I supposed to have done?), meant to conclude a particular chain of reminiscences. This time, too, he felt the urge to give voluble, succinct and strong expression to his annoyance with the foul-tasting canned meat, which was why he followed each gulp with a loud and accusatory howl at the wall opposite:

"Damned canned meat!" – "Fucking life!"

The yelling helped him to calm down a little and made him realise how ridiculous it was for him to swear, especially using words he normally never used. But at least it was a way of unburdening himself to an imaginary interlocutor. He was fully aware that it wasn't the fault of the disgusting canned meat and that there was nothing to stop him from tipping the contents of the plate down the toilet and making himself a sandwich with some cheese from the fridge, but it was doing him good to berate everything that could not be tipped down the toilet and so, after swallowing each chewy piece of the disgusting canned meat, he continued insisting to himself, only now more calmly – as if he had discovered the immutable nature of things – and much more quietly, over and over:

"Damned canned meat!" – "Fucking life!"

The repetition turned his swearing into a kind of idiotic children's game and as he went on mindlessly, he suddenly heard the telephone ring.

He remained seated for a while, not interested in hearing what someone might want to say to him over the phone. But what if it's about something else, he thought as the names of three or four friends flashed through his mind, but then, as he began to walk towards the phone in the living room, he thought again: this was it, irredeemably, definitively.

He crossed the living room, picked up the receiver and spoke. The voice at the other end asked who was speaking, so he introduced himself. The voice gave its name as "Doctor Marton". It occurred to him that there was a time when he used to hear this name more often: it seemed to belong to a urologist he knew and for a moment he wasn't so sure he was going to hear the news he was expecting, but once the voice on the telephone started explaining "I'm calling from the oncology ward. I just happen to be on night duty here tonight," he was quite certain again that he would hear what he'd been expecting.

Actually, he wasn't expecting it at all; it's just that sometimes it had vaguely occurred to him that he would get a call like this one day, perhaps the day after tomorrow, in a week, or in a couple of weeks. But he wasn't expecting it just yet…

However, the voice on the other end of the phone didn't continue with the news he was fearing but instead proceeded to give him a detailed account of how he hadn't been able to find his name in the telephone directory, which was why he had to ring at least three people who he thought might know him, but none of them had his number, and only then had he remembered a fourth person who had finally given him his number. That was why he hadn't called sooner.

The voice on the other end of the phone paused, so, just in order to say something, he offered: "Yes, my number is ex-directory." Then the doctor moved on to the crux of the matter: "The thing is, your wife's condition has deteriorated. Her situation is now critical."

Again, he just said "yes", as if to encourage the doctor to say more but the doctor digressed once again: "I'm sure you remember that before we admitted her we told you that something like this couldn't be ruled out… that you had to be prepared for it."

What does he mean by "we", he thought, annoyed; he had talked to the consultant and nobody else was present at the time. But out loud he just said "yes" again and then finally, as he'd been expecting, the doctor moved on to the reason for this phone call: "And that's why it would be a good idea for you to come in right away."

Again, he repeated mechanically, "Yes, I'll come in right away," to which the doctor added: "It would be a good idea for you to bring someone along."

He didn't understand why he should bring someone along just because his wife's condition had deteriorated, but again he just repeated his "yes" but this time the voice at the other end of the telephone quickly went on, as if it had inadvertently forgotten to mention something important: "Obviously you must be prepared for the fact that your wife may already be dead."

Now the voice at the other end of the line had run out of things to say, so he repeated his "yes, I'll come in right away", and put the receiver down.

For a moment, he stood motionless by the telephone, as if the last sentence had to be chewed first and then swallowed, like another chewy piece of the disgusting canned meat. But he hadn't yet swallowed it. He focused on something that had nothing to do with the content of the phone conversation. Like an editor or a dramaturg editing other people's texts, he reviewed the doctor's last sentences, as if proofreading a manuscript on his desk. Where's the logic in this – first he tells him about the situation getting critical and then he ends by saying the critical situation is over. And then this "obviously you must be prepared…" Obviously! He didn't mind that it was an ugly word; what bothered him was that it made no sense in this sentence. Surely the doctor didn't mean to say "obviously" – what was so obvious about that? Surely he meant to say "of course", in the sense of "but": "but you must be prepared for…"; that would have had some logic to it.

Having finished this proofreading exercise he went back to the kitchen, slowly and deliberately, as if in possession of a secret. Once in the kitchen he sat down on the bench again to ponder something and it took him a while to realise he wasn't thinking of anything, and that all he had to do was go to the hospital and take someone along. So he got up, picked up the plate so that the smell of the canned meat wouldn't linger in the kitchen, tipped the rest in the toilet, flushed it down, put everything away and sat down on the kitchen bench again, as if he now needed a little rest before leaving.

He sat there with his shoulders drooping, his hands in his lap. He would no longer have to... yes, there were quite a few things he would no longer have to ... think about what state he might find her in and what he would say to her... or to think, as he had done so often over the past two weeks, whether she would ever come back to this flat... and if she did, for how long. He no longer had to be petrified, nothing would change, everything had calmed down. She simply existed no longer. He was unhappy with himself for not feeling a sudden sense of alarm that was supposed to shake him up. But then again, could it have ended any other way? That's what she may have been thinking, too. And maybe she'd even wanted it. What nonsense. But still, sometimes in the course of the last few days this thought had crossed his mind. It had lodged itself in his brain and now he felt ashamed for thinking that she had come to terms with it ... with leaving him here. Alone. Surely she must have known that he wouldn't be able to cope by himself. He'd be left sitting in this huge flat from morning till night. Shrouded only in perpetual silence.

And a vast emptiness. Suddenly he seemed to have got a grip, noticing that his mind had gone blank again and that he had to go to the hospital. The doctor had ordered him to come. Although just now it no longer mattered if he went there right away or if he continued to sit here. He wasn't going to the hospital to see her anyway; he was only going there *because of her*.

He got up, went to the hallway, put on his coat, took the lift down, unlocked the garage, opening both wings of the garage door, reversed into the street, not towards the bend and downhill towards the centre of town, but up the hill where some three hundred metres further along lived his wife's cousin. Because he was told not to come on his own although he had no idea why. He had only just been to see this cousin of hers an hour earlier. He had dropped by on his way from the hospital, as his wife had requested.

A few days ago, two patients who shared the hospital room with his wife were going to be allowed to go home for Christmas at their own request. So his wife had asked if she could do likewise and the doctor had given his permission. That's when she suggested that since restaurants were still open on Christmas Eve, he should stop by one and buy some fried carp. They would heat it up, light a few candles and celebrate Christmas Eve at home.

As she had been on a drip for several hours a day, he was surprised that the doctor was willing to discharge her. He had no explanation for this and that was why he went to see her cousin, herself a doctor, to see what she thought. What she'd said was: "Something might happen at the hospital, and something might happen at home. Subjectively, it will make her feel better to be allowed to be at home."

This afternoon she was feeling worse again so she asked the doctor if she could stay in the hospital after all, and the doctor agreed. And that was why she came up with a new plan to do with the Christmas Eve carp: her doctor cousin had a relative who was a manager in some big hotel where they were bound to cook for their guests even on Christmas Eve. Her cousin should order two dinners that he would take to the hospital. They could also light the candles there. But he should go and see her cousin now so she could make the necessary arrangements or find out if it was possible at all.

That was why he'd dropped by his wife's cousin's on his way from hospital half an hour earlier... or perhaps it was an hour.

Was it astonishment that he detected in her face as she opened the door? Or was it startled anxiety ... because she had guessed what happened? He no longer remembered. Instead of a greeting, he said: "I just had a call from the hospital," and she ushered him in without a word. He sat down in the same armchair he had sat in half an hour or an hour earlier, and she sat down too. The room was illuminated only by a standing lamp next to the sofa.

He gave her as detailed an account as he could, concluding with the sentence: "However, you must be prepared for...."

God knows why he had thought that her cousin would also notice the lack of logic in the doctor's call but she just sat there in silence, as if he weren't there at all. She is only thinking about what had just happened, he thought. She's not thinking about her in the same distracted and unfocused way that he is. All that was forcing its way to the surface of his consciousness were some irrelevant trivialities, overlaying the matters her cousin was thinking about. Such as the doctor and his phone call.

She had actually been the first and the only person to tell him the truth, the prognosis for his wife's disease. His wife had been in hospital for a few days when he asked her cousin why she was getting increasingly weak and why the infusions weren't helping. "They do help sometimes, for a while," she said, "but she has..." and she used two Latin words before adding: "And that's about the worst-case scenario in this disease." She went on with some explanation from which he gathered only that it was all probably hopeless. That was why, a few days later, he went to ask her how the doctor could possibly discharge her.

After quite a long time the cousin seemed to awaken. She stood up, and left the room saying "I'll get dressed and fetch a bag and a suitcase".

He was slightly baffled as to why they would need a suitcase and a bag to go to hospital now that his wife had died. He felt embarrassed by her silence, her vacant solemnity. Reluctantly he admitted that his main feeling was that of being wronged because his regular life had been derailed, thrown off track. After all, this woman who'd just died had been a part of his life for nearly two decades. Of course, to some extent, she'd also been a part of her cousin's life. They had known each other since they were little girls and been close long before he met his wife. Yes, that was it, he thought, as if a justification had dawned on him – she had lost someone close or very close, but her life would not change at all. Whereas his life seemed to have been turned completely upside down. She'd shut the door behind her, leaving him in their flat on his own. His life still had a purpose as long as he existed alongside her, since she too needed someone by her side to give her life a purpose. But all that was gone now. Whereas all that happened to her cousin was that something had faded out of her life but she could and would go on living as before.

Silence continued to be all that he could hear in the flat. How come her husband was not at home? He was usually at home in the evenings. Reading his mathematical books. He must have gone for a walk or a run. That was his way of relaxing.

The cousin appeared in the door again, saying "Let's go," and he noticed she was holding a suitcase in one hand and a bag in another.

On the way to the hospital he kept quiet, only once voicing something that had occurred to him earlier: "Today it's Thursday and two weeks to the day that I drove her to hospital."

Two days earlier he sat in the office of the consultant of the department where his wife had been examined.

The consultant didn't beat about the bush. "Your wife has leukemia," he informed him and then paused as if wanting to give him time to come to terms with this before going on.

But the name of this disease meant nothing to him; he had no clear idea what kind of illness it was, to him it was just a medical term. He was familiar with other health problems, such as Paget's disease of the bone, a condition that involves a cellular deformation of the bones of the skull, putting pressure on the trigeminal nerve and causing unbearable pain, for which brain surgery was often the only possible form of treatment. He knew everything about this rare disease, as his mother had suffered from it and eventually died of it. But otherwise he was a complete ignoramus when it came to medical terms, which was why he didn't react to the information with any shock or emotion, as the consultant probably had expected. He asked: "Is that serious?"

"I'm afraid it is," the consultant affirmed.

He didn't find that fully satisfying, so he asked again, with greater urgency: "How serious?"

The consultant addressed him almost personally and very specifically: "Your wife's condition is very advanced. You have to be prepared for anything. It's my duty to tell you."

"But…" he began and suddenly no longer knew what he was going to ask. Probably whether it was treatable at all.

The consultant reassured him: "She will be admitted as soon as a bed becomes available, maybe even tomorrow or the day after." He thought that the consultant gave his wife preferential treatment because they had been referred by a common friend, a doctor, and he had no idea that in this department people died quickly and frequently. "We'll give her cytostatic infusions," the consultant enlightened him but as he must have realised that this term wouldn't mean much to a lay person, he explained that this was a brand-new type of medication, which could have a completely unexpected, indeed miraculous, effect. However, he immediately added: "Initially, the infusions put a lot of strain on the body, and the patients may actually feel worse for the first ten or fourteen days. But that doesn't mean that the underlying condition has worsened. Can you please explain this to your wife? It's quite possible that she can be discharged in three or four weeks. The problem is that there will be a relapse in about three months and your wife will have to be hospitalised again and the treatment repeated."

It was only now that the meaning of the consultant's "very serious" was laid bare to him. He had to be prepared for anything. In the best case his wife would be dying in instalments.

The consultant reminded him: "We will tell her that she has extreme anaemia. That's what you should say to her as well: extreme anaemia."

So he told his wife that she was suffering from extreme anaemia, that there was this new kind of medication, cytostatics, that the infusions initially made the patients feel worse, but she might be discharged as early as about three weeks. He didn't tell her that after some three months she would have to be given the infusions again.

They were just eating lunch. His wife remained silent for a while and then asked: "And is that something people die of?"

He replied grumpily, almost angrily, as if she was suspecting him of not telling her the whole truth: "That's exactly why you're going to the hospital, to get cured, not to die." And that was the truth, after all. He also told her that it was only now that the diagnosis had been made that the treatment could begin.

His wife didn't respond and just looked through him and at the wall as if thinking, oh, go on pontificating, I've learned enough already. Who knows how she interpreted "extreme anaemia". She must have guessed that these two words were meant to soothe her fears. He was sure she didn't believe him. That's why a completely different argument occurred to him: "I was told the other day that I'd had an untreated heart attack. It was diagnosed as angina pectoris. Which is what it said on my father's death certificate. That's also something people die of." This occurred to him because deep down he was still a bit upset that shortly before this his wife had received his diagnosis with such indifference. When he had felt unusually exhausted, had to cut his walks short, and felt a pain in his left arm, all she had said was: "Well, go and see a doctor, then." In the end he felt so unwell he didn't dare drive himself to hospital. And the doctor he saw was quite shocked when she examined him. She told him to lie down on a couch, rang another department where he was examined straight away and given some nitroglycerine and a medical report. When he came home, his wife didn't even glance at it. Only a few days later did she say: "Let me see the piece of paper they've given you, so I know what's wrong with my husband." She read it, folded it up and gave it back to him without a word.

When they discussed her illness later, he got worried that it may have been too harsh of him to blurt this out to her, so he added in a more conciliatory tone: "But it's something one can live with. The doctor said I could live to be eighty."

From then on he had to keep up a constant pretence, both while she was still at home and also later in hospital. Once she was in hospital it would have been absurd for her to believe the diagnosis of "extreme anaemia" he had told her about.

She shared a room with two other patients, both of whom had leukemia with remissions and had to be hospitalised roughly every three months. It was unlikely that they hadn't discussed their illness. And even had she had a room to herself, she knew she was on the oncology ward. Just as well she never asked why he was lying to her. She must have known from experience that this was what people do when someone is gravely ill. In the end, she didn't believe him even when, exceptionally, he told her the truth.

Just a few hours before, the last time he'd seen her today, a nurse had brought in some containers and all sorts of other things, so he left the room as courtesy to the other two patients. While in the corridor he ran into the duty physician, who said "congratulations": he had just seen his wife's latest blood test, which showed a perceptible improvement, quite rare in such a short time. As soon as the nurse left the room, he hurried back to give her the good news. But she just looked at him in disbelief and said: "Really?"

A moment later she said she felt very tired and he'd better go home. He just shouldn't forget to drop in on her cousin about the carp for Christmas Eve.

It was evening now so he was able to park right by the hospital entrance. Over the two weeks when he went to see her in the afternoons – and on a few rare occasions, maybe twice before lunch – he had to look for a parking space, sometimes quite far away, in a side street.

Her cousin picked up the empty suitcase and bag from the back seat. Now it dawned on him why the doctor asked him to bring someone along. It was as if his wife was to be discharged, and the main reason he was told to come was to collect all her stuff, to get rid of all her effects. So that no trace of her remained there.

He expected to find the hospital room just the way it was when he was last there, except that she would be lying motionless and he would no longer be able speak to her or ask her how she was, whether she was feeling any better, how she had slept. But the first thing he saw when he opened the door was a screen that had been placed in front of her bed by the window. He quietly said hello to the other two patients and paused before the screen at the end of her bed. He saw her head and was taken aback to see that even though her face had not changed, her mouth was wide open. As if she was about to scream? No, there was nothing in her expression suggesting that – her mouth was just open. Forming a large "O". As if saying, oh no. He kept staring at her open mouth in astonishment.

A moment later a nurse walked in. Without taking much notice of them, she sat down on her bed behind the screen, took the false teeth from the bedside table, inserted them

the constant feeling that there was something else he should tell her. Then she dozed off again. Once, on waking from her slumber, she said. "It's so nice to have someone hold your hand." Until, finally, she herself told him to go home.

He picked up the suitcase and his wife's empty handbag, flung her coat over his arm and then he spotted a corner of her jumper sticking out from under the blanket. A purple woollen jumper that she had worn every winter for the past few years; in his mind's eye he would always see her at her typewriter wearing this jumper, he thought. He put the coat back on the bed and stuffed the jumper into the bag.

Now all he had to do was say goodbye to the other two patients. He made to shake the hand of the one whose bed was on the other side of the screen. She was the younger of the two, in her thirties, and he had exchanged a few words with her occasionally. As soon as he took the first step in her direction, to his surprise she started talking: "Dear oh dear, who would have thought, it's been just a few hours since you were here…" She had overheard the cousin telling him to go and see the duty doctor: "The doctor won't be able to tell you anything, he was too late, all he knows is what we told him. After you left, your wife fell asleep, at least I think she did, but then I noticed that she suddenly started to toss and turn and all of a sudden she sat up in bed, clutched her head, so I asked if I should call for a doctor but she said no, there's no need, I have a headache pill, but she didn't take it, she just sat there holding her head in her hands and then she said again, there's no need to bother the doctor just for this, and she kept holding her head and swaying from side to side, and then she suddenly fell back onto the bed and I could hear she had trouble breathing, as if she were suffo- cating, that's when we both started ringing the bell to call the nurse, she got here very quickly and when she heard her heavy breathing, she ran out to get the doctor and came back with him a few minutes later but by then we couldn't hear her breathing anymore, and the doctor didn't try to do anything either."

All this came pouring out in a single sentence without any punctuation and the longer she spoke the greater relief he felt: it was immensely important for him to know all this. He didn't have to imagine, to conjecture anything. Her life was now closed as far as he was concerned, at least in the sense of what had been happening to her. And those few words she spoke – no need, I have my pills…. no need to bother the doctor – it was as if he heard her voice, that was how she spoke when it was to do with her – what for, why bother others, there's no need – one shouldn't make a fuss, one mustn't let others dance attendance on oneself. She had suffered from migraines, she had them more and more often and quite badly, and sometimes she would also hold her head like that with both hands as if it were about to burst. And when he heard about her heavy breathing, he thought, involuntarily, that must have been the death rattle. When his father had died many years ago, there had also been this death rattle right at the end. He could recall it to this day.

That was really very helpful, he said to the patient, he would never have found out otherwise. As he said goodbye to them, he was almost moved. He picked up the suitcase, the bag and the winter coat again, mumbled something about Christmas and went out to the corridor.

In front of the duty room, he set down the suitcase and the bag, knocked and went in with the winter coat over one arm. The doctor who had phoned him was at his desk, the cousin was sitting to the side and as he entered it seemed to him that they had been waiting just for him. The doctor stood up, introduced himself and offered him a seat, explaining again that he hadn't been able to get hold of his phone number; he'd even thought he would not get through to him and was about to send a telegram. As for his wife, they had discussed it already – he said, glancing at the cousin – he didn't really have any more information on how it happened, it might have been a stroke or a cerebral haemorrhage; by the time he was called, all he could do was pronounce her final demise. Demise, he thought, what a handy word, how useful. Death is something grim, emotionally loaded… He said he had already heard an account from a patient in her room and then, as instructed by the cousin, he thanked the doctor for going to the trouble of phoning him. Out in the corridor he picked up the suitcase and the bag. The only sounds that could be heard were their footsteps. He had sorted out what he had been told to come for and now the exasperation he felt when he returned home earlier started to creep back.

Only a few hours ago he had told her that he would drop by in the morning and bring her a fresh pair of pyjamas, and she had asked with a feeble smile: "Am I really so far gone?", probably because he said he would come first thing in the morning. She seemed sort of exhausted and frail, as if her strength was failing her, that was why he wanted to see how she would be the next morning. She had managed to work it out somehow.

The hospital had killed her. He kept thinking about this in the car, and eventually said it to the cousin as well: "What was the point of her going to hospital? She could have stayed at home, had some peace and quiet, and everything would have ended the same way." The cousin upbraided him: "Stop talking nonsense! There could have been complications, some haemorrhaging that couldn't be dealt with at home, and you would have reproached yourself for the rest of your life that she wasn't in hospital."

As he drove into the open garage and got out of the car, he announced, out of truculent anger: "This stuff can stay here, I'll bring it up tomorrow." The cousin was surprised: "But why leave it here until tomorrow? We might as well take it up now." And she started unloading the things from the car.

Upstairs in the flat, after putting his wife's handbag under the kitchen table, hanging her black woollen winter coat on the hanger and asking the cousin to put the suitcase and the bag under the table as well – he'd deal with them later – he went into the living room and sat down in an armchair. He heard the cousin taking stuff out of the bag and the suitcase; maybe she was emptying them so she could take them back home. He wished he could be left alone in the armchair with his fury and exasperation.

Gazing ahead in anger his eyes fell on the *recamier* – that was the technical term for what they called a chaise longue, an upholsterer had once told them. It disrupted the symmetry of the room's layout: they had moved it there when his wife became unwell because she was most comfortable in a semi-recumbent position and wanted to be in the room where she always sat at her typewriter and where he, too, had used to sit and read, and as he looked at the recamier he realised that he was now directing his fury and exasperation at everything that came to mind – the hospital with all its bunglers, the attending physician, the doctor who made the silly phone call, the recamier that had turned their living room into a furniture warehouse, the cousin who wouldn't give him credit for anything – yes, she was now on the phone to her husband telling him what had happened and where she was – … and, he finally admitted to himself, he was also angry with her for having died and leaving him here all alone, in fact, she wanted to die and it did not matter to her all that much what would happen to him. Well, to be fair, it must have mattered to her as well, but didn't she tell him herself that she had lost the will to live, although that had been two years ago, but he couldn't get it out of his mind now and kept repeating it to himself: she did want to die.

It was two years ago that they celebrated their first New Year's Eve in this new flat, just the two of them. They never used to have people around for New Year's Eve, and only once had they dropped in on the Trachtas who always held a big get-together in the evening, an open house, but on this occasion they had not only been alone but also felt alone, they didn't ring anyone and no one rang them, they sat there unhurriedly sipping white wine, with really not much to talk about, and didn't turn on the TV or the radio because she didn't want to hear or see people who were cheerful and carefree... And then, all of a sudden, she started musing about life, wondered if there was any point to it, and said that she kept coming to the conclusion that it was actually pointless. He knew she didn't say this because she couldn't work, because she'd been deprived of every opportunity to work, she whose entire life up to that point had been filled with work – I've done my bit already, she once told him – he knew that she was contemplating the meaning of life for a completely different reason, yet he latched on to the subject gratefully. In recent years, having nothing to do himself, he had started reading books on philosophy, although they too lost their appeal at some point and he was hardly reading anything anymore, nevertheless, everything that had been written on the subject, everything he had read about it, now came back to him and he started to pontificate: this is an ancient question, the quintessence of all philosophy, as he tried to find a way of rebutting what she had just said, so many people had chewed over this question, from antiquity to Sartre... but she couldn't give a damn about what he was telling her about Sartre, she wasn't interested in his pontifications and brushed off every argument he came up with a single sentence: "I don't really feel like living anymore."

He knew her state of mind, yet now, as she hurled this at him without mincing her words – that's how it felt to him – something in him resisted, as if she had insulted him, rejected him, and he asked almost indignantly: "But me being here, does that mean nothing to you?"

She didn't reply. What was she supposed to say anyway? That it did mean something to her? But that she had nonetheless lost the will to live? She would have to explain at great length something she was loath to explain, and what for anyway: he was perfectly aware of it himself.

Two months before that New Year's Eve her niece Jelka and a friend of hers had been killed in a mountain-climbing accident in the Tatras. They had taken the wrong trail for their descent and started to climb down a sheer rock face no one had ever descended without full mountain-climbing gear. That was how it had happened.

It had taken him years to understand that there had been something irrational about the way his wife felt about her mother, whom she had regarded as not quite of this world, and about whom everything was good and beautiful. And later on – after Jelka had moved in with them in their city-centre flat – again it had taken him a long time to understand that the way she felt about her niece was the same. On the one hand, she was able to see, and indeed did see, all the girl's flaws, some minor, some major, human flaws typical of all young people, yet Jelka had also been a reincarnation of her mother, an extension of her relationship with her mother: she felt duty-bound to look after her, watch over her. The girl's mother had entrusted her to her care, and she had failed – the niece who had been entrusted to her, perished. And although she was completely blameless, something inside her was broken, shattered, and would not heal. That was the reason she said she didn't feel like living on that New Year's Eve, two months after the accident.

But with time even this wound had begun to close and seemed to have healed. They were living for one another again. But once she fell ill and grew weaker, once she became aware of how things stood with her, the wound opened up again. And maybe that was what reawakened her desire to be together again with those that she belonged with. *Unio mystica*. And although she continued to love him as before, and probably also felt sorry for him, he was someone from this real, everyday world.

The cousin finished her phone call and asked if he would like a cup of coffee. "No, thanks," he said with a determined firmness even though he didn't know why he didn't want any coffee. All he wanted was to sit in this armchair and gaze into the distance, looking for further objects to rage at.

The cousin reminded him: "You should ring your brother." He shook his head in refusal. "No, I'm not ringing him now."

This time he knew exactly why he didn't want to do that. It might be all right if his brother Pavol came by himself. But for this solemn kind of visit he would be sure to turn up with his wife and eight-year-old daughter in tow. Pavol's wife had been hospitalized on many occasions: she'd undergone surgery several times and so, as someone thus afflicted, she talked mostly about her own ailments. Their daughter, meanwhile, giggled at every possible opportunity. She wouldn't giggle now, as they would all sit here in obligatory mourning. And he'd have to talk. But he didn't want anyone around.

The cousin said she would ring Martin and Viera Rázus, a couple who were close relatives of his wife. Goodness gracious, why did she have to bring up Martin in particular. He'd seen him only this afternoon in hospital. The cousin must have told him that his wife didn't want any visitors, and yet he came bringing along some total stranger, and this total stranger wanted his wife to sign a copy of her translation of Pasternak's *Doctor Zhivago*. The novel had won awards in the West and had been turned into a Hollywod movie but had not appeared in the Soviet Union and her translation into Slovak was published virtually semi-legally during the Prague Spring, which made it a sensation. This stranger, a doctor who used to work in this hospital and had for many years been employed by some international organisation in Switzerland, made full use of the opportunity of having a chat with a literary figure. When at long last they left, his wife was so exhausted by their visit that she fell asleep straight away.

He no longer felt like staying in the armchair, for fear that the cousin might say, "Hold on, I'll pass you on to him," and he would be forced to give an account of what had happened and how, so he got up to go to the kitchen to make himself a cup of coffee, but instead surprised himself by declaring: "I'll go down to tell my sister-in-law. Seeing as she lives in the same block."

A few seconds before he had no idea that he was going to say anything of the sort, that he would go and see his sister-in-law, of all people.

Only her cousin and her sister-in-law Mária, no other visitors, his wife had said. But her sister-in-law had not been to see her once in those two weeks. And before his wife was admitted to hospital, she hadn't come for at least three weeks, maybe even four. Her sister-in-law was holding a grudge. She had joined them on one of their last walks, and as so many times before, started to complain about the head of the housing cooperative, who she claimed had made vast amounts of money at their expense. His wife had no idea whether the man had made a little on the side, but when she learned that he was looking for tenants to move into the new building which he himself had planned and organised, he had offered her a flat and, at her request, allocated another to Mária's daughter Jelka, who was still at university at the time. But because his wife defended the head of the housing cooperative, her sister-in-law took offence and, being a person of principle, stayed offended. Two weeks ago, he told her that he'd taken his wife to hospital and why, but she never went to see her.

He rang the door one floor below and heard voices from inside the flat. After her daughter died – it was only then that she had moved into this flat – Mária asked her sister and her husband to move in with her. They were pensioners who went to bed early and never made a sound, so she must have

(28)

had visitors. The sister-in-law opened the door. He remained standing in the doorway and apologized for disturbing her so late. Now he could clearly hear the voices from inside the flat. Young female voices. He recognised that girlish laughter. He stood there uncertainly for a moment before plucking up the courage to say: "I have some news," and getting stuck again before making the brief announcement.

And that's when it happened. All of a sudden, unexpectedly, like when someone has a dizzy spell and keels over, or a tipsy person begins to throw up, right onto the tablecloth, onto his own trousers, unable to control himself or get up and leave, and just keeps throwing up. Just as he was about to make his brief announcement, he felt a lump in his throat, he choked up, his voice faltered and, incapable of uttering a single word, he began to sob, loudly, uncontrollably. He had to lean against the door-frame, felt the tears coursing down his cheeks and covered his eyes with the back of his hand. It was like trying to overcome a fit of cramp but instead he just kept weeping, in choked sobs – he hoped he couldn't be heard inside the flat until in the end he was just breathing heavily, and he finally managed to utter the brief announcement and say what had happened earlier that evening, say those three words. He could now hear cheerful girlish laughter from the flat again, his sister-in-law was saying something he could not yet take in, but eventually he understood that she would come up in a minute.

He stopped on the stairs to wait for his thumping heart to calm down. He couldn't understand what had come over him, and in front of his sister-in-law of all people, a woman who always displayed admirable self-control and iron inner discipline and who was completely indifferent to him to boot. He wiped his eyes and cheeks on his sleeve, as he didn't want the cousin to see him like that.

But maybe the reason it happened was that he suddenly recognised those girlish voices. That girlish laughter.

He and his wife had referred to them simply as "the girls", although they must have been in their twenties. During the two years since the sister of one of the two girls had been killed in the Tatras together with his wife's niece Jelka, the girls would often come to see them, and sometimes he and his wife also went to see the dead girl's sister and her family. Jelka and the dead girl had formed a kind of circle with those two girls. That was why his wife had felt something of a fateful bond with these two girls, who had previously been strangers.

When they phoned from the hospital to say that a bed had become free for his wife and that she would be admitted the next morning, he tried to imagine what that last evening would be like. Would they both pretend that nothing out of the ordinary was happening and that she'd be home again in a couple of weeks? Could the evening pass like any other? No, they needed someone else to be here, someone who would chat about this, that and the other in a carefree way, someone totally removed from his and his wife's world. That could only have been the girls. Even if he told the girls why he wanted them to come that evening, they were the only ones who would be able to come around and not sit here anxiously, with serious expressions, even for a moment. They would talk about all kinds of things, as usual, and they would laugh. Good job he remembered them in time. The dead girl's sister operated some piece of machinery in an optical factory, but her friend worked in an office and even though it was late in the afternoon, he was able to reach her. Yes, they would come, definitely, she promised.

He went into his wife's room and told her he was popping out to the supermarket to get something for dinner. He had to have a bottle of wine and some brandy at home to make everything feel as natural as always, so that the girls would laugh and talk about this, that and the other. He brought the shopping, and soon after he sat down next to his wife, she asked shyly, almost timidly, if he would mind asking the girls to come around in the evening.

He had already done that, he said, he'd phoned them and they were coming. He was elated. He had guessed her wish even before it had occurred to her. That may have been his last opportunity to guess any wish of hers.

The girls had come over that evening, talked about all kinds of amusing things that had happened on their recent hiking trips, how they had to sleep in the hay once, in a shed, they shared all kinds of fun stories about their friends from work, one talked about her father's attempts to make his own wine, he'd even bought a wine press but what came out of it was a horribly sour hogwash, and things like that. They had all laughed heartily, none of this had concerned them, it was all part of a completely different world, he and the two girls drank a whole bottle of wine between them and also had quite a lot of brandy and although his wife stayed in a semi-recumbent position on the recamier, she too was more lively and seemed less tired than on other days. And after the girls left – he'd walked them down to the tram stop – she didn't complain about the visit being tiring.

The cousin was waiting for him in the armchair in the living room. She told him she'd rung Martin and Viera, they were bound to arrive any minute. And he told her that the sister-in-law would come soon; she had visitors. He asked the cousin to make him some coffee. Meanwhile he would ring his brother.

He tried to convince his brother that it really wasn't necessary for him to come over this evening but Pavol wouldn't hear of it and was sure to bring his whole family.

The cousin brought him the coffee and he started telling her what he'd heard from the patient in the hospital. He could recall every sentence as if he'd memorised a script. He was coming to the end of his account when the downstairs doorbell rang and he had finished by the time the visitors came out of the lift.

It was Martin and Viera R. She'd been weeping, her eyes were still red, and the first thing Martin demanded to know the minute he walked into the living room was how it could have happened as he'd only seen his wife that very afternoon. As if he didn't know, being a doctor, that this could happen at any time. In fact, his visit had left his wife so exhausted that she soon fell asleep, and as she opened her eyes she said: "It's so nice to have someone hold your hand." He kept this to himself, as well as another thing he forgot to mention to the cousin: how his wife had told him that, earlier that day, as she went down the corridor, she caught a glance of the cousin coming out of the doctors' room at the far end of the corridor: surely she'd been told something that made her leave without popping in to see her. He tried to talk her out of it, said that the cousin had only dropped in briefly and had to go back to work, but his wife just nodded: "Well, maybe."

There was a kind of obstinacy today to the way she kept insisting that things were looking very bad. This was what he told them about. How reluctant she was to believe that the duty doctor had said to him: "Congratulations". And how, when he mentioned the pyjamas he would bring next morning, what she read into it was only: "Is it really so bad?" Suddenly the doorbell rang again. "That will be my brother," he said, but saw three other people come out of the lift who he would never have dreamt would turn up tonight – Jozef Bžoch, his colleague from his last job, who'd been sacked three years ago on the same day as he was, with his wife Perla, an editor in a publishing house, and her friend Viera Hegerová, a translator who lived near them, so they'd given her a lift. "Goodness, we had no idea, man, none whatsoever," his former colleague said by way of greeting: apparently, they didn't know his wife was in hospital, it was only tonight that a friend had told them – the one who'd given the doctor his number. So he had to start from the beginning, about her first being unwell at home and believing for about three weeks that she'd caught the flu, how she went to see a doctor while he sat in the consultant's room… meanwhile his sister-in-law came, followed by his brother and his wife and daughter… and about the cytostatic infusions she was on. Then he told them what time it was when he left the hospital and when the phone call came, and finally he briefly summarised what the other patient had told him. While he spoke, the cousin was flitting between the living room and the kitchen, making coffee for every new visitor.

Then everyone started talking over everyone else. Martin R and the cousin discussed the likely cause of death. The others, one after the other, recalled the last time they'd seen his wife, where it was and what she'd said. And everyone said, in one way or another, what a great tragedy this was, a great loss to literature, and all the things she might still have done. Except for his brother and his family, who didn't say a word.

The babel of voices was interrupted by Viera R, who said he should ring the state press agency ČTK, as they ought to report it, surely ČTK has to issue a press release when such a major public figure passes away, but he shook his head. "I'm not going to ring them… not now," the last two words occurred to him as an afterthought, as he didn't feel like explaining that he was not going to ring them, ever; Viera R was a bit baffled, and said, well in that case he should ring the writers' union first thing tomorrow, they would draw up an official notice for ČTK. What planet is she on, he thought, but all he said was: "But she's not a member," but then his sister-in-law chimed in, in a firm, belligerent tone, that he should definitely contact a newspaper tomorrow and get them to publish a large death notice in a black frame. He nodded as if in agreement – here's another person from another planet. Now there was no getting round it, he had to explain so he began: he wasn't going to ring anyone, his wife's death wouldn't be reported by any newspaper anyway, because she was no longer a public figure, she'd been expunged from public life, her name taken out of circulation and it was forbidden – "do you understand, forbidden"– he stressed with irritation, to mention her name anywhere, and as for a death notice in a newspaper, it was the same, anybody, including someone completely unknown, could place such a notice in a paper, but if the person who died was no longer allowed to exist in public life, and it was forbidden to utter their name in public, not even in a death notice, a paper would either refuse to print it or it would be censored, well, that was the situation… he spoke quickly and with irritation, it made him quite cross to hear them speak as if they were unaware of the situation his wife had found herself in for the past three years; the ideas they come up with, he thought, as if she'd lived a normal life before… But then another thing occurred to him, now he spoke almost casually, as if telling an anecdote, his fury having evaporated again… the other day, on the spur of the moment, he'd gone to the University Library, he thought he would check in the card index to see which of her translations and books had disappeared and he found no index card with her name on it, not a single one, her name had vanished and… he couldn't help himself and added… so had mine, actually.

The babel of voices resumed, everyone except his brother and his wife considered it their duty to react with an indignant comment. Who would have thought just four years ago that this kind of thing could happen?! But it had. He was only listening with half an ear, as he'd heard all this a hundred times before, in relation to other people as well; when this new era began, he too had often voiced his indignation, but it had turned into endless waffling about the same subject, the flogging of a dead horse, it was now part and parcel of everyday life and therefore it was pointless even to discuss it; but just then, perhaps thinking along the same lines, and in an attempt to move on to practical business – it was getting late – Martin asked him: "By the way, have you given any thought to the funeral, and who might give the eulogy?"

He felt as if someone had whacked him on the head with a truncheon. No, he hadn't given that any thought at all.

He saw the funeral as being somewhere way off in the far distance, but it hadn't occurred to him that a funeral, like a mass, consists of several phases, stages, the eulogy being one of them. He knew at once that he wouldn't be able to come up with the name of anyone who could give the eulogy. The few people they were still in touch with had also been cast aside, so he couldn't ask them to make a public appearance and give a speech, or turn to Jozef B,– "how about you, could you do it?" – by doing so, he would only put his former colleague into an awkward position since he, too, was glad he'd managed to find a job in a building company while his wife was allowed to keep her post at the publishing house. And as for the others, those still allowed to appear in public, to lecture and publish: every one of them would think him thoughtless and impudent to expect them to do such a thing, and in private they would think, she shouldn't have meddled so much, she brought it upon herself, and they would find some excuse or other. Even if he went begging from one person to the next, he wouldn't find anyone. He piped up in a feeble voice: "Not really, I can't think of anyone who could give the eulogy."

Martin must have expected this kind of reaction since he'd kept quiet for so long, then he got up from the armchair and went over to the phone saying, "Let me try something."

He talked to someone whom he addressed as Jožo. Martin first explained what this was about, now the other person would come up with an excuse and apologize, and after a while, Martin would return to the armchair and say, "Oh well, that hasn't worked out." He stopped listening. What a disaster, he thought. Because there has to be a eulogy.

Martin returned to the armchair and said, "Well, that's one thing sorted out." And then turning to him: "He asked me to tell you that he'd be honoured to do it – Dr Jozef Felix."

Jozef B said, almost shouting: "Why, that's wonderful. A university professor. Head of the translators' section of the Union of Writers. That'll be almost official. An outstanding critic, it's a shame he doesn't write more reviews…"

Well yes, all he was writing now were essays on Renaissance writers. He remembered reading Felix's reviews as a student at *gymnázium,* or grammar school, when he first started reading literary journals. But he still couldn't understand how Felix could have agreed as if it were the most natural thing to do. Surely he must have known that it could get him into trouble. He'd been fired from the university long before, in the early fifties, at the time when politically conscious students could decide on these matters. Whereas Felix was anything but politically conscious. That was why he didn't get involved in 1968. He didn't want to have anything to do with this regime and for that reason he didn't argue with it either. He didn't give a damn about this regime, its unspoken rules and prohibitions, its damned, disgusting rules of the game. But now he says he'd be honoured. He is not afraid. No, that wasn't really the point, there were others who were not afraid either, it was just a cliché that everyone was afraid. Everyone had to make a living, that was their main consideration. Should they forget these considerations for a… eulogy – was it worth the risk? It wasn't, and yet the professor thought it was worth it, he was asked to do something he felt he ought to do, and he agreed to do it. And it didn't matter if he was taking a risk for the sake of something small or something large… But maybe that was not what went through the professor's head … he hadn't really known him at all until last summer when he and his wife were on holiday in Orava, somewhere near the Polish border, staying in a cottage their friends the Kollárs had found for them, and it was near there that they met Felix who'd grown up in a village nearby and used to come here with his family in the summer. They had all squeezed into his car and he drove to their cottage, they picked some brushwood, lit a bonfire, roasted some bacon, drank a bottle of wine and sat in the meadow in front of the cottage until sunset.

The people around the table were still talking about the professor, Viera H, the translator, who used to share an office with him after he was sacked from the university and was working as an editor in a publishing house.

He suddenly felt enormous gratitude towards Martin R and realised once again that there was something about him that reminded him of his own father: the burly silhouette, the shape of his skull perhaps, and although there was no facial resemblance, he had exactly the same blue eyes as his father. The image of his father that hadn't quite faded from his memory. He had never mentioned this to his wife.

When the visitors started running out of things to say, Viera H said: "As we're all gathered here, why don't we draw up the death notice together." Suddenly his brother spoke up, he would see to this, his father-in-law was a typesetter who had retired but would still go to the composing room every now and then for a chat with his old friends: if he brought the text, he would typeset it and print it, he could take it down tonight on his way home, provided he had a finished text.

"Well then, let's get started," Viera H addressed those present. She asked for a pen and some paper, then everyone's eyes turned to him. And again, he was caught off guard. He only knew one thing for sure: "I just don't want any of that hackneyed stuff… bowed down in deepest sorrow… mourning our dear… that sort of thing… It ought to be brief and to the point."

"OK, we'll leave that out," she said to encourage him. He thought about it for a while but nothing occurred to him so he started, groping: "This is to inform…", but Jozef B cut in indignantly: "For Christ's sake, how can you start this way, this is not an official document, you might as well start like the village crier: "Oyez, oyez, oyez… Hear ye…" Perla B interrupted her husband's outburst of rhetoric and calmly proposed: "It is with the profoundest sadness that we announce…" that's right, he thought, some clichés were unavoidable… and before long they got to the point in the notice where the name of the deceased would appear in a larger font, his sister-in-law thought the award his wife had been given should be included, it was usual after all, but he dismissed the idea, they may have declared her an Artist of Merit but later blacklisted everything she'd received the award for. Well, in that case, his sister-in-law insisted, it should at least say "writer and translator", but he rejected that too, she was no longer either of those, she was just a housewife and pensioner, that could come after her name, "housewife and pensioner" but that might sound ludicrous, and could even be regarded as a provocation… and some twenty minutes later – Viera H who acted as the recorder had to cross out and rewrite some passages several times, as one person would suggest one wording, someone else another, – it was all done, just one last thing was needed at the end, said Viera H: "The funeral will be held…" but that should be left blank. He would find that out tomorrow, ring his brother and he would fill in these details.

She passed the paper with these few lines and all the redactions over to him to read through but he couldn't see anything without his glasses on anyway so he just stared at the piece of paper thinking that if he tried to do this tomorrow on his own, it might have taken him a couple of hours to cobble together, he would stop at and stumble over every word and end up being unhappy with the result anyway. He was still staring at the piece of paper when Martin asked: "Is it going to be a church ceremony or a civil one?"

He shrivelled up inside, withdrawing into himself: they probably wanted a church funeral, everyone in her family had had a church funeral. But she had left the church long before they met, it was nothing to do with him; was he supposed to return her to the fold now? "A civil one," he replied drily. Martin explained: "The reason I asked was because that will determine what kind of epigraph will appear in the top left-hand corner."

Now he understood. If it were a church funeral, they would pick something from the Bible, they could find five suitable quotes on any page, but in this case? Again, he was at a loss.

Viera H made a tentative suggestion: "It should be a quote from a poet she translated. Lermontov, for example…" That translation of hers had been widely read back in the day, many people knew entire passages by heart, but now no one of those present could recall a few appropriate lines; he himself had never even read it properly, as everything that poet had written was in the grand Romantic vein, demonically dark. No, it would be up to someone else to recall some lines of poetry. But no one said anything.

"All right, a quote from someone else then," Viera offered. All eyes turned to him. He was to come up with a few lines by a poet she had translated that would work as an epigraph. He strained to think, as if it were a matter of life and death. A few disjointed fragments drifted through his mind, some talk of death…, well, if this had sprung up from his memory, it must have come from a translation they had worked on together… as he himself would never have translated any verse… now it was more than just fragments, now he knew these words were spoken by a character in a play, so it could have been only one thing… he walked over to the bookcase, took out a thick volume of Shakespeare, *Tragedies, Part One.* It must have come from that most famous tragedy of his… it was something Hamlet says shortly before he dies, his last soliloquy, here, he's found it… Here are the four lines from which a few vague shreds had surfaced. He read them out in his customary nervous and muffled voice without emphasis, like something from a newspaper report.

He was met with a chilling silence. Everyone was silent in unison. He looked at the faces around him and concluded that it probably wouldn't do. Only after a while did Viera H say: "Let me see." He pushed the book towards her, pointed to the four lines, Viera became absorbed in it as if studying it deeply and suddenly exclaimed: "But this is excellent, we just have to leave out the two lines in the middle!" and she read out the first and fourth line in a firm, expressive, almost exalted voice, and suddenly everyone started to move, nod, yes, that would make an excellent epigraph, and he lapped up their communal agreement as if it were rapturous applause. He breathed a sigh of relief. This was his great victory that evening.

Viera sat down to the typewriter and typed up a clean copy. The room was abuzz again, everyone was talking over everyone else, including his brother who started chatting to Jozef B, whom he had met a few times after dragging the latter home to their flat in the city centre when he was still sharing it with his brother. Everyone was exceedingly happy to have accomplished something useful together, only he remained sitting by himself, smoking a cigarette, proud to have found a suitable epigraph, and one that came from their joint translation at that. And he would have remained sitting there like that if Martin hadn't made a move to get up from the armchair: "Well, we've achieved as much as could have been achieved," he stated contentedly. This sounded like a signal to the others, and everyone started getting up and heading for the hallway for their coats. His sister-in-law came up to him and said that she would of course come along to the funeral parlour tomorrow – of course, he thought, she would now act on behalf of the family. The cousin mentioned that the autopsy report had to be collected from the Institute of Pathology, she would deal with that, she'd take a day off tomorrow and go with them; they agreed on a time to meet. By then the others were all waiting by the front door of the flat and after brief goodbyes and handshakes some took the lift and others started walking down the stairs.

He went over to the kitchen window to watch everyone leave, the way he and his wife used to look out of the kitchen window when their visitors left late at night.

Martin and Viera R were already walking down the hill, the cousin took the street going up, Jozef B was getting into his car with his wife Perla and Viera H, and only his brother still stood by the outside gate, as his wife said something to him. Jozef had already started the engine when his brother went over to his car and stood there for quite a while expounding something, upon which Jozef switched off the engine, got out of the car and rang his doorbell.

As Jozef came out of the lift, he apologised for returning. He invited him into the kitchen. No, no, he was just popping back with a message from his brother, he'd just do that and go, the women were waiting in the car.

So, his brother Pavol wanted him to know – Jozef began, hedging around sheepishly, with circumlocutions and parentheses – he hoped it wouldn't make him cross, this wasn't his idea, and of course he understood very well how he might feel, no one would be happy in these circumstances – and please don't take this the wrong way, for heavens' sake. "Ehm, well, I'm sure you'll understand, so let me get to the point, obviously, it would be completely understandable, I don't know what I would do if I were in your shoes, well, basically, you will be all alone here in this flat," he said, finally getting to Pavol's message: he'd be here all alone and might be tempted to have a drink or two, so his brother offered to stay here with him, while he, Jozef, would give his brother's wife and daughter a lift home, there was enough room in his car, and surely he agreed that it would be better to let his brother stay, to be on the safe side.

Ah, so this was his Pavol's wife's rescue mission, she wanted to make sure that he wouldn't get hammered at home or hit the bottle somewhere on the town tonight. Now he understood Jozef's hesitancy: he was slightly embarrassed to be the bearer of this message and every one of his sheepish prevarications was intended just as a kind of conspiratorial wink-wink – who knows what I'd get up to in your place – and it was because of this wink-wink that his brother didn't come up himself: Pavol was a teetotaller, while Jozef used to drink like a fish, they'd been on a few pub crawls together, a long time ago, when he was still married to his first wife, before Perla domesticated him, and that was why he was a more suitable messenger, one who could show the requisite understanding. He assured Jozef that there wasn't a drop of alcohol in the house. And he'd had enough for today anyway, he really must believe him, he couldn't wait to go to bed and he wouldn't budge from the house. He had to be fit tomorrow.

So can your brother rely on that? – Yes, one hundred per cent, he assured him once more, smiling at the touching care on the part of Jozef, his brother and his wife, he could be absolutely sure of that. "Oh great," said Jozef happily, reaching for the door handle and repeating, "and please don't be cross with me," and then, from the lift, "see you".

He went back to the kitchen window, looked down and a while later he saw Jozef talking to his brother and Pavol gesturing, probably not convinced by his assurances, but his former colleague was already getting into his car and so his brother, his wife and daughter also got into theirs, both cars reversed into the street, turned to go downhill and soon disappeared round the corner.

He didn't resent his brother and his wife for coming up with this, they'd had their experiences with him. But this time what he said to Jozef was true, there wasn't a drop of alcohol in the house and he was sure he wouldn't leave the house for a moment. No, there was no danger of that. Over the past two weeks it happened perhaps three times that as he went shopping for his supper on his way home from hospital he would get a small bottle of brandy which he would slowly sip at home, holding long, self-flagellating monologues. But today the shops had closed by the time he left the hospital, and he wouldn't have bought anything anyway, not even for supper. He was quite shaken by those final hours, and if he hadn't received the phone call from the hospital, he would have turned on the TV, switched off the sound and sat there watching impassively, thinking with trepidation of the following day.

Now he was less shaken than right after he returned from the hospital this evening, everything inside him had quietened down and all he felt was a void. Someone had left, slamming the door shut, never to return. And he was left here in this flat, all alone. Tomorrow he would make all the necessary arrangements, come back home, the door would close and he'd be here all alone again. That was all there was to it.

Quite a while had passed since both cars disappeared from view around the corner below his block. They must have parted ways at the crossroads by now, heading in different directions. Jozef B with Perla and the translator Viera H would soon be home, but his brother lived far away, having recently moved to a housing estate 12 kilometres away, where the first village on the bank of the Little Danube used to be, along a new four-lane carriageway beyond the end of town. He was still standing in the kitchen, his elbows propped up on the wide stone windowsill, gazing at the empty street three floors below. The street was lit by fluorescent lights that shone purple. One of them, a little further down from his house, closer to the bend in the street, was broken and emanated a steady buzz. Nothing stirred in the empty street illuminated by the fluorescent lights three storeys below.

He would wait for a car to pass by.

Goodness, he thought, how many hours he had spent in this flat, at this kitchen window, leaning on the stone. Hours and hours; since the day they moved here the hours would add up to days or weeks, even months perhaps. He was capable of gazing down as if he were high on drugs. Gazing out of the window helped him pass the time. Sometimes he felt like those pensioners he remembered from his childhood, who lived in old houses on the outskirts of town and would sit motionless by their windows, much smaller than this one, staring mindlessly at the street as if they weren't taking anything in. Now he, too, was a little like those pensioners – he was still years away from retirement age although his wife had been receiving her pension for about a year now, but she never stood by the kitchen window watching what was happening in the street, except sometime while cooking, or when he asked her to come and take a look at something – but pensioner or not, he was out of work, spending his time lost in idleness and a void: he had to keep busy and fill the time somehow, so he stared out of the window.

But in fact, there was usually something happening down below.

For example, in the afternoons women would emerge from round the bend and walk up towards the house, women who lived somewhere in this street, with carrier bags full of shopping in both hands. How many times he had wondered how they could lug those loads of theirs up this steep pavement. Whenever he himself went shopping, he would drive down to the supermarket or to the town centre. And every time he would remember his mother, who also used to carry heavy bags up to the third floor of their old flat in the centre of town. In the final years before she died, she would just shuffle about but at least once in a while she had to go out shopping, a sheer joy for her, a form of self-fulfillment, even though she was no longer really up to it and literally had to drag herself up the stairs with one hand on the banisters, stopping somewhere along the way, wheezing so heavily and loudly that he could often hear her upstairs in the flat, making him dash down, take her bags, take her by an arm and drag her upstairs… and if he didn't hear her, she would come into his room, bent double and gasping for air, and tell him she'd left the bags on the first floor, or on the landing between the first and second floor, would he mind going down to fetch them… and she would go and lie down straight away… As late as the end of 1960 she would still sometimes go to the ice stall at the back of the market hall for a block of ice: they had one of those primitive ice boxes you loaded ice into, and even he would be completely exhausted from carrying the ice, and his mother was well over seventy in 1960. She must have been a dreadful sight, lugging one of these slabs of ice in a shopping bag because whenever she ran into someone she knew, they would take the bag off her and carry it right to the front door of their flat; on a few occasions a young man, a complete stranger, had carried it for her... What a dolt he'd been then, a self-absorbed idiot, not to have thought of buying a proper fridge, because he was earning by then, but a proper fridge was a luxury, which was why his mother had never asked him to buy one and his wife had never suggested it either, because she had never set foot inside their kitchen. Only when Edo Friš got divorced and was about to downsize from a huge flat to a studio, he offered to pass on all kinds of things at ridiculous prices, so he'd taken two large armchairs, in one of which his mother would later sit in front of the TV, as well as a smart linen cupboard and several other items, including a proper fridge.

Sometimes he would stand by the window and watch as the fog descended on the city, with thousands of tiny lights blinking as they stretched along the outskirts all the way to the Slovnaft refinery, then the chain of lights below the hill would also disappear and lazily billowing clumps of fog would drift ever closer until even the outline of the house across the street would vanish, leaving just the odd lit-up window and a short section of the street below visible, and he could feel a surge of dampness all the way up here behind the kitchen window... Yes, of course, he thought, there was something to look at down there most of the time.

A car would zoom past every minute or so, entire convoys of them at certain hours on some days, and he'd try to guess the car make from above and read their number plates to see if the cars were local or maybe even foreign. On Sunday evenings many cars would head down the hill on their way home from the three or four restaurants up in Horský park and its environs and from the allotments where fruit trees grew on the sunny slopes facing the Danube; groups of young people would stroll down, usually in high spirits, sometimes singing, or shouting at one another, having fun... but quite often a car would screech before the bend as there was no warning sign and the drivers rarely noticed until the last minute that they needed to slow down. He could never tell if the sudden screech was caused by the brakes or the tyres but he was convinced that some braked so abruptly just before the bend on purpose, to show off, *mancovať sa* – here his train of thought came to a halt: *mancovať sa* was one of those words that was being used less and less and which few in this city knew anymore, while in the old days, in arguments and rows with other boys the word would inevitably turn up as a powerful insult – *ty mancér*, you show-off, you – drivers like these wanted to show off before some young female sitting beside them, impress them with their driving skills or brag about their fancy car, so they'd slam on the brakes hard and the car would judder to a stop in an instant, screeching but without veering off to the side.

But for really dramatic scenes he had to wait until the winter.

It had to get quite cold outside, the icy snow turning solid and freezing on the ground. On such days, if he saw a car emerge from around the bend in the street and come closer, he would sometimes call out to Zora to come and watch: often the cars couldn't cope with the final, steepest stretch of the road and came to a stop just before the bend, their wheels spinning round on the spot. Some drivers would step on the gas in vain, the engine would wail, the car jerk forward no more than an inch, then reverse again and come to a standstill. The drivers used various strategies to deal with this, some would get out of the car, take out a shovel and start to shift the snow or break up the ice on the tarmac, while others would turn the car and drive up onto the pavement at an angle and then tackle the bend almost horizontally, that way they could navigate the bend on the most gentle gradient possible, which, in turn, entailed the risk of another car coming from above crashing into them. Others would get out and ring the nearest doorbell, probably to ask for grit, because after a while someone would come out with a bucket and start sprinkling it onto the final stretch of the slope towards the top of the bend, while yet others just left their car where it stuck fast and continued on foot... yes, on such winter days all kinds of dramatic scenes would play out here.

But then again, he didn't always observe the world from this particular window – in summertime, and generally in warmer weather, he would stand with his elbows resting on the railing of a long balcony that stretched along the entire living room and afforded a view of both sides of the street. On days like these, in the afternoons, his wife would potter around the garden at the back of the house where they had a small plot allocated to them and spend days pulling out weeds that seemed to have been growing there for centuries. At first he used to help her but he found it terribly exhausting, while Zora had been used to gardening from her time in her parents' home and she accepted that this was not his sort of thing, sending him home to sit on the balcony in a deck chair and read. But lately he no longer enjoyed reading, and even though much of his life up until then had been spent reading, he now didn't manage to sit in the deckchair with his book for long before getting up, leaning on the railing and watching both ends of the street. From far off he could make out the faces of people as they got closer to the balcony, always harbouring the secret hope that one of them would be a friend who might spot him up there, turn into the paved courtyard and ring their doorbell, – and someone he knew would indeed walk past, people would still go this way and further up on their walks, but even if they did happen to look up and spot him, they would usually just give him a wave and continue on their way. And so, after a while, whenever he saw someone he knew approaching from one end of the street or the other, he would duck down into his deckchair, with the wooden boards of the balcony forming a kind of low fence and providing cover, while still allowing him to see a narrow section of the street through the gaps between the boards, and he would wait for the acquaintance to pass. He wasn't interested in anyone waving to him from below, it upset him that they merely waved and that no one ever shouted: hello there, how are things, should I pop up for a moment? – not once had anyone shouted anything like that, although at one time he used to see many of these people quite often socially: one of those who went past regularly was Peter K, who lived only a few streets below the bend and passed his house almost daily on his walks. Many years ago, when he was still a dramaturg at the theatre, Peter used to come and drop in on him in the centre of town almost every day: together they would finish off a play, or even rewrite one, but he had stopped being a dramaturg a long time ago, so Peter had stopped dropping in on him while he still lived in the centre... Then there was Albert M. It would make him sad to see Albert walking by and not stopping. Albert had been his best friend for a few years after the war and they always had a lot to talk about, but then various things cropped up and their friendship began to cool off until not even its ashes remained. Yet no matter how often he told himself that he no longer kept in touch even with him, his former best friend, and even though he told himself, never mind, even if someone did come up, it would be just idle talk, they had no longer anything in common and in fact he wasn't specially interested in anything and would only have been disappointed... even so, he would have loved to have someone to chat to now that he no longer had a job and never went out, neither to the editorial office of a journal or publishing house, to a café or the writers' club. A few friends would still drop in from time to time, but most of them came to see his wife, the world of his friends had shattered, they would just give him a wave and keep walking, and yet he kept looking out, hoping to see... maybe not even an acquaintance... only now did it properly sink in that he wasn't really expecting an acquaintance, but rather some unknown acquaintance... someone who would come bearing some amazing news... something completely unexpected, fantastic... he realised that from now on he was living in a different place or at a different time... Finally the right word occurred to him: he was waiting for a *messenger*, like the messenger in Shakespeare's plays who always arrives with some momentous news – Gloucester's army has been routed... Lancashire has fled to France... Burnham Wood was coming... Shakespeare's messengers usually brought the news of some disaster but he was waiting for a messenger who would bring some good news... something so amazing and incredible that as he listened to the message a majestic "hallelujah" would resound in his ears... and if a messenger were to appear, he thought, now slightly scournfully, he would come cantering up the hill on a white horse, a harbinger of good news, a Godot on a white horse... that was what he was waiting for... that was why he kept looking from one end of the street to the other... so, he wasn't, after all, like those pensioners in his youth who would stare out of their open windows with an indifferent, inert, virtually blind gaze... he had always expected someone... only now he no longer expected anyone, perhaps a car at most.

Finally a car appeared on the slope, slammed on its brakes just before the bend, and continued its downward descent.

He turned away from the window. There was nothing left for him to do now but go to bed.

He took some sleeping pills that he kept in the kitchen cupboard so that he could wash them down with water straight away. Lately he also kept his heart medication there, but it was too late to take it now: he wouldn't be able to sleep, he was agitated enough as it was. Instead, he took an extra sleeping pill, filled a glass with water, swallowed the pills and went to his room.

His room was also illuminated by the light outside, but it was much fainter there, since the room faced the slope with the back garden that belonged to their house and another garden behind it that belonged to a modern villa, which had outside steps lit by fluorescent lights. That light was further away and less intense than the lights at the front of the house and all that reached his room was a faint purple glow. He was about to undress, draw the curtains and set the alarm, when he suddenly felt the urge to move his body – he wasn't going to go out, so he walked out of his room, went through the L-shaped hallway into the living room, crossed the long living room and passed through a room at its end into his wife's room, stopping only at the window, through which the same faint light was shining from the outside steps. Had there also been a door by the window of this room, he could have returned to his own and kept going around the flat in circles. But there was no door here, so he turned around, walked from his wife's room back to the living room, from there through the L-shaped hallway to his room where he turned around again… Instead of going out for a walk, he would take a walk around the flat… this was something he could do again in future… He felt quite comfortable walking like this, there was no need to turn the lights on, all the rooms were illuminated by the fluorescent light outside, he didn't have to worry about bumping into anything in the semi-darkness, but he also took care to tread softly so as not to be heard one floor below, where his sister-in-law lived. He was wearing slippers and couldn't hear his own steps, he was only aware of them being light and buoyant.

Having walked from one end of the flat to the other ten or fifteen times he decided to take a little rest. He stopped by the window of his wife's room and looked out at the garden where she had worked so hard for weeks, indeed months. It was now just a solid surface of black and there wouldn't have been much to see there in December even in daytime. He would never forget the roots of the weeds that reached ever deeper into the ground, how he pounded the compacted soil bent double, getting very quickly exhausted and returning to the flat, and he would go back to the garden only in the evenings and even that not every day, to water it with a long hose. He had to keep doing it for at least half an hour because the water would pour down the steep slope, and the newly-planted shrubs, young trees and flowers needed lots of moisture. The garden would now remain as it was – he had never cared that much about it – but it was high time to turn around again and resume his trek, back to his room, then back to his wife's room… at one point, while in his room, it crossed his mind that perhaps he could go to bed now, as the bed was made or, rather, still unmade, for over the past two weeks he had stopped putting the bedding away in the chest: since his wife wouldn't see whether he'd made his bed or not, he could make it or leave it as it was. In general he could now do as he pleased, and once the funeral was over, he could take a train and disappear somewhere, anywhere, or just vanish altogether… his wife was no longer there to see him and for everyone else he existed only as a shadow, a name, but the terrible thing was, he thought, that he wouldn't do any such thing, he wouldn't disappear, vanish, fall through a trapdoor like on a stage, life wasn't as straightforward as that, there was no trapdoor in life, in life there were the wings, that's where he'd been banished a few years ago, he could continue to hang around in this place where no one would see him. But in fact, he pondered… he was quite comfortable in this banishment, one might almost say that he had wished for it, yet he now felt like a deflated balloon, although it didn't happen suddenly, overnight, perhaps not even three or four years ago, when both of them were banished to the wings. It must have started a long time before. He recalled the day he was told that his membership on some film committee had been extended and he said, no, I'm not staying on, and Zora had been very cross with him, why won't you stay on, you know the committee is full of idiots, just remember how many scripts would never have been made into films if you hadn't been on it, so he agreed to stay on, but in fact all he longed for – as he saw it now – was to become smaller, yes, yes, that was it, to shrink. God knows where this longing had come from and why, it may have started when he was quite young. He had barely survived the war, hadn't been accepted for university because his papers weren't sufficiently Aryan, and he started to write for newspapers while embarking on a major theoretical work on the structure of film, he kept writing and writing, he still had fond memories of that time. But after the war he came to the conclusion that someone somewhere, in another part of the world, must have written something of this kind, whereas his work was based solely on films that had been shown during the war, all trashy, so he had lost his nerve, he took two or three chapters from his manuscript and sent them off to Prague, to a newly-founded film publishing house, he didn't hear anything back for a long time, chased them up twice, and eventually a film director replied, apologising profusely, his manuscript had been given to him to review, but he was moving house and a lot of papers went missing in the move, including his manuscript. And since he hadn't kept a copy, it was now gone, all that was left were piles of rough hand-written notes piled up in the pantry, some of which he would throw out from time to time… When the war ended the world had opened up before him and he had been convinced, as many people his age before him and after him, that he would set the world on fire, but years later he admitted to himself that he hadn't set anything on fire and it was too late now, he himself didn't value his own work very highly, even though it had received some praise. It was the work of a dilettante, he told himself, nothing really worthwhile; perhaps only the book on the structure of film that he had stopped writing could have been worthwhile, he thought wistfully as he resumed his pacing to and fro, many people realised after a long time that they had failed in their own eyes, that they hadn't done what they had set out to do, that was the way of the world, the world was one big nuisance, particularly this narrow world he lived in, he was fed up with it, he had no desire to be some kind of luminary in this world. So he deliberately decided to withdraw into himself, until he shrank into a luminary that was invisible, she was the only one who could still see what he was and that had given his life a purpose, but now those seeing eyes were gone, he was now invisible. Though actually not yet, people would still see him up until the funeral, he would have to organise things, like tonight – he would take on the lead role at the funeral, others would judge how well he had played this role, and once his wife was lowered into the family vault... not a grave but a family vault, that sounds quite grand, he thought, and sat down for a while in one of the rooms. Soon after the war, when Zora's uncle, the famous writer Janko Jesenský died, he was given a state funeral: a tomb had been dug with concrete laid over it, all at the state's expense. Afterwards her parents had a six-person family vault made, lined with bricks, it was almost full by now, he thought. The first one laid in it was his wife's brother Fedor, a lawyer, who died shortly after the victory of the working classes*: he'd been a prominent figure in the Democratic Party, which won a landslide victory after the war, and so had to be completely eliminated by the working classes. Fedor had been spared being forced to confess to espionage or high treason and languishing behind bars for ten years or more and was the first to be buried in the vault. When he and Zora had been married for a few years, her father, also called Fedor, was the next to be lowered into the family vault, to be followed five years ago by her mother Milina, and two years ago by her niece Jelka. Now it was the turn of his wife Zora, so there would be five of them there, leaving room only for one more, which would be his sister-in-law Mária, a pediatrician. Her daughter and husband were already buried there and his sister-in-law would be the last to bear the name of the patrician family, Jesenská. There would no doubt be a large crowd at the funeral, since going to the cemetery was regarded as good manners in Martin: the town was particularly proud of the old part of the cemetery, where school groups were taken every year to visit the graves of some of the famous people about whom the children are taught.

He would be carefully scrutinised as to whether he had made the appropriate arrangements, starting with the coffin, which he would have to order tomorrow... suddenly he came to a halt in his wife's room, seeing in his mind's eye the coffin, which he would not only have to order but also pay for, as well as having to have it transferred from Bratislava to Martin, which was also bound to cost ..."Well," he said out loud and continued in his thoughts, just as well that he hadn't gone to bed, this would never have occurred to him in the morning, he would have turned up at the funeral parlour with a couple of hundred crowns in his pocket, who knows how much they were going to charge... He remembered his savings book – his wife had talked him into depositing ten percent of what he earned – he was quite late in starting to do this and his savings amounted to little more than pocket money, and more recently, as he was no longer earning and his fees had dried up, he had had to withdraw some money... this pocket money might just about cover the wake but not the cost of the funeral. He had no choice but to find her savings books. He would get on to it straightaway.

He hesitated for a while, as he felt he was about to do something unbecoming. Her money box had always been untouchable as far as he was concerned, not because she denied him access – he knew where she kept the key and had often seen her take it out from under her sweaters in the dresser, he could have opened the box whenever she had spent weeks or even longer at her parents' – later only her mother's – house, but he treated the box as simply being out of bounds for him. By showing interest in what was in it he would have seemingly validated all the talk and gossip that had been repeated about him even before they decided to get married. And on the occasions when he saw her noting how much she had deposited in each of her savings books, he'd never asked her how much it all added up to. Only in recent years had she said to him once or twice: "Oh well, we'll be able to keep going for a while." He had his own money box, but the one in the dresser belonged solely to her, it was not their joint property.

He opened the dresser, took out the little key and the money box and put it on the desk.

Whenever she had been paid a more substantial fee and deposited it in a savings account, she would always take the latest savings book with her to Martin to show her mother that the money she had earned was safely in her hands. Even though her mother had deigned to accept him into the family and wanted him to feel at home in her house, he'd often noticed that her suspicions regarding money had not entirely disappeared. It was the last reservation she had about him that lingered from the time her daughter decided to marry him, apart from the fact that he had obviously been keen to worm his way into a family with a historical pedigree, whereas his family had none to speak of, or rather, he preferred to keep quiet about it, having been forced to disown his father during, and his mother after, the war*, and he didn't really care what she thought him, she hadn't really known him after all, but there were also quite a few people in his world who thought the same once word got around that their relationship was serious. One sunny afternoon he was sitting on a terrace with an acquaintance of his who remarked, quite casually: "I wonder if you've heard, people say that she has at least a million in the bank." He shrugged his shoulders and said nothing, as if hearing such utter nonsense hadn't shocked him. It happened shortly after the monetary reform*, no one could possibly have had a million in those days, but clearly: the more wealth people ascribed to her, the more they wanted to hurt him, to expose him… In those days her mother had excelled at staging tragic scenes: once she'd gone as far as to make everyone think she was having a heart attack and his sister-in-law – a doctor – rushed to the phone and sent a telegram: "come immediately mother dying". Zora grabbed her suitcase and he walked her to the station on a sultry evening before a storm. She tried to assuage his feeling of guilt but he was certain that at that moment something irreversible had happened, yet the next morning a telegram arrived: "thank god mother fine". That's when they decided to postpone formalising their relationship at the register office. They had to give her mother a chance to get used to the idea, she kept saying. But then, on one occasion, she lost her nerve and begged him to give up the idea: it would be best if they remained just friends, he would find someone else, and so on and so forth. He had almost agreed when he saw how distraught she was, as he too was sick and tired of all the gossip and the fuss at her mother's house; but then again, she would have been unhappy if he'd agreed. Later on, once he got to know her mother better, he realised that those histrionics had not been solely on his account: it was just that her mother was unable to come to terms with the idea that her daughter might leave the family home. And when they were finally married, it turned out that in fact, her daughter had stayed with her and would join him in Bratislava only when she had business there, such as going over a translation with a copy editor at a publisher's, or attending a meeting. On such occasions she would stay on with him for another week or two, very rarely a little longer, so eventually her mother had calmed down, accepted him as part of the family, and the only thing that remained was her concerns over her daughter's money.

Ah, money, he recollected in the darkness of the room. She'd always taken care to behave so that her parents or her mother had nothing to reproach her for. After moving in with him, she had furnished her room with her own items of furniture and carpet. They developed a routine: whenever she came to stay in Bratislava he would note down her share of their joint expenditure, everything apart from lunches, since she soon started having lunch in a restaurant, unwilling to eat the food his mother had prepared. Sometimes there would be some additional expense, and he would explain what it related to and she would pay him back the amount he'd calculated. Initially she found this somewhat awkward, but the arrangement actually suited her, as her parents had also kept a record of every item of expenditure: her father, who had retired years ago, would go out to the shops in the morning and then jot down how much he had paid for the milk and rolls, and a whole series of these little notebooks had accumulated in their house over the years, just in case the need arose to check how much they had paid for groceries on a certain date eight, or even thirty, years ago, say on 3 August 1937. This had been the established practice in their home and this was the way to handle money, so for many years he, too, would itemise her share of their joint expenditure and it seemed almost normal, as theirs wasn't truly a joint household. Until his mother died. At that point, many things changed suddenly. On the day of his mother's funeral she suggested that he put on the Austrian TV news in the evening to help distract him, and a little later she came to his room and watched the news with him even though, until that time, watching TV had "strained her eyes" and her German wasn't very good. His mother, on the other hand, had watched only Austrian television because German was the only language she understood, but now that his mother was no longer sitting in front of the TV set, Zora had no problem understanding German and would watch every play and film with him. And there was an even greater change a year later, when her mother, too, died: he stopped itemising her share of their expenditure, there was no longer anyone to call her to account, and after fourteen years of marriage they had a joint household for the first time… Money and her relationship with his mother were the only things that had caused friction in their marriage. Time and again he had tried to find an explanation for her rude and thoughtless behaviour: it was entirely out of character and he had never seen her behave in this way with anyone else. It might have resulted in their marriage failing altogether had his mother not died in good time, so to speak, just before they moved to this new block of flats.

He opened her money box and took out all the savings books. The one right on top was his, it was his only one containing a fairly large amount. "Emergency reserve," she had once said, as she asked him, quite sensibly, to let her take care of it for him. By then the idea of an "emergency reserve" had become necessary. Thirty thousand-plus had been his fee for a selection of his recent papers and essays for quite a thick tome published as *Pohľad v zrkadlách,* or *Reflections in Mirrors*. At her insistence he hadn't even asked for an advance, deposited the full amount in the bank and handed her the savings book. At this point it was to be expected that sooner or later he would be sacked as part of the post-1968 purges. He turned the page and found just one figure – eighteen thousand. He must have remembered it wrong. But there was also some logic to it. This book of his seemed to be cursed. He'd been unlucky with it in every respect. A few months after the publisher, Slovenský spisovateľ, finally printed it in 1969, he learned that it was on the blacklist, among the books earmarked for removal from bookshops and libraries. They both featured on the blacklist, all her translations, all his, and all their joint ones. This book of his had barely made it to the shops. And it would never be back in the bookshops again. Probably not in his lifetime. And even should everything change one day and the book could be reissued, the things he'd written about would be about all our yesterdays, long out of date. Forgotten. Shredded. And everything he had ever translated, everything she had translated, and everything they had translated together, all of it, down to the last line, would end up being retranslated by someone else. Or copied from their translations. Never mind. It was what it was.

He returned to the bedside table in his wife's room, took out her savings books and went with them to the living room where there was more light, thumbing through them and adding up individual amounts in his head. The total came to over hundred and forty thousand, including his own savings book. He wasn't counting the hundreds that came after the thousands, they might have added up to another fifty thousand or so.

In every savings book, right under the cover, a narrow strip of paper had been inserted with something written on each strip. He sat down at his desk and turned on the light.

With his glasses on he opened one of the savings books again and took the strip of paper sticking out of it, read the single word written on it, put it back into the savings book, and opened the next one. That had two words written on a small piece of paper, then in the next book there was a single word … he didn't need to look at more of these bits of paper. He knew what the single word or two meant. This came as a surprise. A final service she had done for him. She just wanted to make things easier for him. He felt as if she were looking at him now, smiling contentedly.

Each thin strip of paper had the password for the savings book written on it… She knew most of the passwords by heart since she came up with them using a simple key: if her first name was included in the savings book, the password was his first name. If the savings book was named "Danube", the password was the name of the river in her hometown. She had all the passwords written down on a piece of paper that she kept among her documents, among hundreds of pages of manuscript. The little piece of paper was as well hidden there as a needle in a haystack. Impossible for any thief to find. And it would have taken him, too, ages to find it.

He understood and found some comfort in this knowledge. These strips of paper were a kind of deed of gift from her, her will.

She had sorted out her estate. But she could only have inserted these slips of paper after concluding that she would not withdraw any more money from her savings. So she got them ready for him... And that meant she knew what was coming. He started to agonise again: how long had she known? Did she realise sometime during those long weeks she spent in bed at home, while she was ill? Surely not. Perhaps it was after he had spoken to the consultant and fed her all that baloney about extreme anaemia, told her that she might be back home as early as in three or four weeks but that the treatment would have to be repeated? That was when she asked him: "Is that something people die of?" They were sitting at the dining table in the kitchen facing each other – irritated, he mentioned his untreated heart attack and said all the other nonsense about the therapy that could begin now that she had been diagnosed – and all the while she looked not at him but at the wall behind him. She knew. And it was soon after that she had said she would like to see the girls one more time.

But when did she produce these slips of paper? Was it while he had popped down to the shops to buy refreshments for the girls' visit? No, it can't have been then, he could have come back any minute. First, she had to retrieve the list of passwords buried in the pile of manuscripts – surely she couldn't have written down all the passwords from memory, she might have made a mistake – next she had to cut the paper into thin strips and copy the passwords from the list... To do that she needed some peace and quiet as well as enough time. Probably she did it on that last night after the girls had left and he had walked them to the tram stop. He'd gone to bed and that would have given her enough time, all the long hours of the night, with the lonely silence that had enveloped her. She never said a word to him about the savings books, as that would have meant confiding her innermost thoughts. They didn't talk about that.

She had cut up a sheet of paper into long thin strips, located the password for each savings book, written them down on the strips and inserted them in the savings book. He could picture her sitting there and working on it in a focused, calm, dispassionate way.

He picked out from the small pile of savings books one that contained a fairly large amount, put it to one side and returned the others to the money box. He locked it, took it over to the linen cupboard and hid the key under her jumpers. Then he walked over to the living room, switched off the lamp at the desk and sat down in the armchair.

He felt a little strange. So now he had laid his hands on that "million" of hers that Pavel Ličko had mentioned to him back then on the café terrace. Years later, in 1969, Pavel was arrested, held in detention for endless months and eventually sentenced to eighteen months' imprisonment for smuggling some manuscripts by Solzhenitsyn out of the Soviet Union and being in contact with enemies of socialism in the West. Following his release Ličko became a recluse, renting a large allotment where he grew fruit and vegetables, some even for sale, and only rarely descended into the world of the cafés.

So he had one hundred and forty thousand crowns, give or take, but for him this was as good as a million – a fantastic sum, an abstraction beyond his imagination. It wasn't the kind of money he could spend partly in second-hand bookshops and partly on drink, or squander it in some other way. It was an amount that was impossible to spend the way he was used to spending money. He felt like Pushkin's *The Miserly Knight* and remembered the production of this play he had seen before the war, and how in those days it had struck him as the Revelation of St Avantgarde: back then, names such as Meyerhold, Tairov, Okhlopkov, E. F. Burian, Charles Dullin and a host of others that he had since forgotten, had been as familiar to him as the names of his classmates at the *gymnázium*. Until then he had only read about them and seen images, and this was the first time he saw it with his own eyes: centre stage there sat the old miser, perhaps the only character in this little tragedy by Pushkin, surrounded by mountains of coins, he sat there rifling through them, scooping them up in his hands like sand and revelling in their jingling as they dropped onto the pile of gold coins. The scene was set at night, the old miser was illuminated by a single spotlight and the coins seemed to glow with a golden luminosity from below… and now he was sitting here like that, among a cornucopia of coins in the form of savings books.

A new continent had opened up before him, yet there was nothing for him to see there.

For example, should he suddenly feel the urge to buy something, he could just go down to a shop and get it. But he knew already that there wouldn't be anything he might feel the urge to buy. That, too, was something you needed to be trained for from your childhood and youth, that was when the imagination evolved which you need to grasp what money can buy. It wasn't something you could catch up on in retrospect.

When he was still at *gymnázium*, soon after his father died, he took up tutoring children. He would always think long and hard before he spent four or five crowns on the latest issue of a literary monthly, and wondered if he should spend ten or fifteen crowns on a book he spotted in the window of a second-hand bookshop. First, he would stop at the window every time he passed by, pondering before going in and asking if he could take a look at the book. Later, during the war, after he'd been refused entry to university, he would become a regular at the city's pawnshops. He became familiar with all those elderly, always rather potbellied gentlemen behind the counter, their black broadcloth sleeve protectors pulled up to their elbows. There were three pawnshops in town altogether, the one he visited most frequently being in Ventúrska Street, on the ground floor of a former palais; in this enormous, eternally gloomy room with historic vaulted ceilings they would accept almost anything. Standing in the queue before him there would be Gypsies, both male and female, some shady individuals, characters from the underworld, as well as ordinary penurious folk – their neighbourhood was a stone's throw away. People would bring ancient eiderdowns, worn clothes and shoes, a tattered pink slip, old handbags, cheap doilies. On the other hand, the recently-opened pawnshop in a little side street off the main square, which belonged to a bank located in the same building and specialised in gold, silver and jewellery, filled him with awe: he would offer them some object and it would be handed back to him across the counter with the indignant explanation that this was only gilt, not gold. The third pawnshop was more bourgeois. Close to the exit from the cinema, then called Tatra, later Pohraničník, this was the only pawnshop where he had seen every room, even those normally out of bounds to the public. It was when he was still a boy and his father had taken him along because he was going to write a newspaper report about it and the owner or manager gave them a tour of the large warehouse halls; it felt like being in Ali Baba's cave. The staff there were more discriminating and refined, so he could always guess whether to take some object there or to Ventúrska. His mother had gathered a veritable pile of tickets, and took scrupulous care to pay any extension fee in time, even if it meant pawning something else, but ultimately they lost everything they had taken to all three pawnshops, because they were all plundered by soldiers as the front passed through the town in the final days of the war and newspapers soon carried the ideologically joyful news that all pawnshops had been abolished as immoral businesses exploiting the working people. He had no reason to feel ashamed in the pawnshops, as he'd frequented them for the purpose for which they existed, but, on the other hand, he felt ashamed when his mother asked him to take something to the goldsmiths: he would stand there like a beggar next to moneyed people who had come to buy something, whereas he wanted to sell something and leave with money. The man behind the counter would examine the object he had brought under a magnifying glass and just shake his head so as not to disturb the customers who were looking round, so he had to trek over to another goldsmith's, only to go through everything again... Once he had sold his mother's gold engagement ring there was nothing left for him to sell... After the war there were shortages in the shops and a Hungarian peasant from a nearby village started coming to their flat bringing all kinds of goods at black market prices plus a hefty surcharge for taking the risk of being caught by the police... Every visit from this woman was a financial disaster for him, since his mother would buy whatever the woman had to offer, but no matter how angry he got, it was to no avail, his mother would always argue – but we really do need all this. That was what she'd been like for most of her life: except for the twelve years when she was married she had always lived from hand to mouth, and so had never developed any sense of the value of money. Once she got her hands on any, it would just slip through her fingers, although she never bought anything for herself... when the monetary reform came they didn't have even the minimum amount that could be exchanged without losing out... admittedly, he wasn't much better with money himself: when he was paid a fee he would go window shopping but never spotted anything he might have wanted to buy, anything he would have liked to own, and in the end always ended up in the big new second-hand bookshop where he would rummage through every shelf on the ground floor and the first floor, always finding books he would buy but never read, as a way of spending at least some of his earnings, leaving the rest to burn a hole in his pocket, and if he happened to be in the middle of one of his drinking bouts he would spend some of it on booze, or squander it on something else. Either way he would spend it all to ensure it wouldn't bother him anymore… and more recently, when he no longer had a monthly salary, he would from time to time receive royalties from theatres in the provinces where it took longer to discover that his, or their joint, translations of plays were banned. Then, for a while, an editor at the radio would accept some of his writing and broadcast it until one day she also got scared and sent word that it was no longer possible. He had also done some technical translations for someone who needed to improve his professional qualifications, but once he had improved them he no longer needed any translations… but by then he wasn't spending money on anything at all. Last winter he wanted to buy a pair of waterproof boots but couldn't find any in the shops, now he wouldn't be able to find any either, and as for secondhand books, he was no longer interested, as he had plenty of books at home.

Nevertheless, he was beginning to discern this new continent that was opening up in front of him though, in fact, it wasn't new or unknown: he would be able to live free of cares for a few years. He could stay on in this flat, have lunch in restaurants, buy a bottle of brandy whenever he felt like it; he could roam the city's pubs and cafés without feeling guilty, there would be no one waiting for him at home. Now he could go AWOL not just for half a day or until late at night but for weeks, even months on end. There would be no one looking for him anymore. He might as well stay on his old continent.

In the darkness of the room, his thoughts automatically drifted, as they often did these days when he went to bed and couldn't fall asleep, to the idea that, like it or not, he would have to find a job. And since he could no longer do what he used to do in the past, and didn't want to do anything even remotely similar either – becoming a clerk in some basement archive, or an assistant librarian, or even manager of a umbrella repair cooperative – he'd rather do something completely different. Become a taxi driver, for example. He'd been driving for many years and knew every street in this city: which roads were one way, which streets around the *korzo** in the Old Town were closed to traffic; he'd have no problems there. Also, a taxi driver didn't have to work non-stop: he would drop someone off and then sit in his car waiting, reading a book, or he could chat to whoever happened to be in the back of his taxi, and he might even get a tip from time to time. He also had a plan B. The caretaker's wife in their block of flats was a manager in a large supermarket in a mammoth newly-built housing estate on the outskirts of town, where he used to go on Sunday walks with his parents many years ago. The estate had no restaurants or pubs, only a kind of bar-cum-cafeteria that had opened next to the supermarket. The manager once showed it off to him with great pride. Since then he'd often thought that it might be quite nice to be a waiter in that cafeteria. It was never crowded, people didn't spend too much time sitting around, they didn't order too much food, there were always free tables – he saw just a few couples with a bottle of Coca Cola, a cup of coffee or a small brandy on the table, the odd loner having a sausage or a sandwich; the waiter would bring their order and then hang around to the side watching the customers, which might be more interesting than watching people from his kitchen window, and he might get a few tips to boot. But as he pictured these two scenarios, he couldn't help wondering whether taxi drivers had to pass some special driving test whereas he didn't even know how to take the battery out of a car, and whether a waiter, even in this kind of lowly establishment, needed some sort of vocational certificate. And that left him again with the certainty, albeit unacknowledged, that he would never end up as a waiter or a taxi driver.

He went over to his room, drew the curtains, undressed, lay down, and waited for sleep to come.

He had only a cup of coffee for breakfast. As he went into the kitchen, he saw that it was a beautiful morning, with the sun shining almost as if it were springtime. Over the last two weeks, on his daily trips to the hospital, the weather had been invariably bad. On his birthday, a few days earlier, heavy dark grey clouds loomed above the city for almost the entire day.

He made sure he had all the necessary papers, took the savings book he had got ready last night, and somehow remembered that he might also need his wife's ID, which was still in her handbag, as she'd taken it with her to the hospital.

He rang the door of his sister-in-law's flat one floor below and they drove some three hundred meters further up the hill to where his wife's cousin lived. She was waiting for them. "Let's go to the Institute of Pathology first," she said, once in the car, adding, "I'll show you the way," but he said there was no need, he knew where the Institute of Pathology was: at the point where Záhradnícka Street met the town centre. In the old days, there used to be a bus stop there – buses had been much smaller than they are these days and stopped on every corner. He, too, had been smaller then: as a young boy he would pass the Institute of Pathology every morning on his bus ride to school. They lived at the other end of Záhradnícka, at the edge of town. The fields began a little farther off back then.

On the corner of Záhradnícka, where the pot-bellied, sooty, semi-circular façade of the Institute of Pathology stuck out, he turned into a side street and slowed down. "What's going on?" the cousin asked and he said he was looking for a parking place. "But the Institute of Pathology moved from here ages ago," she said, and told him to drive a little further, until a relatively large vacant area opened up, with a new multi-storied building looming up in the middle like a big white box, with a shapeless ground-floor wing jutting out on one side.

Corridors opened in several directions from a large entrance hall and two staircases led to the upper floors. He waited with his sister-in-law while the cousin went about the business they had here, though it still hadn't dawned on him what that would be. They stood there for quite a long time. He had nothing to say to his sister-in-law, under normal circumstances he would have muttered at least "what's taking her so long," but now it would have been inappropriate to seem impatient. At long last the cousin emerged from one of the corridors and gave him a piece of paper. "The autopsy report," she said. "You'll have to hand this in at the funeral parlour."

Could she take a look at her, his sister-in-law wondered and the cousin also said she wanted to see her one last time. He stood rooted to the spot until one of them asked if he would come and take a look at her as well. He shook his head. It wasn't until he he saw them disappear down the corridor that he realised that this was probably a mistake. A sign of indifference, indolence… His nerves suddenly on edge, he started to pace up and down in the entrance hall. He simply wasn't ready to accept that she was here somewhere, he had thought she was still in the hospital, in some basement, in a special room set aside for this purpose. But it ought to have occurred to him that she'd been moved here. He also felt hurt by the question: "Don't you want to take a look at her?" It sounds so stupid, going to see someone who has died, to pop in to take a look. Admittedly, when his mother died, he'd gone to the room where she lay a few times, and a few times he had even sat down beside her and talked to her silently. But that was at home. Where would he see his wife now? On an autopsy table? And he shook his head, out of some kind of defiance perhaps, anticipating a possible rebuke. Let his sister-in-law take a look at her; she hadn't been to the hospital once over the past two weeks and she hadn't seen her for a few weeks before that.

The two women emerged from the corridor again. His sister-in-law praised the deceased: she was looking so peaceful and unchanged, as if asleep. "What a pity that you didn't come as well," the cousin joined in. All he would have seen was what he saw yesterday. But this was a sober, business-like day. He had come to town to make the necessary arrangements for the funeral, and taking a look at his wife was not part of those arrangements.

As they were leaving, his sister-in-law slowed her pace and turned to him: "You know, as I saw her there" – she didn't say where "there" was – "and her face was so composed and peaceful as if she were just sleeping, I wondered if we should have a death mask made."

He stared at her, aghast. A death mask! The idea would never have crossed his mind. What was the point of a death mask? A death mask was something for a museum, to be exhibited in some ceremonial or memorial hall. What would he do with a death mask? Display it in their flat? Instead of a picture? He still hadn't responded and his sister-in-law continued, musing: "It might be the right thing to do. She deserves it."

So that was it. An important figure has died and an important figure should have a death mask cast. She was such an important figure that it was the relatives' obligation to pay their respects. Of course, she deserved it. Now he could only nod: "Yes, you're right."

The cousin said she knew several artists and one of them was bound to know someone who made death masks. She had taken the day off, so she could make a few phone calls and let him know at lunchtime.

It wasn't until they were in the car that she started to talk about the autopsy report and how glad she was to have seen it. She had died of a brain haemorrhage. It was lucky that it all happened so fast, without any serious complications. She threw in some technical terms which his sister-in-law, also a doctor, understood. He listened to her lecture as he navigated the side streets to Záhradnícka. This is where he could drop her off, the cousin said, she would take a tram home. And as she was getting out, she told him to come for lunch: she might as well cook for two seeing as she had the day off. After she got out he drove on towards the city centre.

It seems to be quite common, he thought, to say that someone is lucky to have died the way they did. He could still recall people saying how lucky his father was when he died. To have died of a heart attack. At the age of forty-two, a long time ago now. His mother had been ill for some fifteen years with Paget's disease, a dreadful spasmodic pain in the head, for which she'd had surgery but never fully recovered. Yet when she died, the coroner who determined the cause of death and issued a kind of autopsy report said that there were first signs of what is popularly known as softening of the brain and so she was lucky to have died so suddenly, of a brain haemorrhage. All three of those closest to him were fortunate to have died the way they did.

Just before reaching the far end of the main square he turned into a narrow one-way street where the sun never penetrated. Last time he'd been there was six years ago, the morning after his mother died. The funeral parlour was on the ground floor of a run-down building and, like most municipal services, was located to the rear of a side street. He even remembered that in this municipal office you had to pass two rooms before reaching the third where the customers were seen. With his sister-in-law he entered and walked through the first two rooms, coming to a halt in the doorway of the second where the manager was in the middle of funeral arrangements for another customer. He even recognised the manager. A tall, sickly-looking man, in shabby, darkish clothes, with a permanently lugubrious expression in his face.

They sat down in the middle room furnished with two round tables like a café, each with a few chairs. Otherwise, apart from a portrait of the head of state on one wall, the room was bare. Ever since he started primary stool, there had always been a portrait on the wall, whether it was in a school or a pub: regimes might change, and portraits along with them, but there had always been some portrait on the wall… Soon every school, office, pub and provider of communal services, including funeral parlours, would be graced with a portrait of First Secretary Gustáv Husák*, whom he actually knew personally. He went to congratulate him on his birthday at a time when no one dared to congratulate him anymore. As a matter of fact it was Viera M who had taken him there: Husák would be arrested soon after, as was widely anticipated, which was why people were afraid to visit him. And not long after he was released from jail he and his wife sat with him on the terrace of the Carlton Café, literally turning the heads of passers-by, since few people dared to be seen with him in public at the time. In the spring of 1968 Husák stopped acknowledging him in the street, as by then he was climbing the greasy pole and came to the conclusion that people like him and his wife could hinder his ascent. In the summer of that year Husák refused to take part in a television discussion if Zora was also invited. Someone managed to persuade him to come but as the participants of the discussion were leaving, no one dared to speak to Zora or walk with her to the tram stop, since this man of the future had objections to her. It was for the same reason that many others stopped speaking to her. And to him. But the man of the future had achieved what he had set out to achieve, having climbed up the greasy pole, perhaps even higher than he ever imagined he would.

Eventually, the other customer left and the two of them moved to the other room, which had a counter in the middle. The manager greeted them from behind the counter with a doleful smile of compassion. He explained why he came – about his wife's funeral – took out his ID, thumbed through it to find his wife's name and then reached into his pocket for the autopsy report he had not yet looked at, nor had any intention of looking at later. That completed the first round of formalities and the manager said: "So that's done," moving on to the actual arrangements. He reached into a drawer for an order form, filled it out, and then the placing of the order could begin. He ushered them back into the first room which displayed their various coffin collections, asking him to look around and choose one. The coffins were stacked on top of one another on dark shelving, arranged in such a way that the customers could inspect the ornamentally carved or glued-on decorations on each model at leisure. He still remembered from the time he arranged his mother's funeral that the coffins were displayed by price, from the most expensive at the top to the cheapest at the bottom. Back then he had chosen the second from the bottom for his mother. Now he was looking only at the ones at the top, intending to go for the most expensive one. But he found it distastefully over-ornate for his wife, who had been a woman of refined taste. One shelf below there was a coffin made of the same kind of wood, with more acceptable trimmings. He pointed to it, the manager noted down the relevant number and, being an obliging salesman, began to enlarge on the accessories he could order and what their purpose was. Before he made his choice, he discussed everything with his sister-in-law. When they had gone over every detail, the manager said, "So that's that," and they returned to the office with the counter in the middle and the portrait on the wall.

The manager filled in all the boxes on the form and calculated the total price of the goods ordered. When he was done, he said, casually: "And of course the funeral will be at Slávičie údolie, right?" referring to the only place funerals were held these days, the central cemetery in the hills not far from the Danube where his mother had been buried in 1964.

"No, no," he said, almost shouting, to stop the manager from writing that down; the funeral would be held in Martin, adding that there was a family vault at the cemetery there so there would be no need to find a spot for the grave. The manager took another list from the drawer and informed him that a transfer of 220 kilometres would cost 4,500 or 5,200 – he couldn't recall the exact figure off the top of his head. He was shocked by the sums, but then he remembered the savings books and just nodded. The manager noted down the distance and the cost of the transfer on another section of the order form, and after a pause, as if lost in thought, he asked: "And roughly when were you thinking of having the funeral?"

He told him what he had in mind: "As soon as possible… tomorrow afternoon if possible." A faint smile could be detected across the manager's worldly-wise face, so he quickly corrected himself: "Or the day after tomorrow, perhaps…" The manager continued to gaze at him with a quizzical smile, so he corrected himself again. "All right, let's say Sunday. This year Sunday counts as a working day and the hours are eight to four o'clock."

The manager pulled a calendar closer, and started speaking in a kind of soothing voice as he passed his finger over individual days: "The funeral can't be held tomorrow, because that would mean the transfer would have to take place today but our drivers get their jobs allocated at seven in the morning. I can't arrange the funeral for the day after tomorrow either, as the drivers have already been given their assignments for that day as well. If it were held here in Bratislava, it might be possible, but Martin is quite another matter. And although this coming Sunday working hours are till four p.m., you have to bear in mind that this only applies to shops: funeral parlours are closed on Sundays. And besides, this Sunday is Christmas Eve and funerals are not held on Christmas Day *on principle*." He put extra emphasis on the two last words. "Just take a look at the calendar. These here are the Christmas holidays, so I can arrange to have the coffin transferred on the first day after the holidays, and the funeral could then be held a day later, on Thursday." – "On Thursday", he repeated, dumbfounded, as if he was hearing this in a nightmare – but that's unthinkable, that's a full week. How was he supposed to manage for seven days in anticipation of the funeral? "On Thursday," the manager repeated emphatically, like an immutable prognostication, adding that he would also have to make a phone call to make sure they had a free slot at the cemetery on that day. "Right now," he continued with his instructions, "you need to bring me your wife's death certificate from the register office because I need to record on the order form that I've seen it." Now his sister-in-law spoke up in a kindly and persuasive voice: "You have to send out the death notices first anyway – they have to be printed and posted, to let people know the date of the funeral; it would really be best to leave it until after the holidays, it really would." He nodded finally; he understood, he got it. He hadn't given any thought to the death notices and who should receive them. The reason why he hadn't given it any thought was because his mother's funeral had been held about a day after he had made the arrangements here. But she'd been buried in this town. And he hadn't sent out any death notices on that occasion. There was no way around it, he had to admit. He had just started to button up his coat absent-mindedly when the manager pointed out: "Wait a minute. Let me add it all up." He included the cost of the actual funeral and the other related operations, totted everything up and came out with the figure of just under ten thousand, certainly eight or nine thousand-plus. The manager pointed out that he couldn't start making any arrangements until the bill was settled. "The only thing I can do now is make a long-distance call to check if they have a free slot next Thursday." Yes, please, he would be very grateful if the manager could do that. And as for the bill, he'd come back with the death certificate at around one o'clock and settle the bill then.

"Well, I think we did well," his sister-in-law said when they were out in the street. He nodded helplessly. Yes, they did really well. Seven more days, he thought again.

Now he had to go to the bank and to the register office. The bank was right here, and the register office was less than ten minutes away. He said goodbye to his sister-in-law at the end of the square, in the midst of the crowds. He lost sight of her as she walked towards the tram stop.

He elbowed his way through the crowds. In this part of the square throngs of people always seemed to be on their way to a rally or coming back from one. Years ago, when this city still felt like home to him, when he used to wander the streets discovering its hidden nooks and crannies, the way a village boy would search for hidden spots by a brook, secret hideaways in the nearby woods, a path across a meadow, even back then it had annoyed him that although the city kept growing, the centre always stayed the same tiny size. The same size as under the monarchy. Everything else was the outskirts. Nowadays the city's population was three or four times what it had been in his youth, yet the centre was still limited to this square and a few adjoining streets… and perhaps also the neigbourhood near the Danube where no foreigner would ever stray, he used to think. But now he no longer felt this way about the city and no longer tried to imagine how foreign visitors might see it and which parts they might give a wide berth; he was just annoyed at having yet again to elbow his way through all these people who seemed to have conspired to obstruct him on his way to the bank. The minute he set out for it, he began to feel somewhat restless and insecure.

The main hall at the savings bank was also swarming with people. This was the worst time of the day: when he and his wife had needed to go to the bank, they would go early in the morning or soon after lunch. The lobby was large and airy, open all the way up to the ceiling of frosted glass, and its sides were lined with gallery-like corridors with doors leading to offices. Normally there were very few people here. Now long queues had formed in front of the marble counters, people were walking up and down the hall, transforming the airy expanse into something more like a crowded waiting room at a railway station.

Among the forms laid out on the counter he found a blue one, for withdrawals, glanced at the slip of paper in the savings book, copied the password and joined one of the queues for savings books. He continued to be agitated and although he was familiar with the procedure for withdrawing money from savings books with a password, his mind kept conjuring up all kinds of worst-case scenarios. What if his wife had got it wrong? What would they do to him? They would summon him to an office and start quizzing him on how he came to be in possession of the savings book. What would they do to him then? Oh nothing, his wife can't have got it wrong, this was just a comedy he was playing out to himself. And sure enough, his wife hadn't got it wrong, he handed the bank clerk the savings book and the form with the password. The clerk went to check the password – he kept his eyes on her throughout – came back, retained the savings book and handed him a slip of paper with a number. What a relief! So it did work. Even though out of all the savings books, he picked the one whose password was his wife's name. Quite an impostor he was… But then again, a password didn't stand for the owner; he too had a savings book with his wife's first name as a password.

He had to wait for about fifteen minutes. The clerk had sent a batch of at least ten or more numbers for processing at the same time. He sat down on a leather seat between two water fountains. He saw people leaning on both fountains from every side, holding slips of paper and waiting for their number to be called. The fountains were once functional.

A long time ago, water had come spurting from them and fallen into small pools resting on short thick pillars of stone. How long ago could it have been? Probably before the war. But what would he have been doing in the savings bank then? Those were the times when he started going to pawnshops. And after the war? He hadn't put any money in the bank then. He could not recall… But the image of the formerly airy space of this hall was imprinted in his mind's eye, with the odd person standing at a counter, others sitting on the leather benches waiting for their number to be called, the fountains splashing gently while he gazed at the surface of the round pools to see if the water would ever spill out. It never did. When could it have been… He was on edge again. He realised he felt almost like a hero on a daring adventure, just because he wasn't using his own savings book. Just then he heard a female voice call his number, went over to the cashier, handed over his slip of paper, the clerk pushed the savings book back to him and read out the sum he was withdrawing, picked up a wad of banknotes and counted them out, starting with the thousands, before placing them on the marble counter. So it did work. Of course it worked, and it would work with the other password-protected savings books, too.

The revolving door propelled him out into the street and the stream of people passing the bank swept him along. After a few steps he came to a crossroads where several lines of pedestrians were already waiting for the green light, so he kept walking, crossed the road further on and turned into Štúrova Street. For twenty-five years, until they moved to their current flat up on the hill, he had walked down Štúrova every day, as he used to live just around a corner in a side street; for twenty-five years every time he left the house and headed into town, he would come out onto Štúrova and continue towards the main square. Right now he was passing the huge windows of Luxor, the self-service restaurant. Through the windows he could see people eating and drinking, huddled around tables like bees: he'd walked past this place so many times that he could write a novel about it. One day as he was walking past it with his wife… it was early days and he didn't yet know her very well… he suggested they go to Luxor and have something to eat but she refused, almost in disgust. He, on the other hand, loved these *automats* – as the self-service cafeterias used to be called back in the day – ever since his father had first taken him to the Koruna in Prague: he had thought that it was marvellous that he could order one thing from one counter and another from the next, sausages here, cakes there… He also remembered how, on the first day after the passing of the front, he had done a round of the streets of the neighbourhood and outside the Luxor layers of thick glass crunched under his feet… the glass in all the shopfronts had been broken, the windows of all the shops had been smashed, he could understand that this was the only way to get in to loot the shops at the back of the ground floor but what he couldn't understand was why it was necessary to break the huge panes of glass on the first floor where the café was located, since the only way to get in there was through the door. By now he'd passed Red Army Street, formerly Grösslingová, he would soon have to cross to the other side of Štúrova and turn into Volgogradská where he had lived for twenty-five years and just then two neon signs came on in his head: one said Tulipán and the other Bláha, making him turn around immediately and walk back to the intersection of Štúrova and Grösslingová. Tulipán was a relatively new bar on Štúrova and the corner of his street, and at the far end of Štúrova there was Café Bláha, now called Krym though he still called it by its old name. Across the street from Bláha was the university and quite close to it a big publishing house, which was why you would always find a few intellectuals in the café. He too had spent many an hour hanging around in this café and also at Tulipán, usually with journalists from the now-banned weekly *Kultúrny život* and right across the street from the house where he had lived for twenty-five years stood a publishing house where the editorial offices of as many as ten monthlies and weeklies were located. He was aware that people he knew might come streaming out of Bláha, or someone he knew might come staggering out of Tulipán just as was turning into the street where he had once lived: it could be someone who'd had a drink or two by this time of the day – it was just past noon – they might grab him by the lapels in a show of affection, and start telling him a story he absolutely had to hear, they might try to drag him back into Tulipán or Bláha, peppering their onslaught with assurances of "you have no idea how fond I am of you," or they might just say "hello, how are you", but he didn't want to hear anyone even saying just hello. In no other part of town was he more likely to bump into someone he knew, so he crossed over to the other side of Štúrova and continued straight down Fučíkova, formerly Fochova Street, and only here was he able to relax, take a deep breath, as here he could be certain of not meeting anyone. In the twenty-five years he had lived in this area he'd passed this street maybe four or five times, on occasion he would stop right at the top, at the Mototechna shop, because he had a small Renault for eight years and this was the only place they sold spare parts for all makes of foreign cars, though he would always have to wait for ages for a shop assistant to ask for a certain part and the answer had invariably been "it's out of stock" – in fact, he couldn't remember ever leaving this shop with the part he had come for. Fučíkova Street was always deserted, only those who lived there ever went this way and, feeling certain that he wouldn't bump into anyone here, his thoughts wandered back to the seven days that lay ahead, followed by the big ceremony at the cemetery in which he would play the main part: goodness gracious, whatever was he going to do for the six days that remained after today… in fact he had no idea what he would do for all those days that would follow after the funeral, but after the funeral it wouldn't matter anymore… Fučíkova led to the Danube embankment and from there it was just a stone's throw from the long and large building that housed the Old Town's city hall, his municipality when he lived nearby and also now that he had moved further out of the centre.

He turned into a long corridor. To the left was the housing department he had twice visited before they moved. He seemed to remember, from the time of his mother's funeral, that the register office was on the second floor, and when he checked the notice board he saw that indeed it was, and made a note of the room number. He went up the wide staircase, which was under repair, just as it had been when he had come about their move and his mother's funeral. On the second floor arrows pointed to various offices – he must have come here also about the tax they had to pay on their rental income when they used to rent out one of their rooms to lodgers they had great trouble getting rid of, and after turning in the direction of the arrow he reached the spot where the corridors forked and a very narrow passage led to a door with the number he was looking for. There was quite a long queue here: this was a very large municipality, many children must have just been born and some people will have died. The latecomers were sitting on a bench where there was still enough room for him. The door faced a small window with a view of the Danube. For some reason, whenever he came to this building, he was always reminded that years ago, under the monarchy, the military must have had offices in this place… perhaps it was the headquarters of the K. & K. Danube fleet…

Meanwhile a number of people had made it into the room, so he got up and joined the queue, until it was his turn to enter a big office with officials sitting at their desks and a kind of wooden, lozenge-shaped island in the middle, with enough room for a female clerk who dealt with the files. He went up to the island and when the clerk turned to him, he rattled off the purpose of his visit and what he needed, produced his ID; the clerk thumbed through it, asked to see the autopsy report and his wife's ID – so he had remembered right, he needed to show it somewhere – took all the papers, studied them, typed up some of the information, pulled out the sheet of paper, stamped it and signed it, put the forms and his papers down on the counter, and uttered her first complete sentence: "We'll keep your wife's ID and pass it on to the housing department, so you won't need to go there." He stood there for a while staring at her, an elderly woman in black overalls, but as she said nothing more, he gathered that she was finished with him, so he said goodbye and left.

He felt almost insulted. It was so impersonal – a single official sentence about her ID. But what was he expecting, he asked himself as he walked down the wide staircase, dodging the builders' ladders here and there, was she supposed to give him her condolences or show compassion in some other way? Should she have congratulated those who came to register the birth of a child? Commiserated and congratulated by turns, eight hours a day? And yet, in the old days, that might well have been the case.

Leaving the building, he noticed the small park on the Danube embankment across the road, on the other side of the tram tracks. Trees with bare trunks and branches, black and sickly, stood there as if someone had stuck them into the ground like carved poles, some thick, some thin. He knew this park like the back of his hand, with all its shapes and forms, since in the course of the twenty-five years he had lived nearby, he had come here countless times and walked along the embankment.

As a student at the *gymnázium* he had begun borrowing books from the City Library and one fine balmy day towards the end of spring he had come to this small park with a couple of books. People were strolling along the wide embankment but he sat down on one of the benches, as back then neither the park nor the embankment were as crowded as they would be on every fine spring day many years later, and he had a bench all to himself, and started reading one of the books from the library, but he couldn't concentrate and his eyes kept wandering over to the groups and couples as they walked up and down, and he heard the gentle hubbub of their voices. All these people seemed somehow joyful, gliding past slowly and gracefully, at least that's how they seemed to him now in his recollection. An idyll. And he was a part of it. He was inside a pastel-coloured impressionist painting.

He turned off the embankment again towards Fučíkova and as he walked down the street a memory lingered in his mind, dangling there, familiar and intimate, because he recalled it so often. It was an evening or rather a night, in early summer, and the only ones strolling along the embankment were couples, he and his wife among them, except that she wasn't yet his wife – they weren't even on first name terms at that point, having met only recently, he was holding forth on some topic or other when he suddenly stopped, turned to her, and kissed her. That was the beginning of what ended yesterday.

He was back at the manager's counter in the funeral parlour. This time he didn't have to wait and presented the final document, the death certificate issued by the register office, the man wrote down its number and place of issue on the order form, tore out a copy and gave it to him to sign, and to avoid the manager having to remind him, he said: "I might as well pay now." The manager then tore out his copy of the receipt, signed and stamped the original as well as the copy, gave him some change and told him he'd made the long-distance call about the funeral, everything was arranged, the funeral would be held at three o'clock the following Thursday afternoon. "Is that definite", he asked, "or should I ring again after the holidays to check?" – "No need, it's all confirmed, it's three o'clock on Thursday." So it was definitely seven days from now, six days not counting today. He shook the manager's hand and went back to his car.

Instead of driving into the garage he parked in front of their block: he might have to go down to the supermarket for some groceries in the afternoon.

Upstairs in the flat he first phoned his brother at the Technical University, someone answered the phone and said they'd look for him. Pavol was usually working in a lab where there was no phone and when he did come to the phone, he informed him of the day and hour of the funeral so he could include this information in the death notice. His brother said he'd let his wife know straight away; he wasn't sure if his father-in-law would be able to get it done today but he would definitely bring the printed death notices round tomorrow. Pavol sounded almost cheerful, happy he was able to be helpful.

Back in his room, he could finally settle down in his capacious wing chair and light a cigarette. After finishing it he would lie down, he thought, because he was so tired. But he was barely halfway through the cigarette when the phone rang. The cousin. "I must have rung at least a hundred times, what's going on?" He knew her well enough to understand that when she said "a hundred times" she meant two or three times; she'd had his lunch ready for nearly an hour and would have to warm it up. He apologised, everything took longer than he expected and he would tell her all about it in person. With the unfinished cigarette in his mouth he put on his winter coat again. He'd actually completely forgotten about lunch. He took the lift down and drove over to her house.

The soup was already on the table. As he ate, he gave her a detailed account, starting with what happened at the funeral parlour. Now he admitted how shocked he had been to learn from the manager that the funeral couldn't be held earlier than basically a week from now, on the Thursday after the holidays. Seven days from now, he said with resignation, without going into the detail of why for him these seven days would be an endless limbo and how horrible he found the thought that at the end of these seven days he would have to make a grand appearance before an audience. She brought him a plate of meat and potatoes as he briefly mentioned the bank and the silent rigmarole at the register office, the matronly figure in black overalls and the sole complete sentence she had uttered about the ID. And finally, the confirmation of the time and date of funeral at the parlour, three o'clock next Thursday.

His wife's cousin, meanwhile, had gleaned some useful information from a couple of artist friends: it wasn't sculptors or other artists who made death masks, there were just two craftsmen in this town who worked in plaster, making all kinds of plaster casts at some technical institute or other. She told him the name of the institute and the address. He nodded twice, as no further explanation was needed, he knew where the place was. There was an ice rink across the street where he had learned to skate many years ago, but once he'd mastered skating round in circles his friends mocked him for looking like a buffoon, with his arms gliding like sails in his fluttering winter coat and long trousers, but he didn't say a word about that. He finished his lunch and lit cigarettes for both of them.

Of course he knew where it was. The building used to be called "the vocational school"; that's how his parents had referred to it when he was young. Only recently he read in a technical magazine that before the war the building had been the seat of an outstanding arts and crafts college, second only to the one in Prague. After the Munich Agreeement all the Czech professors were expelled and since most of the teachers had indeed been Czech, that put an end to the arts and crafts teaching, and the building was turned into a vocational school. The original college had probably been housed in some old building, while this new one was built in the Bauhaus style. Sometimes he would indulge in this kind of edifying lecture to show that he knew everything there was to know about the city where he was born and had lived all his life, so he now added a few facts and figures to his lecture on the vocational school that was once an arts and crafts college.

He lit another cigarette; he felt like staying here and resting for a while longer, but the cousin reminded him that it might be better to get going straight away; since the craftsmen were likely to finish work around three o'clock, he might as well get this matter sorted out today as well. She said he would find them on the second floor and handed him a slip of paper with one of their names.

He drove to the wide but short Vazovova Street and parked right in front of the old Bauhaus-style building.

He took the lift to the second floor and spotted two men in boilersuits at the far end of a long corridor. They were having a cigarette and a chat. They paused when he stopped in front of them and asked where he could find the person whose name he had written down. "That's me," said one of the men, tossing the cigarette butt onto the stone floor and stamping on it. He introduced himself and explained why he was there. The two men, both shorter than him, directed their silent, probing gaze at his face. Their first question was how many extra casts he wanted. He didn't understand the question. Did he want just the original or some extra casts as well. Well, maybe one extra, he replied without thinking about it, since they had offered. In the meantime, the second craftsman had also tossed away his cigarette butt and asked: "And who's paying, some organisation or is it a private job, for you?" Almost ashamed he confessed that it was a private job, just for him. He realised that the two men normally dealt with organisations that commissioned death masks for functionaries, political figures, writers, academics, generals and old, worthy members of the party. It was probably quite rare for a private person to commission a death mask. A private person like that would have to be an oddball and must certainly be rolling in money.

"Well, that'll be…" one of them began, and after a while he said, as if he had just worked it out "five thousand five hundred." This figure lingered long in his memory. The man announced it as casually as if talking about a kilo of potatoes but it left him dumbfounded. They would never have charged an organisation so much, there must be set prices for such things. Also, they would have to invoice an organisation and deduct the tax. That is why they had looked at him in such a probing manner, sizing him up before deciding how much to charge. Here was an insecure customer with a shaky voice wanting to get the whole thing over with as soon as possible, who would cough up whatever they asked for, no questions asked. He was in no position to haggle. At least, he certainly didn't give that impression. And they were right. He thought again: sure, what private person has a death mask of his wife made? But the voice of his sister-in-law echoed in his mind. It's the done thing, she deserves it.

They must have seen his shock, so one of the craftsmen briefly explained: "Three thousand five hundred for the original, two thousand for the extra cast." And he added, as if to reassure him: "The extra will be just like the original, a spitting image." But what would he do with the extra that would be the spitting image of the original? And what would he do with the original? Then he heard his sister-in-law's voice in his head again: she deserves it. Yes, she does. And an extra as well. He nodded.

"We might as well go and take a look at her straight away," one of the craftsmen suggested. "The sooner we get started the better." Of course, a corpse quickly loses its firm shape, and they are meant to make the death mask as lifelike as possible. He said he could drive them over to the Institute of Pathology, his car was downstairs. "Let's get going," the two men declared and followed him down the corridor in their plaster-spattered boilersuits.

This time he didn't need any directions to the new building of the Institute of Pathology, and he also knew where to park, but as he headed for the main entrance where he'd been earlier in the day with his sister-in-law and the cousin, the men stopped him. It was the single-storey wing they wanted, a long windowless annexe. There was an iron door at the end and one of the men rang the bell.

The tall, skeletal man who opened the door wore long white overalls and had a sickly, sallow complexion. "My wife is here and…" but there was no need to say any more, the man in the white overalls opened the heavy iron door wide and let them in. He must have known the two craftsmen and guessed why they were there. He went over to a stand by the wall, picked up a large book, ran his eyes over a two-page spread, turned and started walking towards a very long room. As he turned around, he saw a continuous row of metal racks on one side, each holding three large containers. It reminded him of the walls of lockers he'd seen at railway stations in the West, except those were much smaller, meant for suitcases and bags. The man led the way, pausing at one of the shelves and checking the numbers on the containers, then he pressed a button next to the lowest one and the container – at least that's how he later remembered it – slid out or rather, almost shot out. Before he had time to recover, the far edge of the metal container crashed into the front iron wall of a rack. He heard a loud bang on impact. At the same time he heard a much softer but distinct "knock" and as he stared in astonishment at what had slid out in front of him, he realised that it was her head that had made the knocking sound, as the abrupt move of the box had raised it and the sudden impact lowered it again, making it hit its metal mattress.

He stood there perplexed and open-mouthed. He couldn't believe that this fellow had just pushed her out in her container, naked from the waist up. He felt his face blushing with shame and indignation. How dare they? He had never known a woman who was more modest. If they could cover her up to her waist, why not up to her neck? He wasn't showing her to two physicians but to two complete strangers, craftsmen working with plaster. It was her face they needed to see, that was why they had come to take a look at her. There was nothing else they needed to see. His feeling of shame mingled with a sense of embarrassment. The two craftsmen were now probably staring at her noticing that she had only one breast. A single-breasted woman. If only he could at least explain that her other breast had been removed two years ago because of cancer. But he had to pretend that the two men were not seeing any such thing. Even though they were, of course, thinking that he must have had some fun in bed with a woman like that. He kept asking himself how it could happen that they put her on display in this way. Who gave them the right to exhibit her and expose her to mockery?

He didn't know how much time had passed from the moment he heard her head make a knock, when one of the two craftsmen said matter-of-factly: "That's that, then." The two men looked at her with some interest but they saw something different from what he did. They needed to check that they could work on her. Her face had acquired a sallow tinge and no longer had the natural colour she had the previous night in hospital, but its shape, features and expression had not yet changed. This morning, his sister-in-law said she looked as if she was just asleep. But where was it that she saw her? Here in this box? Did she hear her head knock against the metal as well? Or had she still been laid out somewhere on an autopsy table, a sheet covering her up to the neck? Now she was covered with a thick tarpaulin up to her waist. Frozen. Half-naked. Missing one breast. Her face still looked as if she was asleep. He realised that his gaze kept shifting from her face. They shouldn't have done this to her.

One of the craftsmen, who had other things on his mind, turned to him. "It will be done by the end of next week." Why of course: Christmas was coming up; he knew that already, and didn't really care when the death mask and the extra would be ready. "One more thing: we need your phone number so we can let you know when you can come and collect it," he heard one of the men say. He gave them his number.

The men seemed to be in no hurry to leave. Perhaps they would begin work straight away. They probably kept some plaster and some tools here. So he said goodbye and the sallow-skinned man opened the heavy iron door and slammed it shut behind him.

He stood there in the dull light of the December afternoon, facing the feeble setting sun low on the horizon, the winter haze lending it the colour of a lemon about to go off. He walked along the length of the annexe to his car. If his sister-in-law hadn't come up with the idea of a death mask, he needn't have gone through this, seen it, heard her lifeless head knock against the metal. But that, too, was factored into in the price of the death mask.

He got into the car and on his way home stopped to buy some butter, cheese and cold meats. For dinner and breakfast. He added a small bottle of brandy to his shopping basket.

At home he unloaded the shopping onto the kitchen table and went over to the phone to ring the cousin. Yes, he did get hold of them, made all the arrangements, it was all done. Five thousand five hundred. She let out a shriek: "Five thousand five hundred?!" Yes, but that included an extra copy which would be just like the original. But what would he do with the copy? Now he asked himself a question he'd been wondering about all along: what would he do with the original though... but not wanting to sound annoyed, he added: "Oh well, another expenditure of this kind, you only have to do it once..." and then he thought, this was what the savings books were for, after all. He'd also gone to the Institute of Pathology with the two men. So he had seen her now? the cousin asked, almost as if she were excited to have let him have this pleasure. Yes, he had seen her. However, he didn't ask if she and his sister-in-law had also seen her in the container, if they had heard her head knock against the metal, and if she and his sister-in-law had also seen her naked from the waist up. They probably saw her in a different place and anyhow, it didn't matter anymore. He had seen her. And now he was going to have a lie-down and was sure to fall asleep instantly. He'd had enough. So what about tomorrow, would he like to come to the hospital for lunch? Yes, that would be nice. Before putting the phone down, she said: "Have a good rest."

Of course he would go to the hospital tomorrow. He couldn't face going to a restaurant, he'd rather stay at home. The last thing he wanted was to be with people, bumping into someone he knew. He had got used to the hospital canteen. On the very first day his wife had been admitted, the cousin suggested that while his wife was away from home he could have lunch at the hospital where she was a doctor. Now his wife would be away from home forever. Whereas he probably couldn't keep going to the canteen forever, maybe only for a while. But "forever" was something he could start thinking about once the seven days were over.

He put the shopping away: the cheeses and cold meats went into the fridge, the bread into the orange-brown bread bin, made in Denmark, which they'd bought in a special shop after moving to this flat. Over the past few weeks, since being diagnosed with the untreated heart attack, he had quite seriously entertained the idea that something might happen to him. If he now went to have a lie-down and should never get up again, he didn't want someone to find the bottle of brandy on the kitchen table. He hid it in the kitchen cupboard among the vases.

He went to his room, sat down in the wing chair and lit a cigarette. There was one last task left to do: watering the house plants. But first he would have a little rest.

It had been his daily ritual for the past two weeks, the fulfilment of a duty to his wife. On the morning of the day he took her to hospital she gave him two slips of paper with detailed instructions as to which flowerpots had to be watered daily, which every two days, and which needed extra water. Over the past few years, the flowerpots had taken over the flat, sitting on small tables, windowsills, on the parquet floor, everywhere. What surprised him most was that his wife also started collecting cacti, particularly miniature ones in tiny pots. Those were most difficult to water, as he often couldn't manage to fit the end of the small watering can under their tough leaves – or whatever it was they had – and water would spill on the floor, which he had to wipe with a rag. The reason he'd been so astonished by her infatuation with cacti was that only a few years earlier she hadn't regarded cacti as proper, natural plants and actually despised them, thinking of them as some kind of artificial, inferior commodity. In the remaining flowerpots – large, medium and smaller ones – there were all kinds of plants that needed to be watered in different ways, so initially he would carry the watering can in one hand and her instructions in the other. He approached the task of watering the plants in a deadly earnest and fastidious fashion, as he thought that his wife might check in hospital if he hadn't forgotten; she did actually ask him about it a few times and so he treated the watering of the plants as the keeping of a solemn promise to her. And he had kept his promise every day for the past two weeks, even though he found it quite tedious, as the watering always took him over half an hour.

But he wasn't going to spend another thirty minutes watering plants, he'd had enough for today; at most he might water those plants that required an inordinate quantity of water. But then he decided that those plants, too, would manage without it. He got up from the armchair, drew the curtains, took off his suit and climbed under the duvet.

It was about seven p.m. when he awoke. His first thought was that he could now have a sip of the brandy; it would revive him better than splashing water on his face in the bathroom. He'd take care to drink only a little so no one would notice, even if someone were to turn up. He felt for the bottle in the top cupboard between the vases, unscrewed the top and poured himself a small glass. It made him cough, even shed a tear, as he was no longer accustomed to it. The aromatic, rather pleasant stinging sensation abated as the warmth spread through his body and the blood began to course faster through his veins. He rinsed the glass and put the bottle back between the vases. You never knew, someone might drop in. He stood at the kitchen window for a while, relishing the taste of the brandy on his palate. There was nothing happening in the street below. The women who usually trudged up the hill loaded with shopping bags had long returned home. There were no cars with brakes or tyres screeching before the sharp turn. The people driving home from work had already zoomed past by now. No one he knew would be going for a walk at this hour, at the end of December. There was nothing for him to look at. And nothing to think about either… He remembered that the jacket he was wearing today was hanging in the hallway, he found the order form and the bill from the funeral parlour in its pocket and put everything into a drawer in the living room. He would not need it until the funeral. Then he took the money out of his jacket, sat down in the corner of the kitchen where no one could see him and counted how much was left. When he went to the bank to withdraw the money, he already knew how much he'd have to pay at the funeral parlour, and as he wasn't asked for a deposit on the death mask he had enough left. Enough to see him through the holidays. Goodness, the holidays, what could he spend money on during the holidays?

But afterwards he would need to take a train to go to the funeral. And he would certainly need to spend money while he was there. What was left would keep him going until then, he didn't have to go to the bank again. He counted the money one more time, made a mental note of how much was left and put the banknotes away in the desk drawer. He sat down in the armchair in the living room.

So what now? Perhaps it wasn't too early to pour himself another thimbleful? No, someone might yet come by. His sister-in-law perhaps. She might pick up on a topic she had mentioned after they left the funeral parlour, but he dismissed that out of hand and forgot all about it, that was why he didn't mention it to the cousin. His sister-in-law thought it might be an idea to have a gathering in his wife's memory here in the flat or at the cemetery here in Bratislava: she was sure many of those who would not attend the funeral in Martin would come. That may well be, he thought to himself, but one more event to organise here? One more ceremony with him standing before the coffin as the sole bereaved? Complete with yet another eulogy? What else? Why not a whole series of funerals??

No, his sister-in-law wasn't going to come at this time of day, her moral code would deem that inappropriate. If she came up with another bright idea, she would no doubt let him know in the morning. His brother wouldn't be coming either, as he had only rung him at one o'clock, since his father-in-law was unlikely to have gone to the composing room in the afternoon, their busiest time. Someone else might ring the bell, someone who'd heard the news and happened to be passing by… but who would happen to be passing by at this time of the day, in late December, when it gets dark so early… Mind you, anything could happen, he concluded eventually, although it was highly unlikely.

He went back to the kitchen, felt for the bottle between the vases and poured himself another thimbleful, or perhaps

slightly more than he had earlier. He sat down on the kitch-
en bench with his glass and took small, deliberate sips. He
gave a few deep sighs as a feeling of ease started to spread
through his body. When he finished the glass, he held onto
it for a moment, persuading himself that it was all right to
skip supper. He'd eaten enough at lunchtime. He'd rather
pour himself another. But not just yet. He would have to
have a break. There wasn't much in the bottle to begin with.
And someone might drop by after all. No, it was unlikely that
anyone would come now, but someone might phone and the
person at the other end might notice something in his voice.
He would probably sound high-spirited and animated, speak
faster than usual. The cousin for one would certainly notice.
But no, the cousin wasn't going to call, he had told her he was
going to bed, otherwise she would have rung by now, out of
the blue, to ask if there was anything he needed; now she
would think he was asleep and wouldn't want to disturb him.
His sister-in-law, his brother… he started going through the
list of people who might phone at this hour. He felt no desire
for anyone to phone, offer their condolences, except that,
all of a sudden, as he told himself that probably no one was
going to ring now, he became furious that no one was going
to ring the doorbell or dial his number. If he'd been the one
who had died, crowds of people would have come flocking
to give their condolences to his wife. And the phone would
have rung off the hook. They would have come to see his wife,
phoned her to commiserate. But no one cared enough about
him, everyone was going to leave him in the gutter, he was
just a piece of shit. And maybe they were sitting somewhere
and saying: I bet he's now sitting at home or somewhere else
and is quite delighted, because now he can do as he pleases,
and he's pocketed her money too; maybe he's sitting there
all by himself drinking on the quiet so that no one sees him.
Why should anyone commiserate with a low-life like him?
People are scumbags, he exploded, real scumbags beyond

imagination. Damn them all. He was better off spending the whole evening by himself.

That was it, closing time, he decided. He would hole up in his room, the front room window would remain dark. And even if the phone rang, he would just ignore it. He took the bottle out of the cupboard, took the glass in his other hand and made himself comfortable in the wing chair in his room, placing the bottle on the rug by his feet and the glass on top of the radio on the other side. There: now he would be his own, sole company. But he'd be careful, he'd take it easy with the brandy, there were a few more hours to kill before it was time to go to bed, this bottle was all he had, he wasn't going to go out again. He would finish this bottle like a gentleman, while engaging in a steady conversation with himself. He was his own interlocutor and about the only acceptable company at this moment in time. At least until he started getting on his own nerves… How many times over these past two weeks had he sat in this wing chair with a glass of brandy, or without one, like a prosecutor bringing charges against himself in instalments… But now he could stand at ease. He didn't have a clear idea what that actually meant but the expression appealed to him and he kept repeating it: he'd stand at ease.

In any case, he would never have embarked on his affair with alcohol if he hadn't discovered its advantages. He needed a drink to find a way of relating to people, to become chatty, quick-witted, funny, even warm. It used to do the trick with women as well: he would never have got very far with them, known how to approach them, if he hadn't poured himself a little drop of combativeness. Although the list of his successful combats wasn't all that long… There must have been some flaw in him, something that made him so withdrawn, buttoned up, unable to break the glass wall between himself and others. As with his attempt at ice skating, he was beginning to feel like a champion on the ice rink but in the eyes of others he was just a buffoon. They laughed at him. It wasn't

his fault that he was somehow different from the others...
He remembered how, at the age of six, when his parents sent
him to a summer camp for the first time, the other kids kept
hurling insults at him and he even started wetting his bed
there... Fortunately he fell ill and was moved to a separate
room and no longer had to go out for walks with the others.
It had been just like that even before he turned six. He had
never been accepted by the others and had always stood outside the circle. And that is why he ended up feeling insecure
in the presence of others. He was unable to behave naturally.
But alcohol allowed him to shed something, something that
was weighing him down and that was what had driven him to
drink. And that was why sometimes he really needed a drink.

He thought of all the things that would never have happened had it not been for alcohol. Like that time in the little
park on the embankment many years ago, when from one moment to the next, he had turned into a man of action, stopped
talking all of a sudden and turned to kiss the woman by his
side, a woman he in fact respected enormously. He had had a
drop too much before, and many times after that, but on that
occasion something momentous had happened and he still
remembered vividly everything about that day.

On that day he had left home at around ten in the morning,
as he and Chorváth had been invited to talk about literature
with some older students at a *gymnázium*. In those days such
events were organised by the Writers' Union, whose members
would take it in turns to take part. When they got to the
school they discovered that the teacher who had requested
the discussion had been off sick for about a week, and the
school had forgotten all about the talk and assigned someone
to substitute for the class who'd set the students a written
exam for the day, which could no longer be cancelled. Suddenly some spare time opened up before them and they had
to improvise a way of filling it, so they dived into the nearest
pub, which happened to be round the corner. It was one of

those ordinary pubs, with tarred wooden floorboards, the stale stench of beer in the air, and it was quite empty, so they sat down and ordered something to drink. Chorváth, an older critic, had recently published a very scathing review of a novel by Karvaš, which had upset the author quite a lot. They started to discuss this, which took up quite a bit of time. Then there was another recently-published novel on which their opinions differed. They discussed that as well. Some other book had been banned by the censors, and they exchanged views on the manuscript and on censorship in general. They ended up talking about people they knew, writers and critics they'd had dealings with. This was a subject that could be discussed endlessly. And they did discuss it for quite a while. As time went by, the pub began to fill up. Some of the customers ordered lunch, followed by a beer with rum, lorry drivers took a break over a few beers; by then the municipal services workers called it a day, having clocked up sufficient hours for their daily shift. The pub was noisy and getting crowded, so it was no longer possible to have a decent conversation and they moved on, towards the city centre. On their way they took in another three or four pubs, gradually talking less and less, as if they had exhausted every topic. Nevertheless, wherever they dived in, they would have at least one more shot. Chorváth wanted to drag him into yet another pub around the corner from where he lived but there was no point: he wasn't up to talking anymore. Chorváth was fifteen years older, had been drinking for fifteen years longer, and couldn't hold his drink as well as he could, so he came up with an excuse, telling him to go on his own if he wanted to but he'd had quite enough. Having left Chorváth, he turned towards the city centre but didn't bump into anyone. It was now dark. He had stopped in a couple of cafés and in the conservatory of one of them he saw Trachta, his former editor-in-chief, sitting all on his own. He joined him eagerly, having not spoken to anyone for at least two whole hours and went on and on about the kind of day he'd just had. He was in high spirits: the conservatory had been opened up on one side, so people were sitting outside as well, the balmy breeze of a summer evening wafted in, lights twinkled everywhere and he talked and talked… and at one point, as he raised his head from the table and looked round, there she was, by the door, her eyes scouring the interior of the café for someone, so he lifted his hand high in the air and waved until she spotted him, he got up without paying his bill and went over to her beside himself with joy. She had been looking for him, she had come to rescue him from his drinking, he felt that he could lean on her if he weren't steady on his feet, now as well as in future, he felt her protective hand hovering above him and was brimming over with gratitude within. She walked with him to the embankment to get some fresh air. She had spent the whole day at some meeting and then dropped in on him to suggest they go for a little walk, but his mother told her, oh he's been out all day, you might find him at the Carlton or the Savoy, so that's where she went and indeed found him and he explained how he'd ended up going for a drink, it was all the fault of the school but at least he and Chorváth had sorted a few things out. They were now strolling along the embankment illuminated by ancient street lamps. There were no more people milling about, only the odd young couple might pass them, and they could hear their own steps and the gentle swirling of the Danube below. All of a sudden he fell silent in mid-sentence, stopped, turned towards her and kissed her. Quite simply, as if it were the most natural thing to do. He realised his kissing technique left something to be desired but continued kissing her and she didn't object, as if it was something that had to happen one day and now it finally did. They had addressed each other formally until then, since they'd known each other for a relatively short time, yet now they were standing here pressed against each other as if the two of them were a young couple, and with the lights on the embankment shining ahead of them and the lights on the bridge across the Danube further away, his world was full of light and he continued to feel enormously grateful to her for setting out to look for him, for having rescued him, and she, too, was slightly intoxicated. After that he walked her to the neigbourhood of the family houses up on the hill where she was staying with one of her aunts, they walked arm in arm all the way, and at the entrance to the house they sat down on the steps and sat there talking for a long time, discussing the future that they both envisaged would be just like that evening. He would never forget that whole day and remembered it down to the minutest detail.

Later, once she became his wife, she would sometimes come and drag him out of a café or a bar. The last time, as he recalled, it happened at around three p.m., at Café Bláha, now known as Krym. He had told her in the morning that he had some business to attend to at the Slovak Academy of Sciences, where he worked at the time, but instead he tottered from one place to another, having one drink after another, all on his own, until on his way home he came across someone at Krym, this time his wife's friend, a translator, who was there with a man he didn't know. He joined them without asking their permission, and began to hold forth. He could no longer remember what he was going on and on about, by then he could no longer take as much drink as before, all he could remember was raising his head at one point and seeing Zora standing by the tables not too far from the door. She just stood there gazing at him. He got up and went over to her without paying. Her face was hard, as if frozen, her lips pressed tightly together and remained like that all the way home as if she were not listening to him. He understood that she wasn't interested in his excuses. He always had some waffling excuse ready in this kind of situation.

He could still see in his mind's eye all those times in their early days, when he came to the station to meet her and watched her walk up the wide staircase from the railway station underpass, having travelled down from her parents to stay with him, as she scoured the waiting crowds, her eyes bright and her face eager. Back at home she asked him how he had held up while she had been away, and the fact was that most of the time he hadn't held up particularly well, there had been the odd hiccup, to some of which he might admit. With eyes no longer bright and her face dimmed by disappointment, she would, nevertheless, comfort him: it was normal to fall off the wagon, the important thing was to climb quickly back on and so get on his feet again.

And he saw her again in later years, walking up the wide staircase from the railway underpass, her face anxious and her eyes fearful in anticipation of hearing again what she had heard so many times before. He had never owned up to what bothered him most of all: that he could never recall the final two or three hours of one of his bouts. He had never behaved aggressively, or got up to anything terrible, but who knows what he might have ranted on about, blurting out things he would never have said while sober, sarcastic jibes, insulting witticisms, if only he could remember any of it... but try as he might, nothing would ever come back to him. That was what he found most dreadful of all. He could have forgiven himself everything else. Crestfallen, he would sit in the winged chair all crumpled up, a bundle of misery. Sometimes she would stroke his hair, put a hand on his shoulder and say: "Oh, stop worrying, it's too late to do anything about it." And in time she might well have thought it was too late to do anything about him, too.

Come on now, he reprimanded himself; he was overdoing it again, this was another of his bursts of self-pity. It hadn't really been like that all the time, it really hadn't, he assured himself. It would sometimes happen quite often but at other times there would be nothing.

After all, he wasn't a habitual drunkard, someone who can't manage a day or a week without a drink. With him it was an occasional habit. And it had taken many years for this... mechanism of sorts to develop, to make him start drinking for no particular reason and be unable to stop. It evolved gradually, after the war, when he found himself among people who took every opportunity to have a drink. And he would go for a drink with them, before, like everyone else, he went back home. But gradually, it sometimes happened that he wouldn't go straight home like everyone else, and that there were things he couldn't remember. By now he was looking for an excuse and later on he no longer needed an excuse, or other people. Until one morning, about five years after the end of the war, his mother sat down on his bed and said: "You can't go on like this, you have to do something." And she told him what she meant. He underwent a course of anti-alcoholic treatment with a neurologist and managed for nearly a year. Later, by then a married man, he was treated in hospital, followed by twice-weekly appointments when he had to swallow two pills under the watchful eye of a nurse. But this treatment, too, came to an end one day, though its effects lasted over a year. He was capable of stopping and going into rehab at any time. He was what was known as a quarterly drunk. Roughly every three months he had to be on his guard. But this was exactly when he would let his guard down... And sometimes it would also happen in between, when he found himself in company.

After their wedding, his wife stayed with him for one day and then went back to her parents' house. She had to reassure her parents, who must have found out that she had gone ahead and married him despite their opposition, without any advance warning but they had to accept her decision; she was forty-plus and no longer a child. He, too, accepted her decision, but after three days it seemed somehow silly, absurd, unnatural even to be again sitting at home alone, with everything the same, as if nothing had happened. And so he went out in the evening as he used to before he got married, and in that same café with a conservatory he came across two people he knew and joined them. Although he always got back home in a relatively decent state, he had fallen off the wagon again.

It had been his fault, he admitted to himself now, he should have known that it wouldn't be as easy as he'd imagined; she had herself asked him if he would consent to this arrangement, warning him that she wouldn't be able to be with him all the time. She had outlined the whole situation to him, explaining that she couldn't leave her parents all alone, she herself had asked him if he could live with that and he had said he could, and yet he had imagined that things would turn out differently and was disappointed that her protective hand was not hovering above him now that they were married, that she had to hold it hovering somewhere far away, above her parents, and later only her mother. And so he hadn't really changed his ways either just because they were now married, and no invisible halo was shining above his head. Only from then on his quarterly benders, plus the occasional excess – he added only to himself – would be interspersed with periods when she was with him and when she was far away.

From then onwards his life had a dual rhythm. When Zora was with him in Bratislava, she tried to make him change his way of life. She was used to living and working in a disciplined manner and wanted him, too, to work in a disciplined manner from now on. She was cross when he accompanied his mother to the market to carry her shopping bags. He was not supposed to set foot outside in the mornings: mornings were for sitting at home and working. She was right, she was generally right about everything, and he really tried to adapt to her in every respect. And he would have adapted, except that she would soon leave again to stay with her parents. Quite often, after seeing her off at the station and after her train had left, he felt as if he'd regained his former freedom. And that, invariably, meant one thing.

But it wasn't just his former freedom, there were all sorts of other things, her way of responding to his world – admittedly, he now reflected with bitter self-mockery, a drunk, even a quarterly one, could always come up with some excuses, and there was always something; it was cumulative. One day, on their way home, with heavy lorries trundling past, she held her palms to her ears to shield herself from the noise and as she continued walking down the street like that she told him that all this was like a nightmare for her, these crowds in the streets, the noise, the foul air in this city… she felt caged up in the flat, while back home in Martin she had her big garden, a little farther off there were hills and meadows, nature, the landscape of her childhood and youth… so quite naturally she made him feel that this was all his fault, as if he had made her his unhappy victim… And he also had to endure her ignoring of his mother, who didn't exist for her except as some kind of a spectre, which made him reproach himself and think that this went too far, and to despise and castigate himself for being such a piece of dirt to tolerate all this without saying anything. A kind of resentment took root in him about the fact that things had to stay this way: whenever she was with him in Bratislava she regarded it as a temporary arrangement, her real and more beautiful life being far away from him, with her parents, her mother… Now, sitting in this winged chair with some brandy inside him, he tried to make himself stop replaying these scenes endlessly in his head, as if that was what had defined their life together, but that wasn't fair: after all, they had had a fairly normal, contented life, and while all those things that were now entering his mind had happened too, they were not the defining feature of their life together and he knew perfectly well that this wasn't all it was about… all right, it wasn't all their life hadn't been about but it had formed part of it, those things had happened and she had indeed reacted in that way. But he had never blamed her for his own missteps. First and foremost, it was his addiction and he was damned if he knew why he was unable to shake it.

In the early sixties he started a new course of treatment with a neurologist who believed that the problem should be tackled verbally, not by pills or injections. He attended a few sessions and then the doctor told him to bring his wife as well... She spent quite a lot of time talking to the doctor on her own and came out rather upset. At home she threw herself on the couch, sobbing. She was inconsolable and then, all of a sudden, she asked him to take her to this doctor again. Soon she came out completely transformed: he'd given her a strong tranquillizer. She had never said a word about what had upset her so much but she ordered him very firmly: "Stop seeing this doctor."

It wasn't hard for him to guess what the doctor might have tried to do: he tried to persuade her that she, too, ought to do something to make him change his life. As if she had been the cause, as if it had been her fault. It must have made her feel as if a stranger had suddenly stopped her in the street and slapped her across a face for no reason whatsoever. He didn't attend any more sessions. So, of course, the treatment had no effect.

Once, in the early sixties, she had stayed away for weeks on end: her mother was ill with the flu, in addition to some heart problems. He wandered around town, from pub to café to pub again, and when he had had enough of doing that, he bought a bottle of wine and sat down at home doing nothing. In the afternoon he went out and bought another bottle. And wrote her a letter saying he wasn't feeling all that well. She replied, unusually briefly, saying she was desperate, didn't know what to do and that the only solution that she could see was for him to get a grip. The final two lines were crossed out so thoroughly that not a single letter remained legible. What they probably said, he guessed, was that unless things changed the only thing to do was to break up.

(106)

His mother told him: "Pack your things, go and see her first thing tomorrow and talk everything over with her."

That night and the next day on the train he tried to come up with possible solutions. There had to be a way for them not to be living in two different places. Perhaps she might have an idea. The only option he did not consider was the one he presumed had been in her letter. But it turned out that the only realistic solution was for everything to stay the same. Two days later something clicked in his brain. It had happened to him before, though not so intensely, but on this occasion it must have been the result of drinking too many bottles of wine at home, as well as the shock at the way she rejected, flatly and without discussion, all his proposals about how they might combine their two households. And at that moment it dawned on him, finally, that she could not change anything, that nothing could be done, and everything would have to stay the same. She could not provide him with the kind of support he had imagined and she was, first and foremost, responsible for herself and the part of her life that was not connected to him. It had taken him nearly seven years to finally understand and accept this.

He got himself sorted out in hospital again and when he was discharged he was told in no uncertain terms that the even the slightest drop of alcohol would start things off again, and that indeed it would be worse each time and he might never recover. He again went home by himself but now he too appeared to have undergone some sort of transformation: as if he had come to terms with everything. So he would have to manage on his own. He had found his mental equilibrium and was no longer expecting any miracles. He threw himself into his work more than ever. And that lasted for five years or more. Then he had attended some conference or other, he'd given a paper, and there was a gathering in the evening where everyone had some wine, so he had a glassful as well –

and nothing happened. Some time later his mother died and a year after that so did her mother, and from then on they were together all the time. He hadn't turned into a complete saint with a halo. His wife's niece was staying with them in Bratislava, so they didn't have a great deal of privacy, but after a five-year interval he regained his strength and was quite firm on his feet. And eventually only the two of them were left.

He poured himself a little more brandy.

What a success he was, he said, mockingly of himself. Every now and then, he would introduce an element of unrest and anxiety into her life, about himself, about herself. All because of a stupid addiction he was unable to shake. "You have to be strong-willed," his mother used to say. He didn't even know what a strong will meant. He never remembered it when he needed it. By then he was always driven by another kind of will: the will to keep going. Once he put the machine into motion he was never able to bring it to a halt.

He remembered his wife telling him on occasion: "Don't you feel bad about yourself? Can't you see you're destroying yourself?" But he didn't feel bad about himself even when he heard her say that. Admittedly, he could have done more: he wouldn't have felt so insecure in company, his life might have been more pleasant, calmer and steadier without all the upheavals, but perhaps that was something he had also got accustomed to, and that was why he didn't really feel bad about himself... But he did feel bad about her, about the fact that his missteps and lapses, that wretched internal machinery of his, had undermined her and upset her equilibrium. And now there was no longer anything he could do about it. Nothing at all.

But why, it occurred to him, didn't he feel bad about his mother? Why hadn't he agonised and ruminated like this when she died? Why hadn't he delivered such litanies of self-accusation and self-defence then? Probably because she had seen his problems differently. To her it wasn't such a tremendous tragedy, a constant teetering on the edge of a precipice. She had often reproached him and berated him, sometimes even shouted at him and given him a talking to... but it hadn't derailed her, hadn't caused her distress or made her hysterical. She did have a tendency to be slightly flippant about it: oh well, he's having some fun, he needs distraction; he finds it dull being stuck at home all the time; he needs to go out and see people now and then... In fact, she almost rationalised his behaviour. And even on those occasions when she harangued him, it was always with an undertone of indulgence – a brief shower of rain followed by sunshine again: we all have our weaknesses, don't we. Sometimes she too would set out to search for him but when she found him, they would walk home contentedly side by side... here we go again, he had fallen off the wagon once more, but she hadn't lost her trust in him. He was her son, he would sort himself out, she didn't need to worry about him. He certainly didn't cause her any unhappiness and that was why he wasn't racked by any feelings of guilt towards her.

He finished off the brandy. It no longer sent waves of warmth through his body, only exhaustion: he'd had enough. He would just go to bed, whether or not it was made.

He knew he wouldn't fall asleep straight away. But he would no longer think about what he'd been tormenting himself with all evening. He had to call something quite different to mind... And perhaps because his mother was the last thing he'd thought about and in his mind his mother had always been associated mainly with his childhood and youth, a memory came to him, a pleasant and calming one, even though it was also a part of his more embarrassing ordeals.

It was an ordinary working day and he had decided to take the boat to Devín, on his own. The boat ride took an hour upstream, he knew every cove and every meander on this stretch of the Danube. At Devín, he walked along the wide meadow with the ruins of Devín Castle above, and down the embankment of the Morava dotted with restaurants and *viechas*, traditional wine bars. Back in the day, at the end of an outing to Devín with his parents, before they took the boat back they would always go to one of these places, find a table with a white tablecloth, and his parents would order some redcurrant wine for themselves and *kracherlíky* – fizzy lemonade in a special bottle that was no longer available after the war – for him and his brother. He sat down at one of these tables, and as he was almost grown-up now, he asked for some redcurrant wine, a local speciality. He loved it: it was sweetish yet refreshing, and he managed to drink two more glassfuls before the boat left.

The boat swayed gently to and fro, even though they hadn't encountered any other boats and the river was calm. After disembarking, he still felt the gentle swaying as he rode the tram and then the bus, as if still on the boat, but he remembered that this was a sensation that usually lingered for a while after a boat ride, except that it now felt more intense and wouldn't go away. He had to walk only a few steps from the bus stop to the little house with a front garden on the edge of town where they lived at the time, and as he opened the garden gate, suddenly the whole world started to sway. All of a sudden he realised that he was tipsy. That was why the boat, the tram and the bus kept swaying. He thought it was all terribly funny, not least the fact that he had got drunk. For the first time in his life. It felt like an adventure, almost a solemn experience. And he nearly hadn't realised it.

He had enjoyed that outing more than any of the previous ones. He still saw himself sitting there alone, on his own, unlike the times he came with his parents on a Sunday and had to look for an empty table. He was sitting all by himself under an enormous oak, its leaves gently rustling in the breeze with the sun shining through them. Shining at him, too.

The doorbell woke him quite early. He opened the door: it was his brother Pavol, who, seeing him in his robe, said apologetically that he wanted to bring the death notices as soon as they were ready. His father-in-law had gone to the printing works yesterday afternoon, as soon as he was told the date and time of the funeral, and had it typeset straight away, but since only one press was working he had to go back at six this morning and brought them over before Pavol left home; on his way here he had popped into a stationer's and bought two hundred envelopes and two hundred postage stamps. After going into the living room, his brother placed three small piles on the table: sheets of black-framed A5 paper, envelopes and stamps. He picked up one of the notices from the pile and saw the epigraph at the top, and in the middle, in large letters, her name without any of the funeral platitudes, or a profession in the line below, just as he had wanted, just the place and date of the funeral. Further down on the right were the names of the three bereaved – her husband, cousin and sister-in-law, and in the bottom left-hand corner, his address. Everything as it should be. His brother smiled contentedly: he was pleased to have got it done and so speedily at that.

He asked Pavol how much he owed him, fetched a pencil and a notepad, added everything up, took the money from his jacket in the hallway and paid Pavol, who was very scrupulous in such matters. Did he do the right thing buying envelopes and stamps for two hundred death notices rather than for all of them? So how many were there altogether? "Three hundred," his brother said. "Three hundred?" he repeated, as if he hadn't heard right, "Why three hundred?" That's what his sister-in-law had told him last night, he was quite sure she'd said three hundred. "Should there have been fewer?" his brother asked, almost timidly. "No, that'll be fine" he replied, to put his mind at rest, his sister-in-law knew best how many were needed. In Martin alone this would be some kind of social event, he thought. And in order not to offend anyone, he had to send a funeral notice to all the "illustrious families". It was his sister-in-law who had first used this term once when they came to Martin a day late for All Souls'. She had reproached them: "All the illustrious families have already attended to their graves" – even this "attended to" was her special word or a local expression used in Martin, and she'd already been to the cemetery to clean the family vault or, at least, take some flowers.

So how many would he have ordered, his brother asked. He hadn't given it any thought until now. Lately, they hadn't been seeing all that many people. Twenty, perhaps thirty, thirty-five at most, he said. His brother was quite shocked. He was familiar with the expression that appeared on his brother's face whenever he was told the price of something he'd just bought. Pavol believed that the purpose of money was to put as much as possible of it aside and that everything should be available more or less free of charge, or at most a symbolic price.

His brother offered to drop by in the afternoon on his way from work and take the envelopes to the post office. That wasn't necessary, he said as he thanked him. He might not be finished by lunchtime and the post office was just around the corner. In fact, he didn't care whether people received it one day earlier or later. They were silent for a moment. He didn't want to mention the funeral parlour and how much he'd spent there, and certainly not the death mask; that would only upset him. In the end he said: "Don't worry, I'll give you a ring if I need anything." His brother got up to leave; he was in any case already late for work at the technical university.

He might at least have asked, he thought after closing the door behind his brother... actually, what should he have asked?... just generally... how he was going to cope now... He was rather sorry now that their conversation had concerned only the number of death notices, so matter-of-fact, impersonal... but this was how they always talked when his brother came to see him on his own: – he'd talk shop about, say, the relations between the various factories under the auspices of his chemistry department on the one hand, and their Russian business partners on the other, how stringent (or not) their quality control was, the percentage of products that was sent back, although if someone were to test the quality of the raw materials the Russians supplied... the latest news from official circles... who had climbed up the greasy pole and whose position had become shaky ... and he would tell him what was happening in his world... They would also comment on reports they heard on Austrian TV and radio; his brother considered himself particularly well informed because he also listened to the Voice of America, but other than that their conversations where limited to trivial matters... His brother was always able to inform him about any price increases, which he invariably regarded as something earth-shattering. After graduating, Pavol had got a job at the technical university but had never contributed to the family budget unless reminded by their mother, even though it was his earnings that had helped put his brother through school and university. And now he was all wrapped up in his family... There was something slightly impersonal about their relationship. He felt a pang of regret every time Pavol left his house; after all, he was his only relative.

But perhaps that, too, was his fault? After their father died he was often angry with his brother: their mother looked out only for him, she cared only about him because he was younger. Sometimes he would lose his temper and say so out loud and then his brother would follow suit and give their mother an earful, complaining about being treated that way. Their mother would just laugh it off, but some of the old jealousy seemed to have lingered on. He had a classmate whose parents were Czech; they had gone to French class together and he and Pavol used to play cards with this boy, *schnapser* and *mariasch*. And this friend would sometimes say: "Well, sir, it's your turn, sir," with the word sir, *pane,* in Czech and throwing in the odd Czech sentence. He and his brother enjoyed this and started addressing each other "pane" and speaking in Czech. Theirs was a bilingual household anyway – they would speak German to their mother and Slovak to each other. And although there was Czech whirling all around them and they read Czech books, speaking Czech didn't trip off their tongues, as they hadn't actually spoken the language before and would not use it later in life either; and so he would be horror-struck by every "ř" that loomed on the horizon. Others would listen to them and enjoy their clownish double act but this had put even more distance between them verbally. It had become a habit. It wasn't until many years later, after he'd come home a little intoxicated, that he was finally able to bring himself to tell his brother that he thought this whole Sir-ing business and their speaking Czech was just silly, and they started speaking normally again – too late, probably. But perhaps it was all in his head, he thought, not for the first time. He and his brother were basically very different. When Pavol got married and moved into his own flat with his wife, and especially after their daughter Vierka was born, his house became his castle. Even when their mother fell ill, Pavol left everything up to him, she was not Pavol's concern.

He went down to see his sister-in-law and tell her the death notices were ready. She was pleased to hear that and praised his brother for being so clever. She handed him three sheets of paper densely covered in writing – these were the addresses of people she thought of yesterday. She later went to see Martin and Viera Rázus with her list and Viera had added addresses of the people she remembered. And of course, as his sister-in-law reminded him, she was expecting him for dinner on Christmas Eve. Ever since they moved here, that was an evening he and his wife always spent at her place.

Once back home, he took a look at her sheets of paper. There were names he didn't recognize as well as some which he had heard at some point but that meant nothing to him: he had no idea who those people might be. As he went down the list, he kept asking himself: what's this got to do with me? Why should I send death notices to complete strangers? He found only a few names that he noted and ticked off on her list: the address of a relative, Darka Soroková, an ophthalmologist, who along with her husband were the only people they saw regularly on their trips to Martin; Boža Medvecká, also a relative; his wife's old friend Luda Škultéty; and an old gentleman, a friend of his wife's brother Fedor. He made a note of just six names from the three pages.

Then he looked at the second list, Viera's, which was just two pages long. The further down he read, the more astonished he was. This list, too, included some names he didn't recognise, but these were by far outnumbered by names he knew very well and it was beyond him why they, of all people, should be sent the death notice. The editor-in-chief of a publishing house who had written to his wife on six occasions, cancelling contracts for translations she had completed and submitted – four novels she'd translated from the French and two plays in verse they had translated together. The technical director at the state TV – it slowly dawned on him that the man's wife was somehow related to Zora, though she'd probably never even met her... The elderly poet E. B. Lukáč... why? – because he had once been a Lutheran pastor while at the same time writing for a tabloid and representing Živnostenská strana, the Independent Retailers' and Craftsmen's Party, in parliament? Or was he put on the list because years ago, when people were being expelled from the Writers' Union, he had angrily demanded that there be no discussion about the list they had received in advance and that they should all be expelled en bloc immediately? Or Matuška, the high priest of literary criticism... he used to visit them at their old flat – but that was a long time ago; he hadn't shown his face here for at least four years now. And Huba, his former boss from the days he worked as dramaturg at the National Theatre. They had bumped into each other a few times near their house in recent years, as they were almost neighbours; Huba always greeted him as warmly as in the old days, but he never dropped in, because, as a member of the party's Central Committee, he had to be careful who he associated with... Or another elderly poet with whom neither he nor his wife were acquainted... presumably one of the regulars in the *viechas* the Rázuses frequented... Finally it dawned on him: this was a list of illustrious people, the equivalent of the illustrious Martin families on his sister-in-law's list. If he could, he would have scratched out some so thoroughly that they became illegible. Oh well, never mind: let them send death notices to whoever they like, including the President himself and the whole government and all the members of the Politburo.

The only name he copied from this list was that of a former colleague of his, Petrík, who had also been fired: he was not particularly distinguished but he lived in the same block of flats as the Rázuses. He totted up the addresses on both lists that he hadn't ticked off, counted out the requisite number of envelopes and stamps for each list, got dressed and went downstairs to his sister-in-law's.

Again he stood in the doorway while he explained that he knew hardly anyone on her list, that he had ticked off a few names to whom he would send a death notice, but as for the rest... she should send them out herself, giving her name as the sender, as they didn't know him and were unlikely to respond to him in any case. His sister-in-law looked puzzled as he reached into his briefcase for her list, the envelopes and stamps; he knew what she was thinking: he wasn't even prepared to send out his wife's death notices. Feeling awkward, he hastily said goodbye and ran down the stairs rather than waiting for the lift.

Now he had to go through the same thing with the Rá-zuses. This was the most convenient time, Viera and Martin were out, only Viera's mother would be home and she would not be surprised, she'd just pass on the message.

The old lady was nonetheless genuinely surprised to see him standing in the doorway, pulled him inside, shut the door and without a word planted a symbolic kiss on both his cheeks. She ushered him into the hall, as these windowless rooms in the centre of flats were known. Sometimes in the evening, when he and his wife came to visit, they would be offered seats in this room, which had then been lit by a chandelier, but now an inhospitable semidarkness reigned as only a few rays of light filtered in through the door leading to one of the other rooms, which was slightly ajar. Enormous pieces of heavy black furniture bulged out between the doors into the other rooms, making the room appear even darker and more oppressive. He opened his briefcase and was about to start explaining why he was there but the old lady didn't seem to be paying any notice and started talking: she said she couldn't believe it when her daughter told her the news last night, and so suddenly too…

"It's as if a piece of your own life was gone, you see," she said in her elderly, slightly hoarse voice, as she sank so deep into the lounge chair that almost nothing but her hair was visible. "It's nearly sixty years since I first saw Zora in a pram," soon after she herself had married, she continued, as if reminiscing to herself. "And I remember very clearly, even though it's a long time ago, that by the age of four or five she was already a very withdrawn child, always preferring to play by herself." Later he recalled that of all the things she said, this single sentence was the one that told him something about his wife that he hadn't known before.

"And when she was in primary school and was sent to the Tatras for her health, we went to see her a few times" – actually, she was at *gymnázium* by then, he mentally corrected the

(117)

old lady – "because they'd heard some rasping in her lungs, they sent her to a private sanatorium and kept her there for as long as possible before they came clean and admitted that she didn't have tuberculosis after all." He could remember photos from this time, with her parents as well as the old lady and her husband… but there were also pictures that showed her fellow patients; she had confessed to him that she had a crush on one, a boy from Moravia, whose parents were poor, so his stay at the sanatorium had been cut short, possibly also because he was beyond help; he was sent home and died soon afterwards.

"And when she got a bit older, my husband said to his brother" – Zora's father – "a trip to the seaside, to Venice, would do her good." She had only one photo from this vacation, taken on the beach in the Lido, her only trip abroad for a long time.

"Sometime later my husband bought a car," a six-cylinder one, he added to himself, recalling a letter the old lady's husband had written to his wife's father. The car had cost sixty thousand, a fortune in those days, but back then the old lady's husband was the director of a large bank and the owner of a large farm. He needed a car urgently, he told his brother in his letter, because of the farm, so he could go there whenever he needed to and make sure that everything was going well – though apparently without much success, since each letter to his brother explained in great detail why the farm was again not going to make any profit and so he wouldn't be able to send him any money: his wife's brother must have owned a share in the farm.

"In those days we would always take someone along when we went to see them and then we'd go for a drive, either to Strečno and along the river Váh, or to Mošovce, where my husband went to primary school for a few years, and sometimes we would go as far as Liptovský Mikuláš and always stop to look at the house where my husband's brother had a shop before the war." Whenever he and his wife passed through Mikuláš he would also slow down in front of this house where his wife's father used to have a general store until about 1912, selling scythes and nails, and his wife's parents would make bacon or ewe's cheese sandwiches for the workers on their way to the early morning shift. Her parents had never lived in such poverty as in those days, when they had acquired the shop with some irrecoverable debts. Even half a century later the old lettering with her father's name still showed through the new shop sign on the house.

"We would always stop somewhere on the way with a picnic basket and sit down by the roadside" – in those days there hadn't been so many cars barrelling along the road. A haycart might trundle past every now and then; in his mind's eye he could see the old photos showing the family assembled around the car, its driver complete with a driver's cap and uniform. His wife's father had been a passionate and skilled photographer, possibly the only one in the region, and was still taking photos on glass plates and developing them himself. His landscapes, and the people in these landscapes, were quite ordinary and quiet, and therefore strange, with a kind of melancholy and nostalgia about them. Back then it was not customary to seek out scenic motifs, the photos didn't boast loud, contrasting colours; her father captured landscapes that formed a part of everyday life and had equanimity, calm and constancy as their main motif.

The old lady spoke about how his wife Zora, when she was in Bratislava studying at the conservatoire, would come for lunch at their house almost every Sunday and how on weekday afternoons she would practise "here, on this piano," she said, pointing to a large and shapeless object under a thick blanket which no one seemed to have played for an awfully long time – but this lasted, he thought, only until her father bought her an upright; he used to send her an allowance as well as a monthly sum which always included an instalment for the piano. She used to practise at the YWCA in Záhrad-nícka Street where she lived. In those days he actually lived at the other end of that street and would pass the YWCA nearly every day on his way to the city centre. She had been given the use of a room where she would practise every day for hours on end, so much so that her hand often hurt and she had to take a break for a couple of days: she once explained to him that she had short fingers, a handicap for a pianist... "And after Sunday lunch she would also come here and chat with our daughter and her friends; sometimes she and one of the girls would go to the opera or a concert," but that happened quite rarely, he was surprised to discover on reading the letters she'd written to her parents at the time, giving an account of everything she'd been doing... The old lady also recalled the time her daughter spent the summer at a hunting lodge with Zora. "I forget who had rented it, but unless I'm very much mistaken it actually had its own hunt-ing grounds." In fact, it was rented by the father of his wife's cousin; he'd also been a huntsman and his wife's cousin used to traipse around the forest after him, carrying a rifle on her shoulder... he wished she would skip this chapter or at least keep it short, for he knew all there was to know about the hunting lodge, having heard so many stories about it: how they had slept on plank beds covered with spruce branches and how a shepherd used to bring them fresh ewe's milk in the mornings... one day his wife even showed him the spot where the lodge had been, all that remained of it was its charred site, because the Germans had burned it down during the National Uprising of 1944, as indeed they had every lodge in those mountains. The old lady tried to rise, with some difficulty: "Wait a minute, let me show you some photos, we have a whole box full of them." He could have told her he also had several boxes and albums full of photographs of the place at home, as his wife's father had also photographed it enthusiastically. Some of the pictures showed the whole clan, with his wife's parents, herself and her brother, her cousin's parents, her cousin and her two sisters, Viera, and all sorts of other people, whoever had joined them in a particular year, but the most frequent image was of a bunch of girls. Always the first person he could make out was the cousin who, although she was a bit chubbier then, wore her hair just as today, a boyish cut with a parting on one side, the same style all her life… and he also eventually managed to make out his wife amongst this bunch, although she had changed a great deal over the years: back then she was slim, with a longish face and regular, rather graceful features, and always seemed to be lost in thought, as if gazing into herself even while everyone around her was smirking… and in some earlier photographs that were probably taken in her final year at *gymnázium* she was always all by herself in the garden and bore an uncanny resemblance to her niece Jelka at the same age, before she came to live with them in Bratislava, except that, unlike Jelka, she always seemed shy and self-conscious, slightly awkward – this rather unlikely genetic symbiosis, this mysterious likeness, may have lasted only a short time… and then later, during the war, she looked more grown-up, like an emancipated and modern woman… but by the time they met her face was no longer the one in the old photos, her figure had filled out more, her face had widened, the cheekbones becoming more prominent. Of course, she was no longer in the first flush of youth, as by then she was a little over forty, yet she retained her thoughtful, reserved, somewhat shy demeanour… if anything, she looked older than her age, which was probably why there had been so much gossip about the two of them when people started seeing them together. But since then, in the course of the almost twenty years that followed, she had hardly changed at all… fortunately the old lady was unable to find the box she was looking for, and he wouldn't have to look at the pictures, all of which he had seen before.

"And then, after the war, we used to sit in our room and my husband would write letters to his brother, quite regularly, as there was no one else left for him to write to." He recalled both the early letters in which the old lady's husband told his brother about buying the car and why the estate wasn't profitable, as well as the ones written later, in which the old pensioner just complained about life and said that he'd grown tired of everything, was stuck at home, of no use to anyone, and how his daughter was really just doing him a favour letting him live with her.

"Well, but you know all this of course. Sometimes we would visit them in Martin and stay for a week or ten days, as there was nowhere else for us to go." He did remember that his wife's parents were not exactly overjoyed when they announced a forthcoming visit: his wife's father would mumble something, he had probably never forgiven his brother for the farm from which he'd never had any benefit and yet had to pay taxes on, even when it was confiscated after the war – and there was something else: the two of them always had to be entertained, danced attendance on, as if they had a maidservant and a cook…

"That last time you already had a car and my husband was ever so grateful to you, to his dying day." That last visit might have ended in disaster. Zora's father was no longer alive and Zora couldn't help scowling, as she felt this was all too much for her mother. She became increasingly irritable, which was a bad sign, and the tension was so thick you could have cut it with a knife. He felt sorry for them and offered to take them for a drive, though the old man could barely squeeze into his tiny Renault, as he was rather large, and he could feel the car was leaning quite heavily to one side. He drove them to Strečno and on to the River Váh and Mošovce and to various other places in the mountains that were not accessible by car in the old days when they had been chauffeured around in their six-cylinder car; he took them somewhere different each day and the old man kept repeating with touching gratitude that he would never see any of those places again, and he was right: this was the last time he would see the countryside of his childhood.

With this, the old lady's reminiscences came to an end. She leaned back in the armchair and he could see her face as she was apparently getting ready to say something to conclude her account, but in the end she just heaved a sigh: "Dear oh dear, life is hard, let me tell you. Especially when you're old and alone." How true, he thought, though he wasn't yet old.

Silence reigned for a while. Then the old lady asked: "So how many years had you been together?" "Eighteen," he blurted out without thinking, and corrected himself mentally, eighteen and a half, or nineteen, if you didn't go by the marriage licence. He had a lump in his throat and tears welled up in his eyes: he hoped he wasn't going to fall apart again, swallowed hard, and managed to control himself. The old lady sighed again. She and her husband had been together for forty-eight years… such a long time, it was almost unfathomable. But what could he have said to the old lady in response to her forty-eight years, what cliché? He had overstayed his welcome as it was. He opened his briefcase, took out the list, the death notices, envelopes and stamps and launched into an explanation about the names and people he didn't know and to whom he wouldn't be sending anything, though Viera and her husband could do as they pleased. His words came out in a rush; the old lady wouldn't remember most of it anyway, but they'd understand since his sister-in-law was bound to phone and complain about him.

He asked to be excused, as he had to go to the hospital canteen or he'd be too late for lunch. They exchanged holiday wishes and he found himself back in the street.

He wasn't too late for lunch at the canteen, though they would soon stop serving. But he could hardly have stopped the old lady's account in the mid-1930s, at the point where his wife was about to graduate from the conservatoire. She had no one she could chat with to her heart's content. If she'd started reminiscing like this in her daughter's presence, she would interrupt her after a while: "Please, mother dear, we know all his," and when she got together with the other old biddies in a café, she couldn't talk about someone they didn't know... He didn't have to sit there for so long listening in silence either, but he felt sorry for her... he could have interrupted her over and over again by saying – I know, I know, my wife told me all about it – oh yes, yes, I've seen the photos – yes, I remember, I've read the letter in which your husband mentioned this to his brother... no, actually he couldn't have admitted reading letters addressed to someone else that should never have got into his hands... it happened three years ago, when his wife moved some of the furniture from her parents' house to their new flat in Bratislava and was clearing out her parents' house so that it could be rented, all except one room and the kitchen: they had to go through the entire contents of the house and sort everything out. His wife had gone around the house and turned up with a huge pile of family correspondence going back half a century: everything including postcards, telegrams, holiday and Christmas greetings. She no longer wanted to see any of it, wanted to cut herself free of the past and asked him to "just throw out everything you can", so he started reading, sorting and throwing out, and this was how he came across the collection of letters from the old lady's husband and ended up reading them. Most of them concerned the estate and every sentence made him laugh, as their style was stilted yet twisted, florid like a salesman's pitch yet hackneyed and theatrical. He thoroughly enjoyed them, sometimes even calling his wife and reading out the odd excerpt to her; she too had laughed but then frowned, "oh, but it's not a nice thing to do, he was my uncle after all." The letters the old man had written later, after the war, were monotonous and sounded more natural, always the same laments, he just skimmed them, until a sentence in one of the letters stopped him in his tracks: he read it for a second and a third time. Why, but this is about me, he thought, quite stunned, realising that back then his wife's parents had sounded the alarm to their relatives as well. He read the sentence over and over again: it was an echo of the huge storm that had buffeted his wife's parents' house in those days. He kept reading the sentence until he knew it by heart and even now he could recite what the old man wrote in 1953 in a letter to his brother, like an excerpt from some ancient document:

"*We wholeheartedly agree that on no account can we countenance one of these upstarts making a claim on your daughter for financial or any other reasons.*"

What else could the old man do except agree, since he was hoping to spend a week or two at his brother's house next summer, and anyway, he would have agreed with everything his brother and his wife had decided not to countenance. But it had been to no avail. Otherwise it wouldn't be him making arrangements for his wife's funeral now. That's life. If one could order something not to be countenanced come what may and if ordering it would ensure that whatever one couldn't countenance didn't happen... how wonderful life would be if things were that straightforward. ... Like a fairytale.

AROUND LUNCHTIME

He must have been the last person to arrive at the hospital canteen, there were only two or three tables where people were still eating. As he took his tray to a table that was free, he spotted the cousin with a group of doctors sitting at another table and gave her a wave.

Doctors in white scrubs were engaged in animated conversation. They were always engaged in animated conversation at lunchtime. After looking up at them briefly, his eyes started following his spoon as it raised the soup to his mouth. He would have liked to know what it was they usually talked about, but had never asked the cousin. He found it boring to sit here on his own consuming his lunch so he always tried to prick up his ears but all he could hear was a jumble of voices and words he could not make out. The only time he could guess what their animated conversation was about was when it concerned sport. At such times one of the doctors was apt to pontificate at great length: he knew that he had been an active athlete and would sometimes still referee matches on Sundays… the man had such a booming voice that everyone in the canteen was bound to hear his commentary. The previous day's programmes on Austrian TV were never discussed at the table – he knew from the cousin that this subject was covered at their morning meetings: someone always asked for an explanation of a suspenseful scene in a film or a sudden twist in a detective story and those matters had to be clarified first thing in the morning. Sometimes they would lower their voices, and he wondered if they were chatting about some mischief that the head nurse had got up to in the operating theatre, but whatever she had done, her boss never dared to utter a word, as she often insinuated that she had connections with the secret police. And when the doctor with the booming voice exclaimed: "So what else was I to do?" followed by a fist slammed on the table, he thought they might be talking about a colleague on a night shift who had once again turned up drunk at reception in the morning and prevented the receptionist from making phone calls or giving information over the counter, until someone gave him a lift home. And when everyone guffawed, he imagined this had something to do with a lab assistant. Some fifteen years ago he had been treated at this very hospital, his wife's cousin was syringing his nose and that's when he first saw the new lab assistant, a rake-thin blonde, a dazzling Hollywood pinup. She had since married, had two children, filled out and with her hair now turned black was no longer particularly attractive, but remained kind and warm-hearted, and out of the goodness of her heart generously dispensed sexual favours to all those who showed interest, whether they worked at the hospital or not – which sometimes led to dramatic scenes, such as a screaming fit from a jealous lover, or to other kinds of trouble. For instance, when a woman accused her of stealing her husband, the lab assistant comforted her: "My dear, I've had so many pricks in my lifetime they wouldn't even fit into this lab here." When the doctors' conversation sounded calm and businesslike, he thought that perhaps they had started to discuss the recruitment of new cleaners and how they would now be able to reopen a wing of the hospital that had to be closed because of a shortage of staff. He could have asked but he didn't want to be nosey, and anyway, the cousin had been giving them the low-down on what went on at the hospital long before he started having lunch here.

Only once the doctors got up and continued to talk for a while as they stood there was he certain that they were now discussing the patients they'd operated on earlier in the day and possible complications.

When the doctors were gone, the cousin joined him at his table. As he tackled the meat and dumplings on his plate, he told her about the lists he'd been given that morning, about returning his sister-in-law's list, and the long and offended face she had made. "Don't worry, she'll get over it, and actually, I could use about twenty notices myself." The cousin was related to his wife on her mother's side, something probably not reflected in the lists. "Will you come over tonight?" she asked. She and her husband were going to stay with some relatives over Christmas and she wanted him to come in the evening as she was expecting a call from her sister in Zurich, who would also want to speak to him.

He nodded in surprise and became anxious once again. Another unpleasant chore. He couldn't imagine what he might have to say to her sister in Zurich. But that, too, was one of his duties in the run-up to the funeral.

When he finished his lunch, the cousin suggested they go to her office for a cigarette. Over these past two weeks, when she wasn't too busy, she always suggested they went for a cigarette after lunch, so he gave another nod.

They crossed the hospital courtyard and went to an annexe, where her office was located on the first floor. He lit up and noticing her mocking glance, offered her one, too, and lit it for her. "Coffee?" she asked as always, as that too was a part of the ritual of their get-togethers. Standing behind him, she put a mini immersion heater into a pot and waited for the water to come to the boil. Staring out of the window, he saw the same view he did every day: the rear wing of the hospital, and three large windows covered with coarse, black, heavy canvas – the operating theatre. He'd also had surgery there but that was a long time ago. And the murky, bleak skies, as almost always over these past two weeks, now caught his attention.

She asked: "Another?" They always had another cigarette.

The cousin inhaled the smoke deep into her lungs, puffed up her cheeks and exhaled the smoke through the thin crack she made of her mouth, as she always did when she was thinking hard. "There's something I've been meaning to tell you," she said eventually in a quiet, soft voice. He assumed it would be something unpleasant, as she couldn't bring herself to begin. She said she'd been wondering if she should tell him now or later, but then again, why keep it to herself. It's just that it was all rather strange. And so she began.

Last Sunday, when she visited his wife, Zora told her about a strange dream she had the previous night. In it she saw her father and mother, looking just as they did when they were alive, except that they seemed tiny and very distant.

They were waving to her and her mother called out: "We'll see you on Thursday." She realised what this meant and it really frightened her, but her parents continued to smile at her, so she said: "But I can't come, my husband is here, I can't abandon him." And her mother said, to reassure her: "Don't worry about that, he'll join you before too long." This was what his wife had told her last Sunday. On Wednesday evening the cousin went to see her again. She couldn't get the dream out of her mind but what she told his wife was that she'd had a call from the hospital to see a patient, and decided to drop by on her way out. But Zora said: "Well, I've got over it." "What have you got over?" the cousin asked, as if she had no idea what she was talking about. "The dream, of course." The other two patients in the room started to laugh and the one closer to his wife reminded her: "But it's only Wednesday today." If she hadn't dropped in on her it would never have come up and Zora would have believed that she'd got over it. And then on Thursday the cousin became anxious and went to see the duty doctor later in the morning, and he told her the same thing as he told him, that her overall condition hadn't changed but the blood tests were showing clear signs of improvement. She hadn't dropped by to see his wife that day so as not to make her think she had come to check whether the dream had come true after all, and after speaking to the doctor she quickly took off. That was precisely when his wife was out in the corridor, he thought, she did see the cousin come out of the doctors' room and take off, and concluded that things must have taken a turn for the worse and that she probably didn't drop in on her to avoid having to tell her. – "And on Thursday night," the cousin concluded, "when I heard you ring the doorbell for the second time, I knew straight away that her dream did come true after all."

The doctors' room suddenly took on the appearance of the cabinet of Dr Caligari. He asked, quite absurdly: "She told you all this in the corridor?" – "No, it was in the hospital ward, that's the reason the two other patients overheard it." – "So she told them about her dream as well?" – "No, but they were both there when she first told me about it."

He finally got it. He felt a bit hurt, offended even, that his wife hadn't mentioned this to him at all. She had told her cousin, she had let her fellow patients overhear it, and he was the only one who didn't need to know about this. A message from the hereafter. But then again, after a while, he remembered that the dream involved him too. That was the reason why she couldn't mention it to him. Since she expected the dream to come true... she must have believed the other half of it would come true as well... so, obviously, she couldn't have said a word about it to him. But now he understood why she was suspicious when he told her so excitedly on that last day that the duty doctor congratulated him on her blood tests and that's why she asked, as if not believing him: "Really?"... and later, when he said he was going to bring a fresh pair of pyjamas the next day, she asked "are things really that bad?" She must have been convinced all that time that her dream would come true.

He couldn't think of anything better to say than: "But that's incredible." He was thinking of the final hours when he was sitting by her side, hours that now seemed half-unreal to him. Something was going on inside her, something he had no notion of. Something long buried started to emerge from the deepest recesses of his soul, but as he waited for the recollection to gain a clearer form the phone rang. The cousin took the call and then said she'd been summoned to a patient who'd been operated on earlier that day. He hurriedly put on his winter coat and they went down the stairs together. Out in the courtyard she reminded him: "So see you tonight – you haven't forgotten, have you?" He hadn't. Outside the back door of the hospital's wing she suddenly reminded him of something else: "Don't forget to send a death notice to the consultant as well." He looked at her, taken aback, and shook his head uncertainly, but the cousin was quite resolute: "No humming and hawing, just go ahead and do it. The man did what he could." And she disappeared behind the door.

Outside the hospital he found himself in a street that was dirty grey, as if drenched in dishwater. But this time yesterday, he thought, the sun was shining... no, everything was just like this yesterday, and it was only a couple of hours later, as he was leaving the Institute of Pathology, that there was a faint lemon-coloured light illuminating the scene.

He would probably not tell the cousin what it was that he had suddenly remembered. It was something that hadn't occurred to him for a long time. It also had to do with a mysterious dream, one that his mother had had. Some two weeks before his father died, she had dreamt that he had a heart condition that would kill him. Without telling his father about her dream, she persuaded him to go for a check-up, and the doctors had indeed prescribed some medication for his heart, so his mother calmed down and stopped thinking about her dream. She brought it up again only after his father died and every time she did so, she would add with tears welling up in her eyes, that it was her fault. He no longer remembered what exactly she was blaming herself for. His father had been travelling around Tunisia for a newspaper shortly before he died; maybe she thought she should have stopped him going, talked him out of it, told him about her nightmare. Tunisia was incredibly hot and it must have made his condition worse, maybe that was what she had in mind as she went on and on about it talking herself into believing that it was her fault – he could no longer recall. It was possible that his mother had modified her dream slightly after his father's death. She was a little unhinged in those days, on the verge of losing her mind. That was what made him think that the dream hadn't been quite the way she described it. For his mother, though, the dream remained quite real. She took to reading books on mysticism. But in time that, too, passed. She was frantic with worry about making ends meet with two children (his brother was nine and he was twelve) on his father's pension, which was small, as he died relatively young. And she probably tried not to think of the fifteen minutes or so that it had taken his father to die, or of her dream.

But now, as he walked down the street, he kept thinking of the dream he had just learnt about; in fact he could think of nothing else. He could neither disprove it, nor convince himself that his wife had modified it in retrospect: he was simply unable to escape it, nor was he able to put it down to coincidence, but was obliged to accept it, if for no other reason than because it had come true. And his wife, it now seemed to him, had been almost impatient for it to come true.

Actually, that wasn't really accurate either. Didn't she tell the doctor that she'd rather stay in hospital over the holidays even though, only three or four days earlier, she had asked to be allowed to go home?... maybe the dream was the reason why she wanted to stay in hospital, perhaps she had been afraid of being at home, out of the doctors' easy reach... and even on the last day she told him to go and see the cousin about the new arrangements about the carp for Christmas Eve dinner, which meant that she must have been thinking beyond the Thursday, the day everything was to come to an end. And yet, in those final hours that he spent by her side, she had been so certain that things were *so* bad with her that it almost seemed to him as if she tried to talk herself into believing it. As if she were just waiting for her dream to come true. To be kept, like a promise. The thought even flashed through his mind that this dream had driven her to her death: were it not for this dream, she might still be alive.

But what about the slips of paper in the savings books then? No, she must have thought about it earlier. And when he told her the diagnosis of extreme anaemia, she stared above his head at the wall opposite before asking him: "Is that something people die of?" Because, of course, she knew that this was something people died of. And she had translated the two words into a medical deadline. She did once actually say: "I'd like to have a couple more years," only he no longer remembered when that was… probably when she already knew that she would have to go to hospital. But did she say that because she felt that those two years wouldn't be granted to her? Something inside her had been ready for that dream.

But how could she have predicted the exact day?… Something inside her did know. Her subconscious. He didn't like that word. It could mean everything or nothing. A warehouse crammed full of boxes that contained, neatly packaged, all those things one is not aware of until a specialist comes and pulls them out with his Freudian forceps. Either way, the subconscious is not a prophet. It was something in her body, something that knew. Somewhere inside her brain, that matchless computer, there was a cell that knew. And the computer in her brain had sent a message, an assessment of the data. Everything until then had been just an inkling. An apprehension. A vague guess. A foreboding. And when the dream delivered the information complete with a date, the inkling became a virtual certainty.

But why and how did that cell in her brain, responsible for processing and evaluating a constant flow of data from the whole body, manage to inform her of the final date? If it worked like that, the same thing would happen to everyone, and yet it hardly ever did. Maybe this piece of information had somehow slipped out of the circuit. Or perhaps it was just a coincidence. In fact, it might all have been just a coincidence. A person might feel unwell and grow weak, as she had done in the weeks she had spent still at home, and that person might connect the dots and realise that something was happening inside them, something that was unstoppable. People may be gravely ill and imagine they are about to die, but when they recover, they put it all down to self-delusion, a state of hypochondria before dying, and no longer see it as the work of mysterious supernatural forces. At other times, when this inkling, this conjecture, the virtual certainty comes true, it's as if something inexplicable has happened. Both scenarios could be just a coincidence... But sometimes that single cell in the brain, the core of information, has assembled so much data that it can't be wrong. And if that's what has happened, how is it possible that this calculation had somehow crossed into her consciousness, even if through a dream?

The most plausible explanation was that if that central cell in her brain was indeed aware of everything and calculated everything, it translated the message into a dream. A human brain might resemble a computer but none of us perceives its information as shapeless digits. The digits must be turned into images. Dreams may appear as a confused, chaotic mess, as in this case, but they invariably represent our modified, distorted experience of the past. That is the material that dreams are made of. And this dream of hers contained the essence of her life: home, her parents' house, which was her refuge, her sanctuary from the world – that was what her parents had meant to her. Whenever she stayed with him here in Bratislava, she would be tormented by guilt about her parents, though later only about her mother, who were waiting for her, that was where she was supposed to be and now she felt they were calling her. That was what this dream was about. But then again, when she stayed at her parental home, she was tormented by guilt about having left him on his own since, in fact, she had taken on responsibility for him as well. That, too, was reflected in this dream. She could not just embrace the dream's promise of a reunion with her parents – it had immediately made her aware that she could not leave him by himself, just leave and slam the door behind her. That was why in her dream her mother made the promise that he would be joining her soon.

He suddenly realised that he wasn't frightened to learn that he also featured in her dream. He interpreted it as an epilogue, an embellishment, rather than a prophecy. Not for a second did he imagine that if the part of the dream that concerned her came true, the part concerning him ought to come true as well. Even if a cell in her brain could have known something about her, it can't have known anything about what was outside her. It did not store any data about him. Only about the waning strength of her body... Everything else was just wishful thinking that it would all work out for the best in the end.

But what about his mother's curious dream all those years ago? But then again, how would he ever know what had happened and why it happened, why both those dreams had come true...

Now he was ashamed that he had been unfair to her when that first night he had thought: she has left me here alone. She made the dream go on until it told her that he would follow suit. She was aware that she could not leave him alone here.

By now he'd been home for quite some time, had made himself a cup of coffee and sat in the armchair thinking that her dream also contained in a nutshell the story of their life together.

LATER IN THE AFTERNOON

He awoke from his musings, which had almost turned into slumber. He still had work to do. The death notices, the ones he was sending out on his own behalf.

He sat down at his desk. The cousin told him to send one to the consultant at the hospital. His initial recalcitrance had by now dissipated. He wrote his name and the address of the hospital on the envelope. Then he copied the names from his sister-in-law's list onto the envelopes – the two girls here in Bratislava and three families in Martin. And from the list compiled by the Rázuses, his former colleague Vlado Petrík. Right. He'd have to come up with the rest himself.

Only where to begin? He suddenly remembered their neighbours' tenants in this block of flats: four names apart from his sister-in-law. These four envelopes he would put through their letter-boxes himself. He counted what he had so far: eleven. So far, so good.

But then his brain ground to a halt. All sorts of heads and faces started to parade before him without any rhyme or reason; long forgotten moments emerged from the depths of his memory, someone would say something and he would respond. He forced himself to bring the images to a stop, along with their audio accompaniment. There was only one thing to focus on: names.

He would have to pick a starting point... He would begin at the end. The people who came last night. His wife's cousin, Martin and Viera Rázus, his sister-in-law: he didn't have to send them anything. Then Jozef Bžoch and his wife Perla and Viera Hegerová, who came with them. He found their addresses in the phone directory. Two more envelopes. His brother Pavol and his family. He had to send them a death notice because if he didn't, they would take offence and think he didn't deem them worthy of one. Another name. Envelope number fourteen.

The two girls who came to see them before his wife went to hospital. He'd done their envelope already.

On the last Sunday that his wife was still at home, they held a small gathering at their house. It was his birthday, his fiftieth. The cousin again. The Rázuses and sitting next to them, a little to one side, Agneša K, the journalist, who was alone, as her husband was in prison. She didn't say much even though normally she was very chatty and sociable, and everyone else was very gentle with her. That was one more envelope done. And to his surprise Martin R brought along a colleague, Dr Ujházy, a neurologist who worked at his hospital. She had been prescribing him his medications for many years now, mostly imported pills to lift or dampen his spirits, to help him sleep, or against depression, whatever he asked for – he belonged to a circle of intellectual hypochondriacs that the doctor cultivated: she was a bit of a snob in this respect, taking pride in her privileged clientele, made up mostly of actors and actresses. And although two other doctors were present this evening, she was the only one who thought there was something strange about his wife's mysterious flu and arranged for her to see a specialist the next day, who diagnosed her extreme anaemia. Maybe she had guessed the diagnosis just by looking at his wife. Two more names, the doctor and the journalist. So that's sixteen envelopes done.

He served his birthday party guests Soňa Čechová's special trifle in small sundae cups; she had made the trifle specially for him and brought it over in a big bowl. Soňa may have been the favourite among "Zora's students", as the group of women translators she used to teach at university called themselves some twenty years ago, around the time Edo Friš divorced his first wife for Soňa. Edo was older, infirm and in ill-health, which was why she had come alone. Another envelope done.

Earlier that day Martin and Renée Kraus had dropped by, a couple who lived in the house diagonally opposite theirs. The cousin had introduced them when they moved to this part of town. They turned up in the morning, out of a kind of shyness, presumably expecting a huge crowd in the afternoon and not wanting to impose. Another envelope, eighteen done.

And earlier... another former translator had dropped by, one who also used to visit them in their old flat. She had since changed jobs several times and would always seek their advice as to whether she had taken the right decision. Eventually she settled down at *Kultúrny život,* but was now forbidden to publish and then she was banned from translating as well. But she knew people who worked in publishing houses and on a couple of occasions they asked her to pass a message to Zora that they might have a translation for her, provided she found someone to "front" it. His wife had never succeeded in finding anyone. On that occasion she asked Luda Škultéty, her friend from their young days, who would indeed have done it, but she lived in Martin and by the time they got around to speaking to her, the translation had been given to someone else. Sometimes this translator would come and see them on the spur of the moment. They, too, sometimes dropped in on her. The last time she came to see them, on a Sunday morning, they had a bottle of Metaxa brandy at home and they got through almost all of it in about two hours. Zora was quite cross with him for having drunk most of it. Envelope number nineteen.

Another person who would sometimes drop in was Gabo R, an old friend of his wife's, most recently deputy chief editor at a publishing house. He knew all the latest gossip, rumours and intrigues, and would assiduously report all the news. Once, in a fit of self-pity brought on by God knows what, he began to pour his heart out and complain about how tough it was to hold a position of responsibility nowadays, the kinds of awful things he was obliged to do, and how they had no idea how lucky they were to be happily sitting at home, not having to get their hands dirty. Gabo got so carried away by his lamentations that he made himself out to be a kind of martyr, which made his wife blow her top – she could be very short-tempered sometimes. What on earth was he on about? His publishing house had repeatedly written to her cancelling contracts for translations she had completed and submitted – and some of those letters bore his signature. And what made him think they enjoyed being stuck at home with nothing to do, knowing full well that given her age, she would spend the rest of her life stuck at home with nothing to do, so what on earth was enviable about this? Since that day Gabo hadn't shown his face in their house again. But he felt grateful to him for many things he'd done in the past: he had thought of him when commissioning new translations and, most importantly, it had been his idea to publish the selected works of Shakespeare in four volumes, which included a number of the plays he had translated jointly with his wife. And admittedly, Gabo couldn't really afford to rock the boat too much. After the war he had risen to the rank of director of the state radio but had been ousted because he had not reached this position as a representative of the party of the working people after 1948, so he should count himself lucky to have his current job and should watch his step. He looked up Gabo's address. Envelope number twenty.

And now for the writers… he was stuck again and started scouring his memory… they had spent decades among writers: his wife would spend hours in meetings and on committees and addressing plenary meetings, while he used to review their writing, hang around with them in cafés or in the writers' club, yet now he couldn't recall any names, they had scattered to the four winds, not out in the world, just far away from them… in fact, he mentally corrected himself, it was not so much that they had scattered, more that they had never been all that close… and as someone who used to write about them he couldn't expect them to lavish their affections on him, while his wife had a special predilection for speaking her mind without mincing her words, indeed, a gift for being undiplomatic and making enemies… and if they occasionally befriended someone, they would be isolated from them by the times that they lived in… This reminded him of Mináč, with whom they used to be on such good terms that they used to go and see him almost every Sunday, to chew the fat on all key issues of the day, always managing to kill a bottle of vodka. They got along famously until 1956 – and the Russian tanks in Budapest – on that day, they rushed over to his place in complete shock and keen to know what he thought, but to their surprise he was quite calm: "So what else were the Russians to do?" He was actually surprised and irritated to see them so upset and it wasn't until later that they learned that he hated the Hungarians with a vengeance and would not have minded if the Russians had dropped a nuclear bomb on Budapest. After that their visits grew less and less frequent until they stopped seeing him altogether and would barely acknowledge each other in the street. Mináč had come to detest Zora especially because they would often sit in the same meetings and she would invariably adopt positions he deemed harmful to the Slovak people, and he, her husband, was to blame... Then there was Matuška, the high priest of literary criticism, who once used to deliver lengthy and exhausting tirades in their old flat, and the more he drank, the more he would curse the Hungarians, the Czechs and, coincidentally, also the Jews: this was his standard line whenever he received an invitation to speak or, in the absence of invitations, he would hold forth in the Writers' Club. In the summer of 1968 everyone listened reverently, as if he were Confucius, to his wise speeches at meetings of writers, his bitterness mingling with unconcealed outrage as he declaimed in a trembling voice: "Nothing is good enough for these democratisers of ours, not even Husák is good enough for them, not a good enough democrat" – by then in certain circles the term "democratisers" was already a slur directed at those who preferred democratisation to federalisation*, people like himself and his wife and a handful of others, mainly people associated with the journal *Kultúrny život* that was later duly banned. And, once excommunicated, they became black sheep, heathens who had not put their faith in the new redeemer and saviour, and so this friendship too imploded and he had never set foot in this new flat of theirs... but never mind the writers and the high priest of literary criticism: even close relatives, like Viera and Martin R, started to look upon his wife as if she had lost her mind for having turned into a democratiser and the nation no longer meant anything to her... but wait a minute, wait a minute, there was this writer who would still turn up at their place, on and off, sometimes with his wife, a stylish lady, and very beautiful too; many years ago he had been widely savaged for his novel *Pokolenie v útoku* (A Generation on the Offensive) and Zora had stood up for him, something he'd never forgotten... and whatever his other attributes, he had not disappeared. So that made twenty-two.

And sometimes... every now and then they would bump into someone on their walks around Slavín Hill or Horský park, exchange a few words, ask an old friend round for a cup of coffee, the friend would spend an hour or so sprawling in their armchair, never to show his face again... But how come, he wondered, nudging his memory, how come he's groping around in a void, they had always been surrounded by people, crowds of people who would throng around them... actually, people had never thronged around them, he thought, immediately correcting himself, and even if they had been surrounded by some people, they were just fleeting acquaintances, not friends...

He had to come up with a system, find a thread that would lead him from one point to the next... so that the names would parade before him across time, across various periods... Then he had an idea: he would draw up a list based on the jobs he'd held. The workplace is the only venue where you come into daily contact with people with whom you share a common bond.

His first job, in the first three years after the war, was on the newspaper *Národná obroda*. He could see its entire editorial staff in his mind's eye as if in a group photograph. They were a small bunch, more or less the same age, a well-oiled team, all young, confident, fearless intellectuals – maybe that was the reason that the paper had a rather small readership – and because they were all just starting out, writing came to them easily, it was playful and ferocious... he spotted Marenčin among them, his best friend in those years – until he discovered that he had stolen his girlfriend at the time, the first great love of his life; in retrospect he ought to have been grateful, for this "love of his life", just like many before and after her, turned out to be a figment of his imagination, made of very tough material rather than brittle porcelain, but by the time he got over it, which had taken him rather a long time, they had both moved on to other jobs, and the times had changed too; soon this former best friend got married, and after that he got married too... and now he would just wave to him up on the balcony when he passed by his house on one of his walks...

As for Trachta, his first editor-in-chief, he would drop by his place in the evenings whenever he didn't know what to do with himself, then in later years he would just spend a few hours at Trachta's wild birthday parties that would go on for a whole day and night, on one occasion even taking Zora... the last time they had spoken was about three years ago, when someone had offered him a translation provided he came up with a "front". A publisher was planning a new edition of a novel he had translated soon after the war, but since in the old days many translations had been sloppy, done in a very slapdash way, it would have to be retranslated and who better do it than he, since he had translated it once before – so went the message conveyed to him. He bumped into Trachta in the street and explained what he needed, but was met with a very sullen look: surely he knew that he was quite high up at the radio and that meant paying a high tax on his salary, on top of which he was also writing scripts for TV quiz shows; if he took a translation now, that might push him into a higher tax bracket and that was out of the question, Trachta said, looking very annoyed... he then approached another former colleague whose response was as amiable as a warm embrace, "With the greatest pleasure, my dear fellow, of course I would love to help," but as soon as he heard the conditional mood, he knew there was no point listening to the rest – this friend had recently returned from the US and often received new books that he would pitch to publishers who would in return let him translate whatever he wanted, but if he took on yet another translation, it might arouse suspicions about his capacity to cope... he was about to ask who would check up on this, or how, but there was no point, back then this was the standard response to supplicants like them; his wife had been told the same thing by her former students when she asked them to be a front for her.

Then there was his next job, at *Pravda*, another newspaper and another five years of his life. By then independent opinion was regarded as virtually a criminal offence, which was why this newspaper wielded the authority of a communist party mouthpiece. In his mind's eye, he conjured up another group photograph. It was so crowded it was almost impossible to fit everyone in, so many people were required on this paper as almost no one could write, most of them had had the benefit of only a perfunctory education and were untrammelled by any views of their own, by any 'intellectualism', as it was called, so they had no need to get rid of it, as he had to promise to do whenever he was attacked for this vice. It was customary at this newspaper, whenever a new ideological campaign was launched, that a pack of wolves would gather and start sniffing around for anyone who might make a suitable target. He had never experienced so much malicious hatred as at this newspaper. In the end he was quite lucky to get fired simply for not being a member of the party and thus avoiding other, much more serious forms of punishment.

No, he wouldn't find a single name here, he was quite sure, but those were truly strange years and he found it hard to drag himself out of that mire immediately. Though he never quite managed to get rid of his 'intellectualism', a stick he was often beaten with, those years left him dumbed down and professionally damaged, having to re-learn how to read and write, with one article in particular he'd written in those five years staying branded on his forehead and continuing to itch, yet he never quite managed to toe the line and march to the same tune as everyone else. At first he thought he might take shelter on relatively neutral ground by joining the arts desk but after describing a book by Tatarka as the best post-war Slovak novel, he was reprimanded so vehemently that the walls shook, just for daring to mention the novel in the same breath as socialist realism. But when a year later the same author wrote another novel, quite a lousy one, and he said so, he was reprimanded again, so vehemently that the walls shook again, for failing to notice that this, at last, was true socialist realism, and how could he not see that here, at last, was the first person to conquer this Himalayan peak. So he had himself transferred to the foreign affairs desk where life was much more comfortable and all he had to do was cut-and-paste the news from the one and only news agency to produce the requisite number of lines each morning... He stared again at the group photograph, the face of the edi-tor-in-chief Marko loomed over the blurred faces like a rock. The others regarded him as just a senile moron but to him he was the very embodiment of that era. He would spend all day sitting in his editor's office designing mock-ups. The daily edition of the paper had eight pages while the Sunday edition had twelve, and the editor-in-chief would prepare a mock-up of all these pages a month in advance, meaning he would de-cide some three hundred pages ahead what editorial would appear when, what would be the main headline across three columns on page one, what would appear on pages two and four and five and six and seven each day, what copy the indus-try, agriculture, ideology, foreign affairs, arts, letters, sports and perhaps some other desks would supply on which day. He would leave the odd blank frame on pages three and eight perhaps, for the foreign affairs and sports desks, since he was unable to predict and determine what schemes the American imperialists might be up to in a week's time, what threat to world peace might come from the German revanchists in three weeks, what fresh act of betrayal Tito's fascist gang might commit in two weeks' time and what fresh peace proposals the Soviet Union might present to the UN General Assembly, just as he was unable to predict the course and outcome of sports matches over the next four weeks. Once a week Marko would call a big staff meeting where everyone sat with notebook in hand, ready to take down precisely when their desk was to supply an editorial or the main article across three columns of page one, or a reportage, or a more detailed report on page five, the editor-in-chief having given all his pages headlines, which he accompanied by a briefing that was quite unnecessary since the content was clearly expressed in the headlines:

URGE THE MASSES TO VOLUNTEER IN OUR FACTORIES!

OUR COOPERATIVE FARMERS ARE WINNING THE BATTLE
FOR HIGHER YIELDS!

THE SOVIET UNION HAS ESCALATED ITS STRUGGLE
FOR WORLD PEACE!

GUARD THE UNITY OF OUR WORKING CLASSES
WITH YOUR LIFE!

THE USA – A BASTION OF GLOBAL IMPERIALISM

WE MUST START PREPARING FOR THE SPRING
SOWING SEASON!

WEST GERMAN REVANCHISTS – THE LINCHPIN
OF AMERICAN IMPERIALISM!

WE WILL DO OUR UTMOST TO BRING
IN A SUCCESSFUL HARVEST!

LET'S RIGOROUSLY COMPLETE PLANNED TASKS
IN ALL SECTORS OF INDUSTRY!

SOCIAL DEMOCRACY – THE ARCH-ENEMY OF THE UNITY
OF THE FORCES FOR PEACE!

OUR OPERA ON THE PATH TO SOCIALIST REALISM

NOT EVEN IN WINTERTIME DO OUR FARMERS REST
WITH THEIR HANDS IN THEIR LAPS!

THE UNSHAKEABLE FRIENDSHIP WITH THE SOVIET UNION –
A FIRM FOUNDATION FOR OUR COUNTRY'S INDEPENDENCE!

LET'S BRING THE MASS SPORTS MOVEMENT
TO THE FACTORIES AND COOPERATIVES!

In the agricultural section, deviations from the standard headlines were dictated by the changing seasons, while in the industrial section it was the changing names of voluntary workers' brigades and innovation movements that were meant to help our industry be at the cutting-edge of global productivity, hot on the heels of the Soviet Union. Although the targets of the ideological campaigns changed and sometimes contradicted each other, requiring some variation in terminology, the pattern stayed the same, for there was always something for the masses to condemn, as the enemies that had been exposed invariably failed in their attempts to betray our country to someone – the US, West Germany or Israel – so that the editor-in-chief didn't need much imagination to keep cranking out the headlines for this section either:

THE BOURGEOIS NATIONALISTS – OUR PEOPLE'S
ARCH-ENEMIES!

ALL DEVOUT PEOPLE ARE UNITED IN THEIR CONDEMNATION
OF THE TRAITOR BISHOPS!

THE ZIONIST AGENTS FAILED IN THEIR EFFORTS
TO SUBVERT OUR PEOPLE!

FACTORY WORKERS, COOPERATIVE FARMERS AND THE PEOPLE
EVERYWHERE DEMAND THE HARSHEST SENTENCES
FOR THE TITOIST-ZIONIST TRAITORS!

And each campaign of this kind was accompanied by the same expressions of gratitude:

OUR SECURITY SERVICE IS A DEPENDABLE GUARDIAN
OF THE PEOPLE OF OUR COUNTRY!

WE ARE GRATEFUL FOR THE VIGILANCE OF OUR SECURITY
SERVICE – THE IRON FIST OF THE WORKING CLASSES!

On major annual holidays and the most sacred of anniversaries the headlines and texts were repeated every year without any variation:

J.V. STALIN – THE TEACHER OF ALL NATIONS,
THE ARCHITECT OF THE OCTOBER REVOLUTION,
THE BUILDER OF THE SOVIET STATE!

THE GREAT OCTOBER REVOLUTION – THE GREATEST HOLIDAY
IN THE HISTORY OF PROGRESSIVE MANKIND!

For those who had lived through this period, he thought, these headlines would continue to convey its essence for decades. It was an era of slogans. Man could not live by bread alone, but he lived by, and was fed, slogans. Slogans victoriously declaring that Time had stopped, that History was frozen and the Word had surpassed reality. However, he also recalled the dual nature of the slogans – there were those that were triumphalist, victorious, basically harmless, all-purpose lies, and then those that were murderous, dripping with blood.

No, he wouldn't find any names among this lot, and yet he couldn't drag himself away from those five years, for he had not experienced anything like that since, and as he glanced again at the group photograph he noticed for the first time that a face had been airbrushed out of it: Laco Mňačko, an expert on the working classes, who had created a number of heroes of innovation and socialist labour, and had acquired a privileged position since his reportage always contained some scintilla of reality, something that was very rare in those days and brave, too, for his aggressive literary ambitions always made him inject that scintilla of reality. That is what brought them together and soon they would be inseparable, like a pair of enigmatically whispering heretics. There was a time when Mňačko would turn up in his office almost every day, impatiently waiting for him to cut-and-paste his daily quota of lines and cobble together the final captions and subcaptions to go with them, restlessly walking up and down the room, urging him on: „C'mon, get on with it, it's not some bloody masterpiece," and after he handed in his copy they would always dive into the same café and Laco M would begin by sharing the latest news: "Have you heard… so-and-so was arrested yesterday… And in Prague… And did you read that disgusting speech from yesterday? Beats the Stürmer… And do you know who's teamed up with who at the newspaper?… Be careful, those bastards in the Writers' Union, they're plotting against you, they say you want to sink our literature… Yesterday I saw so-and-so… he was shitting himself… he told me that, apparently… Things are going downhill… now that a factory director in the back of beyond was locked up, too." In the course of these exchanges they would get through several brandies, smoke quite a few cigarettes, and after settling their bill they'd go out into the long narrow park in front of the café, which was once called a promenade and where pensioners could rent little deckchairs on sunny days, before cars started whizzing by on both sides. Their walks in the park, however, took place during a cold and wet autumn, the wind rustling in the trees and the damp leaves crackling underfoot, and only here could they move on to comments and interpretations. "You know the chap they arrested in Prague, he was basically a nasty self-important fellow, a typical Comintern cadre, but the only reason they locked him up is because he's Jewish…" – "But how come he's still around, can you understand that, he was a 'Londoner'* after all and nearly everyone who was in exile in the West has been locked up by now…" "You know that greenhorn, the one who used to share your office on the arts desk, apparently he's confessed to everything, that he spied for Tito, that it's all his fault, he should have stayed where he was born…" "But you know, the ones I feel most sorry for are those who fought in the Spanish Civil War, they got away from Franco but back home none of them got away…" The wind murmured in the trees, it often rained, and there was usually not a soul around as they walked from one end of the park to the other, their collars turned up, against the rain, two whispering conspirators. "Unbelievable, this damned mafia that's taken over here…" "But if those high up say nothing, it means the mafia's got something on them, something to blackmail them with… but what is it, and how…" – "And the Russians keep mum as if they had nothing to do with it all, as if it didn't make them, too, look bad in the eyes of the world…" "Oh well, what riff-raff, let me tell you, but those up there, they must be able to see through it…" They reached a dead end again. So they would try a different angle: "What if it really is Tito's people behind it all, trying to discredit the regime?" – "Don't be silly," – the Yugoslavs were close to his heart, he had even studied Serbo-Croatian before the war – "all that stuff about Tito's people is just bullshit," but how could he still believe this if he didn't believe anything else, "either it's all true", he told Laco off, "or it's all a lie." But he wasn't able to come up with anything other than the Titoists. Neither of them was an Alexander the Great and they never managed to cut the Gordian knot. Before too long the great show trials* began and they learned from the indictment that nearly all the defendants were of Jewish origin, with one Slovak "bourgeois nationalist", one alleged German and someone else thrown in for good measure, and once this puppet theatre show with real-life puppets was over, they stopped playing political detectives, their hypotheses having yielded nothing, and once the socialist camp – camp, what a brilliantly apt word for our part of the world, they would often say to each other in those days – had discovered that Jewish doctors, Jews – for the second time in history – had plotted to murder the Lord of the Kremlin along with all the Apostles, their heads were purged of all criminal conjectures, there were no more mysterious gangsters, no more secret mafia, there was no more enigmatic fascist conspiracy but quite simply Moscow and Stalin… From time to time his friend still felt the need to raise some marginal issue and to exercise his brain cells, but by then he had stopped wondering, everything was possible in this camp of theirs, the only thing that still remained to be invented were some new slogans, so he preferred not to think about anything, not to rack his brains over anything, and so the great Sherlock Holmes and his dim-witted partner Doctor Watson, instead of trying to solve mysterious crimes, started to play chess at the café, only downing a brandy now and then, their conspiratorial debates in the park over, and Doctor Watson, with his undisciplined and unsystematic way of thinking, kept losing every game, prompting the Great Schemer Sherlock Holmes to come up with a little jingle, and announce, full of himself, after each victory:

"It's checkmate,

Says your Czech* mate,"

until once, in the middle of a game, quite late at night, the great Sherlock Holmes reproachfully reminded him in a sentimental, almost trembling voice: "Here we are, playing chess and in Moscow meanwhile the old bugger may have kicked the bucket," and this reprimand elicited from little Watson, who was losing again, such a state of euphoria as to immediately suggest that a brandy was called for to mark the occasion… they never finished the game that night, as one brandy followed another, they even went over their limit of ten doubles and not a drop more… The next day his mother had to shake him awake and as he opened his eyes she came down on him with unusual fury: "You're kipping here like an old wino and the whole world outside is in chaos. They said on Austrian radio at seven in the morning that Stalin has died and by the time I went out to get some milk and rolls the streets were packed with people," and she went into the kitchen to make him a white coffee and butter a couple of rolls. As she left the room he had exactly the same feeling as on the first day after the war… now, now, he thought, only now would real life begin… and although this euphoria proved premature, most likely influenced by enduring fairytales from his childhood, for only in fairytales does the monster breathe its last and the whole world heave a sigh of relief, transforming everything and allowing things to blossom again, whereas after the monster's death the socialist camp retained its guards, Kapos and assorted lesser monsters, yet as a result of this event their unique friendship started to fade, they no longer had anything to whisper about, they were no longer bound by common heretical ideas that nobody else was allowed to hear… and later on his friend began to write books, one of them a bestseller, which he, as a critic, was expected to review but he assumed that someone else would lavish much more praise on them, which indeed proved to be the case, and his friend started to regard him as an intellectual snob, and that made the last leaves of their friendship wither and fall from the tree, but the memories remained, and now he thought with nostalgia that this was definitely someone he ought to send a death notice to, but he knew he wouldn't, as Mňačko had lived somewhere abroad for some years now, and he didn't even know what address to put on the envelope.

Finally he tore himself away from those five years and tried to remember a name from his third job, another five years of his life. Dramaturg at the theatre… but his drowsy musings on the people he had known in that position were interrupted by the doorbell. He started, quite stunned, he could not imagine who it might be – his brother? the cousin? his sister-in-law? – and went to the hallway to press the buzzer and let the visitor in.

The lift door opened and out came Viera H, yesterday's note-taker, who solved the problem of the epigraph by cutting out two lines. A shopping bag in each hand, she marched into the kitchen and announced: "Here is your Christmas dinner." She took a saucepan out of one bag, set it on the table and continued her announcement: "Sausages, mashed potatoes – *fučka* and sauerkraut." Then she took a paper carton out of the other bag: "*Trúbeľky*, home-made". Her friends, the sisters Magda and Marta lived nearby – more names he had to make a note of – and they would make these wafer rolls every year in the same way they used to be made back in the day in their village, and would always give her some. And since Viera went to pick them up, she thought she could bring him some Christmas provisions. He confessed that until this moment he hadn't thought of how he would feed himself through the holidays when everything was closed, so he really appreciated her… She interrupted him to say that she also brought a message from another friend, Soňa Č: first of all, she was inviting him to lunch on Christmas Day, and second, Soňa had phoned around some people in publishing and learned that some thirty people might come to the funeral, so perhaps he should book a city coach… and yes, they would go to any destination, and did he know… of course he knew, you had to book it in the Luxor arcade, that's where he had booked a coach for his mother's funeral, just for a small group of neighbours from their block, and his brother and his family, since he hadn't informed anyone else to make sure there would be as few people as possible at her funeral… no, no, it wasn't the Luxor arcade any more, cross-country coaches now had to be booked at the bus terminus… oh, all right, he knew where that was, to the left of the bridge across the Danube… exactly, the office was by the bridge, that's where he should go to make the arrangements – by the way, did he have a time for the funeral… so in that case, he could leave it till the first day after the holidays, she and her friend would phone around and tell people where and when the coach would be leaving from, he could organise everything the day after tomorrow, she had to dash now, someone was waiting for her in a car downstairs. And she was gone.

He went over to his desk, wrote a name on an envelope and looked up the address of Marta L, the friend who had sent the wafer rolls. She, too, was a translator. And her name automatically brought up that of her sister, Magda T, also a translator, if he was not mistaken. Both were certain to come to the funeral. But he wouldn't have remembered either. So that makes… twenty-four names.

And now, as he came to the third job he had held, he thought that no one had probably ever kissed his wife's hand as many times as the actors and directors at the theatre club after a premiere. For some reason actors took great pride in maintaining the chivalrous manners of the old days. And in their eyes his wife was of a piece with that bygone world, she represented the language of the classics and a family from classical times, so to speak. He, by contrast, was just "a man of letters", someone they respected and knew as a theatre critic – he started writing about the theatre during the war – and that was why he had been offered the position of dramaturg. Initially he had turned it down. A few days later, as he was strolling along the Danube with his wife, she gave him a talking to: he really ought to give it serious thought, even though he had enough translating work since he left the newspaper, it would be truly helpful if he accepted the post, as it would make a profound impression on her parents back home: a dramaturg at the National Theatre, now that was something, her parents would have to admit that he was somebody to be reckoned with, that he enjoyed respect, that he had some standing… and so he took the job. Before long all the actors started to hate him – what use was it to them if the plays were critically acclaimed when the casts were kept very small and the rest of the company had nothing to do. He really didn't know how to choose plays with roles for everyone; he probably wasn't the right person for the job of dramaturg and the actors sensed it – they didn't understand that there was a strategy behind the repertoire he had devised, while he, in turn, did not understand where the actors were coming from. They all craved a major role and once they were cast, they would learn their lines during rehearsals and never even glance at the script at home; they were always too busy, arriving for the rehearsal in the morning from the radio studio, then being driven to the TV studios, and in the evening to the film studios, and at night they were busy dubbing films… They wanted to star in the theatre but otherwise their main concern was making money. Their conversations revolved around cars, weekend cottages, trips to the West… sometimes also around the fantastic play shown on Austrian TV last night, but of course our dramaturgs would never go for anything like that. They didn't take the rehearsals seriously, treating them as a necessary evil, and yet, when the play opened, he was stunned and almost moved, and had to admire them for what they had made of their role as if by magic. He used to rub shoulders with them at the theatre club, was on first-name terms with them, and yet he never stopped feeling the way he did when his parents sent him to scout camp as a child. As if he were in an alien world. And the more time he spent hanging around and drinking with them, the less respect they had for him.

Eventually he found a few drinking mates to go to wine-bars with; he would pick up the bill and they would entertain him by badmouthing the theatre and everyone in it. One was an assistant director, who was very ambitious and as a result disdained to carry out his obligations as an assistant to such an extent that he had to be fired because he seemed to be doing nothing at all. The other was a sound technician who also ended up being sacked from the theatre, after getting so drunk that once, during the performance of a tragedy, he put on the soundtrack from another play and made the audience roar with laughter as if they were watching a slapstick comedy.

He, too, had ended up being fired, in his case for a grave ideological misdemeanour: his revisionist dramaturgy. He had never come across this term before or since: he was the only revisionist dramaturg in the entire country and was happy to share the story with everyone. An elderly director, who was due to stage a play by Gorky, had fallen ill, and thus he lost a Russian classic from the repertoire. So he replaced it with a play by Bulgakov since that had recently been allowed to be staged in Moscow; however, the local moguls decided that our audiences weren't as mature as the Soviet ones and promptly banned it. So that was another Soviet play gone from the repertoire. Around that time Arthur Miller lifted the prohibition on his plays being produced in Eastern Europe, so he quickly included one of them... But rehearsals had already started of a piece by a Brazilian writer, one he had picked partly because the author did not ask for royalties to be paid in foreign currency. And there was also a Shakespeare. Three Western authors and none from the socialist bloc. And to cap it all, the mercurial Khrushchev had just decided to start another row with Tito, when he had already planned a mournful play by a Croatian author set on the periphery of Zagreb, so that could not be allowed under the circumstances. Once all this was added up the sum total amounted to revisionist dramaturgy.

The idiots, he fumed again. He got up from the desk, picked up the plastic watering can and filled it up in the kitchen. He had already skipped the watering once, yesterday, he hadn't watered the plants he was meant to water every day, not even those that needed extra water. He took the slip of paper with the instructions and started out at the window in his wife's room. He had to take special care when watering the cacti so the water didn't spill over their thorns and onto the parquet floor. He filled the watering can again and stood by the small table next to his wife's sofa, over a large plant that soaked up water like a mushroom. As he stood there, his eyes alighted on a Weiner-Král* painting above the sofa. It had irritated him from the very moment his wife had put it there, though he had never told her. It suddenly occurred to him that he could take it down now. He would do that first thing tomorrow. On the other hand, he understood why his wife had bought it and hung it where she did. It brought back memories of her youth, of the hunting lodge where she had spent so many happy summers. One day she showed him the burnt-out spot where it had once stood. From there they embarked on an almost hour-long climb on a trail up a steep grassy slope. He hated trails on steep slopes from which he might fall. But he managed to climb this one, which led to a round plateau. She led him to a spot from where woods stretched down endlessly in every direction and right by them, bathed in the rays of the sun, lay a little village, looking like a scattering of large dots. And the painting depicted the view from above, from this very hill, down towards the valley and the village, shown as tiny dots right at the end of the woods. In a way, a perfectly painted landscape, not a piece of kitsch. Except that near the bottom, where the blackness of the woods almost touched the village lit by the sun, there under the trees, as if buried, lay the face of a woman, young and plump, wearing lipstick, rather like a porcelain doll, standing out from the dark of the trees: the artist couldn't help inserting a private symbol of his, a secret code, even into his realistic paintings. The face belonged to Alma M, the woman who was looking after him and who had introduced them, his Beatrice, only some twenty years his junior. Anyone looking at this painting would know straight away, oh yes, that's his mistress; even in aesthetic terms that little face stuck out like a sore thumb, the very centre of the painting. And that was what irritated him. He would take the picture down first thing tomorrow.

They had seen many paintings by this artist at their friends' houses and loved them for their particularly lyrical quality. And although they never found the kind they admired in his studio, they always ended up buying some he had available.

Yes, Alma too, should get a copy of the death notice. In recent years they had been seeing her more and more often. She had contacts who supplied her with émigré journals and books and she'd been summoned to the secret police about it a few times. Afterwards she would give him detailed accounts of the interrogations and he was always impressed with her uncanny ability to wriggle out of things. Until his wife said to him: don't be so naïve, the secret police don't believe a word she says, but what matters to them is that they know who she receives the émigré journals from and who distributes them and based on who her friends are, they can work out who gets to read the stuff. And if they ever think that it could come in handy, they will have all the information. Zora was probably right. He returned to his desk and put Alma's name and address on an envelope. Twenty-six.

And how about Weiner-Kráľ, the painter? The last time they went to see him was soon after the death of Zora's niece Jelka and her friend. They picked a painting and were about to leave when the artist dug out another – a present for his wife. It showed two girls trying to cling on to a perpendicular rockface. It almost made him dizzy, so powerful was the depiction of height in this painting. His wife stared at it uncomprehendingly at first, as if she could not believe that he wanted to give her a painting that depicted the final moment in the life of Jelka and her friend, then gave a muffled cry and began to sob. She was so stunned and wept so bitterly that she almost choked, and then stormed out of his studio without saying goodbye and bounded down the stairs, away from the nightmare. But all the painter wanted to show was that he'd been thinking of her, that he empathized. That made twenty-seven names.

Having got started, he had to finish. There was still his last workplace. He was certain that it wouldn't yield a single name, but he had spent eleven years at that institute of the Slovak Academy of Sciences, longer than anywhere else. The only memorable thing about this job was the long, large room, with two secretaries sitting by one of the walls, and two long tables running the length of the room: every three or four months between thirty-five and forty scholars, the institute's employees, would gather here for a meeting. Each one had been assigned a long-term project and those who were due to complete their assignment had to explain why they hadn't yet done so. This was usually followed by a learned discussion, of which he remembered only the very first, which concerned the periodisation of literature, and whether the beginnings of modern literature in their country dated back only to the 1980s, the time a new kind of poetry came into being, or to 1918, when literature found itself in a very different situation. Behind the large room was the office of the institute's head and his secretary. About six months before he was fired, they moved to a refurbished building where people were two to a room, one meant to be there in the morning, the other in the afternoon, though not necessarily every day. When he joined the Institute, he knew most of the other researchers, though not particularly well. He was better acquainted only with those he knew from before; this wasn't a place where you could get to know anyone intimately. Ďuro Špitzer came to mind, a journalist they had turned into a scholar, who once asked him, when they were already in the new building: "So what will you do when they sack you?" He was a little surprised that Špitzer assumed this was a certainty, and replied, with equal certainty, "I'll be a translator." Špitzer smiled: "And you think they'll let you do that?" Taken quite aback, he said: "But of course I will translate…," but Špitzer continued to smile so he stopped and said that surely they wouldn't prevent people from translating. Actually, by the time he was sacked Ďuro Špitzer was no longer at the institute. When did he leave and why? Strange, only about three years had passed and he could no longer recall. When his mother died, Ďuro was one of the two people who had written to him. He should send him the death notice. But he had always been ex-directory. And he didn't have him in his address book. He would have to ring someone and ask. But he wasn't going to ring anyone. So that was that… Oh yes, another person who had found a job there was Števček, a former editor-in-chief of *Kultúrny život*. When Zora was on the editorial board, she backed him for as long as she could, and he had often written for the paper. The frequent clashes with the censors and high-ranking party officials had given Števček a heart attack, and when he was discharged from hospital, he got a job at the academy, a quiet place for a convalescent. If for no other reason, he ought to send him the death notice because of those editorial board meetings, when Števček and his wife had pulled together. Well, he ought to – but he wouldn't, because now he also remembered what several people had told him – he and his wife had stopped reading the press at some point, out of disgust – that this former editor-in-chief had published a lengthy and comprehensive piece of self-criticism, starting with his proletarian origins, to which he said he had remained true for a long time until he had somehow succumbed to deviationist temptations. He didn't even feel like reading it. He might take the death notice as a sarcastic reminder of the past he wanted to erase. Rather, he ought to send the death notice to the Institute's director, who had given him his job and had always treated him quite generously if he failed to complete his long-term projects. On the other hand, this same boss had also been on the committee that sacked him: he wasn't to blame, of course, for the list had been handed down from above, but ever since then, whenever they bumped into each other, his former boss said hello as if he was someone he had briefly met at some symposium five years ago. And there was something else... the Institute's journal started publishing a detailed study about him, in instalments of roughly thirty pages. Someone had shown him the first instalment: he took a quick look, saw that it mentioned Sartre, and, after turning a few more pages, there was Sartre again, in another context. He gathered that the author, a young simpleton he had met, was trying to prove that he was guilty of existentialism and all kinds of other horrors to boot. In fact, he had never read a single theoretical work by Sartre, as he could never identify with his talk of the freedom of the individual and the idea that everyone was free to forge their own future. What his own experience taught him was that life was determined by history and circumstances, and the option of freely choosing one's own path was a luxury that he had not been granted by fate. But details like these were immaterial, and once he had been eliminated, any moronic scholar could cobble together any kind of scholarly bullshit about him to earn himself a doctorate; he ought to be flattered to be regarded as that important – never before had anyone paid him such detailed attention, no one had ever tried to get to the top using his back, but it was his former boss who was most likely behind the idea for this piece, and finding a volunteer to take on this long-term assignment could not have been difficult. And with no little Schadenfreude he also remembered that soon after the purge in which he had been eliminated, new, almost military-style procedures were introduced at the institute, maybe even a punch clock, but what he knew for certain was that if anyone wanted to be absent during working hours they had to explain where they were going, why, and for how long, and the receptionist would log the precise time of their return. That was not a regime he could have endured anyway.

So, summing up, he concluded with an impish smile, not a single name... But maybe he was barking up the wrong tree. After all, it wasn't names for his own funeral he was looking for. It was his wife's employment history that he should be looking at, the jobs she had held... In the years he knew her she worked as a part-time editor at a publishing house for a while. Then she went freelance. He had already picked one name from her publishing house, Gabo Rapoš... then there was the former translator, the one who had tipped his wife off about the three translations if she could find a front and with whom he had downed almost an entire bottle of Metaxa one Sunday morning... as well as Soňa, the translator whose husband had given him a fridge, who had also been sacked since. Ferenčík, one of the two chief editors, had once been the best man at their wedding but now it was his job to inform Zora which of her translation contracts had been cancelled... And suddenly it dawned on him that while she was still working there part-time, another person employed at the publishing house was Jozef Felix, the university professor who said he'd be honoured... this was after he had been fired from the university, in the early fifties, when decisions of this kind were taken by students... How could he have forgotten him, of all people; he should have topped his list... but in fact, he had not met him in person until the previous summer, in Orava near the cottage close to the Polish border. That made one more name.

And of course, there were the Kollárs, the couple who helped them find that cottage in the Orava region, close to Námestovo where they lived. He was a senior engineer, she a teacher at a secondary school. One day she turned up at his wife's parental home – they were spending the summer there as they could no longer make use of the writers' retreat in the Tatras, even should the whole place have been empty – to invite Zora to give a talk at her school. His wife said no, and seeing that the woman took offence, Zora – he still remembered this well – burst out laughing: "I suppose it hasn't occurred to you that if I gave a talk, it might cost you your job?" This was at the dawn of the new era and the young teacher didn't have a clue. Ever since then, whenever they were in Námestovo they would stop by and his wife had to tell them all she knew because those two were interested in everything, being the kind of folks naïve enough to still believe in ideals and values and God knows what else.

The last time they saw the Kollárs was last summer, when they dropped in to pick up the keys to the cottage that the couple had booked for them. They arrived late in the afternoon and, as usual, spent a while at their house before checking into the new hotel where they had booked a room for the night. A big village wedding was in progress on the ground floor with all the requisite whooping, singing and stamping of feet, like in a village pub. The following morning his wife wasn't feeling well: it must be some kind of flu, she said. They went back to the Kollárs to tell them they wouldn't be going to the cottage after all. The couple wouldn't hear of it – come on, it will pass – they themselves were leaving later that night for a holiday at Lake Balaton – for people from the mountains this was like being on a beach by the Pacific – and said they could stay in their flat, she was bound to feel better soon. Zora let herself be talked into it, took to her bed and stayed there for three days, not really herself, unwilling even to get up; and then, all of a sudden, she felt better and they set out for the cottage. She just remained somewhat subdued. Now, it seemed to him that this was their most wonderful holiday ever. Without a single cloud of mis-understanding throughout. She had accepted that he didn't feel like climbing the nearest high peak, went up on her own and returned rapturous about the wonderful view, how she could see ever so far into the distance, and those tremendous mountain peaks... That must have been when it all began, he now realised, that time she was in bed in the Námestovo flat, so weak and lifeless, and later at the cottage, so content with everything, somewhat subdued.

So there's this couple and the university professor to add. Twenty-eight names. He was sure he'd forgotten someone but no one else came to mind just now.

He put four envelopes to one side, stuck stamps on the rest, stowed everything in his briefcase, picked up about a score of death notices for his wife's cousin, put on his coat, took the lift down, posted four envelopes through the neighbours' letterboxes and walked around the corner. The post office was a little further down and was already closed, but the post box outside would be emptied one more time before the holidays. He dropped the envelopes into the box. The locals would receive theirs first thing in the morning, the others straight after the holidays.

EVENING

The moment he dropped the envelopes in the post box, he stopped thinking who he might have forgotten. The only thing on his mind was what he would say on the phone to the cousin's sister in Zurich.

He kept thinking about it, trying doggedly to concentrate, but couldn't come up with a single sentence. And he was unlikely to come up with anything. To get to the house where the cousin lived he had to go up the hill again before turning into a street that ran parallel to his own higher up the hill. He was fond of this street, lined mostly by three-storey buildings in the Jugendstil style on one side and on the other by family houses and villas, one of which, at the very end of the street, was more like a small palace, all lit up as if for some pre-Christmas celebrations. Whenever he passed it he remembered that during the war it had served as the embassy of the Third Reich, in the wartime Slovak Republic, and whenever the Germans were unhappy about anything, an editorial devoted to the issue would appear in *Der Grenzbote*, the daily of of the local German Volksgruppe. This happened quite often. Even the name of the street had been changed, as Moyzes* Street probably sounded provocative to German ears, too close to Moses, so they ordered the name to be changed to Schiller Street. In those five years his life had been controlled by whatever went on inside this building which he had never set foot in and for this reason alone he would have liked to know what purpose it served now. He knew that a certain institution had requisitioned many a family house although there was no sign indicating who owned it now, but it was unlikely that they would have confiscated a building as prominent as this. Why had he never asked anyone what was there now, he wondered as he passed its illuminated windows, and a little further on, in the middle of a large lawn, he saw a yellow family house where, until twelve years ago, Friš had lived, the man who had given him a fridge, a chest of drawers and two massive armchairs. The house once belonged to the composer Alexander Moyzes, with whose sister Friš had broken up not long before. He also recalled that in the early 1930s his wife had studied under Moyzes at the conservatoire. But then that phone call again encroached on his thoughts: what on earth could he say to someone he hadn't spoken to in person or on the phone, someone he hadn't seen for… exactly four years and four months.

It was actually due to a chain of coincidences that, for many years in the summer and quite often also in winter, they used to see his wife's cousin who lived in the Tatras, or the Tatra cousin, as his wife sometimes referred to this relation of hers, whose actual name also happened to be Zora. Their first encounter was quite unexpected: they had come to the Tatras shortly after their wedding – the only time they stayed at one of the Grand Hotels built in the early twentieth century in the imposing Alpine style, since all the other hotels had been commandeered by trade unions – and one day, while on a fairly long hike, they stopped at a chalet high in the mountains. It was late autumn and it started to rain… or at least this was how he remembered it now… the chalet was deserted and then, all of a sudden, they saw the Tatra cousin running towards them. She was working at a sanatorium in the Tatras but he hadn't met her yet because at that time his wife had been written off and shunned by the extended family – but it turned out that in this cousin they had found someone who didn't share the family's outrage at her marriage. On the contrary, she told his wife off for not having sought her out, started to address him by his first name straight away and introduced them to Harry, a tall slim man about his age or slightly younger, who worked as a stoker at the chalet and whom this cousin later married. Ever since then, they maintained contact through of a chain of coincidences, so to speak. His wife discovered that her former pupil Magda, to whom she'd given piano lessons, was in charge of a trade union resort in the Tatras. Magda was the daughter of a butcher, the graduate of a hotel management school in Switzerland – two facts that in those days disqualified her from taking more prestigious positions in the hotel industry – but she could find them a cheap room with full board whenever they needed one and once when she went on holiday, she even let them stay in her own flat… Sometime later the Writers' Union bought a former private sanatorium and had it refurbished, and they could always get a comfortable room there, though without board, so they had to take their meals in a restaurant nearby. Ever since their first encounter at the chalet, they had always gone to see his wife's Tatra cousin at the TB sanatorium, where she had a large room, initially on her own and later with her husband. Harry had studied law, having graduated in the year of the triumph of the working classes, and since he had been involved in some student demonstrations just before the change of regime, he left Prague after the victory of the working classes and moved to the Tatras. He had gone mountain-climbing there during the Protectorate and met his wife's cousin on one of the hikes. He must have been among the first to be driven by ideological reasons to seek refuge from civilisation in Nature. Nowadays, it flashed through his mind, one would say that he was fleeing the establishment.

Whereas he and Zora, even though he had repeatedly been fired from job after job, had nevertheless always remained at least halfway a part of the establishment and civilisation, no matter how far it was affected by ideology. No wonder that whenever they got together, they would start talking about these matters and passionate disputes would flare up between them. Harry had plenty of time and used to listen to Radio Free Europe all day long – the broadcasts were not jammed in the Tatras, an area not populous enough to make the effort worthwhile – and as he spoke English and was able to listen to any station he wanted to, he was well informed about everything that went on in the world. He had spun for himself a web of unassailable opinions, partly supported by his experiences, and they found it impossible to convince him that he was wrong about anything. Whatever the topic under discussion, be it potatoes and why in this part of the country, where there used to be a glut of them, they were now scarce and of poor quality, or anything else – he no longer remembered all the subjects they used to argue about – they could never agree on anything. Had they got into an argument with a party official, he would probably have sounded like Harry, belligerent and picking holes in everything the party secretary would have said. As it was, they had to admit that much of what went on in this country was absurd and some of it was outright nasty, but nevertheless, one had to draw some distinctions... not everything was the same as a few years back... one could see some stirrings... although he now remembered that it was mostly in neighbouring Poland that things started to stir. The Tatra cousin and her husband were in touch with Polish mountaineers, and had entered into a kind of barter trade with them: the Poles would deposit some wool or jumpers in a cavern – he recalled that once rodents had eaten their way through the consignment – while they, in turn, would bring spare parts for cars. And it was on one of their trips to the Tatras that he and his wife had first come across a pile of Polish weeklies from 1956, the year Polish intellectuals had gone crazy overnight, getting drunk on freedom. He found those journals so fascinating that he learned to read Polish just so he could take in these revelations, imbibe this intoxicating and fascinating revisionism that he had never before encountered… on the other hand, the only Polish periodical the Tatra cousin and her husband were interested in was an easily digestible illustrated weekly aimed at the masses and with zero interest in profound and enlightening intellectual journals that looked forward, wide-eyed, towards a future of reformed socialism: the Tatra couple were firmly anchored to the gloomy, unshakeable reality around them, so all their arguments remained unresolved, not least because utopias were completely alien to the other couple, and so they kept playing with words, doggedly if amiably, for hours on end. One evening, after they finished the wine he and his wife had brought as well as all the wine their hosts had at home, the Tatra cousin went to her lab one floor up and came back with pure alcohol, which she mixed expertly so that they could continue putting the world to rights, the world immediately around them as well as the world north and south of the equator… but that happened only once and, as time went by, their arguments began to lose their edge and they ended up agreeing with their hosts with increasing frequency, although they had not yet lost faith in the illusions of the Polish intellectuals who had, meanwhile, lost all of theirs. But things might still change, they argued, it was worth pushing against the door that was no longer slammed completely shut, in order to open it up a crack and then a further crack: they still bore the marks of the interwar Czechoslovak intellectuals' naïveté, when people marched to optimistic lyrics about the millions who would one day march a thousand kilometres against the wind. The authors of the lyrics, Voskovec and Werich*, had got it all completely wrong and when push came to shove, they had had to flee to America: that was their thousand kilometres. But he and his wife had clung to the tattered remnants of those silly, naïve ideas and still believed that if not millions, then perhaps if some smaller groups of intellectuals pushed against the wind, they could inch ahead at least a few metres, maybe even half a kilometre: all they had to do was to keep pushing against the door that was slightly ajar, until one day it would open into a new world, but when the day finally did come and the door which the two of them had been pushing against was finally flung open, what was on the other side was not a new world but Russian tanks that came bursting through that opening. However, back in the days before disaster struck, they still thought that it was worth pushing against that door, by then even the couple in the Tatras started to feel the wind of change, Harry was no longer a stoker in a mountain chalet but the legal adviser in a large factory at the foot of the Tatras and now told them about arbitration proceedings he was pursuing on behalf of his large enterprise. He had to explain what arbitration was and why socialist enterprises were involved in disputes that required arbitration, and even though he had by now become a seasoned revisionist, thanks not only to training via the Poles but also the Italians, he was surprised to learn that the workers of this factory spoke so highly of the old days under Baťa, a private enterpreneur when, after all, everyone knew that he had been a slave driver just like Ford – entire novels had been written about that – but now he was obliged to hear that under that capitalist everything used to run like clockwork, everyone could calculate what their earnings would be, whereas now everything was a mess: one day the raw materials would be delivered late, the next management would fail to obtain spare parts for the machines and the workers would be left hanging around twiddling their thumbs, cursing the regime and praising the old days when the factory was run by Baťa, the private enterpreneur. But otherwise the couple had lost all interest in issues of communal welfare since they were now allowed to travel abroad once a year, their first trip in their own car – for which they had managed to save up – took them to the Caucasus in the Soviet Union where they climbed Mount Elbrus, and more recently they had been to Turkey, to Mount Ararat – Karakorum – and so now they would sometimes not see them when they came to the Tatras in the summer...

He paused in the middle of a flight of steps – a shortcut connecting the upper section of the street to the lower: ever since he'd been diagnosed with a heart ailment even the slightest effort would make his heart thump, or at least that's what he thought, so he took a short breather here, and suddenly out of the recollections of their stays in the Tatras there surfaced one that had not occurred to him recently. The Tatra cousin had once mentioned that they would like to take them on a hike, though nothing too strenuous, somewhere that was off a marked trail: "Yes, the Nefcerka!", his wife exclaimed excited as this was a nature reserve without any marked trails. said to be the most beautiful part of the Tatras. "We could organise that, couldn't we?" the Tatra cousin asked her husband, who nodded, "Of course, no problem," but just in case, he checked whether this was going to be a mountaineering expedition – it was not just narrow trails along steep slopes that scared him, he also dared not set foot on those sections of trails that ran above precipices where there were chains for people to hold on to for safety. His wife's cousin conceded: "Well, right at the top we may have to help you abseil some two or three metres." Her husband had his doubts: "Oh, come now, I don't think that will be necessary." Well, that was it as far as he was concerned; this was definitely not his kind of thing, but his wife, who had been hiking in the Tatras from a young age, was used to unmarked trails and wasn't scared of precipices, was all for it, so they agreed to meet one more time before Sunday to hammer out the details, but just then his wife announced, to everyone's surprise, that she wouldn't go, she didn't dare to, it would be too much for her, she was no longer a spring chicken. They all tried to make her change her mind, he even asked what she was suddenly so scared of and that was when she looked at him with flushed cheeks and blurted out: "I see – you want me to go, so that I'll get killed there." He was shocked into silence and listened as the other two tried to talk her round, until she finally agreed. Early on Sunday he drove them to the agreed spot, and in the afternoon took the car again, drove all around the Tatras, turning onto a road that passed through a village, and then trudged along a dirt road to reach the point where he was supposed to meet them: they should have been there by now – perhaps they got lost, or it was too much for her after all, he thought – and then, at last, he heard voices. As they drove back his wife waxed lyrical about how wonderful it was, there was no need to abseil even right at the top... but she agreed, it really wouldn't have been his kind of thing, and the view... But where did that absurd accusation come from? By then he'd been on the wagon for several years, never even touched a drink, had had no affairs – nor did she suspect him of any – and they lived in perfect harmony... It was only now that he started brooding over that sentence again. Perhaps she was frightened of her own courage, gripped by some dreadful anxiety, and there he was, trying to talk her into going... But maybe it was just like with that dream of hers, he wondered as he stood on the steps, that, too, was driven by concern and anxiety that she lacked the stamina, she panicked that she wouldn't be able to cope, maybe there was nothing more than that, too, like behind the dream he spent so much time brooding about…

He continued up the steps; the cousin lived just off to the right. He admitted that the Tatra couple had been right in most of their heated arguments back then and that it was only their own clouded brains that had made them defend every kind of position and attempt to refute many of their arguments… On the other hand, if back then everyone had decided that it was all hopeless and that was that, that nothing could be done about it, and if there hadn't been fools like him and his wife, and many others, who kept pushing against that door that was slightly ajar, until it finally opened to let the Russian tanks in, the two of them and hundreds of thousands of others might not have ended up in this shit that they may never climb out of, and the other couple might still be stuck in a single room in the Tatras instead of being in a spacious flat in Zurich, happily living the life they wanted to live…

He stopped thinking of what he would say on the phone. He wouldn't come up with anything sensible anyway. He rang the doorbell.

"Ah, there you are," the cousin said by way of welcome, "we've been waiting for you." He mumbled something about it not being that late but then remembered that in this household they went to bed at an outlandishly early hour – and also got up at an outlandishly early hour – so their evening began earlier as well. Gusto, the cousin's husband, helped him take off his coat in his usual, exaggeratedly obliging way, this time without making the face that was meant to show that he was imitating an English butler. Once in the dining room he apologized again and explained that he had to go to the post office – and had spent three hours or more cudgelling his brain about who he should send the death notices to… He gave the cousin a couple of dozen from his briefcase. During the conversation that followed he kept trying to think of a suitable sentence to say on the phone, but the cousin got up and said, "Let me place the call to Zurich, they must be waiting for us." She gave the number to the operator, since in those days you couldn't dial international numbers directly, and as they sat there waiting in silence, he no longer tried to think of what to say, as the main thing was that it would soon be over. Finally the phone rang, the cousin picked it up and after a while she said: "Yes, he's here, I'll pass you on," and held the receiver out to him. He took it, got up and said, "Hello." It was as if he'd heard the voice on the phone only yesterday, so familiar was its intonation, every distinctive "r" and the kind of accent that many Slovaks who speak Czech a lot tend to acquire, although she'd probably never spoken to her Prague-born husband in Czech – on the contrary, he used to speak Slovak making many, often slightly funny mistakes, and always the same ones. As soon as he heard the first words, spoken in a quavering voice, he felt a sense of relief and somehow understood that he might not need to come up with the sentence he was trying to compose in his head, as the cousin had already told her sister what had happened and since then an entire reservoir of memories must have accumulated in her head, some long forgotten, some fresh, blurred shadows having taken on a definite shape and come to life, turned into words that came pouring out of her in a torrent: she spoke without pausing, in sentences that chased and jumped over one another. His memory retained only one thing from this deluge of words, about how, when she was still a young girl, Zora had started to take this cousin on hikes in the mountains and so had it not been for her, she would probably not have taken to mountaineering or looked for a job in the Tatras after graduating. In his befuddled and subdued state everything else just slipped his memory, but gradually the torrent of words slowed down, she started choking up as if her own words had darkened her mood, and he realised this was probably the point at which he ought to say something, but then she was off again, sounding more composed and almost calm, telling him there was no need for him to say anything, for she could imagine very well how he felt, – and was there anything she could do for him, anything she could send him –, and only then did he finally manage to come up with a sentence, without thinking:

"Yes, could you please send me some Tacitin…Tacitin…" Yes, of course, she would send some, and after adding a few more words asked him to put her sister back on the phone. He handed the receiver back to the cousin, who had been standing next to him throughout. She asked her sister something, probably about her own daughter who also lived in Zurich, but he was no longer listening. He thought he really could do with some Tacitin; she had sent him the tranquillizer from Zurich before, sometimes his wife would also take one… and he felt relieved the way one does after some tremendous exertion or great excitement, or indeed as if he had taken a Tacitin. She didn't really want to talk to him, she just needed to pour out to someone everything that had accummulated inside her and he was the only person she could tell all that.

The cousin put the receiver down, said something to her husband, presumably to do with their daughter in Zurich, then she told him she would now serve him dinner and disappeared into the kitchen. He was left alone with her husband and it took him a moment to realise that he was telling him something, oh, that he was going to spend the holidays with his relations but then had to be back… this was probably to explain that he couldn't come to the funeral, but this was not something he needed to be told, as Gusto had never attended any family funeral and never went anywhere with his wife; he regarded all this as waste of time, as he had to go home straight after the Christmas holidays, his maths books were waiting for him, he still had some difficult equations to solve, that was why he didn't have time for anything apart from brisk walks to keep fit. But of course, he nodded understandingly and then fell silent as relief spread through his body after the phone call, not because he didn't have to stammer out anything – it was as if he had been speaking to someone from another planet, all he represented to the voice on the other end of the phone was a past made glamorous by memory, and not the person he was for everyone else here in Bratislava, those who knew him well and constantly rebuked him for something or other, though he had no idea what. For the voice at the other end of the line he was just a person deserving of compassion, of words of consolation, and therefore the conversation didn't elicit the vague sense of guilt he otherwise carried with him wherever he went.

The cousin came in with a slice of meat in some kind of brown sauce. He'd actually worked up a decent appetite, he said contentedly as he began to chew on the first bits of meat and squash the potatoes with his fork, taking care not to make the sauce slop out of his plate. He launched into an account of the morning's events: the visitor who brought the casserole, the home-made wafer rolls, the coach arrangements – and the cousin exclaimed, that's wonderful, she would also take the coach on her way back.

Did she know, he asked her, when it was he'd last seen her sister and her husband – no, how would she know, but of course it was here, at her place, he had come for lunch with his wife, she had rung them to say that the two of them would stop by before leaving the country, so they came over straight away. Harry said they were headed for Switzerland before stopping abruptly and asking him: "So what about you? Are you going to stay? Can you imagine what it will be like here? Do you really think that someone like you won't end up wiped off the map?" And Harry went on to answer his own question: "Things will get horrible here, you'll see!"

He even remembered the exact order in which his questions came. But why – though he didn't say it out loud – had he addressed him alone? Did he think his wife wouldn't end up wiped off the map?"

After repeating the salvo of questions that had rained down on him on that occasion, the cousin asked: "So what did you say to him?"

"Oh, just some nonsense," he admitted, angrily. "I'd be too embarrassed to repeat it now but back then everyone made dramatic speeches like that: that things wouldn't get all that bad. That the wheel of history could no longer be turned back. That this time the masses were mobilised and the momentum could no longer be stopped." That was exactly four years and four months ago, and now sounded so silly that he just concluded: "And more stupid nonsense like that."

"You two were idealists," the cousin said. That made him a bit cross. "We were neither the first nor the last. Just remember our literary classics from a hundred or hundred and thirty years ago," he replied, quoting lines of poetry about the nation that schoolchildren had to memorise to this day. "They were idealists all right, but their justification would have been that they didn't have a clue how political power operated and what it meant." And he began to spin them his theories. "For the past two hundred years all the intellectuals have had a bee in their bonnet about how our nation, this tiny David, could smash Goliath at the drop of a hat. The nation just had to get its act together." The song from the interwar years again came to his mind: "When millions of us will march, all against the wind…" "You're not familiar with the song?" he asked her. "Yes, I am, I still know it by heart." "You see, we're all a part of the same generation of idealists." He continued to spin his web of theories. "Except that the nation is just an abstract concept dreamt up by intellectuals and it has absolutely no aspiration to smash any Goliaths. Only when it realises there are no powers-that-be looming above, for a brief moment it feels the world is its oyster. But that moment never lasts very long, soon enough some new power-that-be will loom above the nation, turning it into a powerless little David again. And it keeps his mouth shut."

The cousin ignored his grandiose ideas. "But what he said was true. You have been wiped off the map."

"Indeed we have. But was it quite as terrible as Harry predicted? Harry and his wife wouldn't have come to any harm because they had never been involved in anything. And we haven't been locked up or deported to Siberia either, we've just ceased to exist. And that's actually quite gentle treatment considering what this regime is capable of." He contradicted the cousin, even though deep down he agreed with her.

"This regime has to wipe everyone off the map, otherwise it would probably not survive," said Gusto, and told them his story, not for the first time. He had set up a new department at the technical university and had to rustle up every single screw himself, hammer every bookcase together himself, locate every single machine himself. He would be in his office from five in the morning every day. Only to be fired a few years later, in 1958, ending up as a labourer and mechanic in a cooperative somewhere out in the sticks and he could count himself lucky that it was for only three years. And what had he done to deserve this? It was all because there had been no technical university in Bratislava before the war, so he had to study in Prague, and after the Germans closed down the Czech universities, he graduated from a German university as a foreigner, since he held a Slovak passport. Had he returned home, he would have been called up. That was his only crime. And that was why he had to be wiped off the map. He got rather worked up as he told his story again, and he concluded with his credo: "There's only one thing I wish for in this life. I'd like to live long enough to see this red fascist regime go belly up. I wouldn't mind if I died the very next day."

They went on chatting for a while but there were all kinds of things whirling around in his head and he wanted to be alone, and they had to get up at four the next morning to catch their bus. He said it was time for him to go and they didn't try to keep him from leaving.

Suddenly, everything he should have said back then started to come together and swirl around his head in the same way that, after a discussion or a meeting, he would start to compose the speech he should have given. L'esprit de l'escalier, as the French put it.

Back then… Back in August 1968 he didn't think that one day they would be wiped off the map. The thought had never occurred to him. He believed it was their duty to stay in this country because something could still be salvaged. He realised how foolish that sounded now, when he knew that nothing had been salvaged, but back then that was what all the newspapers were saying, and people were convincing each other that this was the case. And in his own mind he actually felt some scorn for those who joined the long caravan of cars heading for the Austrian border. Not for ordinary people, like the Tatra cousin and her husband, each of whom had their own reasons and were entitled to try their luck somewhere they could live a normal life. He didn't hold it against anyone who was fed up with the kind of life they'd had in this country for the past two decades. His scorn was directed at those he knew in person, who had prided themselves on being loyal communists, a class above the common people, who had spouted lies or half-lies in the newspapers or on television whenever party discipline had demanded it. He, by contrast, had been deemed a clueless intellectual without internal discipline, an exhibitionist loudmouth, just like his wife, who wouldn't listen to reason and learned that truth had to be handled with care "But you can't write that," Loebl* implored him when he showed him the manuscript of his newspaper article on Mňačko who had defected a year earlier, in which he said that people had the right to leave their homeland. "How can you say such a thing?" said the shocked Loebl, even phoning him later, begging him not to publish the piece. When was that?... sometime in March 1968, but by August that year Loebl himself had crossed the Austrian border, claiming the right to leave his homeland. He accepted it: the man had spent many years imprisoned under this regime; but why were people like him incapable of thinking normally in public until almost the last moment? But it wasn't really about these people. He just felt that anyone who had been somehow involved in stirring things up in the past few months ought to stay put, if for no other reason than to be here if ever someone called them to account. Those who bore some responsibility, even if only indirectly, should at least have waited to see if something dreadful happened here. Although that wasn't the point either; it was up to everyone to decide for thelmselves...

As for himself, he didn't want to leave... and there was actually another reason why not. He'd seen so many regimes collapse and and he didn't want to miss it when it happened again. He was drawn to reversals, upheavals and disasters, perhaps because he'd been through so many of them himself. He had experienced Munich* and the collapse of democracy. Six months later he witnessed the collapse of Czechoslovakia and the creation of a Slovak state. Six years later he saw the Slovak state collapse. And after another three years, the collapse of the first postwar Czechoslovakia, when political parties still existed. The only thing he hadn't really seen collapse was Stalinism, which had crept away almost imperceptibly, like a thief given police cover for a safe getaway.

After the Russian invasion he expected the thunderous collapse of 1968, that crazy, amateurish, and absurd attempt to rebuild a house shoddily built by habitually sloppy people out of cast-offs, according to nineteenth-century designs yellowed with age, in the outdated architectural style of a remote backward country – an attempt to use some reformist jiggery-pokery to refurbish a shabby shack and turn it into a state-of-the-art building to be admired the world over. For a moment, he too had believed that it was possible, having lost all sense of proportion and suffering from delusions of grandeur like everyone else, except that this hubris of men longing to be equal to the gods, a David hoping to smash a Goliath, all this was doomed to end in fiasco and retribution. Just like every one of the past regimes he had witnessed. These fiascos were part and parcel of the world he'd been born into.

A good hour had passed since he walked by his house yet he still couldn't bring himself to go home. He had to keep walking up and down and get it all off his chest, having got into the swing of it.

Well, each of these historical fiascos had brought some benefits, he thought, for those who could take up vacant posts, flats, armchairs or government positions. These people benefited but otherwise what purpose was served by this historical see-saw, which brought some people up and others down, and threw yet others off altogether, before the next cycle turned everything upside down again? And one day, after this latest fiasco – that day may be far off but he was absolutely certain that it would come – everything would indeed turn upside down again. But what sense did this all make, if any? … He recalled a plumber who had once explained the sense of it all from his perspective. They would call him out when they still lived in the town centre, and he had gained the plumber's trust as he had spoken to his mother in German. The man claimed to be a Hungarian but in fact he was one of Bratislava's old trilingual Pressburgers, and the last time they bumped into each other in the street a few months ago and the old man asked how he was, and when he told him about his situation, the plumber felt he could trust him even more now and offered his own take on historical upheavals the Slovak way:

"I'm sure you remember," the man said, "what happened after 1938. The first who had to move out were the Czechs. How many? A few thousand, perhaps twenty thousand, nobody knows. And who took their place? The Slovaks. Then came the Slovak state and the deportations of the Jews began. How many were deported from this city? Ten thousand, twenty thousand, maybe more, nobody knows. And who took their place? The Slovaks. Then the Russians came and in one fell swoop deported all the Germans and, while they were at it, the Hungarians, too, for good measure. How many? Twenty thousand, thirty thousand, nobody knows that either. And who rolled in instead of them? The Slovaks. At least two-thirds of the population of this city have been evicted, expelled, driven out, and their place has always been taken by the Slovaks. And what's been left from 1968? – fuck all, if you'll pardon my language, only the Slovaks got their federation. Everyone suffered the consequences, and only the Slovaks ever came out on top."

Then the plumber gave a description of the Slovaks crawling out of their villages and small towns as if from molehills, until they occupied this city, reaching the bitter conclusion: "Only a couple of hundred years ago they were living in the trees." Well yes, he thought, I've heard that before. Whereas the Hungarians, the plumber had forgotten to add, had a great culture going back a thousand years. But come to think of it, this city had been more or less purely German around the thirteenth century, and certainly in the fourteenth, and after that it was the Hungarians crawling out of their molehills for about five centuries, until World War I.

But he didn't hold the plumber's prejudices against him. All his life he'd been listening to the Slovaks cursing the Hungarians as evildoers, so hearing the opposite view seemed to restore the balance somewhat. Ever since he was very young he was used to everyone badmouthing everyone else. This city was Europe in a nutshell.

Nevertheless, ever since his encounter with the plumber he had tried to find some kind of continuity between these various reversals of fortune. And he did find one which was quite indisputable: ever since Munich there had always been one or other large group of people that was persecuted.

After Munich, Czech teachers started disappearing from his *gymnázium*, from all *gymnáziums*, everywhere. The theatre director whose production of *The Miserly Knight* and other tragedies by Pushkin he had once watched open-mouthed as an avantgarde revelation, had to leave for Prague and, as he learned after the war, had subsequently been expelled from there because he was a Jew, to some place from where he never returned. A few Jews started leaving, mostly those with money and connections in the outside world. This was the first time the city began to be depopulated. In every street and on every third building there would be a sign advertising a flat to let. He had viewed dozens and dozens of flats in those months, as he and his mother and brother were keen to move out of the district on the town periphery where they'd lived since he was a tiny baby, and suddenly found themselves surrounded by belligerent Nazis. Eventually, after spending a long time picking and choosing, they moved into a large three-room flat in the town centre, a choice that proved particularly advantageous in later years when he had no income, as they were able to rent out two of the bedrooms and the maid's room: there was never a shortage of people looking for a room in the centre of town. And after some time, someone – they never discovered who – had even sent a classy Czech woman their way, one who trusted them and confided that she was regularly receiving money from abroad to support those persecuted by the regime and, if they agreed, she could send them Jewish families to board with them, whose expenses she would cover. Of course they agreed, as having people pay for board and lodging would help them maintain their standard of living. There was something absurd about the whole thing. In those days he and his brother were suspended in an uncertain limbo as semi-citizens: he was one document short of qualifying for full Aryan papers and wasn't allowed to enrol at university as a result, while his brother had been kept out of school for a whole year before being allowed to return to his *gymnázium*. Nevertheless, they both lived in constant fear that they might not be able to survive on such thin ice. And it was, in fact, in this precarious situation that he began to write for the newspapers. In those days you would often see people in the street, always in a hurry, holding a briefcase over the lapel of their coats to make the yellow Star of David less conspicuous. One day the Jews of this town were assembled into a several-kilometre-long column, with him and his brother also being hustled into the line by two men from the local Jewish Centre who had come for them to their home. Wielding heavy rifles they drove the several-thousand strong procession to a branch railway station, loaded them onto cattle trucks and disgorged them some twenty hours later at the German concentration camp of Sereď, sixty kilometres from Bratislava. Their mother ran from pillar to post until she managed to get them out. Forty thousand people passed through the camp at the time, mostly Gypsies towards the end. Soon afterwards the house they lived in (whose roof he had spotted that last night from the hospital window) was requisitioned by the Slovak army, but by now the town had again lost much of its population so they had little difficulty securing a small secluded family house far out on the outskirts surrounded by a large undeveloped plot; as the Russians started to advance towards the city, a Wehrmacht soldier at their door informed them that the house had been seized and that he wanted to take a look around to make sure no one was hiding there and that the house was suitable for their purposes. The Wehrmacht soldier walked from one room to another, inspecting everything including the toilet. They had a Jewish lodger at that point, an elderly man, and they were on tenterhooks wondering when the soldier would discover him but his room was empty: they thought the lodger had climbed out of the ground floor window. After the soldier was gone the man reappeared – it turned out that the soldier had opened the bathroom door but took only a cursory look inside and went on without spotting the old man standing behind the door. Since their last move the town had lost even more of its population, the front was approaching, this time the housing department allocated them a four-room flat in the centre of town, which they heard stood empty. From there they were again taken one night to the local branch of the Gestapo, though this time only for a few days. Transports were still being assembled, no longer to Auschwitz as a few months ago, just much smaller transports to Mauthausen. Soon cannon and machine gun fire could be heard in the city and the streets were completely deserted. And after the front the new, as well as the old, police had their hands full deporting Germans and Hungarians. His mother, as an ethnic German, was also notified where and when she should report along with the members of her family: that is himself, his brother – and twenty kilos of luggage. By then he was working for a newspaper and had some influence to ensure that they were taken off the list. One of his colleagues in the editorial office always had bundles of keys hanging above his desk and when they asked him what these keys were about, he said: "Come, let me show you," and he took them down to the old town, to a small, run-down flat with unfinished cups of coffee on the table. "Interested?" They shook hands, but after seeing the unfinished cups of coffee they no longer felt like seeing any more flats. The police got a bonus depending on how many Germans and Hungarians a day they evicted, so thousands of flats fell vacant, and all were immediately occupied. A few Jews also began to drift back, some of them wandering around in their concentration camp rags for the first few days, to the dismay of the well-dressed burghers: this was the first real flare-up of spontaneous hatred towards the Jews, those people who until recently had been the lowest of the low and anyone could take whatever they fancied from them, but now suddenly they were supposed to have equal rights again and none had collaborated with the Nazis to boot. In fact, everyone was fighting everyone else: the communists were set against the democrats, everyone was waiting to see who would be the first to bump off someone else. Only after the victory of the working classes did things calm down. Initially there were no more deportations but, on the other hand, an increasing number of people were landing up in prison until – lo and behold – the next wave of deportations began, labelled Operation B, whereby this time the bourgeoisie, and prominent members of old political parties, were forced to move out to the countryside and had their flats allocated to institutions and factories. By now people were being arrested indiscriminately, although on an individual basis, following some kind of system, and once the relevant authorities seemed to be exhausted by these incessant arrests, Stalinism began to run out of steam, almost imperceptibly at first. Then for many years nobody was expelled, until 1968, when very large numbers of people left again, though this time they did so of their own accord. Of those who stayed, some were exhausted by the total extinction of their hopes and saw the future as black clouds on the horizon, while others joyfully anticipated the sun rising in a bright blue sky and felt national self-confidence bubbling up inside them: Slovakia was off its knees, its shackles would now ease, federation it would seize. And federation duly arrived. It was accompanied by dismissals, sackings, redeployment, demotions, transfers to villages and small towns, and it also affected many of those who thought that achieving federal status within Czechoslovakia would be their salvation. This time he too had sunk even lower than he had during the Slovak state. Now it wasn't on account of some document he was lacking: on the contrary, this time they gathered piles of documents against him – his articles. His wife was also wiped off the map, for the first time in her life. And it was for life. Both were wiped off the face of the earth so thoroughly that not the slightest mark or trace of them remained.

So was this the kind of continuity that he craved, another collapse followed by another rallying cry to have a go at another section of the population? Was this what he wanted to go through again, yet another iteration? Was it this that had stopped him from leaving?

He had by now returned home and sat in the winged armchair in his room, still feeling that he had not found his way to the very end of the thread, that he hadn't yet found the single, fundamental answer to the question of why he stayed here after 1968. There must have been something else, he thought, as he focused on this period.

Of course there was something else. Something very simple. What would he have actually done abroad? He knew no one out there, had no connections, no friends, no one who might have offered him a job. Since the end of the war he had got used to everything falling into his lap. Whereas before... yes, there had been a time when he had guts, was able to wriggle out of trouble, exploit every opportunity, was used to being a drop-out living on the margins of society. And a drop-out can't survive without a few dirty tricks and some scamming, without grovelling and demeaning himself every now and then, or holding out a begging bowl when necessary, picking up a few crumbs and the odd cigarette butt when no one is looking. But things had changed with time: he had grown comfortable.

Two weeks after the front had passed, in mid-April 1945, he went for a stroll in the main square with a friend, the painter Guderna – the last time he had seen him was in another historical era, before the whole town had burrowed down into shelters, but now there were crowds of people everywhere, in the main square, along the Danube, on the couple of pedestrianised streets in the Old Town known as the *korzo*, in the main streets, since everything was still closed, businesses and offices were not open, people had nowhere to go, all the shops, restaurants, cafés and wine bars had been looted, all people could do was stroll in the streets and squares, which is what the two of them were doing when, all of a sudden, amidst the crowds of people walking towards them, Guderna spotted a man he knew and called out to him: they hugged each other overjoyed, and it turned out this friend of his had fought in the Uprising last autumn and spent the winter hiding in the mountains, they talked animatedly interrupting one another, and the stranger mentioned, among other things, that he had just arrived from Košice* as the government's plenipotentiary with the task of getting radio broadcasts and newspapers organised, and at this point Guderna made the introductions: "Meet my friend, a wonderful fellow, he's written about our surrealist poets and would now like to work for a newspaper." Though his writing about the surrealist poets amounted to no more than a few amateurish reviews, as he hadn't understood many of them, just as he didn't understand much about poetry in general, nevertheless Guderna appreciated his reviews: they provided a kind of reference point – and that was all it took, before long the stranger took him to a building where his father had once worked as an editor, showed the doorman a decree stating that the building in which the wartime government's daily paper had been published was being requisitioned, and the doorman just shrugged, opened the door of the lift for the stranger and said that the editorial offices were on the third floor and showed him to the office of the editor-in-chief. He expected the stranger to take a seat and start organising other people to put the paper together but instead of sitting down, the man reached into his briefcase, took out a stack of papers, flung them on the desk in front of him and said: "Here's the new government programme, you'll publish it in two instalments and that will fill up half of the issue, as for the news, you'll just have to listen to the radio." The man gave him the phone numbers of a handful of compositors and a maker-up, and off he went, saying he had lots of other things to see to. He was left by himself, the only person on the entire floor, the only person in all these rooms, and as he passed through them all, he couldn't find a single radio anywhere: in all likelihood the doorman had handed them in to the authorities in accordance with the decrees plastered all around town, so he hurried home with the joyful news that he had a job, the first in his life, and as he had to start immediately, he picked up a small radio they hadn't handed in, wrapped it in a tablecloth and took it back to the office, where, as a token of respect, he sat down in the room where his father had worked years ago, and started to read the government programme, but he found the stilted sentences so boring that he just turned the pages until he came to the end of the section that would appear in the first issue of *Pravda*, then he listened to the news on the radio, from the front and elsewhere, he even knocked out an editorial, something along the lines of: here is a brand-new newspaper arriving on your doorstep, rejoice! Then he phoned the compositor and maker-up, and stood by them in the composing room, and finally, in the morning, someone else took care of the paper-boys, and that was the start of his career.

His stint at *Pravda* was brief, though before he left he managed to recruit a few staff writers who had to wear the tightest of blinkers to work there. Soon other newspapers started to appear and he was offered a job on an independent daily, *Slovenská obroda*, and three years later, after that paper was discontinued because it took too independent a line, he was offered a job with the communist daily *Pravda,* and when he was dismissed from there because he wasn't a party member, someone offered him the position of dramaturg at the theatre, and when he was fired for revisionist dramaturgy, he was offered the chance to write on literature at an academic institute, and after a long time there was sacked for being a counterrevolutionary, and since then no one had offered him anything and he didn't even try to look for anything because he knew he wouldn't find anything he would be able to do. But until then someone had always given him a leg up, and even if he was kicked out, all he had to do was wait a while until someone gave him a leg up again. But who would give him a leg up if he were abroad? He would be lost and helpless.

In those days he had an idée fixe that now made him laugh. Whenever he imagined himself abroad, for some reason he would picture himself in front of a microphone – as a newsreader on the radio. He had spent decades covering issues of every kind, but all he would be able to do abroad would be to read the news. And that was not something he was particularly keen to do. Here at home he could always take on translations, he'd thought. So what would be the point of making a leap into the unknown?

A newsreader on the radio… what a crazy idea, completely idiotic. Ever since his early school days he'd been mocked for not being able to roll his "r"s, and later, whenever someone wanted to do a mocking impression of him, they would make a point of pronouncing every "r" in the most contorted way possible and everyone would split their sides laughing. And whenever he got up to speak at a meeting or in a discussion, before he got to the end of the second sentence people would start shouting: "Speak up, we can't hear you", as he was simply incapable of articulating a single sentence in a clear, even voice. And his accent bore all the marks of a city like this one, where people once spoke four different languages, whereas the pronunciation regarded as "proper" was the hallmark of those who had come here from the provinces as adults… A newsreader on the radio… the prospect was about as realistic as seeing himself as a taxi driver or a waiter in a cafeteria he thought as he lay in bed in the dark before going to sleep.

And how could he have entertained this idea seriously anyway: he was married… His wife had once said to him: "If you decide to leave, I will come too, but it will be up to you to organise everything, it will be your responsibility." She gave a clear indication that she wouldn't stand in his way. And she knew that he would not ask her to do the impossible. It was out of the question for him to ask her to take off with him into the great big world outside. She was not someone who could be re-planted elsewhere. She was like a flower that would begin to wilt if transplanted into different soil, until it withered away.

It was slowly dawning on him that all the arguments he used to give about why they had to stay in this country were hers. He had just parroted them because he had adopted her way of thinking, right down to her actual words: it was necessary to stay here because they may still be able to salvage something… this was what she would say and she would act accordingly, continuing to write and speak up in public, even when he no longer believed any of it. But in a way Zora had been right, he thought now. If you are jointly responsible for something, it is your sacred duty to throw yourself to the wolves, put your head on the block – those, too, had been her words, her position. To leave would have amounted to betraying those who stayed behind, a sign of cowardice – that was how she had been raised, that was her credo. She could not betray it. And he had adjusted to her, repeating things he thought she might say. He was like her doppelgänger and had to stay with her. End of story.

Here was another decision in which he had allowed himself to be pushed, this time by her. Not that he held it against her; she didn't do it consciously after all. And he had no choice in the matter, for her life was also his life. He didn't exist in the singular. Until now.

He returned to the present. It no longer really mattered why they hadn't left back then. It was she who had left now, and he who had stayed behind. These pointless musings brought on anxiety and left him exhausted. This is where his home was, he had the savings book, so who knows, perhaps this was better than struggling through the thickets of an unknown world. He was tired of everything and more than anything else wanted to stop thinking, about anything at all.

Anyway, it was time to go to the kitchen for a sleeping pill and to go to sleep.

Tomorrow morning he would set about organising the coach. And rehang that picture. Something else that needed to be seen to was bound to crop up. Just as well he had things to see to all the time. Right until the funeral.

He woke up suddenly in the middle of the night, feeling surprisingly lively – something in him had been alert, at work while he slept, he realised as he glanced at the clock and saw it was not quite four in the morning, too early to get up. His head was awhirl and he wasn't sure whether it was the tail end of a forgotten dream, or if he was in a state of wakefulness. It was something to do with the funeral but neither he nor anyone else seemed to be involved. It was probably no longer a dream, so he listened to the mellifluous flow of words he could hear. Before he was able to make out any actual words he realised that this was the professor giving his eulogy. He could hear his soft, confident voice, the firm cadences of the individual sentences delivered in a minor emotional key. The professor's voice rang out all around him, there was a restrained solemnity in this eulogy of an illustrious person who had left an indelible mark…, had masterfully enriched…, will go down in… we bow our heads in respect before…

Now he was lying in the dark fully awake as more and more high-flown phrases poured out of him, just disjointed fragments, keywords, not necessarily full sentences, he was spinning them out, waxing lyrical to himself, though delivered in the professor's voice, this was what a eulogy should sound like. And then suddenly, the voice trailed off, having exhausted all the ringing words of praise, and although nothing further was needed, he felt that it was wrong for it to have come to an end, it was too soon to put a full stop at the end of a lifetime. Something was left hanging in the air, something that remained unsaid. And it would be up to someone else to complete it.

For surely the last three or four years also formed part of her life? Was there really nothing to be said about these years? Just because she had ceased to be a public figure, a luminary, and was merely a private person? Just because she was no longer publishing translations or articles, but receiving notifications of cancelled contracts instead? In fact, her life was just filled with different content. After they moved to this flat, she had spent weeks furnishing it. This was the first home she had ever furnished, as before she had a large room in her parents' house, with a view of the garden, and all the furniture had also belonged to her parents and had been moved there from other rooms; when they got married she had arranged one room in the Bratislava flat where he had lived with his mother and, initially, also with his brother. When they moved here, they brought over some furniture from her parents' house and much of the furniture from his old flat, and she went shopping for various additional items. For about three weeks she turned away all visitors except for her cousin, who was astonished on each occasion to see how an amorphous mess was taking on the shape of a place fit to live in. The enormous windows had not been fitted with blinds, so she went shopping for curtains, thick colourful drapes as well as thin net curtains. Fittings and accessories of every kind began to appear, such as a brand-new Swedish vacuum cleaner. Eventually the place turned into the home she had envisaged. Then came the final touches: the cleaning of the windows and window frames, the vacuuming of the carpets, and the varnishing of the parquet floor. Only once all that was done were the first visitors allowed in. And she had kept the flat spick and span ever since, as if she were a maid in the employ of an excessively fastidious lady of the house. But the flat had come with a section of the garden on the slope behind their building. Nothing but weeds and grass and whatever the wind blew in had grown there, perhaps since time immemorial. Only an enormous pear tree stood sprawling at the top edge of the garden, with just the odd tart crab pear hanging from its branches in the autumn. The gardens further up and on both sides boasted manicured lawns, and when they moved in, behind one of the fences a thicket of lilac had just burst into purple bloom, its intense fragrance filling both of the back-facing rooms in their flat in the evenings. He invited a childhood friend, Karol Weinberger, to come over. Over the years Karol had turned into something of a garden designer, even though he had actually studied law and found a job at the French cultural institute after the war, only to end up being imprisoned as a French spy after the victory of the working people, and after his release drove a lorry that collected waste and delivered manure, eventually working his way up to becoming an expert at the botanical gardens. He inspected their section of the garden first from the balcony, then went down, pulling out a bunch of grass and some weeds here and there, poking the soil with his fingers and offering the advice that it wasn't worth planting any flowers, because should there be any heavy rain, it would wash everything down the slope not least because the soil was packed stone-hard and wouldn't absorb much water. What would make most sense would be to plant a few shrubs which would give the garden a kind of unified architecture; he even wrote down the shrubs' Latin names and explained that they needed little water and could withstand the baking sun. What about a rockery? his wife asked. A rockery, as the crowning glory of her garden, had been her dream. Yes, she could plant a few rock plants, provided they were as low as possible, some soil would have to be dug out to create a small plateau, he said, and wrote down the names of plants for a rockery. But initially there was nowhere to plant shrubs or start a rockery, since everything was overgrown with thick, tall grass and weeds, so his wife had to clear everything with a spade. But she was undeterred, slaving away on that slope as if it were her mission in life, and sometimes she would come home at the end of a day so exhausted that she'd just go straight to bed. After days of prolonged rain, when at least the surface of the soil loosened making it easier to dig out the weeds, he would give her a hand. As the weeds gradually retreated he would drive her to the big garden centres located at the other end of town, and as most of the shrubs Karol had suggested weren't available, they bought whatever caught their eye, as long as they were assured that it would withstand the searing sun and poor quality soil; there wasn't much choice, as most of the shrubs had sold out in the spring, some time before they had moved to their new flat, so they threw in a few slender trees and planted them, but by next year it was clear that hardly any of them had taken. They started doing the rounds of vegetable markets around the city and picked up flowers, seeds, young plants as well as more mature flowers, large clumps of moss for the rock garden and large patches of moss with tiny white and blue dots of something that could have been flowers, taking care to choose a range of flowers so that something would be in bloom throughout the year. And while his wife kept digging up the weeds, he'd go around bookshops hunting for books on gardens and gardening, rockeries, shrubs, ornamental flowers for the garden as well as house plants, cacti in particular. Come summer they would water the garden with a hose; this had often been his task. He went to see his childhood friend in the botanical gardens: though he wasn't allowed to sell anything, sometimes the flower beds had spread out too much, sprawling luxuriantly onto the paths, and Karol would dig out bits of the beds that jutted out. At the same time flora also began to proliferate in every room of their flat. His wife took special care of her cacti, allocating to the collection a small table that used to be reserved for dictionaries, manuscripts and proofs. These were mostly miniature cacti that needed a lot of care and attention. In fact, all the plants required care and attention, of various kinds.

It was here in this flat that Zora first began to cook, as it was her mother who had done all the cooking in her parental home. When she came to stay with him in Bratislava, she would take her meals in restaurants and for the last two years or so of his mother's life, he would join her and bring meals for his mother, who by then was too weak to cook: whenever she decided to do some cooking, she would let everything burn, leave the pot on the stove and have a lie-down, doze off and by the time she went back to the kitchen it was too late. But on their part of the hill there were no restaurants, and they would have had to drive down to the city centre, so Zora gradually began to cook: starting with *lečo*, a pepper and tomato stew, omelettes, pancakes, tinned meat, gradually branching out into a wide range of dishes. He bought her every kind of cookery book, setting aside a special shelf for them in the kitchen, but the only one she regularly consulted was an old cookery book her mother had used before her. Nevertheless, her specialty was less traditional dishes, such as chicken with curry powder, which had a sweetish, apple-like flavour.

No cleaner had ever set foot in this flat. Zora regularly cleaned the rectangular window panes, even unscrewing the metal frames to reach inside the double glazed windows. She bought a washing machine and they stopped taking their clothes to the laundry. And along the entire ten metres or more of the two balconies she planted geraniums and begonias, which she would cut down before winter and store in the cellar. And then there were all the decorative plates that she'd hung up in the entrance hall...

As he lay in his bed, suspended between night and day, these memories effortlessly began to turn into sentences which together added up to an account of how she had created an alternative content for her life. His words, precise and without any need for rephrasing, flowed effortlessly from one into another, maintaining a stylistic register that was on the light-hearted side, as if observed from a distance by a complete stranger. He was certain that his memory would retain this script and he would be able to retrieve it in the morning as if reading it from a typewritten sheet. He covered all the aspects of her life that needed to be mentioned at the funeral as an addendum to the professor's eulogy, complementing his oration. Personal memories of a life that had suddenly turned perfectly ordinary. Nothing subversive. Only those who knew would understand. He went over in his mind what he had composed and as there was nothing more for him to do, he fell asleep satisfied with what he had accomplished.

In the morning, still in his pyjamas, he looked out of the kitchen window: a murky, sleepy sky had descended even more oppressively onto the city, the heavy clouds an opaque grey; the street was wet and small puddles remained on the small paved yard in front of the garages.

He got dressed and made himself a cup of coffee. But he didn't feel like breakfast. He realised that he couldn't just type up what he'd concocted at night and take it to some editorial office. He'd forgotten that however good he was at writing words in the air, he wouldn't be able to make them materialize by means of a typewriter, as the sentences he had formulated during the night would get all jumbled and start to fall apart in an operation that required a degree of physical exertion and concentration. He needed a second person to write up what he'd drafted in his head and a third person to deliver it, and the second person would have to tailor it for the third. And he knew exactly who should be the person to write it up according to his instructions and who should deliver it later, although he was no longer sure if it had occcurred to him at night or only in the morning. He needed these two links in the transmission chain. Otherwise, he might as well bury the whole idea.

He had already decided what he'd do first thing: he'd go and see Agneša, the sacked journalist who'd been at his birthday party two weeks ago and whose husband had been locked up for the past six months. Over the past two or three years she and her husband had visited them quite often and had first-hand knowledge of some of the things he wanted included in the text, and with her years of experience, and being someone to whom writing always came easily – she could complete an article in one go, without fretting over it and rewriting it endlessly the way he did – writing this up wouldn't pose a major challenge for her. But what if she said no? He avoided thinking of that; there was no alternative, he couldn't go around asking one person after another, word might get out and that could not be allowed to happen. If she said no, that would be that. He would also tell her who he wanted to deliver it: one of the girls, the sister of the girl who had died with his wife's niece Jelka in the mountaineering accident, this fact should also be mentioned at the outset to make clear that it was in these past few years that the girl had got to know his wife. And what if the girl said no, if for no other reason than because she had never spoken in public before? Well, that would be that, too. It wasn't crucial; after all, until yesterday it hadn't even occurred to him that something of this sort ought to be said at the funeral, but now that he had the idea and composed the entire text in his head, it would be nice if it did happen.

Wondering whether one or the other of them would agree to take this on made him nervous but, at the same time, also contented, because it would give him something to do all morning, keep him busy. It annoyed him that he had to wait a little. Today was a holiday and Agneša would be having a lie-in. Over the past decades she had developed the habit of going to bed late as there were always visitors at their place, although since she and her husband had found a listening device in their flat, they often visited others instead. For decades she didn't have to be at her desk until quite late in the day, but now she had to get up early for work, so he couldn't show up on her doorstep too soon. And he couldn't give her a ring to ask what would be a good time, he was sure her phone calls were still being tapped. He had to bide his time.

He started to pace up and down the living room, hallway and kitchen, rehearsing the speech he had composed overnight. It was good. Each point flowed quite naturally from the preceding one, and it was all in the right key. As he recited the text, he would come to a halt every now and then but each blank would always be automatically filled by a word that at least resembled what he had come up with at night. To be on the safe side, he repeated any passages that had begun to fade, editing them in his head before moving on. Once he had gone through the entire text in this manner, he divided it up into bullet points to commit their order to memory, just in case. In fact, this was what mattered most. Knowing himself he suspected that he wouldn't be able to recite the text to Agneša exactly as he remembered it now, and that as soon as he had to say it out loud, hear it in his own voice, his nerves would at some point compel him to start shortening the text, leaving out this and cutting that, and condensing the more complicated passages. That wouldn't be too bad; after all, he couldn't present her with a polished text that she would just parrot off. The important thing was to remember the individual points and their ramifications.

Suddenly he didn't know what to do. It was still too early to drive to Agneša's. Perhaps he should have something to eat. But that could wait, too. He was worried that on a full stomach he would mess up the clear outline of the text. Eating always made him ease off a little, prevented him from staying focused. And just now he was nauseated by the very thought of food.

He could expand the text. Actually, though, it was best not to, it was perfect just as it was. But simply because he didn't know what to do with himself until it was time to leave, he started scouring his memory. For instance, he thought of how, after returning home in the evening having spent the day working in the garden, she would go to her room and stand at the window for a long time gazing into the gathering darkness and surveying her day's labours, checking how much of the garden she'd cleared of weeds and trying to work out how much there was left to do, how many days it would take. She couldn't get her fill of looking at the shrubs and flowers that she had planted that day, her thoughts perhaps wandering back to her room in her parents' home, which had also looked out onto the garden.

It was still too early for him to leave, he'd have to wait a while longer. Suddenly an idea flashed through his mind, instantly making him happy. He went over to the long coffee table covered with dozens of tiny pots of miniature cacti and behind them piles of books on shrubs, cacti, rock gardens and gardening in general that he'd bought her over the years, he carried the books over to his desk, and wrote down their titles and the authors' names. Next, he went to the kitchen, took the cookery books off the shelf and also carried them to his desk but this time he just wrote down their general subject rather than copying the exact titles. Some of this information might be used to enliven the text.

He pocketed the sheets of paper and since he really could think of nothing else to do, he decided to go, even if it meant he would be early.

As soon as he got into the car, he was gripped by fresh pangs of doubt. Why should anyone want to take on this kind of extra burden, that could easily get them into trouble? If she said, "But you know the situation I'm in, I just can't afford to do that," there would be nothing he could say. If he told her that no one needed to know she was involved, she would just shrug her shoulders, thinking that perhaps he would be the first to blurt it out somewhere when he had a drink or three. She might well imagine that he was the last person she could rely on.

But then again, he'd known Agneša for years. Her husband Laco introduced them soon after they were married, just after the war. And in the decades that followed they had met countless times. Partly because they used to live very close, less than ten minutes' walk before he and his wife moved to the hill. Sometimes he would bump into Agneša on her way to the editorial office, which was around the corner from his flat, or on her way home. Sometimes he would see her down in the street when he looked out of the window: even back then he would sometimes gaze at the world below, watching strangers in the street. It hadn't yet become a part of his daily routine in those days; he would just lean out of the window to take a break from whatever he was working on. He used to see her quite often in the editorial offices of *Kultúrny život*, as he worked for them even when he was employed by another paper. He often wrote on film and theatre, the sections in her remit. They rarely spoke very much when he went to her office: he would hand in his copy, she'd read through it and say, that's fine, it'll go out in the next issue. She rarely had any comments. On occasion she might give him a great idea for something to write about, but he hadn't talked to her any more than to any of her colleagues. Sometimes he'd hang around with *Kultúrny život* staff at the Café Bláha drinking shots of rum, brandy, slivovitz or whatever intellectuals happened to favour at the time – and she would show up around lunchtime and have something light to eat. Or he might be at the Tulipán, the bar that opened sometime in the early sixties on the corner of the street he lived on – and on occasion she would show up there in the morning, if she had nothing to do in the office, and would join him and they would just say hello or perhaps have a chat. In a sense, she knew everything about him because when he was on a bender, it was usually in one of these two places; on days like these he might turn up at the editorial office just to see if he could find a drinking buddy and wouldn't have to down shots of rum or brandy, or glasses of cinzano all on his own, and she knew that if he got going in one of these places first thing, he wouldn't stop anytime soon. And besides, she knew everyone who knew him and heard everything people said about him at the time. And it was also the case that he knew everything there was to know about her, everything others were saying about her at the time, that is.

They were in each other's line of vision, as it were, and for that reason they rarely visited each other. As far as he could remember, over those twenty-five years she'd been to his place only a few times, her husband almost never. He was more likely to visit them, sometimes at her invitation, when so-and-so was coming, someone from Prague or from abroad, and she asked him to join them. They had a host of friends and generally didn't mind him coming along, they'd always welcome him with open arms, although he was less keen to hear so much talking all the time. Alcohol was almost never served at their house and he found it boring to sit there without a drop to drink. That was quite lucky, in a way, otherwise he would have barged in on them more often on his way home, for one final drink with someone he could also talk to. She had become a kind of fixture in his life.

Except that *Kultúrny život* was shut down in 1969, with Agneša sacked even earlier. Meanwhile, with his wife no longer spending so much time at her mother's and now being based in Bratislava, he no longer strayed into cafés before lunchtime, having mended his ways in many respects, and even if he might sometimes still go for a drink it would be quite rare. They still lived quite close to one another but their paths rarely crossed anymore, though it was around that time that he and Zora began visiting them more and more often. The lives of Agneša and Laco had changed, too: they had far fewer visitors from Prague or abroad, many of their friends had left the country around 1968, while quite a few of those who had not, no longer showed their faces at their house. The hustle and bustle quietened down. It was only then that their relations became warmer. For they shared the same fate and views. Sometimes he and Zora were really keen to spend time with Agneša and Laco, who still had quite a few friends and were always well informed. In those days, when it was still far from certain how the situation would develop, it was good to get the latest news, to learn what X had done and why Y had been fired, and who was now too frightened to stop for a chat with an old friend in the street, and all sorts of other things that would not necessarily have interested them in the past.

There was only one occasion – it happened after they had already moved to their new flat on the hill – when Zora got terribly cross with Agneša. They had bumped into her somewhere in town and Agneša greeted them almost jubilantly, as she was dying to tell them that there was an article about them in that day's paper, almost a whole page spread; they were the heroes of the day. His wife, however, wasn't best pleased about the paper devoting so much attention to them and didn't want to know the details; she quickly said goodbye before Agneša had time to utter another sentence. The meeting happened on their way to a restaurant in town, and over lunch he noticed that Zora's hands were trembling: "Why on earth did she feel the need to pass on this news? She knows we don't read the papers and don't want to know what they say," she complained. He understood why she was agitated and indignant. This was a time when not a day would pass without some revelation about someone who'd done or written something in 1968, and his wife found the papers horrid and disgusting, truly repulsive. And Agneša had now forced her to take a glance, however brief, at something that was like a nest of horrible worms that tarnished everything. But later on she and Laco started visiting them again in their flat on the hill. Once they even mentioned that it would be better if they didn't come to their place because they now had a "sound system". They were baffled until they told them that what they meant was that a bug had been planted in their flat and connected to a transmitter.

Shortly after that the Kalinas were arrested. Agneša was released after a few weeks, and one day, just before Laco's court hearing, she rang their doorbell quite unexpectedly.

She was standing there with a grim and bitter, almost hostile, expression he'd never before seen on her face. She'd just seen her husband's defence lawyer and was told that when the secret police questioned him, Rozner, as a material witness, he had uttered a sentence on which they built her husband's indictment. He was completely stunned to learn that. When he came home from his interrogation, he'd run everything past his wife as well as Alma, who was very experienced in these matters. He'd made no mistakes. He hadn't told them anything they wouldn't have known already. Agneša quoted the relevant sentence in his statement. He responded indignantly: "But that's just some ideological drivel! I have never said he'd done anything he could be prosecuted for! The interrogator asked if Laco could have been of the opinion that a series of articles*, about people from 1968 that appeared in the party press and was broadcast on radio and TV, might have represented the party position, and I said he could have been of that opinon. That was all." Gradually she calmed down – the secret police were past masters at blowing things out of proportion. They would now summon him to testify in court, when he would have to put things right by explaining that he had never heard Laco express such a view. He was prepared to give his testimony. But the judge allowed each witness only about five minutes and brought his statement to a close before the point he was meant to challenge came up. In legal terms, the only thing that counted was what he said in court, not what he had said during the interrogation. Nevertheless, the court verdict included the sentence from his interrogation, to the effect that Laco might have been thinking something. He told Agneša to ask for him to be called as a witness for the defence at the appeal. But the judge didn't allow any witnesses to be called at that hearing.

They continued to see Agneša now that she was on her own – she had come to his birthday party, for instance – but now, as he pulled up outside her flat, close to where he had lived for nearly a quarter of a century, he wondered if she might still hold it against him… But then again, she might agree for the sake of his wife whom she couldn't blame for anything. Still, his heart was in his mouth when he rang her doorbell.

She opened the door, still wearing her dressing gown, as he expected. He said he'd come to ask her advice and hoped she could help. Agneša just nodded and didn't ask any questions. Nor did she say a word about the fact that his wife had died, almost as if she didn't know although she must have; but they had known each other for too long for her to come out with the usual clichés and shake his hand with a concerned expression; instead she just asked him to wait a moment while she brushed her teeth and had a quick shower; she'd put the kettle on and they could have breakfast together. In a voice hoarse with nerves he said that he'd already eaten. "Oh well, then you can just have some coffee," she suggested good-humouredly. Whenever he came to their house, he'd be offered a cup of coffee; she would also make some at the editorial office when he brought her an article on the theatre or cinema, and she would drink it while she read.

He sat down. She'd said a moment, which meant she would be ages. He knew Agneša and her moments. She would pop out "for a moment" to take a call from a friend while reading his article, making him wait a good twenty minutes while she was on the phone. By the time she brushed her teeth and taken a shower, quickly slapped on her make-up, put the kettle on and brought her breakfast on a tray, he was bound to forget everything he had so painstakingly worked out in his head.

How come the flat is so quiet, he thought suddenly. Shouldn't their daughter be home? She should be up by now but maybe she had gone out to see some friends. She had found a temporary job, as she hadn't been allowed to go to university and was hoping to start her studies next year. But today was a holiday, so she must have gone to see one of her girlfriends. She had as many friends, male and female, as all his old schoolfriends added together. But when he was young, it was not common for everyone to have a group of friends.

He liked their flat. The furniture seemed tailor-made for each individual room. He'd first seen it soon after the war, completely furnished. After the war people "organised" things for themselves as best as they could. He didn't manage to organise anything for himself; he just started working for a newspaper straight away, like an idiot, just him on his own to begin with, then there were two of them, later three. There was no time for organising, and besides he wouldn't have known how to go about it.

Last time he'd been here was about three months ago. He and Zora hadn't gone to Martin, as he was expecting to be called to testify at the appeal hearing. But no one had called him. At about five in the afternoon Agneša rang to say: "It's all over, the appeal court has confirmed the verdict. No witnesses were admitted. It was horrendous. A large room this time, and all the seats in the public gallery were taken by secret policemen. Whenever Laco said anything in his defence, they all roared with laughter. Every single time." But she wouldn't say more over the phone, she said they should come over.

He told his wife what Agneša had said. It made her really upset and furious: she started yelling about gangsters and mafias, then she wound a wet towel around her head and said she had to lie down. He should go on his own. Agneša asked at the door if Zora was coming and he explained how upset she was and that she had to go and lie down. He could see she was disappointed. He was just a piece of furniture in her life, a lifelong colleague, but the person she wanted to talk to was his wife, someone who meant something in society. But she hadn't come. And she repeated more or less the same thing as she had said over the phone, only in much more detail. How all those people roared with laughter and how utterly pointless the whole hearing had been. Her face was drawn, her movements visibly slowed down, as if something had snapped inside her. They were sitting in the same room where he was waiting for her now, drinking coffee. Then someone rang the door, a loyal friend. Agneša went to make him a cup of coffee and when he heard her telling the visitor the same thing he had just heard, he took his leave.

He recalled with great clarity an afternoon, an hour or an hour and a half, spent in this flat after Laco's first hearing. He had come with Zora, the flat was packed with people and booming with their voices. The fifteen or so witnesses who had testified in court were there and at least as many other friends. And perhaps the same number of their daughter's friends. And something unprecedented for this flat was happening: bottles of vodka or gin or brandy were served in every room. People were standing or sitting, talking over one another. A party. For a while he was sitting next to Agneša whose husband had been sentenced to two years' imprisonment only a few hours earlier. She was talking animatedly, almost on a high, but he could tell that she'd been crying. "So that sentence I said is no longer in the indictment, as it hasn't come up in court," he said. "That's what you think," she snapped back derisively. "It's still in the verdict. It's against the law but the judge said that if the court had not raised it with the witness, whatever he had said during interrogation was valid. They picked a senile old judge who hadn't bothered to read all the witness statements properly and had no idea what questions he should put to whom. But none of it really mattered anyway. The verdict had been decided in advance. The court took five minutes to consider it before returning with a typed-up judgement." Then she asked if she could suggest him as a witness for the appeal hearing. Of course she could. But it might be in the summer. That was no problem, he said, they could stay in town.

But that time when he came to see Agneša on his own, he didn't tell her the whole truth. After he had told Zora about the outcome of the court appeal she had flown into a rage about those gangsters, the mafia, the entire mob, but then she also began to deride Agneša and her husband for all the things they'd been up to, the endless letters of protest they'd been sending left, right and centre: what were they thinking, what did they expect!? He was tempted to say: What do you mean? Should they have just sat on their hands and said nothing? Shouldn't they have stood up for themselves, done everything they could? But he kept quiet because he suddenly realised that she was right. He could still hear her now: they kept complaining, citing legal provisions, protesting and demanding justice – didn't they know what kind of world we are living in, did they really think it was a normal world? She stayed at home because if she had come to their flat these things would have been on her mind the whole time and she would have had to make an enormous effort not to say a word: yes, you should defend yourself, you could stand on your head if you wanted to, but you had to accept that you wouldn't achieve anything. Once you are caught in their net, once you let them ensnare you, you have to recognise that you've lost.

Of course she had been right, but she could say this only to him. He knew immediately what she meant, except that it was in his nature to give up even before he tried to stand up for himself. This time, too, he'd given up, he thought. Even though he was making all the arrangements for the funeral. He had, surprisingly, managed to do something on his own initiative. But it would last only until the funeral.

Then he just sat there without any thoughts, waiting for Agneša to appear with her breakfast on a tray.

After she had tucked into her breakfast and had her tea, he could finally begin. Instead of saying that he'd woken up in the middle of the night he told her that in the morning he had run through what the professor might say. He would say everything that needed to be said, and was sure to do a great job. But that was not the end of the story. There were also the last three years, when she was no longer doing any of the things the professor would speak of. And something ought to be said about that, too, a kind of short feuilleton, without anything that might be controversial or construed as provocative, just a straightforward description of what those years were like. It could even be rose-tinted if need be, but the important thing was to tell the story all the way to the end. And he launched straight into it:

The final three years during which she'd been reduced to being a housewife. How she furnished the flat, the first one in her life, having until then lived in her parents' house and her husband's flat, furnishing it just as she wanted it to be. At first he cleaved quite closely to his prepared script, although some of his brilliant turns of phrase had slipped his mind. The garden. The weeding. The shrubs. The moss. The fruit trees. The clearing and planting. The longer he spoke, the more his voice started to shake, so he cut his sentences short. The view of the garden, yes, why not mention that as well, he thought, as he found himself adding this detail. The kitchen. The lunches. His voice was tiring. Perhaps this whole idea was ridiculous. What was the point of saying all this at the funeral? Curried chicken tasting of apples. He managed to recall how he wanted it to conclude although he forgot most of what he had prepared in his head. When he was done, he reached into his pocket for the pieces of paper with the titles of the books on gardening together with the names of their authors, and the cookery books, without mention of their authors.

"It should read a bit like a feuilleton, a kind of genre painting, simple in style, more like a collection of facts that would add up to a coherent whole, a kind of recollection, that sort of thing, and it could also be moving, if necessary," he said in conclusion.

He realised that he hadn't yet told her why he was there. "I know what it should say. If I were able to concentrate I could articulate it more clearly than I just have, but I'm not up to writing anything coherent right now. Not even a few lines." It was almost as if he were appealing for her compassion. But he still hadn't said why he had come. He had just hinted at it. "You came to see us many times, you know what it was like even without me telling you. It should just all be mentioned in some way."

That made things quite clear, the ball was now in Agneša's court. She finished her yoghurt, nodded and after thinking for a moment she pointed out: "But I hope you know that I can't be the one delivering it. That would be seen as a provocation. And besides, it could get my husband into more trouble."

"It would certainly be a provocation," he agreed. He would not tell anyone that she had written it and it had never occurred to him that she would be the one to deliver it. He started telling her about Jelka who got killed in the Tatras. "I remember," Agneša cut in. "Yes, but she was not alone, a friend of hers also died in that accident," he said and explained why he'd brought it up. "The other girl who died had a sister, and she used to come and see us quite often with another friend. They were there that last evening, before I drove Zora to hospital. That girl knew all this and could also write a piece of this kind, except that she has probably never written anything in her life. I can't ask her to write it, but I can ask her to read it." And after a brief pause he added: "I think she'll agree. Maybe I should have started with her, the girl who would give the speech. Because this can be delivered only by a someone who is completely unknown, someone outside literary or journalistic circles. Someone without a past. Someone anonymous. That's the only way to make it sound natural and not provocative." He explained because he was hoping to convince her at the same time. "This girl, she works in an optical instrument factory, she's an ordinary worker. Young and somewhat gauche, she looks so ordinary that no one who hasn't met her before would remember her face. It should sound like the girl's own recollections. And the main thing is, she hadn't known Zora in her earlier life. The accident happened shortly after we moved to our new flat. So, in fact, she only knew her as a pensioner, basically, as a housewife who spent her time gardening. So that's another good thing about her, she didn't know Zora before, she may not have even heard her name." He had run out of things to say.

A moment's silence followed. If she says no, he thought, that feuilleton I will never write will stay in my head. "All right," Agneša said. She went on to say when she might be ready as if they had swapped roles and she was now a contributor and he the editor waiting for her copy. "I won't manage to do it today, though. I have to do the shopping now, we have people coming for dinner." Her daughter had invited a few friends who were in town on their own. She didn't know these girls herself, had no idea who they were, so she hadn't invited anyone else. "But I can get down to it tomorrow and might be able to type it up by the end of the day. Then I'll sleep on it and take another look at it in the morning. I think I could bring it to you the day after tomorrow, in the evening. Early evening. Not too late, so that you can still take it over to the girl." He kept nodding, as if he had the shivers. He felt a surge of relief. "Does this girl live far away?" she asked.

"Yes, quite far away," he said, explaining roughly where; but it's no more than twenty minutes by car. "I'd better go and see her now," he said and got up since he'd done what he'd come for. "I hope she says yes," said Agneša. "She will," he assured her although he was by no means sure. If she said no, he would ring to let her know that the whole thing was off. If he didn't phone, it meant she had said yes.

He had come here on a mission and, mission accomplished, he said goodbye and left.

He got into the car, and as he no longer needed to recite his text to anyone, his nerves calmed down, his agitation and worry about finding the right person was gone. Had Agneša refused, there was no one else who could do it. During the drive his thoughts wandered back to when she said "it could get my husband into trouble": he was sure it wasn't meant as a reproach just something she stated in a matter-of-fact way, but that was how he took it. Why did she have to remind him? She knew as well as he did that her husband would have been convicted anyway, even without his stupid sentence; they would have found some other stupid sentence in someone else's testimony, as in fact they had done. His words weren't proof of any criminal activity on the part of her husband; he had managed to navigate these waters better than he'd expected under interrogation. The previous day he and his wife had been to see an American movie that Zora hadn't seen before, *The Best Years of Our Lives*. It was extremely long, he needed something like that to help him kill time and not think that he'd been summoned by the secret police to appear the next day, but he had held up well. He could be pleased with himself.

The next morning the interrogator had ushered him into his office and left him on his own for about fifteen minutes, but he didn't lose his nerve. When the man came back, he brought a pile of journals, told him to look through them and left again. They were émigré journals. After returning the policeman asked if the accused had lent him any of these journals – he had noted that in this place Laco's name was "the accused". No, none. And he wouldn't have accepted them anyway, he didn't want to have anything to do with such stuff, and all his friends knew it.

They had nothing on Laco, Alma had told him (apart from the fact that he had found a bug in their flat and made sure everyone knew about it). Then there was the Karel Kryl record* – the interrogator asked if the accused had played it to him. He almost laughed: why should he? His wife had bought it in a record shop, and they'd heard it on the radio before. "We have that record at home."

This was followed by typical cop questions such as: how long had he known the accused and his wife, how often had they met and when. He would deliberately give a convoluted reply: they first met during the war, but it was just a casual acquaintance, thanks to the fact that they both wrote about film, and for a long time they had been the only two who wrote about film, as intellectuals in this country were not interested in film, regarding it as something like a circus show. They got to know each other better after the war but didn't meet very often although they used to live close to one another and would sometimes meet in the street; he sometimes went to see the accused's wife in the editorial office, but had no reason to visit them at home. And what did they talk about? About the newspaper she worked for, articles he would write, their mutual friends. And what about recent political events? That was what the interrogator had in mind. Why should we have discussed those? We had more or less the same views; Laco and his wife had both lost their jobs and soon after that I lost mine, and then my wife was cast aside and now she's not allowed to do anything. Had they discussed a certain politician (Husák)? After all, he and his wife, as well as the accused, had been acquaintances of this particular politician (Husák), who now held high office in Prague. This dragged on for a long time, as he made a point of giving long-winded replies. He was sure his conversations hadn't been recorded as he hadn't been to their flat for a long time. Then the interrogator showed him a series of newspaper articles – had he read them? No, he hadn't – how come you hadn't, you used to be a journalist, - well, reading newspapers is not compulsory – but the accused had written a pamphlet about those articles, surely he'd showed these articles to him and his wife along with his pamphlet? No, Laco knew that neither he nor Zora read newspapers, which sometimes had articles attacking them and why should one read nasty things written about one? It was conceivable that their names had also been mentioned, so they told Laco they didn't want to even look at them. But he did show you that pamphlet of his, didn't he? He did mention it to us but we said no, why should we read a rebuttal of an article which we hadn't read a single word of. But the accused had told you what that series of articles was about: yes, he said there were lies in the articles. Did he say what lies? He mentioned that the articles said that Goldstücker* was born in Mukachevo and had gone to a yeshivah school there, although in fact he was born in Orava and he attended a Slovak primary school, followed by a Slovak *gymnázium* and then a Czech university in Prague. So why did the accused think this was an indication of antisemitism, couldn't it have been a simple mistake? Come on, if you say that a distinguished cultural figure attended a yeshivah, it's pretty obvious why such an error might have crept in and what it was meant to imply about the people who took an active part in 1968. The interrogator offered him the pamphlet, but he refused to read it: what was the point? Did he happen to know who Laco had sent the pamphlet to? He really had no idea. Was Laco of the opinion that these articles expressed the party's official position? This was the first question that took him by surprise. He remembered that the accused – as Laco was called here – had once mentioned that the articles had been discussed at the highest political level and that someone at the highest echelons had been very critical of them. At that point the interrogator addressed him as if he were a child, an idiot. He said: if these articles appeared in instalments in the central paper of the Communist Party of Slovakia and subsequently in the central newpaper of the Communist Party of Czechoslovakia in Prague and if, as the accused had said, they had been twice broadcast on national radio, surely it was possible that the accused regarded them as the official party position. As a former newspaper editor, he knew that what was printed in the papers or broadcast on the radio was holy writ, so he said that he may indeed have regarded it as the party's position. The interrogator summarised in a few sentences the part of the conversation concerning the articles that had gone on for an hour and a half, then typed it up. Then he let him read a notebook in which Laco had been recording jokes as a testimony of the times. He then pointed out three jokes he had allegedly heard Laco tell. That brought the interrogation to an end. The policeman gave him the statement to read: the section concerning the series of articles was drastically shortened, the fact that according to the accused high-ranking official X had spoken critically about the series of articles at some high party forum was cut, and the only thing that remained was that the accused regarded the series of antisemitic articles as representing the party position. He wanted to say that the statement failed to make clear why he might have regarded this as the party position, but that might have made the interrogator labour some obvious point again, so he said nothing and signed the statement. Back home he related everything faithfully to his wife, and neither she nor anyone else he told about it had found any fault with his testimony. He was quite satisfied with how well he had done, but now he was supposed to feel guilty – even though the verdict had been drawn up in advance and they would always have found a sentence like his to hang everything on.

He pulled up in a side street on the outskirts of town, in front of a small family house. The girl's mother came to answer the door, a short, rotund woman. She seemed surprised, perhaps because she was expecting a neighbour. He knew they were friends with one of their neighbours who had a phone line and was happy to pass on messages. After the initial surprise the chubby woman's face turned sad, she held his hand in hers for a long time without saying a word – she never said much as she could barely manage more than a few words of Slovak, while he didn't speak any Hungarian. After holding hands for a while, he said he had come to see her daughter. She took him to a covered veranda with a dining table and two benches and called to her husband in the cellar through an open hatch. They had started doing up the cellar soon after the tragic accident with Jelka and their elder daughter; that was when he and his wife had gone to see them for the first time. Her husband intended to produce wine in the cellar, and did indeed start doing so soon after. His daughter would go into the vineyards with her friend "barrel-scraping" for grapes – he'd not heard the expression used in this specific sense before – and her father would turn these "barrel-scraped" grapes into wine that his family and neighbours thought was quite acidic and everyone else thought completely undrinkable. A man emerged from the hatch, carrying a carafe of wine, presumably for their Sunday afternoon get-together with the neighbour. He put the carafe onto the highest step, and shook his hand for a long time, saying "what a tragedy…" He just nodded, so the man kept repeating, "what a tragedy…" in a deep, sonorous voice. He was heavily-built and broad-shouldered, as one might expect of a master carpenter, now manager of a carpentry cooperative. He talked a lot and almost exclusively about himself, and all his stories invariably boiled down to how he was a jack-of-all-trades, a man for all seasons able to cope with any problem life threw at him. He spoke to his wife in Hungarian, and sported a moustache worthy of a Gypsy baron, and always wore a heavy black suit like a peasant dressed up as a gentleman. Eventually he pointed to the table and they sat down on two benches facing one another.

Meanwhile his wife ran over to the kitchen. He knew she would come back with some freshly baked filled pastries, as whenever he and his wife had visited, freshly baked pastries filled with jam of some kind would instantly materialise. His whole body was now aching with hunger so he decided he would have a pastry, but he wasn't going to touch it before he had dealt with the matter in hand.

"Yes, it's a tragedy," he said, not knowing what to say, so he just kept echoing the sentence, adding a profound thought: "When it happens so suddenly," – "I know, I know", the man nodded, "although people say that with an illness like that…" and he left the sentence hanging in the air, allowing for a variety of possible conclusions: what can you do; you have to be prepared for it; that's the way of the world and you have to come to terms with it. It suddenly occurred to him that this was the perfect cue for what he had to say. "It's not too bad at the moment, there is so much that has to be sorted out in the first days, all the funeral arrangements," he said and after a brief pause decided to get down to business. "Actually, I've come about the funeral. But that's something I need to discuss with your daughter."

The heavily-built man with the broad, manly moustache was clearly at a loss to understand what his daughter might have to do with this funeral, but he got up from the bench immediately, went over to the stairs leading up to the attic, and called out their daughter's first name. Meanwhile his wife came out with a big plate of pastries, of two different kinds, explained what they were filled with and just as he reached for the nearest one despite his decision to wait, biting into it like someone on the verge of starvation and starting to chew away frantically, he heard the sound of shoes on the wooden stairs as the girl came down to join them. She wore light pumps, which she also wore the last time she came to see them, next he saw a skirt made of thick fabric that came down to her knees, a jumper and a windcheater. She always wore the same clothes, but he thought that there probably wasn't any proper heating in the attic. When she came down they exchanged greetings and shook hands. She was neither pretty nor plain, he was glad to confirm, with a face that was exactly the kind that is quickly forgotten; just right, anonymous, he thought with satisfaction, as if appraising her. There was something exceedingly shy about her face and posture, which put a distance between her and other people.

He was embarrassed, as he now had to chew and swallow the pastry as unobtrusively as possible. But she started talking straight away, almost apologetically – allowing him to sink unconsciously into her clear monotone, the voice of someone who was unused to speaking in public and certainly never gave speeches in public – saying that she had heard the news already, as that evening she and her friend had been to see his sister-in-law – he remembered that moment, heard the carefree girlish laughter: that was the point when something in him snapped, when he was suddenly overwhelmed; it hadn't happened to him before or since – they didn't want to go up and see him that night as they knew he had other visitors and they were sure that he had a slew of official matters to attend to and they didn't drop in the following day either, but they definitely intended to come. Listening to her you couldn't tell from the way she spoke that her mother was Hungarian, he thought. In this city, it used to be difficult to guess the background of someone's father or mother, at least until recently, though in Martin things were different. A number of people at the funeral might say: couldn't he have found someone else, someone more appropriate, to talk about her?

When at last he swallowed the last bit of the pastry, she asked: "So that time when we came to see you, was that the last night before she went into hospital?" – "Yes, that's right," and even though he hated to say so, he added: "She specially asked me to invite you." He hated saying that not because it sounded somewhat solemn, but because he felt compelled to say it in order to make the girl feel some sense of obligation.

He could no longer dodge the issue. He'd come to see her about the funeral… that is, he had a favour to ask – she raised her greenish eyes towards him, her hands still resting on her thick skirt. "You see, a professor will give the eulogy, and I'm sure it will be about all that my wife accomplished and what she represented, professionally so to speak, and that sort of thing." But yesterday an old friend of his had come to see him – only a second earlier, as he started talking, he had no idea that he would be telling such a lie, but he was very pleased with it at this moment – and the friend suggested, among other things, that there should be another speech, something quite brief, because in recent years his late wife no longer lived for her work, she had no professional life, so to speak… and he launched into an abbreviated version of how she had furnished the first flat of her life, about the garden and the weeds and the cacti and the shrubs and the moss and the cooking and the cookery books, and that's when he thought of her – and he looked into her greenish eyes and paused for a moment – because she knew his wife only during those years and only in that way, so there wouldn't be anything in this speech about literature or that sort of thing, just a personal recollection: he had found someone to write it up, but this particular person was not the right one to deliver this speech, as he was a literary critic who used to review his wife's translations and it would look strange if he now shared such purely personal memories – to cut a long story short, this friend would write it in such a way as if these were her – the girl's own – recollections, memories of someone who knew her only during the last three years of her life.

The girl remained silent for a long time, and then, instead of an outright no, she came out with: "Hm, I don't know". At this point her father turned to her and said in a tone that brooked no opposition, as it sounded more like an order or an expression of her father's will: "Well, surely you could do that, couldn't you?"

His daughter's greenish eyes continued to stare directly ahead. She can't have been happy at the thought of appearing on stage and reciting something written for her by someone else, and to do it in front of complete strangers from a world so totally alien to her own to boot. But in fact, it flashed through his mind with a certain satisfaction, it would be hard for her to refuse. At the time of the tragedy, when her older sister and his wife's niece had died together in the Tatras, his wife had decided to give a speech at her sister's grave without anyone asking her; that murky day in November at the cemetery in Sláviče údolie appeared in his mind's eye for a moment, a powerful autumn wind was blowing from the Danube, a minor gale at times, scattering his wife's words, so that only those standing closest to her, right above the grave, could hear anything and connect the words. Surely, he thought, this must be going through her mind, or by now she would have said no, I'm not up to that, I can't do it.

The girl lowered her eyes to her dark skirt and slowly, almost unhappily, promised as if addressing some nebulous figure: "Very well then, I'll do it."

He began to reassure her again that there would be nothing about literature or stuff she didn't know about and couldn't speak of, it would concern just things that could be her own personal recollections. And if something didn't feel right or she found it too long, she could cut the text and leave out anything she wanted to. Finally, he moved on to the practicalities and said that his friend would bring him the text the day after tomorrow, in the evening, and that he would come over with it straight away. Should any problems arise, he would ring their neighbours to let them know he would be coming round later or the following morning, or that the whole thing was off.

At last he was able to reach for the unfinished, jam-filled pastry and tried to suppress the crunching sounds as best he could. He felt slightly guilty about being rather economical with the truth and not mentioning that this speech was meant to be a kind of counterpoint to the one given by the professor, complement it in a way.

But he didn't chastise himself, as he had no intention of rectifying this omission anyway. He also didn't mention that everyone else would have refused, fearing that it might be seen as a provocation. And wouldn't it? Perhaps not, if it was delivered by such an unassuming and unknown person. But then again, he might get her into trouble. He was exploiting her, making use of her, but he felt he had no choice.

He took a second pastry, more calm now, and remembered that he had to tell her when the funeral would be held, that she would have to take a day off to travel there, but of course he would cover her travel costs. Oh dear, why did he have to say that last bit – that was just embarrassing.

She said she was planning to come to the funeral anyway, along with her friend, of course, and there was no need to cover any travel costs.

He also told her about the coach. But that was something he had yet to organise. In any case, he would let her know in good time when it would leave and where from.

He didn't help himself to another pastry although he was still ravenous, to avoid giving the impression that he wanted to stuff himself. They weren't to know that he hadn't had any breakfast. He wanted to add something reassuring: she need not worry, she wouldn't have to learn the speech by heart, all she would have to do was read the text out aloud in advance a few times so she knew what was in it; and if she was worried about stage fright, he could give her a tranquillizer beforehand, to steady her nerves. He had some that were guaranteed to work.

The girl's father invited him to stay for lunch even though it would be just a modest affair before Christmas Eve dinner. He thanked him and told another lie, that he had to go and see someone else, also about the funeral – to do with the coach, someone who might be able to organise it for him. They accepted that. He didn't feel like having lunch with anyone and wanted to be by himself again. If he stayed here, he would keep repeating himself, reproaching himself deep down because giving the speech would entail a risk that he should have told her about but didn't. Though then he dismissed it out of hand: how much of a risk was there when even the professor had taken it on?

"Have a glass of wine at least," the girl's father offered. "Thank you, but I really can't, I'm driving," he said with a quick and doleful smile, as the broad-shouldered moustachioed craftsman brought two glasses of wine and ordered his daughter: "Well then, let at least the two of us have a drink then." But she just shook her head, got up, reached out to shake his hand, said they would see each other soon and went upstairs, in that thick skirt reaching down to her knees and a jumper under her windcheater. Maybe there's no heating in the attic at all, he thought, and at that point he noticed that he hadn't taken off his coat the whole time and didn't feel too hot at all…

"I'll have a drink on my own then," announced the maker of his own wine and poured himself a glass. He pointed to the pastries, inviting everyone to help themselves, and then explained that he had finally worked out why his wine tasted so acidic, but if he tried it now he would surely enjoy it. And bringing a thumb and an index finger together to his pursed lips, he gave a smack and said: splendid. He had read a book about wine-making, but in the end he'd worked it out for himself, he said with an unintentional chuckle as he sipped his wine. When he finished his pastry, the man asked, quite unnecessarily. "So are you about to go?" and went to get his wife from the kitchen. She brought some more pastries wrapped in two layers of paper, for the holidays, she said; of course, he couldn't refuse.

As he left the house and got into his car, he felt a weight lifting from his chest. A feeling of gentle jubilation coursed through his body. Only six or seven hours had passed since he dreamt up this idea and already he had organised everything, and succeeded on both fronts at that. Some three hours ago he was still striding up and down in his flat, all on edge, because had either of them said no, the entire plan, this brilliant addition to the funeral that he had come up with, would have fallen by the wayside. But everything worked out just as he had planned. On the first evening, he had also come up with the perfect epigraph on the first try. Suddenly he felt like the jack-of-all-trades he had just seen; he had reason to be pleased with himself. To a certain, if only a very limited, extent. Because when it came to life… by and large – he remembered that Shakespeare had a great metaphor for this which was not so easy to translate in such a striking way – when it came to life he wasn't really that good at managing it. No, when it came to life, he had never been a jack-of-all-trades.

He left the car in the garage as he knew he wouldn't use it anymore today, and as he opened the gate he noticed a bunch of envelopes someone had stuffed under the part of the gate that was never used. He bent down, pulled them out and lo and behold, they were all addressed to him: the postman must have delivered these telegrams and express letters. Inside the house he opened the mailbox and found four unstamped letters there, presumably from the neighbours in this building, which he added to the rest and then took the lift upstairs.

At home he tossed all the envelopes onto the kitchen table, then took out a small pot and ladled out a portion of the sausages, mashed potatoes and sauerkraut from the cooked meal he was given yesterday, put it on the stove with a little water and turned the gas on. How long does this need, he wondered, oh, never mind, he would taste it in a few minutes, this time he wasn't going to have food that was only half warmed up, he thought, this was the first meal he was heating up at home since that evening. He sat down and opened the unstamped envelopes first. It seemed as if everyone had sat down this morning right on cue to respond to the notices he'd posted through their letterboxes yesterday afternoon. One of the letters threw him slightly off balance, though, as it praised his wife as a great personality and then, in the final paragraph, it addressed him and said that the nation continued to expect great work from him, that he owed that to the nation… He could scarcely believe his eyes: was this comrade not aware of the position he was in? He couldn't offer the nation any more great works, even if he wanted to.

Meanwhile the food heated up, he put it onto a plate and when he finished eating, it occurred to him that he'd left the pastries in the car. He went down to get them, put them on a plate and went into the living room. Now that he wasn't so hungry he could savour them instead of wolfing them down. Once he had had his fill, he suddenly noticed how tired he was. He'd sorted out everything he'd planned for this morning – not without some excitement – he was entitled to take a nap. He went to his room, undressed and fell asleep almost instantly.

The minute he woke up, he knew he had two phone calls to make: one to the professor and one to Darka in Martin.

First he rang Professor Felix. He should really have thanked him at once for agreeing to give the eulogy. But as he rang him now, he realised that every stage leading up the funeral brought the relevant associations to his mind, so now he offered to collect the background information and bring it to the professor. The professor was taken aback – what background information? – well, he explained, he could gather a list of all the books she had translated and written with all the dates, a kind of overview, surely that would … I see, well, why not, – he gathered from the professor's voice that nothing of the kind had even crossed his mind and that he probably didn't need any of it but since he had now offered… in that case, tomorrow afternoon would be best, that's when he would start writing up the eulogy. And he told him when to come.

Darka was an ophthalmologist who lived in Martin, whom they used to visit whenever they were there. She already knew: he didn't need to explain anything, she would book him a room at the new hotel. They were bound to have some vacancies, and he should definitely come for dinner.

He still had three hours to fill before going down to his sister-in-law's for the Christmas Eve dinner. This was the time to shave and make himself look decent. And he could also choose a couple of records to be played at the funeral, although he could leave that until tomorrow if he found he was short of time. Two years ago, before her niece's funeral, Zora went down to her sister-in-law's flat, taking two records, something by Tchaikovsky and a Sibelius symphony, which Jelka had played quite often and at quite a volume in recent weeks: they could hear it in their flat one floor up. Once at home she put both records on the stereo, making a note of which passages should be played. Then she had taken the records to the funeral parlour in Martin and left them with a note explaining which piece they should play at what point during the funeral... As that was how his wife had done it two years ago for her niece's funeral, so this was how he, too, had to do it now for his wife's.

His situation, however, was different. It was around the time they got married that the first LP records became available and they had been buying records continuously ever since, even if they had never played some of them. In the evenings they would sit together listening to music in what became a kind of cultural ritual for them, with him trying to appreciate music, let it conjure up images or evoke a particular mood, though he couldn't help thinking that he didn't appreciate music the way he was supposed to. He had once confided to his wife but she just laughed it off, everyone appreciated music in their own way, she had said. He had no doubt that Zora's way was the right one, as she had a flair for music, and having studied at the conservatoire, she knew theory of composition and the history of music and was able to hear in each piece everything that he would also have liked to have heard, except that he didn't know how to grasp that abstract notion of "music", put together according to some exact, almost mathematical, rules of composition and counterpoint and polyphony, in the way that she did, and appreciate it and hear it in an analytical and focused way.

After Jelka moved in with them, whenever they put on a record she would join them in the living room with her knitting or a book, and listen along with them. It used to annoy him that even while reading or knitting she might have been much better at appreciating music than he was, but what particularly bothered him was the fact that the intimacy of their private evenings with music had gone. He would get up and go to his mother's room to watch TV. There was nothing he could do about it: Zora was really happy to see her niece spending so much time listening to classical music, even if she was studying her maths books or knitting while she did so.

By the time Jelka became independent, they had lost the habit of listening to music together. Later, in the new flat, his wife would spend her days gardening and was too tired to listen to music in the evenings. And after her niece's tragic death she probably wouldn't have put on a record anyway as it would have reminded her of the time they had listened to music together. And that is why he was now at a loss as to where to start, how to choose music that would be appropriate not just for the intervals during the funeral but that would bear some relationship to his wife… music that would be her music.

He could pick almost any record by Bach, of course, that would have met the first condition, but in fact his wife had rarely listened to any Bach, even though they had quite a few Bach records. She had never been particularly attached to Bach and although no one at the funeral would know that, he did, and so felt that by choosing Bach just because it was the easiest option, he would be betraying Zora in some way. Having shaved and changed, he made some coffee. Gazing at length and attentively out of the kitchen window he saw that at this time of day, just before nightfall, the street was deserted, as was to be expected on Christmas Eve, empty of people and cars, with a powdery yellowish mist descending from the dark blue sky.

He set to work. It was useful to have, or to have given himself, another task. He went over to the shelves and cupboards where they kept their records and took out their entire collection apart from the jazz records, as those were not appropriate and his wife couldn't stand jazz anyway, the jazz he loved so much. That still left plenty of classical records to choose from: a hundred, or perhaps two hundred, maybe more. He piled them up on the table and the bench.

First, he eliminated one major genre, the symphonies. She had always preferred chamber music, that he knew for sure. He thought of a few Beethoven piano concertos, but they were either too well-known or too abstract, too elusive to play only a short excerpt from. Mozart's piano concertos on the other hand were mostly too graceful or contained some spark of humour. The Largo of Dvořák's cello concerto: the cello struck him as too emphatic and serious, with even the gentlest passages followed by the full orchestra rising to fortissimo. He recalled that she had played Debussy and Chopin during her graduation concert at the conservatoire. He tried out a few sections of some Debussy records: too playful, not appropriate to a funeral. Chopin was out of the question. Perhaps Ravel instead? For a moment he considered a Ravel violin concerto or piano sonata. No, Ravel wouldn't do either.

He stood by the record player for a while, listening before lifting the arm on the stereo and lowering the needle further on, then turned the record over, lowered the needle once or twice, then picked another record. Sometimes he remained standing, sometimes he sat down in the armchair and had to keep jumping up, as he never spent very long listening to a single excerpt.

Shostakovich – that was it, he said to himself, the chamber music. His wife would play it over and over again. She once described a particular record of his as ravishing. So he put on one record after another, only to conclude that the people gathered at the House of Mourning* would most likely respond to the music the way he had done in the past. Shostakovich was also out.

So he continued to stand by the record player or sit in the armchair. He'd leap up, make a dash for the stereo, putting on one record after another. In some two hours he had sampled dozens of records.

Eventually he got to Janáček. His wife had bought every single Janáček recording. The only complete operas she'd ever bought were Janáček's *The Cunning Little Vixen* and *From the House of the Dead*. He began with the *Sinfonietta* but had enough after the first few bars, with their blaring fanfares. As for *Taras Bulba*, the very title made it unsuitable for a funeral. The *Glagolitic Mass* wouldn't work either. The *Lašské tance*, well, that was folk music, he thought. But the very first piece made him prick up his ears, freeze almost. He knew he had found what he was looking for. Each short piece was a world in itself. A plaintive, doleful and yet at times joyous world. In the second song a female voice suddenly rose abruptly high, only to fall just as abruptly, and he was as moved as he sometimes was in the theatre or the cinema. This brief excerpt touched something in him, it made him tingle. He was sure no one would be left unaffected by this brief passage. He continued lifting the arm of the stereo every now and then, before the end of a song. He knew he would choose at least a couple. Next he put on Janáček's *Moravian Songs*. These were just for the piano. Melancholy improvisations. But the tunes on both records were reminiscent of the plaintive Slovak folk songs called *trávnice*, only without their shrieking and hollering. This was music that would speak to everyone everywhere, including in a House of Mourning. And at the same time, this was her music, even if no one else knew. He had made his choice.

He felt proud and exhilarated. Yet another piece of the puzzle had fallen into place, the puzzle that had begun with the search for an epigraph for the death notice.

This is exactly what I was looking for, he thought, something more personal, surely everyone would understand that. It wasn't a waste of time to spend two hours sampling records, leaping up from the armchair, putting one record after another on the turntable in search of something he had only the vaguest notion of, like a painter making his preliminary sketches… or rather, like a theatre director looking for music that would knit everything happening on stage, his entire production, into a single whole. Although he hated funerals and would much rather have done without this particular one, preferring to get everything over with as quickly as possible with only a few people by his side, he was nevertheless creating the funeral as a production, like a director staging a play.

But now he had to stop. It was very nearly time to go for dinner at his sister-in-law's. He had to smarten up. He went over to the wardrobe and took out a black suit, a white shirt… a black tie… and, almost as an afterthought, black shoes. He admired himself in the mirror. It had been a long time since he had seen himself like that. In the old days he used to wear his suit to theatre premieres, shows by visiting foreign theatre companies, to concerts. But recently he and his wife hadn't gone anywhere, hadn't seen anything. His sister-in-law would be pleased to see him looking decent: it would stop her worrying that he might turn up at the funeral dishevelled, in some worn-out dark suit and brown shoes. That was the sort of thing she was likely to expect of him. And besides, this would be the last time. Since their sister-in-law moved to the flat on the floor below, she invited them over for dinner on every Christmas Eve: twice so far. If his wife hadn't fallen ill, they would have gone this year too – if for no other reason than to make up with her, even though Zora had been quite cross that her sister-in-law hadn't visited her in hospital, or even inquired what was wrong with her.

Every time they returned home after visiting his sister-in-law, he told his wife that those had been the three most boring hours of his life. But he couldn't contemplate spending Christmas Eve next year here in this flat, alone.

He hadn't thought of any presents. But she probably didn't have a present for him either. They usually gave her a book, something illustrated or unique in some way. And his sister-in-law would also have a book for them, usually one they already had, as they were constantly buying books. But that, too, was just a ritual. The times of festive gift-giving came to an end once Jelka grew up and his wife's family in Martin started to fall to pieces or, to be more precise, to die out. In the early days, gift-giving used to be rapturous and full of excitement: Jelka would always be showered with presents of every kind, and the family ritually required her, on receiving each wrapped present, to exclaim: "oh, how wonderful!" or "what could this be?" Jelka always managed to improvise and vary her exclamations of joy, anticipation and pleasure with consummate skill, even if she received twenty presents. He, too, had tried to convey his joy and happiness, despite usually receiving a shirt from his wife and a tie from his sister-in-law. He himself had never bought a present: Zora would always go shopping before Christmas and would get something for herself on his behalf, and also for her parents, for her sister-in-law and her daughter, telling him what she'd had bought so he would know what they were about to thank him for. On one occasion, very early on, his wife had presented him with some cloth for a suit. He invariably found this ceremonial exchange of gifts depressing, since he was expected to be present and therefore had to leave his mother all alone at home, with his brother and his wife the only people who might drop in briefly to keep her company, in that room with the TV and without a Christmas tree. All water under the bridge. His mother was dead, his wife's mother was dead, as was Jelka, the main protagonist in the Christmas gift-giving show, and now his wife, too, was dead. The only ones left were him and his sister-in-law.

He glanced at his watch and saw he still had ten minutes before seven o'clock. He was expected to arrive on the dot.

So he sat down in the armchair in the living room and started to imagine what would be awaiting him. According to a long family tradition, everyone would find a tiny glass with a thimble-sized shot of some white spirit, slivovitz or cherry brandy, placed on the freshly ironed white damask tablecloth. After that, soup would be served and then everyone – his sis-ter-in-law's sister Amálka and her husband were also going to be there, his sister-in-law had offered them two rooms so she wouldn't be in the big flat alone – everyone would stand up, clink glasses, and drink the minuscule thimbleful, as dictated by the tradition in his wife's parental home, where aperitifs were served in tiny vials. Next to each shot glass there would be a half-filled wine glass. This, too, was symbolic, like tak-ing a sip of wine from a goblet in a Lutheran church since, as far as he remembered, no one had ever asked for another glass with their meal. If sauerkraut soup was on the menu, his sister-in-law would apologise for it not tasting exactly as his wife's mother used to make it; though she had been told where she would find good home-made sauerkraut, it didn't taste anything like the real thing, the kind that Mother always bought from the same peasant woman. His wife always coun-tered that the soup was delicious, but his sister-in-law would start disparaging it again, listing the spices Mother had used, some of which she couldn't get hold of here in the city. His wife claimed that there was one particular spice in the soup that Mother had never used, but his sister-in-law insisted that she had. Next up were sausages with the obligatory potato salad, and his sister-in-law would apologetically declare that she got the sausages from a butcher who had been recommended and had ordered them in advance, but they weren't as good as those another village woman used to bring from the most recent pig feast. His wife would declare that, on the contrary, these were just as good as the ones they used to have at home, but his sister-in-law insisted that their flavour was not as delicate, they were a little bit too fatty and less spicy. Only in the case of the dessert, *opekance* with honey, did his sister-in-law not apologise for not making them the way Mother had done, as in baking these mini-doughnuts she used exactly the same kind of flour, eggs, honey and other ingredients as in her own parental home. He, on the other hand, used to dread this third course, as the honey on the *opekance* always got down into the roots of his teeth, exposed by gum disease, and he needed the utmost effort to manage this course. The dinner conversation always revolved around various Christmases long ago. His sister-in-law would recall that the young Jelka had been so happy to be given a doll that she started jumping up and down around the Christmas tree, cradling the doll until she bumped into the tree, making it tilt at a dangerous angle, but Daddy – that is, his wife's father – had come to the rescue at the last minute. His wife, too, remembered being frightened that the lights on the falling Christmas tree might set the curtains or the carpet alight and rushed into the kitchen, filled a bucket with water, and came running down the hall and into the dining room – and it was just as well that she had because one of the curtains by the window had indeed caught fire, but they managed to extinguish it without having to empty the whole bucket on it. And so time would pass in nostalgic conversation. Then they would play a record, always the same one, a folk Christmas mass. When the record finished – having exchanged their gifts of books immediately on arrival – they began saying their goodbyes. But now it was high time that he went.

His sister-in-law welcomed him with the warmest, kindest smile, as if seeing a beloved, long-lost friend. There was no trace of the forbidding face she had the night he rang her doorbell, when she still didn't have a clue as to why he was on her doorstep, why he was trying to barge in; perhaps she had assumed he'd heard she had visitors and wanted to join them. Her forbidding expression was a basic part of her personality. She was uncompromising with herself and uncompromising with others. Life was a serious matter, not a joke. You had to keep calm and carry on, maintain strict self-control. Fortunately, it occurred to him, surprised by this warm, kind, and smiling face, Jelka hadn't maintained strict self-control, and hadn't been uncompromising with herself or others.

His sister-in-law ushered him into the festively decorated living room, whose chandelier used to hang in the dining room of his wife's parental home. Her sister Amálka and her husband were already there. He hadn't seen either of them for ages. Certainly not in the past few days, or in the two weeks his wife was in hospital. Amálka came out with some very warm words of condolence, while her husband just smiled as he shook his hand. Everyone seemed transformed. Amálka had never before had a kind word for him and he had no doubt that she held him in the lowest possible esteem. She had spent her entire life in toil: she would bring typing home, while her husband would bring home accounting work to make a little extra, because they had two daughters who were now grown up and needed help with the grandchildren. Only recently had they begun to live more like a retired couple, while he and his now-dead wife had got themselves into some kind of trouble with the regime, done things that normal people like them couldn't permit themselves to do and just worked and did what they were expected. Only people who considered themselves superior could allow themselves to clash with the regime. But now they seemed transformed.

With the formalities out of the way, his sister-in-law remarked that he'd made them wait, and when he glanced at his watch, he realised that he was indeed about ten minutes late. Of course, once he started to reminisce, unfurling images in his mind, he had to do it thoroughly, in detail; this was his favourite game, his preferred pastime, as every recollection was an immersion, and so once again he had miscalculated the time needed for the mental replay of the last two Christmas Eve dinners in this flat.

He apologised and explained that he'd spent the entire afternoon choosing music for the funeral. He must have expressed himself too laconically, since he was met by astonished looks. He explained that his wife, at the previous funeral... Now they understood, and said: it was Tchaikovsky on that occasion, wasn't it. It was, he nodded, but that was followed by a passage from a Sibelius symphony. Seeing that the name meant nothing to them, he added that this was the music Jelka had listened to most often towards the end, making it clear that he meant Tchaikovsky and Sibelius, so that they would understand that the latter was as famous as the former.

That exhausted that particular topic, and his sister-in-law invited everyone to come to the table, and after showing him to his place, disappeared into the kitchen. There was the freshly pressed damask tablecloth, the small shot glass with something colourless inside by each plate and a wine glass that was just over half-full. Only Amálka's husband had a bottle of beer and a tankard by his plate, as he suffered from diabetes or some such condition and never drank wine. His sister-in-law returned with a tureen of sauerkraut soup and set it down on the table, but instead of sitting down, raised her shot glass and when everyone else got up as well, she said: "As this is a sad occasion, we're not going to drink to anyone's health. Let's just clink glasses as a sign that we are all a family." Well planned, he had to admit to himself.

They began to spoon the sauerkraut soup and Amálka sang its praises but, strangely enough, his sister-in-law didn't contradict her and didn't say a word about Mother's sauerkraut having tasted quite different and why. They chatted about something else. When the sausages with mashed potatoes and salad arrived, Amálka and her husband praised the sausage without any objections from his sister-in-law. He realised that now that his wife was gone, there was no point comparing the various versions of the sauerkraut soup and the sausages, as Zora was the intended audience of all the talk about why Mother's version had been better.

Instead, Amálka started to talk about how they used to make sausages for Christmas in the old days. They made them on other occasions, too, but her father, who was a butcher, used to make special ones for Christmas. He was astonished to hear her mention this in such a matter-of-fact way at this festively laid table, over this snow-white damask tablecloth. His sister-in-law would never have breathed a word about her father being a butcher over dinner at "Mother's", in this patrician and highly civilised family in which everyone, in one way or another, had been involved with culture, newspapers, literature, cultural institutions or politics – in the days before the victory of the working classes. Perhaps in order to become an integral part of this illustrious Martin family, she, too, had to keep quiet about certain matters and adapt; perhaps it was only at that point that this excellent doctor acquired the demeanour of an English governess from the time of Queen Victoria.

In response to his question, his sister-in-law, too, started to talk about the family butchers', where it was located and where they used to live – the two sisters seemed pleased to hear that he knew the street, half of which had since been demolished and turned into a cul-de-sac – but of course he remembered it, although he didn't mention that it was next to the former College of Crafts, now a branch of the Technical University, where he'd gone to organise the death mask. Highrises were now being constructed all around the area for various departments of the Technical University. It was once a quiet street, rather out of the way, although every other house used to be owned by a German vintner, with a *viecha* on the ground floor. "Yes, exactly," Amálka agreed, and his sister-in-law nodded with a spontaneous smile: suddenly they had become compatriots, with him having grown up on the outskirts of the city, in a neighbourhood called Ružinov, and the sisters in the old part of town known as Blumentál, after the nearest big church. Recent immigrants to the city, he thought, had no idea that a neighbourhood called Blumentál had even existed. What amazed him even more was when his sister-in-law said, yes, the street was full of German vintners and their sons – or *štricáks* as they were known in old Pressburg – so she, too, knew this long-forgotten word that young people didn't know anymore – who would shout at her on her way home from school: "Here comes the beanpole", because even in her student days she had been tall and thin. Yes, she said with a quite natural laugh, I used to be like a beanpole, but she would just pass the heckling boys as if she didn't see them, she gave another laugh and said she could still hear them shouting at her and when she said, in the flawless German of old Pressburg, "Da kummt die Telegrofstange", he was dumbfounded as he had no idea that as a young girl she spoke not only standard German but also Pressburg German. His mother, who came from Sudetenland, only spoke German, this was the only language one could have a proper conversation with her in, but they had rarely met, as Zora took great care to keep their encounters to a minimum, being embarrassed that people might see his mother in her shabby, worn, comfortable clothes. Sometimes though a meeting was inevitable because his sister-in-law's daughter Jelka was living with them at the time in their old flat in the centre of town. However, even on those occasions his sister-in-law could never have a German conversation with his mother or she would let on that she was fluent in Pressburg German, that she had something in common with his mother. He couldn't suppress a smile: Blumentál and Ružinov suddenly found themselves sharing a table.

He realised with a start that he'd let his guard down and was sitting here with his head buried in his hands and elbows propped on the table as if he were in a café, smiling as he listened to his friends reminiscing around the table. After all, he was feeling quite at home here. He had to recalibrate and switch mood. He had a flash of inspiration: he remembered the song on the Janáček record with the soaring female voice that broke off suddenly and unexpectedly, full of grief and sorrow as it fell. Having convinced himself that his face had regained a suitably half-absent expression of melancholy, he felt once again pleased with himself.

He recalled the first time he had used this technique. It was during his adolescence: he might have been around thirteen, and the whole class had burst out laughing at something and even after everyone else quietened down he still couldn't stop laughing, caught in a kind of spasm, similar to hysterical sobbing that was impossible to suppress. The eyes of the entire class were on him, the teacher stared at him from his lectern, indignantly waiting for a chance to continue. In this incredibly awkward moment he recalled a theatre production he'd seen recently – later, when he was dealing with theatre professionally, he realised that it was probably Maeterlinck's *The Blue Bird,* in a production by Stanislavsky's theatre company – he remembered very little of the play, apart from a scene with an organ-grinder and a little girl, and now in the classroom, as he desperately tried to stop laughing, he called the scene to mind and was overwhelmed by a sense of sadness, despondency and loss. This time he would use the excerpt from the Janáček song to rectify his facial expression. The honey-doused *opekance* now appeared on the table and instantly brought the sisters' reminiscing to a halt, as everyone around the table delighted in this sweet crowning glory of the dinner – except for him, painfully aware of the honey flowing into his roots and under his gums in an unstoppable flood, like needles jabbing his exposed teeth. This time he didn't feel like making the effort to disguise his pain. Didn't he like it, someone asked immediately. He did, it was his teeth, his gums that didn't. "Oh well, that's what happens if you don't brush your teeth regularly as a child," said his sister-in-law in a jocular but also schoolmarmish way, slipping back into Victorian governess mode. He readily confessed to the sins of his youth.

Now he began to talk, telling them how he organised the death mask the very same day that they'd been to the funeral parlour together, how his wife's cousin had discovered who made them, also that he'd ordered an extra copy and that they would be ready in a week. Then he mentioned that there would be another speech at the funeral, a kind of personal recollection of his wife at the time when she was no longer translating, since that was something the professor wouldn't deal with, and when he told them who would deliver this speech, his sister-in-law wondered, quite logically, "is she also going to write it?" So he explained that he'd found someone else to do that, having instructed this person on the points that ought to be covered, and asking them to word it in such a way as if the girl had written it herself. There was no reaction; they didn't lavish praise on him, as they found it hard to imagine what kind of personal recollection this could be and especially what the point was of talking about such things: first the professor would present her as a major figure, and then some unknown person would say that rather than being a major figure, she was someone who spent her time gardening and cooking. They could not understand why it was necessary to knock his wife off the pedestal on which the professor will have placed her. No one seemed to think that this was a great idea, so he moved on and told them that the next thing he was going to do was organise a coach: city coaches could be booked for out-of-town journeys of any length. He had not yet made the arrangements, but would organise it very soon to make sure that everyone planning to go to the funeral from Bratislava could take the coach.

This immediately elicited praise from his sister-in-law: that was really a great idea, Amálka would also take the coach on the way there, he just had to let her know the time and place of departure. Everyone would be informed by phone, he said. Oh good, one less thing to worry about, said his sister-in-law, though she would actually travel to Martin earlier, the day after Christmas Day, to be there the evening before the funeral, as there was a lot that needed to be seen to, "as you may imagine". One thing in particular, which was "seeing to the tomb" – her usual expression, which she'd probably picked up from one of the illustrious families. In the eyes of the illustrious families and all the patrician Martin residents, their dead lived on in the form of tombs or vaults that needed to be "cleaned up", as his wife used to say, once a week as she set out to "clean up the tomb". This set off a firework of associations in his head linked to the cleaning of the tomb, walking up to it equipped with a broom, a rake and a watering can and carrying flowers picked in the garden or bought in town: first, one had to rake the leaves that had fallen on the marble headstones from the nearby trees, then sweep the tomb and everything around it as clean as the parquet floors in their flat; remove flowers that had wilted in their glass holders and take them to the cemetery's rubbish dump; empty the glass flower holders, bottles and preserving jars and fill them with fresh water from the tap in another part of the cemetery; trim any shrubs that dared to stick out too close to the tomb; break up the soil around the tomb's edge with a small spade, and perform many other tasks that he no longer remembered to ensure that the tomb was like a part of a home, or rather, a shop window that could be admired on a Sunday or on a quiet morning by members of the illustrious families or any other crazy old residents who came to check whether and how well individual graves had been "seen to" or "cleaned up", a subject on which they would no doubt exchange opinions and then appraise the descendants of those buried in the graves, as people would visit the National Cemetery, as it was officially called, with schoolchildren brought here from all around the country. Only after the job of the seer-to and cleaner-up of the grave was over would he or she spend a moment before the tomb and perhaps give a thought to the person buried there, but always to take a rest before going home to see to their flat, clean up the garden or type up a translation. Of course, he agreed with his sister-in-law that the tomb needed to be thoroughly seen to before the funeral: "You know as well as I do that we can't rely on the little woman who is supposed to look after it, and the path from the garden gate to the house also needs to be swept clean, his sister-in-law continued with her list. A wide path, virtually an allée, lined with magnificent old trees, ran from the street to the house with its large iron gate; on his first visit he thought he'd got the street number wrong and walked past, assuming that an avenue of trees that wide could lead only to a manor house, a small chateau, but in fact it just led to a long, single-storey house with an entrance at the other end, by the garden;

– "the yard will also need to be swept," his sister-in-law continued: the yard being the area in front of the entrance to the house, opposite which stood another, smaller single-storey building where his sister-in-law now stayed when she came for the summer; there was also a woodshed and a kind of larder as well as a barn where he would park his car: all of this would, of course, have to be cleaned, washed, scrubbed down...

– "refreshments will have to be prepared for the guests from Bratislava and also for any locals who might turn up because they used to visit in the past…

The funeral wake! he suddenly realised. He'd been thinking only of the funeral, organising everything to do with the funeral, devising and expanding the programme; it was the funeral that filled his days, that provided a focus for his attention, since behind the focus there was nothing but the back of the lens: he saw nothing there, he was unable to see that far, it was something he didn't want to imagine, his every waking moment was dominated by the funeral, and it had never occurred to him to think of a funeral wake! The wake, since time immemorial an essential part of the funeral: of course everyone would expect something to eat at the funeral, and to be offered a drink, perhaps even to get drunk, whereas he associated a funeral only with the House of Mourning, the scene of various activities with him as the master of ceremonies; it would never have crossed his mind that a funeral went on to a wake held where the deceased had resided, and he had to be reminded by his sister-in-law. Quite spontaneously he blurted out a thank you to her for thinking of this;

– that went without saying: of course she would deal with that. She thought it could be held "in the two rooms that you didn't rent out after Zora's mother died", if he had no objections, she would open the windows to air it the day before, the room by the kitchen was large enough to take quite a few people and they could all gather there for two or three hours before travelling back, refreshments would be served…

– she was quite right, the room would need to be thoroughly aired beforehand. Since his wife's mother died there was no one left to switch on the electric stove from time to time, and when they arrived in spring, for the first time after the long winter months, dampness had seeped through the outside wall all the way to the lower edge of the window, so that the whole place reeked of damp. His wife would go immediately to the woodshed to fetch some kindling and firewood which she would pile up by the tiled stove and light a fire while he sat down in a deep leather armchair to rest after driving for four hours or more, and after lighting the fire – the tiled stove would soon start emitting pleasant heat, it would always heat up very fast – she would start dusting because the room was also full of dust and stale air, so of course it would have to be thoroughly aired now.

Yes, – he said, chipping in – there was a mattress by the door with two sets of duvets and pillows piled on top which will have to be moved, and the bedding stuffed into the wardrobe in the hallway. He'd give her a hand with that, of course – but his sister-in-law interrupted him: "Don't worry about that, I'll get someone to help." – after all, he would be taking a train and arriving a day in advance to go to the funeral parlour in the morning, so he could help her in the afternoon after he was finished there. But his sister-in-law butted in again: "you really don't need to worry, I'll find someone to give me a hand." So he moved on to his last point – he decided not to spend the night in the room they had kept in the house but had asked Darka to book him a room at the new hotel instead: "you know Darka, the ophthalmologist, don't you?"

He didn't feel like offering any further explanations, and indeed there wasn't anything to explain. It was not because everything in the house and the room would remind him of something that he decided to stay in a hotel… well, that too, of course… staying there would bring back memories of their trips over the past few years, when this room had been the only one they had used, or of the many years before that, when her parents were still alive and this was where he slept, when the room had been her study, her private space… yes, he might be haunted by these memories but that wouldn't be so bad: he felt the same in their flat… it was just that he didn't want to be in that house alone, to be on his own for the first time… that would probably make him sort of discombobulated and frightened, it might even drive him to get a bottle of wine to get over it… a hotel room, on the other hand, was neutral territory, the hotel had been built for people coming to this small town on business, for instance at the armament plant that manufactured peace doves, as the locals used to call tanks, and more recently, diesel engines; others, like him, had matters to attend to at Matica Slovenská and indeed he wanted to go to bed at night feeling like someone who had some business here and was going to leave soon, and that was why he decided to stay in a hotel;

– "basically, all the bedding and anything else in that room that might be in the way, can be removed, so I will just drop in to say hello," he said to his sister-in-law, "and will give you a hand with anything you might need."

Once everything had been cleared off the table covered with the snow-white damask tablecloth, with only a candlestick with a burning candle remaining on it, the second part of the evening began.

Amálka and her husband sank into a deep leather sofa and he into a deep leather armchair, identical to the one that had stayed in the room they retained in Martin and where refreshments would now be served. His sister-in-law stopped in front of him with a mischievous girlish smile, her hands crossed behind her back and leaned over like a schoolgirl about to whisper something a little confidential not meant for everyone's ears and said, still with a kindly smile: "And now, seeing as you're here, can we ask you for a favour?" Then she whipped out a record from behind her back and said what he knew was coming: "Would you be so kind and put it on for us, we're no good at these things", and handed him the record with a flirtatious smile.

This was the third year he had been asked to put on the same record because she was no good at it. He placed the disc on the turntable and switched the stereo from the radio to the record player.

His sister-in-law now joined her sister and her husband on the deep leather sofa and he returned to the leather armchair, all of them putting on serious faces, ready to listen to the festive music. It was a recording of a Christmas Mass that an unknown village priest composed some two hundred years ago for his parishioners. The main charm of the piece was its naiveté. The organ was accompanied by folk instruments and the lyrics were sung by a group of village folk in the somewhat amusing dialect of the region where the priest had lived and worked. He and his wife had also bought the record when it appeared on the market some six years ago, sometimes they, too, had put it on at Christmas, so this would be the fifth or sixth time that he had heard it. He wondered how many families up and down the country might be listening to the same record now. He was fond of one particular section with the gruff voices singing naïve doggerel about the three magi. These days he found those sections where the lyrics were hard to understand rather boring. He'd always preferred the final parts on the other side of the record, and after mentioning this to his wife, she laughed and told him, as he also read later on the record sleeve, that the final sections were no longer part of the Christmas mass, but old Christmas carols. The slightly comical passage about the three magi was now over, and the Christmas carols on the other side of the record were still far away, so he gradually stopped listening. He laid his arms on the wide armrests of the leather chairs, the kind he used to see in lawyers' offices after his father died and all kinds of merchants took them to court for not paying for various items he'd bought. The leather was quite worn where his arms rested. His wife's father had probably bought the entire suite back in the early nineteen twenties, when he was director of a bank: he had the house renovated and bought all kinds of furniture, and nothing had changed in her parental home since those days. They had kept one of the armchairs from this suite in his wife's room in Martin. Over the past eighteen years he had often sat in it when he was visiting, reading the papers when they were delivered in the morning and a book in the evening, because there was no television in her parents' house and they hardly ever went out. He would sit there when he felt bored or depressed, or when he wasn't thinking of anything, and now, too, he was also slightly bored as he sat in the armchair. He looked at the enormous cabinet and, as always when they came here for Christmas dinner, was amazed at how enormous and ugly it was. He had first seen it many years ago in the reception room of his wife's parental home, and it didn't seem so colossal to him there, maybe because the house was quite dark. Here, however, in this modern building, where one room consisted entirely of large windows and each room was lit by strong light from the side and from above, the cabinet loomed in all its humongous ugliness. Zora and he had agreed that they didn't want to take the cabinet to their new flat but what were they to do with it? To their utter astonishment, Jelka almost jumped for joy when they offered it to her. He couldn't understand it, Jelka had been a modern girl in every respect, adhering firmly to the conventions of her generation with all its categorical imperatives and its lifestyle, so what could she have seen in this cabinet? Perhaps she thought it was something of an antique, something that young people now considered fashionable, or perhaps she regarded it as some kind of antique pop art.

The record finished playing. He got up to turn it over and play the other side, the continuation of the Christmas Mass followed by the Christmas carols. But to his surprise, his sister-in-law also got up, turned half towards the couple and half towards him, gave another gentle theatrical-girlish bow, extended her arms and announced: "So that was the concert." Apparently, none of them noticed that the Christmas Mass hadn't finished: his sister-in-law never played records and must have assumed that once one side of a record came to an end, that was the end of the whole piece.

He knew that his sister-in-law would now ask him to show her one more time how to switch the stereo back from record player to radio. She asked him to do it every year, and she did not disappoint: she asked him again now.

He pointed to the record player setting on the stereo, then showed her how to switch to ultra short waves and explained "you switch to this button that says ultra short waves"; that tuned the radio to Österreich 1, as local short wave stations were not available on the Western-made machine. He reminded her once more: "This is the record player, this is radio, it's all ready now, tuned for you." His sister-in-law remarked that it was actually quite straightforward but he was convinced that if he turned up here next Christmas Eve, she would ask him the same questions again.

During the demonstration and explanations he glanced surreptitiously at his watch: it was a quarter to ten. As far as he knew, his sister-in-law as well as Amálka and her husband went to bed around ten o'clock.

As he straightened up he said he ought to go, he wanted to give his brother a ring and wish him merry Christmas. This was met with understanding and made insincere and redundant any insistence that he should stay longer. Everything here followed an established order, and on this occasion there was even a playful moment to the proceedings, as well as the customary concert, every topic had been covered and it was time to leave. They went over the arrangements once more: the coach, how he mustn't forget to let Amálka know where and when to come; the time his sister-in-law would go up by train, and which train he would take. After they wished each other Happy Christmas one final time, the door closed behind him.

Upstairs in his flat he turned on both ceiling lights in his room, thus flooding it with light, as the special occasion called for it, unlike the past days or even weeks, and he sat down in the winged chair and put on the TV but without turning on the sound. He wouldn't ring his brother until he had some news regarding the coach; all he wanted now was some peace and quiet – he pressed the buttons on the TV set, switching from one channel to another, but as he had no intention of watching anything, with or without sound, he switched it off again. For a while he sat in the armchair motionless and without any thoughts, staring at the illuminated room and telling himself how nice it was to be back home and not have to talk to anyone. Even though this time it hadn't been too bad down there, and not quite as boring as he'd feared. There were even moments of warmth – Blumentál – Ružinov. He smiled. He knew a district called Blumentál existed, he had known its every street from when he was a child, although they had actually lived further out. This was the first time he had talked to someone from the real Blumentál.

So what was it like when they had had visitors, he wondered, people with whom he had more in common? Actually, that had not been so great either, he thought, after their visitors left he never felt he'd got much out of the evening, in fact, he'd got nothing out of it; they had talked about this and that, they'd gossiped, poured their hearts out to each other, but in the end he was left with the same void inside as before. So what was the point of gazing out from the balcony or the kitchen window in the hope of spotting someone he knew, someone who might come to visit them, turn into the courtyard in front of the garage, go through the gate and ring the bell with his name beside it? What was the point of waiting for someone? And what was he expecting from people anyway? He simply expected something, something that only people could offer. Many years ago, when he went on assignments as a journalist, whenever he boarded a train he realised that he expected that trip to provide... an adventure, an encounter with some astonishing person with whom he might feel at home. And though in recent years he no longer expected that, every single person who dropped by had the potential to jolt him out of his day-to-day routine, to bring into his life something that his own imagination was unable to define. So what about now, when he no longer expected anything from anyone, no longer even hoped that someone might turn into the courtyard in front of the garages and ring his doorbell? Now that he could no longer imagine waiting for something… could he go on living like this? Perhaps only in a kind of stupor, in a state of sluggish lethargy. But then again, what was the point of wondering about that? He would find out soon enough.

He got up and went into the kitchen, remembering the still unopened telegrams and letters. Once there, he surveyed the situation outside the window. The street was empty in an annoyingly convivial way, a pernicious way. It must have turned colder, for the mist in the air seemed to be freezing and the lights of the city down below had vanished again. But the heavy clouds weren't completely black and here and there let through a bluish dim light, suggesting that maybe a full moon was lurking somewhere behind them.

He opened the remaining telegrams in the winged chair in the living room. What could one expect of telegrams? Anyway, three were from people he didn't know, only one from an old friend… someone smart enough to realise that sending a telegram was the easy option. It took him fifty years and something out of the ordinary had to happen for him to figure this out; he was sorry that he hadn't responded to death notices in this form in the past as he wasn't aware of the opportunities for cliché that a telegram offered. There was also a letter that went on and on about what a distinguished figure his wife had been, in which he felt, possibly without justification, the sting of a covert reproach… she had been one of the pioneers, one of the generation that had paved the way… as if he needed reminding, as if he weren't sufficiently aware of that himself. Finally, he was quite moved by a brief letter from a woman he didn't know very well, who wrote how she had visited them once, and what a lively conversation they'd had and how cosy it had felt, and how fortunate he had been to have enjoyed such a beautiful, safe, and truly enviable relationship; many people admired them for this, and she repeated how comfortable, happy and cheerful she had found the atmosphere in their home. He had no recollection of her visit. The letter concluded by saying that he wasn't alone, there were people around who loved him and who were there for him. Well, that's a step too far, he thought. Empty drivel. He wasn't alone? A load of nonsense. He was all alone and had no one to turn to; there was no one here for him.

He came to the end of the condolences. The last letter was the only one he found truly moving. It took him a while to tear himself away from it. Yes, theirs was an unusual relationship. And despite all his failings, he too had taken great care to make it secure. Admittedly, there were times when he'd fallen for someone else, but nothing had ever come of it. He knew that it would have humiliated her, dishonoured her, exposed her to ridicule, and to forestall that, he always got a grip on himself and nipped the affair in the bud. Theirs wasn't a shallow kind of relationship, which was precisely why it had upset him that it had made his life complicated because of her strained relationship to his mother, and her strong attachment to her own mother and her niece. But on the other hand, it also made him unhappy that he had made her life complicated, as there had been times when he had fallen off the wagon, unable to focus on anything properly, and may generally have disappointed her. That's what happens in life: you make each other unhappy in all sorts of ways, but nevertheless theirs was… yes, a secure relationship. Every wound would heal eventually. When all's said and done, she had really been his… he searched for a suitable, non-melodramatic word… his home. His home was not located in some geographical space, some natural landscape or residential area: his home was being with her. Some of his old hopes had come true after all, not in the magical way that he'd once envisioned but in their everyday reality, which, in spite of everything, had not been all grey. On the contrary, it had rarely been grey. It had always glowed in intense colours, whether light or dark. And since she had been his home, now he no longer had a home. He no longer had a place to rest his head, as they say, from now on he'd be a vagabond, a tramp who could set out at any moment on a journey to... nowhere.

He sat there for quite a while pondering how someone had come and blown apart, carelessly and inconsiderately, the tiny blocks that made up his life, scattering them randomly, leaving each block lying quite senselessly in a different place, on its own, but he no longer had the strength to put them together again, to make one block support the next and re-assemble them as they originally were, or make them into something new.

He sat in the winged chair for a long time thinking that there was nothing to be done about that now. As she sometimes used to say the day after one of his benders, when he sat there dejected, battered, flaked out, a very picture of despair: don't worry about it anymore, she would say, nothing can be done about it now. The only thing that worried him now was that indeed nothing could be done about it, absolutely nothing at all.

He turned off the lights, took his sleeping pills, undressed and went to bed. He let a film of mental images roll that he found most calming: he was driving the car with her by his side, both of them watching the road ahead with equal concentration; in a minute he would ask her to light a cigarette for him, she would do so and hand it to him, he would take a long drag on it and they would both keep their eyes on the empty road ahead. After Svätý Beňadik the road wound its way between the trees, the river Hron coming into view occasionally behind them, the odd tree trunk having fallen into the river, then coming round a bend they would come upon a lorry, catch up with it, and he'd say, "That's all we needed", as they both knew they wouldn't be able to overtake it for quite some time. After they passed the ridge above Kežmarok, the road sloped downwards among thick coniferous forests, to a place where they would always stop and when they got out after three hours in the car they would be literally engulfed by the green fragrance of pine needles. On their way to the Tatras they once passed through a village where the road went quite steeply downwards and suddenly, down in the hollow ahead of him he spotted a hay wagon with people coming home from work; all of a sudden it was right in front of him, much sooner than he expected, and he had to use all his strength to make the car screech to a halt; the women on the haywagon didn't realise that he had almost crashed into them and merely turned to look at the car that had made the funny screeching noise and laughed. Or there was the time they drove along a road and a lorry coming towards them was overtaking another car, he had to slam on the brakes abruptly so that the overtaking lorry wouldn't crash into him on his side of the road and his wife exclaimed indignantly: "What an idiot!". Or there was the memory of that dreary Sunday, on their way somewhere, when all the villages were deserted and he didn't have to slow down even in the built-up areas. They discovered a newly-built road that went all the way to the chalet at Roháče, the sun was beating down, and he had to keep shifting into low gear as the road kept getting steeper and it made them happy to be able to get so high up by car. He was passing through a loop on a plateau, a car would have been visible all the way from the far end of the long arc, but the road was empty, so he asked her for a cigarette and took a drag. Or on the bank of the Danube, at the other end of the city, they discovered a new road leading to the nearby woodlands; when they reached the very last stretch of embankment they got out of the car by a group of trees with big clumps of green mistletoe high up in their canopies, somewhere close by they sensed the presence of a broad arm of the river with stagnant green water. And then driving down an empty road again, no need to concentrate, and he asked her to light a cigarette for him…

Many more images of that kind passed before his eyes, often the same ones again and again, until he fell asleep.

All dressed and refreshed by the obligatory cup of black coffee, his elbows on the stone parapet of the large kitchen window, rather than looking down on the deserted street below, he was gazing up at a sky that appeared to be vast, composed of heavy, dark purple clouds of down that seemed neatly arranged one after the other, with an occasional narrow gap between them allowing the sun to shine through and illuminate, through the longest gap, the landscape somewhere far beyond the city, on the other side of the Danube, and even though the river itself was obscured by the buildings on the embankment, he could have traced its arc exactly as it entered, and left, the city. The illuminated stretch of the countryside was bathed in a yellow glow, just as it would be in summer, since it was flat and almost treeless. The city was asleep, crouching under the sad, heavy eiderdown, its houses huddled together and shrunk below the vast dome of the sky. As he took in the view, he was conscious of coming to life and felt as if he were the only person in this city standing by the window and gazing down at the empty street below, even though he had a job to do today, to which he would apply himself assiduously and with concentration, because it had to be completed by a certain time. Today, it being Christmas Day, none of his colleagues would be typing up any pages of their latest novel, none would be churning out any particularly penetrating insights into the complex relations between literature and society, and if his wife were still alive, he would not be embarking on any important work today either, but since she was no longer alive, he couldn't take a day off, there was something for him to do every day in preparation for the funeral, and that filled him with deep satisfaction. However, the city down below was not, in the main, populated by people who came up with new mathematical equations, musical chords, pages of a new novel, or who contemplated the evolving relations between literature and everything else: most people down in the city simply lived, raised children, earned their daily crust, felt frustrated with life, fell in love, were jealous, hated someone, and now they were having breakfast, happy that they didn't have to go to work. They were driven by life's monotonous routine and it was quite normal for them to feel safe and confident that everything would be just the same tomorrow: that they would have their breakfast and look after their children, snap at their wives or be with someone else in their thoughts, bound to the other person by a paralysing attachment called love, which was at its greatest and most powerful and most astonishing when the other person wasn't there and everything still lay ahead… except that for him nothing lay ahead anymore. He had a few days left in which he'd have something different to do each day, and the job for today was to sit down and cover blank sheets of paper with writing, while later on he would just trundle from one day to the next as if his head were inside a sack, but he didn't want to think about that now, when he still had a few days of being able to pass the time in a purposeful way.

He drew away from the window and his eyes alighted on the bag he'd brought home from hospital that night and had yet to unpack. He pulled it closer, took out two bottles of mineral water, one full and one half-full, and a small bottle of Coca-Cola. At first he was at a loss as to what to do with them, then he opened them all and poured their contents down the sink. If he ever poured himself a drink out of one of these bottles, it would remind him of the fact that she had left it unfinished. He took out a tin of Greek peaches and took it to the larder but put it to one side; he wouldn't open that either, he would throw it out later. Next he unloaded the books she didn't manage to finish and carried them to the bedside table in her room: he would have to return them to the University Library. Then there was her underwear, some used and some not, which he shoved into the rubbish bin, all except for her jumper and skirt, which he put back into the built-in wardrobe in the hallway with her other clothes. There was a big pile of jumpers there but the one he now placed on top of the rest was the one she'd worn most of the time, winter and summer, for years. He saw her wearing it as she sat at her desk, typing away and looking at the open pages of a book she was translating; she had worn this jumper when cooking, too: it was her home outfit, sometimes she would even wear it on top of her pyjamas when she strolled along the corridor in her dressing gown, which was why she took it to the hospital as well… Under the shelf with her underwear hung her dresses; she had lots of them, like some lady of fashion – that was the term she used – in fact, it was the same with her dresses as it was for him with his books: she would buy them and then never wear most of them… Since they married, whenever she received an invitation to a meeting in Prague, she would pop into Dom módy, the clothing department store, and every time come home with a few new dresses. About three years ago someone recommended a seamstress and she had at least five dresses made, but as far as he could recall, she would wear the same dress all summer, and when they went to the theatre or on a more formal visit, she always wore the same two-piece suit. He ran his hand over her clothes… at least half of these dresses she had worn no more than once, and at least half she had never worn at all, because, before they were married, she had only one dress for all occasions, but later felt she needed to have a variety of dresses, to wear this and then that, to show off, but she had never managed to get into the habit, being unable to learn new tricks… what was he to do with all these dresses now? he might give them away… to the two girls, who would be quite happy to have them altered…, there was no rush though… and what about her pyjamas and the rest of her underwear? give it all away, as if she had never been here?… he'd see… then he remembered her winter coat… yes, it was hanging in the hallway… he gently touched it with his fingertips… he would probably give that away as well… but now it was high time to get down to work.

He went into the living room, sat down on the ottoman and looked at the bookcase. It was so big – tall, but especially long – that it had to be dismantled in Martin for loading into the removals van. It once stood in her room, for, oh, some thirty-five years, he estimated, ever since she graduated from the conservatoire. Her translations were in the middle section of the bookcase's highest shelf, she had arranged them according to date of publication, with anything published in the first months after they had moved to this flat added at the end. Now he'd have to take all these books down – he'd need to bring a chair from the kitchen to reach them – stack them up on the table – though he couldn't fit all the books on there so he would leave on the desk those he could not fit onto the table and bring them over later, while those he'd made a note of he would pile up on the floor, making sure they remained arranged by year of publication. Next he needed some paper: he'd have to draw vertical lines with a ruler, with the first column for all her translations, each with a number, the second column for author and title, the third for year of publication, and finally, in the fourth, the number of pages. That was it; he was ready to begin.

The first book he picked up from the pile before him was by a Bulgarian author, which rather surprised him. He looked inside the book, saw the names of two translators and he knew at once: the publisher had received a totally unusable translation and asked her to turn the text into something intelligible and readable… she agreed, and that was how she got into translating. Maybe she would have started to translate anyway at some stage, after all, it was a family tradition: her brother had been a translator, her father had tried his hand at it many years ago, her uncle had done some rather poor translations of poetry, so she might well have ended up doing it eventually, but thanks to this Bulgarian tome she embarked on this career in one particular year, and from then on stopped devoting all her time to teaching piano to children from upper-class families, something they were expected to learn in those days, even if they had no musical talent whatsoever. Three French novels followed, including *Madame Bovary*, perhaps the best novel of the nineteenth century. Some years ago he had come home with a Czech translation and his wife had asked, rather testily, why he'd bought it when they had a copy at home, as she had translated it years ago. He couldn't tell her then that when it came to such an extraordinary novel he didn't entirely trust a translation she had done at the start of her career, so he put on a surprised face as if he hadn't known, but after that she focused on translating from the Russian and stuck to Russian almost to the end, with all those classic novels featuring minor landowners and their manor houses, little villages and hamlets, and sometimes comical petty bureaucrats in sparsely furnished ministerial offices. And then there was Lermontov, the greatest Russian Romantic poet. This translation, he recalled, had caused a furore when it was published during the war and from then on everyone with even the slightest interest in literature knew her name, though in those days he hadn't himself bought this book of poetry praised by all and sundry around him, many quoting entire stanzas by heart, as this kind of extravagant Romantic grandeur was alien to his nature, as was extravagant despair and extravagant melancholy; in those days he had been preoccupied with quite pedestrian worries like scraping a living and keeping the wolf from the door. Next came the thick tomes of Dostoyevsky, forever agonising about guilt and redemption... by the time he reached the end of the war he'd got to number fourteen, the first war novels, written while the war was still raging, then the three volumes of *War and Peace,* generally regarded as the greatest novel of the nineteenth century, which he had also bought but failed to read at the time; only when they were already married had she forced him to take it on holiday one summer. After this came contemporary novels from that country which he had not read and had no regrets about not reading. He was now up to number nineteen and two thick volumes lay before him: Sholokhov's *And Quiet Flows the Don*. He knew he would get to these, there was no one to relieve him of this duty, and he had to reach for the two volumes, open them up, make a note of the number of pages and year of publication, and although something in him resisted, he had to record them, of course, albeit with a sense of shame, humiliation, even a kind of revulsion. It was so embarrassing, everything to do with these two volumes or rather four, in that first edition: it was embarrassing and, at the same time, absurd to think that if it hadn't been for these four volumes, they wouldn't have met and married… his journalistic self-confidence at the time and the slap on the face she had given him were to blame, but above all the era when those four volumes were published, a time when every molehill could be made into a mountain. This was not to say that her translation was a molehill – it was one of the most difficult translations she had to tackle, few other books had given her so much trouble, starting with technical terms, such as the names for parts of a wooden haycart and ways of dealing with the use of dialect – and her translation must have been a masterpiece, but it happened to be published in the middle of the churning and murky currents of those times.

Some time earlier Genialissimo Stalin had penned a treatise on linguistics, clearly a masterpiece of scholarship, and all the peoples of all his subordinated gubernias and colonies were overwhelmed with gratitude for the bucket of wisdom he had poured over their heads. The crème de la crème of the intelligentsia – architects, biologists, archaeologists, choreographers, et al. – were eager to apply in their scientific or artistic fields the findings of this work of a genius who made Aristotle and Socrates, Descartes, Hegel and Immanuel Kant, and even Karl Marx, look like Lilliputians. The translator Ján Ferenčík published an essay which said that in light of this treatise the Sholokhov translation did not deserve unequivocal praise. He argued that one of the many brilliant points made by the said treatise was that every language included some words that were dying out and some that were newly-emerging, and since this translation featured many words that were dying out, little-known, or almost completely unknown, and were therefore to all intents and purposes unintelligible, the translation as a whole evinced certain negative tendencies. Someone else responded to his critique by defending the translation, while yet another asserted that if a translation manifested such negative tendencies, it was a reactionary translation, even if it manifested some positive qualities. Yet others defended it and others still wrote that all this digging up of unknown, extinct words, this negative tendency, was evidence of bourgeois nationalism in translation. Another critic spoke up on behalf of the translation and in response another elaborated on its bourgeois nationalism.

One day, when the polemic had been raging on the pages of the literary weekly *Kultúrny život* for weeks, he went to the editorial office with a review of the Italian film *Miracle in Milan,* which had made a deep impression on him. As he waited for Agneša to read through his review, the editor-in-chief Kostra spotted him, ushered him into his office and poured his heart out: their readers were fed up to the back teeth with this endless polemic, and no one could make head or tail of it anymore; it was high time to draw a line under the whole thing. Then came some words of flattery: "Listen, you're so clever, you're so good at analysing, putting things into perspective: why don't you summarise the debate and draw a line under it so we can wind the whole thing up."

The editor-in-chief was a poet who cared only about his own poetry, so he couldn't suggest that he could do this himself, nor could he be asked for advice. He tried to wriggle out of this awkward task, but he couldn't just say a firm "no", as the editor continued: "Come on, all you need to do is juxtapose the opposing views." He pleaded that this wasn't really his line of work… but the editor-in-chief assured him that it was precisely because it wasn't strictly his field that he was being asked: the issue should be settled by someone who wasn't involved, an outsider. In those days everyone obeyed that axiom of Lenin's which stated that even an ordinary cook should be able to rule, that anyone with the right kind of thinking had the ability to decide matters they knew nothing about; the whole system relied on dilettantes and amateurs, they were in charge of everything… So he agreed to take it on.

From the purely journalistic point of view the task wasn't too difficult. He went to the archives and took out every issue of *Kultúrny život* in which the translation had been discussed: after all he was expected to draw conclusions from the polemic, not to come up with any pearls of wisdom of his own. He read through everything carefully and tried to draw a line under it in a way that would allow the cake to be simultaneously eaten and to remain whole (folk sayings were all the rage in those days). The translation was outstanding, that was indisputable – he felt a certain respect for the translator, who for him represented the highest echelons of the translating world; on the other hand her language was to some extent marred by archaisms, as some of the words in the translation were either not frequently used or even unknown to the wider readership, so in a sense the translation did cultivate elements of the language that were dying out. On yet another hand, the translation had nothing to do with bourgeois nationalism, as that was a phenomenon that could be found anywhere in the literary language and was not limited to translations alone.

All of this could have been said in one page but because of all the compulsory references to the work of the Genialissimo, which opened with the statement: "Language is a means of communication between people," he permitted himself some philosophising on the subject. He quoted statements made by one side, then by the other, basically padding out his few pronouncements with so much material, some of it quite unsavoury, that his article ended up being excruciatingly long and boring. It appeared on the front page of *Pravda* and everyone was convinced that it represented the position of the highest official spheres, even though he hadn't discussed it with anyone – and wasn't even a party member. To his astonishment, at a translators' conference held some time later, the translator gave a speech and exercised self-criticism. He didn't understand why the matter had to conclude with such a loud and theatrical finale but he was pleased that no one had challenged his piece and nothing more was heard on the subject.

Very soon afterwards, before he had time to forget the matter – back then days galloped by like a horse foaming at the bit, in the words of a contemporary poet – bourgeois nationalism was no longer on the agenda, no one was writing or giving speeches about it, and it suddenly transpired that the true archenemies of the proletariat were some nebulous cosmopolitans. And if anyone was predestined to serve as an example of a rootless cosmopolitan, who better than he, someone with a father he never mentioned and a mother with whom he spoke German at home. He'd written a few damning reviews of a few lousy books and plays. Would that make him want to destroy homegrown literature? That wouldn't have been very convincing. But the polemic around *And Quiet Flows the Don* was still fresh in everyone's memory. It had affected a person with a good reputation and family lineage. And although he wasn't the one who had started it, and didn't add a single argument to it, he was the one who had summed it up and brought it to an end, conceding that the translation did include some words that were little known or even unknown, thereby championing some kind of scrawny, bleached out, emaciated basic language and compelling the translator to exercise self-criticism to boot. He, the bastard who had no business to be involved in this kind of thing in the first place.

This caused him great distress at the time. Finally, he had an idea. He went to see Ferenčík, the man who had started this whole campaign and was the first to blast the translation with heavy cannon. "We ought to draw a line under this matter once and for all," he said."Ideally all three of us ought to be involved: the person who started it, the one who concluded it, and the person it has affected." After all, the debate wasn't held in the spirit of genuine scholarship, as the entire discussion had taken place in an atmosphere of hysteria with bourgeois nationalism being dragged into it, and then, for some reason, she had ended up exercising self-criticism. Her translation may have had the odd flaw but overall… in fact… Oh, come on, what's got into you, Ferenčík said in dismay, we didn't say anything that was wrong. He was quite reluctant to open it up again. He'd been in touch with the translator and she didn't hold a grudge, he said, and Ferenčík let him read their correspondence to show that as far as she was concerned, too, the matter was closed.

And sure enough, the letters were very friendly. She had enquired about Ferenčík's personal problems and those of his wife, offering all kinds of advice; she clearly stood by him and tried to be supportive and helpful and to stay in touch. As for that scandal… there was only one reference to it: if she blamed anyone, one of her letters said, it was he, the "upper-class lad" – this from the daughter of a former bank director – he understood perfectly that this turning of him into a "lad" was meant as an insult: an upper-class lad from Košice, a city that epitomized Hungarianness.* In fact, he was anything but a lad from an upper-class family and he'd never been to Košice or anywhere in the country's far east, and he couldn't speak Hungarian – but this was the confirmation that he was to be the scapegoat.

Soon afterwards he went up to her at some writers' conference… she was rather unpleasant and ungracious, but as he insisted on having a talk, she suggested that he come to her aunt's place where she was staying. This was in the middle of winter. He followed her as she walked ahead of him in the snow and the freezing wind in her heavy black boots and thick sheepskin coat – a powerful, forbidding, confident figure. On the way she turned to him once with the words: "You really should have stayed out of this." It felt like a hate-filled slap on the face. What could this kind of upper-class lad from this kind of a city possibly know about our people, our nation and its language. It made him feel the way he had felt in primary school when the other children hurled abuse at him because of his father. He wished he could turn on his heels and leave. But he preferred to be insulted by her now, face to face, than finding something like this written about him in a newspaper one of these days. So he went along to her aunt's flat and told her why it was time to draw a line under the whole business by writing a joint article. Perhaps it crossed her mind that anyone, even Ferenčík, with whom she was exchanging such friendly letters, could be turned into a rootless cosmopolitan. Or perhaps she had got it out of her system with that single sentence, but for whatever reason, she agreed in the end. He wrote the article, sent it to her, and she signed it; Ferenčík was initially reluctant, insisting on crossing out a few things, but eventually he signed too, and the article didn't cause another scandal. They started corresponding. After a while they started meeting when she was in town. And about eighteen months later they were married.

There was nothing romantic about the way they met. It was actually fear that had driven him to speak to her, while she needed someone to correspond with, to meet, to talk to, to look after. Back then he'd been a very conflicted and highly-strung person, and she seemed to need someone just like that. But he had never written about translations again. Nor had he ever said another word to her about any of hers.

Eventually he moved on to another book, noted the data, then picked up the next... he now needed more time, as each title reminded him of other things that had happenened to him, and generally in the world, at the time she was translating it; in her letters she would often mention the book she was working on, for example, that she was enjoying the work because it was really well written, or that it would be hard work because it was stylistically very demanding, or that it caused her a lot of headscratching since it was poorly written and she couldn't translate exactly what the author had written because it would come across as her being sloppy as a translator... again he felt a pang of guilt that he had read so few of her translations... but he focused mainly on books he was reviewing, written by Slovak and Czech authors, sometimes these were indeed translations, but from other literatures; he'd also read books on politics and literature, lots of theory and all kinds of journals in all kinds of languages whenever he could get hold of them... as for the Soviet literature that she translated, he'd read a lot of that before the war, back when it seemed almost like a description of what the future would be like; that was certainly how he had read the books then, but now that the future was being built all around him, works of fiction were also expected to say more or less the same thing as the Soviet novels he'd read before the war – and which she was translating; the books written now all seemed to run along the same lines: someone was sent somewhere in the back of beyond to manage some failing factory or construction site where everything kept breaking down, where chaos, carelessness and an absence of accountability reigned, but the protagonist would manage to turn everything around, making sure that production at the factory flowed without a hitch or that the building was completed ahead of time… Actually, he admitted that she hadn't translated any novels of this kind, although he had to read such plays in his capacity as dramaturg at the theatre: this is what plays by Slovak as well as Soviet authors were about, all the films also featured managers like these, men brimming with vitality and energy, and powerfully built as well, who overcame every obstacle in their way. Whereas he was enchanted with Flaubert's *Education sentimentale*, a book he read soon after they got married, feeling a kind of intimacy with its characters even though they lived in the previous century rather than being powerfully built and brimming over with energy and vitality – as a matter of fact, its characters lacked all these qualities and were actually rather like him… she waxed lyrical in one of her letters about a wonderful book in which the author described the wilful destruction of forests in his country that had been going on for decades… and he recalled that back in the nineteen-twenties the same Soviet author had written about the merchants who in the old days had the forests chopped down for profit, and once the world was turned upside down, even though no merchants remained, the chopping down of the forests continued, as it transpired from this author's novel that a saboteur somewhere high up in the ministry had deliberately ordered the chopping down of the forests. As soon as he realised that this was what plot of this novel revolved around, not only did he lose all interest in it but he felt outright revulsion towards the author, even though this was before saboteurs, too, had been decried as just figments of the writers' vengeful imagination. Zora had agreed that he had a point, but to the extent that the novel focused on the dying forest, it was an extraordinary achievement, and challenging to translate, but even so he'd never been tempted to finish it… Well, he had in fact read some of the classics she translated, although not very many, since the Russians had a great many great classics and she kept translating them, alongside contemporary authors… There was something in the dialogues that he found baffling, as if he could detect another voice in the background, behind those of the characters in the novel, who all sounded like her father and mother. Perhaps these were all excellent and appropriate solutions to the problem of the various voices, perhaps that was what made it sound natural, but he couldn't help feeling that all the characters had been turned into clichés resembling her nearest and dearest. That was the only thing he found somewhat jarring, but whenever he found in the final paragraph of a review any critical comments about her translation, he would get cross, as if he had himself been the target of some completely fatuous criticism because, even though he hadn't read most of her translations, he still felt as if they were in part his own work. As a matter of fact, the reason he hadn't read most of her translations was that he didn't read much fiction in general; people thought him incredibly well-read but they were mistaken: he had to focus on the books he reviewed, by home-grown authors that he often found extremely boring, and he also kept up with literary theory, continuously discovering that everything about yesterday's theory had been wrong, whether it related to literature, or the world, or society as a whole, and eventually, when very gradually books written in the West began to filter through to him, he felt he had missed out on a great deal, that he had become dulled, that he'd been reading textbooks for secondary schools and had only now got around to reading books for graduates… Most of what he read from the West seemed to him incredibly clever, which was quite understandable as he was discovering material he had been cut off from for fifteen or twenty years; there was so much to catch up on that he had no time for, as well as not enough interest in, the works his wife was translating, by writers from a country no longer able to offer anything new, where instead of thinking, people just built factories and fulfilled five-year plans… Actually, he was now looking for excuses: as a matter of fact his indifference and his indolence had also played a role, as those books didn't seem to exist for him: he'd heard so much about them from his wife that he felt as if he had assisted at their birth and so didn't need to read them. But the question of how it might have made her feel if she had realised that he read almost none of her translations had never crossed his mind and now he felt guilty again. Whenever he translated something, his wife would look at his manuscript and mark everything she would have translated differently and he would then revise his translation along those lines and she had always found the time to do that. On the other hand, he had no need to feel guilty, he thought, since he would do the same with her articles, rewriting whatever she had written, leaving her to recast it in her own words. Or he might suggest that she add this point or that, immediately typing up his suggestions, which she would ponder and turn it into her own article. So it can't have been just ignorance and indolence behind his failure to read so many of her translations, whereas she had checked every one of his. She was the expert when it came to translating, while his own expertise was in writing articles, theorising, speculating, attacking, disproving, arguing… It wasn't that he didn't care about her work, quite the contrary: he just didn't want to meddle in her translations and, besides, he had really not read much fiction: his head was pumped full of theories of fiction, he was very well-read in those, but he'd lost the habit of reading novels, reading them only if they could be made use of, exploited, processed. Nevertheless, he couldn't rid himself of a feeling of guilt… and yet, in the end – yes, it was really almost at the very end – he did contribute quite substantially to her decision to take on the translation that had made her a household name even with those who were previously unaware that she'd been the country's foremost translator for the past twenty-five years.

It happened in 1967. The two of them managed to make a trip to London, invited on the back of their joint translations of Shakespeare, an ongoing project – and one day, as they were walking from the British Museum to the underground station along small streets boasting specialist bookshops of every kind, they stopped in front of a shop window displaying only Russian books in Russian, mostly ones published abroad. And suddenly he spotted a pocket edition of *Doctor Zhivago*, a novel whose author had never lived in the West but was living *there*, in the Soviet Union. Pasternak had been active as a poet in the nineteen-twenties and -thirties and then he fell silent until he wrote this novel, which had almost been published at home, but instead he was lambasted, torn to shreds. The novel did make it to the West, however, and its author was awarded the Nobel Prize in literature, which resulted in him being harrassed into turning the prize down. They went in and asked to see the book. He noticed the colophon on the verso of the title page – the book had been published *over there*, by a publishing house he had never heard of: that of the Ministry of Agriculture. His wife couldn't understand how a publishing house like that... He paid quickly and they left. A lightbulb went on in his head. The book was published in the West, of course, he said, enlightening his wife, the publishing house and the place of publication was fake, but for a reason: so that, should Soviet customs find it in someone's luggage, the traveller could claim that the book had been published *over there*, by the publishing house of the Ministry of Agriculture. Back at home he encouraged Zora to take the book to a publisher and argue in the same way as if speaking to a customs officer: the book had been published in the Soviet Union after all, albeit in a publishing house she'd never heard of (or at least she hadn't been aware that it published fiction), but as it did appear that meant that it could be translated and published in this country as well. The staff at the publishing house were initially sceptical but in the end agreed that they, too, could use this line of argumentation with those higher up and said she should get started on the translation. This was the beginning of the era when the high-ups could no longer meddle in everything, partly because of the rapid turnover in the echelons of power. When did she even manage to translate it? Throughout 1968 she constantly sat in meetings, appeared on television, wrote articles, received invitations of all kinds – she must have translated the book in any odd moment she could snatch. It was typeset and printed at lightning speed, just as in the capitalist West. Every day copies of the book printed the previous day would be loaded up and distributed. And although by then the Prague Spring had wilted, normalisation* was yet to get underway. Everyone knew that the book had been condemned by the Soviets for slandering the most glorious period of the Soviet Union, and now there was an opportunity to find out what really went on during this most glorious period. And of course, everyone knew that the book's author had received the Nobel Prize and even those who knew little or nothing about that had at least heard that the novel had been adapted as a Hollywood blockbuster featuring major stars, and even though no one had seen the actual film, everyone had heard the theme music on some Western radio station or other. So everyone had to buy the book, even if they ended up never reading it. He remembered going to a bookshop one day for some new publications and heard everyone asking for this novel. As he stood there browsing, he overheard an assistant say that they had sold all their allocation of copies for that day, but more would be delivered tomorrow. Everyone he visited after that had a copy. Although recently some of those he visited and who saw him scanning their bookshelves admitted they had moved the novel to a back shelf, but of course they kept it; it hadn't been banned after all...

Of all the books he had piled up only one remained now. A slim volume, by the same author, though written and published some forty years earlier. In some complicated way they managed to get hold of the original. He clearly remembered his wife working on this translation, not just because she did it quite recently. It was during the summer they had spent at her parents' home, as they were no longer eligible to stay at the writers' retreat in the Tatras and he had nothing left to write or to translate, so he buried himself in books on philosophy in the hope of understanding the reasons behind the state of the world he lived in and the woeful failure of the utopia he had envisaged. His wife, meanwhile, was making notes for her translation of the almost esoteric short stories of Pasternak's youth. Before writing these, the author had attended some lectures on philosophy at Heidelberg, where the university had attracted many famous Neo-Kantians. His wife was making notes at a small table she had brought out into the courtyard, while he was reading Hegel's most difficult book on logic, where on every page he found himself buffeted at least five times from the Absolute to Nothing, but found it impossible to picture either Nothing or the Absolute: although the book felt as if it had been written in some unknown language, or as if its author were playing a practical joke on his readers by making everything revolve around Nothing and the Absolute, he tried to make at least some sense of it. But his wife kept interrupting him with questions such as: is it Neo-Kantians or Neo-Kantianer, or should it be New Kantians or perhaps New Kantianer? And – since all the names had been transcribed into Cyrillic – she wanted to know how to spell Cassirer –with a K or a C – and whether "Kogen" might be Cohen, and having read philosophy books by writers other than Hegel, he guessed that it would have to be Cohen and that Simmel was spelled with two "m"s; she had no regard whatsoever for the fact that, sprawled though he was in the deckchair, he was trying hard to work out the meaning of at least one of Hegel's sentences, and just kept bombarding him with questions day after day, leaving him unable to understand the extremely complex relationship between Nothing and the Absolute, although he really wanted to understand this, since this idea, turned on its head – as the famous adage* would have it – proved that the revolt of the proletariat was inevitable. But never mind: at least the names of all the German philosophers together with their complex terminology were correctly transcribed and translated in Pasternak's Heidelberg stories.

He wrote down the year of publication and the number of pages of this last one and started to carry the books back to the bookcase, one pile after another, since he had to climb onto a chair each time, taking care to put them back in the same order as he'd taken them down, so that he wouldn't have to arrange them again.

As he sat there casting his eye over the lists – they looked like sheets of accounts, with each title assigned a number and a line, followed by more numbers – suddenly he felt that everything he'd done this morning – it was past midday by now – was pointless. This, quite illogically, gave rise to another idea: after he had something to eat he would take the number of pages in each book and add them up. Now that would be not only pointless but also made absolutely no sense. Nevertheless, he looked forward to the total figure, which would no doubt be very large, though even that would not be the whole picture, since she often returned to some of her translations after a time, revising them thoroughly, or making substantial changes, but it would be impossible to express that in terms of a number of pages. But just at that moment it seemed to him that this dramatically high figure would in and of itself, without any further commentary, be evidence of her lifetime's achievement. He was sensible enough to realise that after nearly thirty years spent translating and never being short of such work – which had been a full-time job so to speak – the final figure would inevitably be very high, as for the entire thirty years this was what she did every morning and afternoon and often also in the evening. On the other hand, it occurred to him that if he tried to add up all the articles he had written just since the end of the war – actually, it would be an impossible task, since he hadn't kept most of them and some had appeared unsigned – it would amount to, say, eight hundred, perhaps a thousand pieces. Most of it was not worth the paper it was printed on, especially the articles he wrote while working for newspapers… he might have kept two hundred articles perhaps – but how many was he truly proud of? Though his work was a completely different kettle of fish… one article could be like this, another like that, whereas her translations – precisely by virtue of being translations – had maintained a certain consistent standard. A few had been extremely difficult to do, but others might well have been translated by someone else in more or less the same way… So there was some analogy with his articles after all. But then again, none of this really mattered. He wanted to come up with this high total, but he would do so later. It was proof of something after all. Even if the professor didn't need it and didn't make any use of it. It was just another brilliant idea of his: to provide the professor with background information…

He went to the kitchen, opened the fridge, and took out the two pots he received yesterday, and ladled a lunch-sized portion into two smaller pans and set them on the stove to heat up. They had to be stirred, he knew that much, to ensure that the sauerkraut soup was hot and the sausage and mashed potatoes didn't stick to the pan.

With most of his labours done, there wasn't much left for him to do. In fact, he didn't feel like doing anything anymore. It was all too exhausting. Every title he noted down gave rise to a memory. If not every single one, then certainly the translations she did over the past eighteen years. This was less background information for the professor than a backdrop for his own reminiscences. He had come up with another way of summoning memories of his past life to mind, including many that were not related to her translations at all, just the year a particular translation was published. Whenever he recorded something in that mechanical, accountant-like manner, some reflections flooded into his brain, a kind of processing. But he would much rather put a stop to it. Have a rest. Stop picking away at it and allowing these images to curl upwards like smoke.

He emptied the two pans onto a plate and sat down at the kitchen table. He still had to write down all the works of Shakespeare that they had translated together, some twelve comedies and tragedies… he would soon have the exact figure. They had translated them jointly, but they were really her translations. He would supply a literal version, as close to the original as possible. Whenever an English word had two or three different meanings, he would write all three possible translations underneath each other and if the annotated edition had a footnote on a particular word or a line – to say, for example, that the Folio edition had this and the Quarto that, the meaning of the word in Shakespeare's day but also something quite different in the vernacular… for instance, "get thee to a nunnery" could also mean to a brothel – he would write all that out as a note below the relevant line and having had to write everything by hand, he remembered those pages, covered in tiny letters: fiddly work, quite tiresome, especially when he had to spend most of the time leafing through dictionaries. All he did was supply the literal wording; she was the one who turned it into verse. In time her brain had developed a special chip for processing Shakespeare's lines: she would take a look at his dreadful literal translation and his notes, stare at it for a while and before long come up with a perfectly formed line… sometimes, after returning to her parents' house, she would tell him in a letter that on the train she'd translated sixty lines… or eighty… he no longer remembered exactly. Once a play was translated, she would always let him read it, he might have thought that perhaps it could have sounded a little more solemn, theatrical, stylistically more complex and archaic, but actors were always full of praise for her translations, finding their roles easy to perform... simplified, so to speak... he would read one of her translations as he lay on the couch, scribbling a comment once every twenty pages or so. At the beginning, when she let him read one of her first Shakespeare translations, he didn't dare express his opinion... this wasn't another sign of his indolence, it was that he just didn't dare. However, when it came to *Hamlet* – his longest play – they spent four days poring over it, from morning to night, as she slowly read out every line of her translation to him, and he would check the original and have something to say about each line. Had someone been listening to them then, they might have thought they were having a row, but it happened only with this play. The last of Shakespeare's plays they had translated was *Henry IV Part One*; they went to the publishing house together with the final version, discussed the deadline for *Part Two* and for another tragedy or comedy with the editor, but only a couple of minutes after leaving the building and finding themselves in one of the streets of the Old Town on a chilly and damp autumn day, Zora said: "I don't think there's much point going on with this," and he said "You're right, there isn't," and once they got home he put away the English dictionaries and the annotated editions of Shakespeare and everything else they had to have at hand while translating, stopped thinking about the deadline for *Part Two* and sure enough, soon they were informed that the contract had been cancelled, both for *Part One* as well as for another Shakespeare play that had yet to appear.

Well, yes, but apart from Shakespeare there were also the four plays from the German that they had translated jointly, because they were written in verse and he was useless at verse. The first was a classical play and what his wife had done with it was quite phenomenal, while the other three were by contemporary authors from West Germany, who for some mysterious reason all had a predilection for writing plays in verse in the nineteen-sixties. The first one was a five-finger exercise for her, the German author being quite bad at verse, another also threw up no problems, only the third had provoked a real row: when he read her final version, something in him rebelled against it, he thought it should have been left more or less as he had translated it, but she insisted on her own version. There was something crudely provocative about the play and he felt she had smoothed its rough edges down too much, made it too literary, so he argued with her about every single line and once it was clear that this wasn't getting them anywhere, he said, fine, let's leave it, but you will be credited as the sole translator to which she agreed, but he couldn't help feeling offended. After that there were only three titles left to deal with… He had finished his sausages and mash and comforted himself with the thought that there wasn't much left to be done. Because, since it was completely pointless, he no longer felt like writing it all down, and besides, he'd have to go quite soon. But mostly, he didn't feel like it because going through the titles made his head spin: there had been enough of it in the morning, he wanted it to stop.

He continued with numbering her translations but started a fresh sheet of paper because he was now dealing with numbers of lines, not pages. So, there were the twelve Shakespeare plays and four German ones. This time he didn't bother with the page count, adding the note "unpublished" in brackets in two places, nor did he record the number of lines, since, though he remembered that *Hamlet* had around four thousand lines and the other plays between two and three thousand, he had no idea about the number of lines in the German plays, so he left the relevant boxes blank.

Finally, he took a pile of unpublished manuscripts from her desk drawer. She had kept a copy of only two of her translations, as she'd delivered the originals to the publishing house and then the contracts had been cancelled; the third manuscript wasn't even retyped, and still had her corrections and revisions. These were all translations from the French, by contemporary authors. He really ought to read them. But then again, he hadn't done much reading lately. And these were demanding modern writers... No, he was unlikely to read them in the foreseeable future. How strange, though, that she went back to translating solely from French after so many years, having started out as a French translator years ago. He recalled how Soňa Č, who had been asked to write a publisher's report on one of the translations, waxed lyrical about it: "The play is set among young people in a metropolis and the translation reads as if it had been translated by one of them, a young person..." So why had she argued with him so much about that German play in verse, why couldn't she let it be crudely provocative? Maybe, he mused, this was after her mother had died and she was no longer trying to make her translations sound the way they used to speak at home and perhaps started to become aware of how people around her talked... Perhaps, perhaps... but now he would never find out. And nor would her biographer, if ever there were to be one.

But in the end he did start counting the number of pages of translated prose after all, just tallying the figures on each sheet, noting the total at the bottom, and then adding them all up. It came to more than twenty thousand pages. Perhaps this really was a phenomenal number. But perhaps it wasn't quite so spectacular. At least, he didn't find it all that impressive now. He tried to do a rough mental tally of the number of lines of verse in the plays but gave up before he got to ten thousand. What was the point? He would have to count rhymed and unrhymed lines separately. The whole thing was a pointless exercise.

So that was done. He put all the sheets into his briefcase. He was ready to go. He looked at his watch. It was more or less the time they had agreed. Suddenly he remembered that he didn't actually know where Felix lived. He found his name in the phone directory. The street name rang a bell but he wasn't sure where it was. He went to the phone and rang Martin. On a day like this, he was home, of course, and told him how to get there. He asked if it was in one of those blocks with glass-fronted balconies. Yes, that's right. Now he knew exactly where it was. He said thank you and put the receiver down. It was about twenty minutes' walk, past a small street market where he often went shopping – not so much for vegetables as for seedlings for the garden – in fact in the next street down from the square where the market was. When he was young and often walked around the city, he used to cast envious glances at the buildings where every flat seemed to boast a balcony. The glass-fronted balconies on every floor gave the blocks an appearance he thought very chic and sophisticated at the time. But that was before Felix came to live in Bratislava, after having taught at a *gymnázium* somewhere in the back of beyond.

As it wasn't very far, he decided not to drive, perhaps with the thought at the back of his mind that once he was there the professor might pour a little something into his glass. Only now, as he left the house, did he notice that the clouds that had been pressing down on the city for days, or perhaps weeks on end, had dispersed, leaving the sky overhead blue and rays of feeble sun shining right into his face as he walked around the corner. The perfect time for a walk. On the first day, too, the sun had come out for a moment as he left the Institute of Pathology. But now the sky was all blue and it had turned considerably colder.

And then, at the professor's... well, what would happen when he visited the professor?

He put his briefcase down by his chair and watched as the professor slowly leafed through the papers he'd put together earlier in the day. Why would he need to look at all the titles? He knew that she had translated many major works of literature, famous classics as well as some more recent ones, translations Felix could quote by heart, at least in part, as he also taught the history and theory of translation; she had translated some less important and some completely unimportant books as well that he may not have been aware of, but those weren't really worth remembering. He could see that Felix didn't actually read it, he just glanced at the sheets of paper, allowing his gaze to pause on every page for his benefit, to satisfy him that he was reading the names of authors, the titles of their works and numbers of pages, and before turning a page, he would nod his head sadly. On reaching the final page, the professor gave a smile – he guessed that he had reached the title published by subterfuge, the book for which Pasternak had been awarded the Nobel Prize and that had been all the rage but had not appeared in Russia, where its author lived, and since the professor had reached the end of the first, main part, he pointed out, a little diffidently but nevertheless boastfully, that just out of curiosity he had added up the total number of pages of prose that she had translated – the total was shown under the last title on each page, in bigger lettering, underlined twice, it would have leapt out at the professor even without him pointing it out. "Well, what an enormous body of work, a truly admirable oeuvre, albeit unfinished," said the professor, or something to that effect, he forgot his exact words but the word "unfinished" prompted him to say that the list wasn't finished either: there were also plays in verse that were really all her work where he had just provided the literal translation; he hadn't added up the total number of lines but they might come to some fifteen thousand. "That alone is extraordinary," the professor remarked and seemed to be about to push the papers to one side, so he drew his attention to a page of translations that had been, with one exception, completed and submitted, but the contracts were cancelled. The professor turned the page, this time reading with close attention; these were translations he can't have known about but that were bound to interest him, as they were of modern French authors and he had begun his career as a scholar of French literature. He checked that he really had come to the end of the sheets and said, this time not out of courtesy, but with genuine sincerity: "Now that's really unprecedented. Even during the war we didn't see anything like that, and that was under the Fascist regime." – He felt a sting of reproach, as if the professor wanted to remind him that he, too, had written about the Fascist regime as the worst thing imaginable, while regarding the period that followed as the beginning of better times, the "bright tomorrow", to use the cliché so common in the 1950s but not these days, although, of course, the professor didn't mean it personally, it just felt like that to him; admittedly, he might well have used this kind of language once but that was a long time ago now, it was surely only his neurotic, egocentric touchiness that created this impression, while the professor continued, with growing indignation that could not possibly be directed at him – "and not a single line in the newspapers, not a word in the news on the radio." He remembered hearing this on that first evening, when Martin and Viera R, and Bžoch with his wife Perla, and his wife's colleague Viera H came over; he was sure this was something he would be hearing many more times in the coming days: "not a word in the newspapers." That was it in a nutshell for most people, but the professor didn't leave it at that: "This is outrageous," he declared in a rather stentorian voice, "barbaric and outrageous, there are no other words for it" and then, as if this was the end of a speech, he fell silent, walked the length of the room, apologised and left.

He returned with an almost full bottle of Metaxa and two shot glasses – he'd been secretly hoping for something of the sort, which was why he hadn't taken the car – hell, who was he kidding that he only decided to walk because it wasn't that far, the sun was shining and a walk was long overdue. He was pleasantly surprised that it was Metaxa that the professor produced, that was the brandy they also used to buy when they were expecting visitors, not because it was cheaper than French cognac but because they preferred its wine-like aroma, even if it was a little on the sweet side.

The professor put the shot glasses down on the table, took the cork out of the bottle and politely asked: "Will you have one as well?" He nodded and after they clinked glasses the professor started talking: "Every time I think of her, I remember the last time I saw her, only a few months ago, by that spring…"

He remembered that occasion, too, their last summer. Their friends had booked a cottage for them by the Polish border for two weeks and they went for long walks along mountain paths, in the shade of conifers and across broad meadows, and once, as they were driving back to the chalet, they stopped at a sign pointing to the spring and bumped into the professor who happened to be there with his wife and daughter. He explained that this wasn't any old spring, people called it "the water of life" and flocked here for it from far and wide, and when his wife asked how come he knew all this, he told them he grew up in a village nearby, then they all squeezed into his car and drove back to their cottage. They fried some bacon over an open fire and had a bottle of wine – or two? he no longer remembered… they must have bought it at a hotel on the way to the cottage… it was a Romanian Traminer, he remembered that because Romanian Traminer had an unusually spicy yet slightly sweet flavour… and as he'd had a few glasses of the Traminer, afterwards his wife wouldn't let him drive the professor and his wife to the village where he'd grown up and where they were now staying with relatives, but the professor said it wasn't necessary, he knew exactly when the last bus left from the hotel below the cottage…

The professor started to reminisce about that evening, how they sat there in the setting sun frying the bacon – he remembered the fat dripping from it every time he pulled some out of the fire. In fact, it was the professor who had proposed the barbecue, after they had engaged in mocking banter about what was happening in their world, in the city where they lived, which seemed so remote in the country, then the professor stood up, followed by his daughter, and they began collecting twigs; everyone was in a light-hearted and carefree mood. Now the professor said something similar about his wife: – "You could tell that she felt light-hearted and carefree there, as if transported to a different world, full of life," while he thought: actually, that was when she first fell ill.

Before leaving for the cottage, she'd been unwell and they had to spend three days with the Kollárs, who had made the booking for them. Now he also recalled that she had still not completely recovered on their first day at the cottage and he thought they might have to return home, but then she felt better. Something had happened to her though, she suddenly seemed at peace with everything, quite content, as if this were the ideal place for a holiday; she didn't reproach him for anything, or make any demands on him; for example, when she decided to hike to the top of a mountain for the wonderful view that could be reached only via a steep path and saw that he didn't feel like the climb, she just climbed the hill on her own, without holding it against him, and when she came down was happy to tell him all about the view…

It occurred to him that the professor was probably delivering the first part of his eulogy here; having already put his ideas into words in his head, he would complete it in this seemingly impromptu style, but when read out, every sentence would sound as it he had painstakingly written and rewritten it, thanks to his relaxed delivery and a voice that rang out as naturally as if he were breathing… At that moment he almost envied him this ease, which was exactly what he lacked: he invariably sounded stilted, defensive, his voice strangulated, as if constantly on his guard, scared of something, especially – though perhaps only – of people: he was always scared of them, unless he had consumed the requisite amount of alcohol, otherwise he felt permanently hemmed in, pathetically running away from something, a threat of some kind … Now he remembered that back in the days when he had only just met his wife – the professor was a colleague of hers at the publishing house, having been recently fired from the university – she had asked Felix what he thought of him and Felix had told her – he's very bright, highly intelligent, but something of a cold fish – these words had stayed with him because the professor hadn't even met him and this was not how he saw himself, rather than being a cold fish, he thought of himself as scared and insecure, and his wife understood that, maybe that was a reason why she'd taken him under her wing, to heal something in him. She used to say: "I wish I could rid you of that stiltedness, it's as if you are scared of people. There's no reason for you to be so insecure, you of all people"… but she had never quite succeeded. Perhaps she might have if they hadn't spent long periods apart and he'd been under her constant tutelage.

They were on their third shot of Metaxa when the professor's wife came in with an assortment of Christmas pastries on a tray. He rose to say hello and she gave him a smile, placing the tray on the table by the bottle, and he knew that soon everyone would know that he'd been to see the professor and was drinking brandy, word of this would have got around even if this hadn't been three days before his wife's funeral, the professor – as he well knew– was a regular at a *viecha*, where he would meet his friends without ever getting drunk, whereas with him it was quite certain that he would be drunk after a few glasses of brandy; the news would reach Martin and Viera tomorrow, and a few days later the cousin would tell him, smiling, that she heard he'd been to see the professor and that they had some brandy, and the professor's wife would tell others too, of course, but the cousin would be the only one to tell it back to him... Meanwhile the professor was holding forth about his trip to Paris last summer and how he had brought back two suitcases of books, two full suitcases, never mind that he had to go hungry in Paris... they were all books on Dante – the professor made a sweeping gesture with his arms and indeed, there were books covering his desk as well as the chairs. He felt a twinge of envy... back in the nineteen-sixties he too managed to get to West Germany, twice, each time bringing back at least one suitcase-load of books, except that unlike the professor, he had put the books on his bookshelves, enormously pleased to have got hold of them but had read hardly any of them. He asked the professor if before leaving for Paris he remembered to get a certificate for customs confirming that he would be bringing back books for study purposes, but of course the professor had thought of that, he got one stamped by the university. He too had always got himself such a certificate from the institute at the Academy of Sciences, where everyone had their own long-term work plan, he remembered the customs officer's eyes nearly popping out of his head when he opened his suitcase, thinking probably that the suitcase should be confiscated for some higher authority to decide which of the books may be imported, but he had produced the certificate from the institute and was allowed to bring them all in. "I've recently been working solely on Dante," the professor went on, "there's a Dante anniversary coming up, but do you think anyone knows anything about him these days?" He fell silent and stared at the professor's library deeply ashamed as he, too, knew very little about Dante but the professor continued elaborating on Dante, or maybe Cervantes, whom he had translated earlier, he had also written about him... and Petrarch, he was next on his agenda, in a year's time at the earliest... and finally he asked what he was working on, was he writing anything, and topped up his glass.

He explained that he hadn't been feeling too well lately, heart trouble, not that long ago he was still reading all kinds of books he hadn't got around to reading before, mostly philosophy, but now he'd given up on those as well… so, no, he hadn't been working on anything recently. The professor thought for a moment and admitted that there wasn't much he could do except to write reviews "for his drawer" and then, perhaps to cheer him up, he confided: "You know, you wrote mostly on contemporary literature, which I'd also written on for some twenty years," and he cut in: "Yes, I was still at *gymnázium* then," as he recalled reading a few things by the professor at the time. The professor smiled and went on: – "but now, let me tell you, even though no one is trying to stop me, I feel no desire to write about… the kinds of things that get published nowadays," he said, dismissively, as they weren't close enough for him to say, instead of a wave of his hand, "it's all bullshit, anyway". He nodded with a smile, as if he had in fact put it that way. "Every time some sort of upheaval happens out there," he began expounding to the professor the way he used to expound to his wife and any visitor, "literature stands to attention, obeys whatever command comes from the Appellplatz, writers rush to their barracks and start writing something opposing it, as ordered." Integrity was another thing that could no longer be mentioned in literarary reviews. He recalled that many years ago, a young Felix had provoked considerable scandal by proving that the writer Dobroslav Chrobák* had plagiarised something. These days, however, if someone brought out a translation of his wife's under their name, he couldn't say it was an act of plagiarism. Well, those were the days, the professor conceded with a laugh, and that brought them back to what the professor said at the start, that this sort of thing was unprecedented. They went on talking about this and that and as their conversation had come full circle and there was nothing left to say, if he stayed any longer it would look as if he was just waiting for another tot of Metaxa, so he got up, thanked the professor once again, and went out into the hallway to put his coat on. At the last minute he remembered to mention the coach. Yes, he would take the coach, of course, and so would his wife, said the professor, rather pleased; he just mustn't forget to let him know where it would be leaving from and when.

He went out into the street and could hardly believe his eyes: it was snowing. The first snow of the winter. During the visit he had been looking at the professor all the time, or at the wall behind him; he may have been aware of it getting dark outside, or maybe not even of that, because by then the professor had drawn the curtains and switched on the light. It had been sunny on his way here. A faint December sun, lemon-yellow. Like late in the afternoon of the first day, when he came out of the Institute of Pathology annexe... But now that the skies had been clear for a few hours, it had turned cold, and the clouds that had briefly retreated from the city had returned, seemingly out of nowhere. They had just withdrawn, awaiting the right moment to make a comeback. Now snow was falling out of them. *Sniežik,* his wife would have said, using the diminutive form of snow. Tiny snowflakes floated around the streetlights like white mosquitoes. The ground was a little slippery, and he really watched his step, to be on the safe side.

Subconsciously, he decided not to take the shortest route home, down the narrow streets. It was now dark, with snow flurries in the air; he might easily slip. He turned towards Valy, now Malinovského Street, which he had driven down yesterday lunchtime; the pavement on that street would be a bit slippery too, clear of cars or people, but at least it had neon lighting. There were swarms of snowflakes chasing each other around the large neon lights when a blast of wind came from below, or they would fall calmly, deliberately, revelling in the neon lights as if spotlit on a stage.

As he walked up Malinovského, he slowed down when he saw that the lights at the pedestrian crossing were red. There was a woman waiting there, blonde hair, slightly old-fashioned hat, and when suddenly a car went down Malinovského, the woman turned to look at it him and he saw her face. Why, it was Viera M! His first, instinctive reaction was to go up to her but then he realised that she probably didn't know, as she was now moving in different circles, and she would only hear the news after the holidays when she went back to work; if he spoke to her now, he would have to tell her. In recent years, whenever they bumped into each other or sat in a café, for some reason she had never mentioned his wife, she never said, "so nice that you're married to her"– nice being her favourite word, it stood for good, wonderful, fantastic… and his wife had never mentioned her either: once, many years ago, he had said something about Viera and his wife had cut in: "You were in love with her"; he tried to refute it but Zora was adamant: "Yes you were, even if you didn't know it", so he dropped the subject and stopped talking about her… Now the woman in front of him made a move, since it was now green for pedestrians, but he waited a while before setting off again; even if she looked back now she wouldn't recognise him, her eyesight was poor even when she wore glasses… not so long ago he let her pass him in the street in summer, in broad daylight, and on that occasion, too, he was sure that unless he stopped right in front of her she wouldn't have recognised him. He didn't feel like listening to her usual spiel, the same one she would go through these days, always concluding the conversation by asking how he was and what he was doing now and he would reply, "oh well, you know, I can't publish or translate anything" and all she would say was, "what a waste of someone as smart as you." He would shrug his shoulders and they would go their separate ways; she couldn't very well start fuming about why so many people couldn't publish or translate, as she was married to a man who had climbed the greasy pole to unexpected heights at the same time as others began to lose their jobs and some people, like him and his wife, had been completely eliminated. She had by then been married to Husák for two or three years and was as loyal to him as she'd been to her first husband who had been in prison many years ago and although she would often seek out his company, nothing ever happened because she was a faithful wife. But after his release from prison, her husband went back to his philandering, and when they met in those days, she would always tell him who her husband was sleeping with, until in the end she divorced him.

He couldn't tell her his news as she might think: good for him, he's free again and can find somone else and start from scratch, but then again, if he didn't tell her and she found out a few days later, it would be rather awkward, even though they had long ago stopped being friends. He was right to let her walk ahead and not catch up with her, even if nothing had happened and he had come up to her, their conversation would be like a worn record; she was unlikely to even be aware that she kept rehashing the same old script about the good old days so many years back, when, after the war, they worked on the same newspaper – that she'd bumped into another former colleague and that his name had also come up, then she would ask if he still remembered the time he came to her office and asked if she could type something up for him... – he usually typed his pieces himself but this time he had something he thought would impress her – and he dictated to her an article by one Georgescu, our correspondent in Bucharest, describing the life in the city three years after the war. Of course he remembered, or rather, he might have forgotten but now that she reminded him it always came back to him: he'd been annoyed with their editor-in-chief who was only interested in articles from "our own correspondent" somewhere, preferably a very remote country; whenever he heard that someone he knew had travelled anywhere in the world, for example to Argentina to procure supplies of hide for the production of shoes. So he wanted to prove that given the standard of such articles from these correspondents from around the world, he could just as easily churn them out from his desk in the editorial office, and indeed, the editor-in-chief had not realised that Georgescu from Bucharest was a spoof, until one day he confessed and Trachta wouldn't speak to him for two weeks. She thought this was an incredibly daring feat, the way he had dictated the whole thing to her, without notes, a report from Bucharest, a city that had been closed to foreign journalists. She had admired him ever since and whenever they met she asked him if he still remembered..., yes, he did... and very gradually, if he walked up this street for a while longer by her side, she would leap back in time and ask him if he sometimes thought back to the days they used to go out together... admittedly, there had been a time he used to take her to the cinema or the theatre and to cafés, they used to wander the city together and she would tell him all about her life... back then hardly anyone would so much as look at her, she'd been fired from another paper, *Pravda*, where he was also working at the time, she'd been fired on the spot after her first husband was arrested – in the heat of the political campaigns waged in those days he was accused of having forged certain documents to advance his career – and around that time someone on a film journal for which he occasionally wrote reviews mentioned that the editor-in-chief was looking for a typist and was willing to employ her, if he pulled the appropriate strings, so a few days later he went back having pulled all the strings and she started working there as a stenographer; what mattered was that she had a job and was able to make a living, and that was what brought them so close, as close as if they were a couple, although in fact she was just waiting for her husband to be released from prison. And once he was back home it was indeed all over between them, they stopped meeting, no longer went anywhere together, he suddenly stopped existing for her – this was what he had told his wife and that's what must have given her the idea that he'd been in love with Viera, because he was bitter about being ditched by her, so to speak. He would have forgotten all about it except that whenever they bumped into each other in later years, she would remind him of those times, once at some press conference where a film director was answering questions from journalists, she leaned towards him out of the blue and started gushing about those days, said she'd had the time of her life, he was quite astonished, having all but forgotten about it and it had left him quite nonplussed. But that was when she was still married to her first husband, the one who always had a mistress on the go, so she must have been depressed, she wouldn't say any such thing now that she had a husband who was not interested in mistresses, all he thought about was that he didn't have many years left, after more than ten years inside and a few more waiting to be rehabilitated, so there wasn't much time left for him to climb to the very top. Surprisingly enough she didn't quit her job at that newspaper even though she no longer needed the money, having by now progressed first to editor, then to deputy editor-in-chief, and while editors-in-chief kept changing, she stayed. At this point she would make another leap forward in time, he thought – she'd start talking about the years that followed when she started writing about film and would go to screenings at the film club with Agneša, whom he had visited yesterday and who was now – at least he hoped she was – writing her speech for the funeral – the two of them had become bosom friends, they'd sit together gossiping and it was Agneša who told him that Viera was going to marry the party functionary of hers – he was sure she would ask him what Agneša was doing and he would tell her that she was currently a typist, and maybe also that her husband had been in jail for about six months now but he still had no idea what he'd been sentenced for... suddenly he stopped imagining their further conversation because the lights changed and the woman in the black coat in front of him walked off in another direction – of course, it dawned on him now, that was the way to the building where all the functionaries had their flats... by the time he reached the crossroads the lights had changed to red again, and although he could easily have crossed the street as there were no cars, he dutifully waited for the green light and watched as she walked up the street that was built up only on one side, with a high fence on the other, behind which warehouses flanked the railway line nearer the main railway station.

He crossed the road as well, no longer compelled to continue his conversation with her as she was now out of his sight. Surely he couldn't really have been in love with her, he thought again, as if trying to reassure himself. And even though later she was prone to get carried away when she recalled that rather brief period, she had probably not been in love with him either; she may have admired him, but only in an intellectual way. When she fell in love it had always been in a romantic way: she met her first husband at university, and he remembered her telling him that he had been in the resistance and was still involved in some dangerous missions, which made her feel as if she were in a movie, walking down the street with someone involved in some clandestine activity who could be imprisoned any minute... And her second husband... that was – at least initially – a fairy-tale romance.

Now he had to smile. Not so long ago someone told him that her mother was Jewish. This was the only thing she had never confessed to him. Her greatest secret. She hadn't confided even in him, even though she had told him things he was sure she had never told her second husband... But in fact, he thought, he'd never told her about his father either. But everyone knew that he was Jewish. And everyone assumed the same thing about his mother, since she spoke German. And he had never said anything about her either. It was nobody's business. He was born in this city, he was just like anyone else and never wanted to be different. Only others had always regarded him as different... He recalled that she had talked a lot about her father, some kind of aristocrat, even his name sounded aristocratic. But never a word about her mother, where she or her family had come from.

At home he stuffed himself with the pastries and Christmas wafers left over from the previous morning. He'd had lunch earlier and some cakes at the professor's, so he wasn't hungry; he just needed something to steady his stomach, as he could still feel the effects of the brandy he'd had there.

He went into the living room, switched on the light, and paced up and down for a while. Faint voices could be heard from the flat below. His sister-in-law had visitors. Her sister's daughter with her husband and three children always visited on Christmas Day. So the children are still there, he thought. Actually, it's still early evening, it was only the empty streets that made him feel he'd come home very late. He kept pacing up and down the room for a while longer but was unable to focus on anything. The shots of brandy had jerked him out of the state of torpor and depression that had triggered these painful reflections. He switched off the light and went into the kitchen, to his observation post at the window. But there was nothing to look at there. It can't have been more than eight o'clock and the street was deserted, no cars screeching round the corner, no people coming back from their walk in Horský park, nothing. Tedium. What he needed now was to see some activity, something that would catch his attention. But on Christmas Day people tended to sit at home, and only the next day, St. Stephen's Day, would they go out and visit each other and spend their time drinking, as his mother once explained to him. Suddenly he remembered what she said next, this hadn't occurred to him for decades, and why should it have, it was nothing of consequence, only as he recalled what his mother had said about Christmas, her next sentence came to him: "Let's go out now and see what the city looks like with everyone sitting at home."

So they went out of their little house in the working-class neighourhood on the outskirts: him, his mother and his brother; his father was away, on an assignment for his paper, perhaps abroad. They walked down Záhradnícka Street towards the centre of town and not for a moment did they feel bored. There was something to talk about the whole time – he would have been about eight at the time and his brother five, at that age one would talk about anything all the time. The city centre began around the place where the old Institute of Pathology used to be. They passed the Café Metropol with its large dark windows and continued past the State Hospital where he'd been admitted a year or two ago to have his appendix taken out, spending some time in a room overlooking this street… there were never many shops or people around there. Soon they reached Obchodná Street, which was called Uhorská in those days and was renamed Schöndorfská during the war, after Schöndorf, as a village just outside the city gates was known in the twelfth century. Obchodná was normally bustling with life, Bosnian street vendors would stand with their large baskets on the corner of a long square, and further down the street was lined with single-storey houses with shops that were all dark now (this was before the days of neon lights) and they didn't come across a soul; it was as if Obchodná, and not only Obchodná but every street they passed, was nothing but a stage set deserted after everyone had left and they were the only ones allowed to walk around on the stage. They stopped in front of a small shop that sold shirts and was owned by an old friend of his mother's; at that point they turned round – this was an important milestone, as his mother would often pop into this shop when they went to town, even though she never bought a shirt there – and started walking back home amidst the stage set of this strange town. For that night the town felt strange to him, not so much because there wasn't a soul around but because he had never walked its streets after dark; he could still remember the moon shining in a clear sky, he could clearly see the old houses, the new buildings in the square, the State Hospital and the Café Metropol, and then boring old Záhradnícka Street again, with its coal and timber warehouses and empty plots still without any houses and, finally, the abbatoir close to where they used to live; all of this made it appear to him as if he had found himself in a strange city, one he'd never been to before, it was the first time he had seen it like this, in this kind of light; had he been much older, he thought now, it would have felt like walking around an unknown Italian city, because the moonlight cast everything in an unfamiliar, new, beautiful, almost intoxicating glow, and because this was the first time he'd seen such a thing: a deserted city at night.

Before he knew it, he was putting on his winter coat: yes, of course, that was what he would do tonight as well, he would re-live that expedition to a strange city devoid of people, frozen in its dark sleep; it would be safe to go down the city streets, tonight of all nights he need not worry that he might end up in some boozer and then move on to another, and then yet another. Tonight it was not his good resolutions that protected him but the ancient decree that ordered all pubs and bars to stay shut on Christmas Day; tonight he was not in danger, even if he stuffed his pockets full of one-hundred-dred crown notes, tonight he would stroll around the city that had become unreal, transformed into a set on a deserted stage. And so here he was, walking around the bend where you would rarely see a soul late at night; however, the moon was not shining tonight. He had now come down to Štefániko-va Street with its tramline to the railway station; he had seen this street so deserted when, coming from the city centre late at night, he would scurry down to the far end where he would still find an open pub or bar, or, more frequently, to the

Writers' Club, which also used to stay open late. He now passed Štefánka, its windows dark, no sound of Gypsy music… this might have been the only café in the city where there was still live Gypsy music – where on other nights large knots of people would hang around outside after closing time, some waiting for a cab, others trying to decide which woman was likely to tag along to the next dive or to accompany them home. Štefánka standing all dark at the end of this wide street with no one outside was also a familiar sight from nights when he passed it on a tram or, in earlier days, when he came out of the Writers' Club just across the street, ambling towards his flat in the city centre the worse for wear. He now reached the top of the main square but instead of walking down towards the lower end where where he had lived for many years, he turned into a narrow street that marked the beginning of the *korzo*… when still a student at *gymnázium* he sometimes used to walk this way on Sunday mornings and had been here thousands of times since, at all hours of the day and night… but since this time he wasn't being swept along with the crowds or fighting against them he noticed again that the beginning of the *korzo* was actually a wide bridge over the former city moat, with trees down below, in a kind of a garden… many years ago he tried to take a photo of this place… and to the side of the bridge, on the wall of a building with its foundations reaching to the bottom of the moat he saw the faded shop sign "Fornheim's", the city's biggest carpet store before it was Aryanised* in 1938… he had once been there with his father to buy a carpet. He walked under St. Michael's Gate and remembered that two wine bars had opened quite recently in the street on the left, both having a smaller room with a bar upstairs and a large folklore-style cellar downstairs… sometimes when he went around checking out bars and pubs, he would order a glass of wine at the first bar and another in the other place, drinking up and hurrying along… now he was going past a dilapidated old palazzo, from the gate of which, more than two years ago, he emerged with Zora and after a few steps, she turned to him and said: "What if we don't even get started on *Part Two*? What's the point anyway?" and she was right, by then there really was no point, and they had never set foot in this publishing house since... instead they both began to have their contracts cancelled... If he took the street on the left, he would reach the second-hand bookshop but its window would be dark tonight and he had in any case stopped going there for books... besides, he suddenly heard some high-spirited male voices coming from the square in front of the Old Town Hall so he didn't turn left and continued straight ahead, past the University Library... this is where he would have to return the books he'd taken out for his wife when she was in hospital... past another dilapidated old palazzo encased in wooden scaffolding. He noted that it had been like that for at least two years... all those palazzos that Hungarian magnates had built here after their estates were overrun by the Turks, sending them scuttling to these parts for a century or two... and next to this scaffolding there used to be the big pawnshop that would accept absolutely anything... and in the square he was now approaching there used to be the Sokol patisserie, named after its owners even though they were German, which was the reason the patisserie was no longer there... this is where you came in the old days for the best macaroons in town. Suddenly he paused in surprise, what's got into me, why does my brain suddenly register everything I'm passing... he had set out for a stroll around an unreal city expecting to see it how he'd seen it as a young boy, he had set out for a strange city, not streets in which invisible threads connected him to everything, ensnaring him... it was because he wasn't going anywhere or stopping anywhere in particular, because he didn't see anyone and that brought on these bouts of reminiscence about every place he passed: here on the left there used to be a philatelist's that he had visited a few times before the war to buy stamps, and next to it on the corner there was a German bookshop during the war, which hadn't been there before and he'd never set foot in it. The little street ahead of him would now take him to the arthouse cinema, or the Cinema for the Discerning Viewer, as it was officially called, and out to a small park. On the opposite side of the park he saw the neon lights of the Carlton and Savoy hotels and the cafés Carlton and Savoy... many years ago he'd be at one or the other almost every day with Laco Mňačko, who now lived God knows where abroad... one rainy November evening they went out of the café to exchange subversive speculations in the park in whispers, as the wind ripped the leaves off the trees and no one else was walking about in such weather... He would walk past it on his way back, he might find a taxi outside the Carlton Hotel that would take him home, though first he headed towards Rybné Square, but as he emerged from the little street into the square, he noticed that the pavements were much more slippery hereabouts, which wasn't surprising, as the Danube flowed very close to the back of the two hotels, and this part of town was always more damp because of that ... one night he and Zora had come out of the Cinema for the Discerning Viewer and as he started the car the fog ahead of them was so thick that you could have cut it with a knife, though only until they turned towards the centre of town, where, just a short way from the Danube there was no trace of the fog... now he would walk as far as the end of the square, to Rybná Gate and then turn and start walking back, there was nothing but rubble behind the gate anyway as access roads and flyovers for the new bridge were being built there. In the old days the area right behind Rybné Square was the liveliest part of town, with this end of the square boasting pubs and seedy dives and with whores flanking Vydrica Street on the far side of the gate, where there was another brothel and a noisy pub across the street, and in two other narrow streets further down only the cheapest whores used to ply their trade... but all these buildings had been torn down, with the elimination of prostitutes beginning immediately after the victory of the working classes, even though in later years they turned up again, if only here and there, at random and quite sporadically. Now that all these buildings were gone, who knew where the ones who survived the persecution had relocated... they were probably sitting in pubs drinking... even if he really wanted to know, there was no one to ask... but why should he bother going all the way to the end of this big square, to Rybná Gate, the café on the corner had closed down anyway and even if there were no longer any prostitutes sitting around, neither there or in the city brewery across the square, which had also been demolished... he could see some rubble on the other side of the park, all that remained of the brewery, which he had passed hundreds, if not thousands of times, even when there wasn't a soul about... there was nothing there to stop him turning around and walking to the far end of the little park, towards the National Theatre, he might find a cab outside the Savoy or the Carlton, even on a night like this. No one but he could have come up with such a silly idea, to go for a walk around the city in the same way as when he was a little boy, hoping to find an unfamiliar city he had never seen at night before. Back then it was the first time he had seen it like this, dark and deserted, beautiful, like a stage set, but now all the roads had been trampled on, each house brought back a memory, everything was covered in the spittle of his recollections, dilapidated, commonplace, run-of-the-mill... but actually, he needed to stretch his limbs, the shots of brandy were troubling him, he had to hit the streets, and let the alcohol be absorbed...

He heard footsteps behind him for the first time since leaving the flat... someone was following him... the way he had followed in the footsteps of his old friend up Malinovského earlier this evening... it could even be two people... the only thing he found surprising was that earlier, when he had turned round at the end of the square, he didn't notice anyone walking this way… perhaps they'd come out of a house… perhaps there were two of them… the steps were now getting even closer.

When he came round, he was lying on the pavement on his side, his knees pulled up, and the first thing he saw was his hat, lying a few feet away. He reached for it, still slumped on the ground, pushed himself onto his knees and then rose to his feet; he was a little woozy but otherwise he didn't feel anything, there was no pain, he looked one way then the other, but still couldn't see anyone… he wondered if he could have simply fallen over, he touched his face then looked at his hand, touched his head and felt his scalp, then glanced again at his hand, next he touched his neck and glanced again at his hand: there was nothing, no blood, he was still standing in the same place where he got up from the pavement, he reached into his pocket, it was empty, the money was gone, to hell with it, it was less than a hundred, he wasn't sorry about that but then he was seized by a feeling of panic: his keys, good Lord, if he'd lost the keys to his building and his flat and had to ring at a neighbour's door and explain … phew, the keys were there, they hadn't taken his keys… what about his ID, he dreaded the idea of having to go to the police and explain, apply for a duplicate, but his hand felt the ID in the inside pocket… so all they had taken was money, thirty or forty crowns, and they had to whack him on the head just for that… only now did he realise what had happened… the ghost he'd heard behind his back that had evaporated again into the dirty night air by the time he opened his eyes. He would now have to trudge home on foot, his left leg was hurting a little, but it wasn't too bad, he had no money for a taxi, he couldn't tell a cabbie: "Let me just pop upstairs for the money", he couldn't show his face to a cabbie, who knows what state his face was in. After passing the Cinema for the Discerning

Viewer he turned into the street he had come along … he'd fallen down, there was probably a gash on his face from taking a tumble and being out cold… or a bump on his head… and this would happen just now, with the funeral only three days away… suddenly he felt incredibly sorry for himself: he was innocent this time and yet he'd been disfigured like this, just when he was completely blameless… how many times had he wandered around the other side of Rybná Gate among the tarts and the Gypsies and the rest of the underworld without getting into harm's way, how many times had he staggered home so hammered he couldn't even remember how he got there the next morning, anyone could have whacked him on the head in that state without having to lurk behind his back, but nothing had ever happened… and it had to happen just now, when everyone would be able to see… he started to feel desperately, unutterably, indescribably sorry for himself, choked with a grief that was quite irrational; he was sobbing and tears ran down his cheeks as he walked back home, all alone, up the street with its dilapidated houses… he couldn't stop his tears, the sobbing and weeping… he must have shed more tears and sobbed for longer than on that first evening, as he leant against the doorframe of his sister-in-law's flat… if at least he'd been guilty of something… he kept wiping the tears away with the back his hand and felt nothing, his brain stopped registering the familiar places, he didn't even look ahead, only down at the ground, his only thought being to get back home, to reach the other end of the *korzo*, Štefánka, where he would turn into a street that went up the hill. Eventually he managed to drag himself to the bottom of the turn, climbing slowly, exhaustedly as if climbing his own Golgotha … as if he had smashed all the past few days' preparations for the funeral to smithereens.

Once home he headed straight for the bathroom and inspected himself in the mirror. He couldn't see anything on his face. He was baffled. He felt his face and head again: nothing.

But he had fallen down on the ground, he had lain there, with his cheek on the pavement. And yet there was no trace of that to be seen anywhere. Perhaps it was just his brain as it reacted to the brandy, after being worn out by the woes that had intensified over the past weeks and days, and the steps he heard behind his back were merely a hallucination before he lost consciousness triggering an uncontrollable burst of self-pity. Still breathless, yet exhausted by the events, he decided to take a slightly bigger dose of his sleeping pills than usual. He went to bed without checking what time it was. What an idiotic idea, he kept repeating to himself, how could he have come up with such an idiotic idea, going back into town to see it the way he'd seen it for the first time, as a child, on a walk with his mother.

Even after climbing under the duvet and turning off the light, he kept telling himself: what an idiotic day, stupid day, it was pointless spending hours scribbling notes, pointless paying a visit to the professor and completely pointless giving him the notes, the only point of sitting there was to have his glass of Metaxa repeatedly topped up. Then he had a conversation with his old not-quite-flame, maybe it wasn't even her, he'd only caught a brief glimpse of her face as she turned for a few seconds and looked at a passing car, standing a few steps behind her in the dark... it might have been a complete stranger that he had obsessed about on his way home, imagining a conversation during which she kept reminding him of the past... most likely it hadn't been her at all, just the brandy taking over his brain... and after he got home he came up with this idea, this chimera of seeing the city through the eyes of his childhood ... what an idiotic, stupid day... stupid, stupid day, idiotic and stupid day, stupid day, idiotic day, stupid day...

He kept repeating this, holding back his tears, until he fell asleep.

THE FIFTH DAY

This section of the manuscript has been lost. In it the author gave an account of a visit he paid Edo Friš and his wife Soňa. An important part of the context is that she helped him organise the coach to take the funeral guests to Martin and inform them of the arrangements.

When he came home, he found his bed just as he had left it after getting up in the morning: he hadn't made it, so he couldn't now stretch out in his jumper and trousers and cover himself with a blanket but would have to put his pyjamas back on. However, he couldn't get Edo out of his head and sat on the sofa thinking of him. Edo had always been thin, of a slender build, but now he looked as brittle as glass, or precious china… and given his insanely high blood pressure he was likely to be the next to go. So how come he was so focused on the future? Zora had stopped caring about the future long before she fell ill. Nor did he believe that any kind of future awaited him in this country. Something would change one day, but he was too old to live to see it… Yet this friend of his, although he had very little time left, hadn't given up hope that he would live to see it… not least perhaps because he had a ten-year-old daughter… and a relatively young wife who could still translate many more books… but even Edo himself… perhaps subconsciously, might be reluctant to leave the world in its current state, this was the world he had fought for after the war, in those years he was brimming with self-confidence, in his arrogance he disdained everyone who still thought with his own head, regarding him as a café creep and would find it easier to depart this world if he could leave his mark now that he no longer held high office, had no official car and had turned his back on his own past, the past that had caught up with him… now when he had so little time left and had turned so fragile and brittle.

A long, insistent ringing of the doorbell startled him awake. He scrambled up from the bed and went over to press the button in the hallway, hastily pulling on his trousers and slipping on his jumper.

Peter the writer was standing in the doorway dressed all in black, like a smart messenger sent by some otherworldly undertakers. "Hello," he said in a mournful, subdued voice. He lived nearby, lower down the same street on the hill above the city. Peter would turn up at their place only three or four times a year, and so was the last person he was expecting to see now.

"Is this a good time? You weren't about to go out?" Peter asked. "No, not at all," he assured him, adding: "Some friends invited me for lunch and I dozed off afterwards."

Had Peter come to offer his condolences, he wondered? Would he be the one to present them in the most clichéd way? Several days had passed and he had met all sorts of people, but nobody had yet offered their condolences. It was as if they didn't think it appropriate to express their condolences to him, since he could now, after all, feel liberated, unconstrained. Having settled in the living room armchair and stretching his long legs out far in front of him, Peter said: "You can imagine how this news has affected me." He was sitting upright, rubbing his forehead with his hand. Then he said: "Someone called me the very first evening." So he wasn't going to offer his condolences, although something of the kind was bound to follow, otherwise he wouldn't have come.

"Your wife was an exceptional person," he began, after taking a deep breath, and paused after this first brief sentence. Then he went on.

A custom had developed, not only in *Kultúrny život*, which had been banned for three years now, but lately also in the dailies, of marking the death of a distinguished person not just by a black-framed obituary written by another person of distinction who was still alive, but also a series of brief "reflections" as they were called, solemn meditative pieces by other writers or, if the distinguished person wasn't a writer, by other colleagues from their profession. Since Peter was also a banned writer, he had now come to deliver his "reflection" in person. Apparently deep in thought, he proceeded to sketch a portrait of Zora, as it gradually took shape in his mind, transforming it into articulate, cliché-free sentences.

He must have worked on it at home, he may even have typed it up, not for his sake, not so that he could recite it to him here, but for future reference, so that – once the ban on him was lifted – he could publish his notebooks, including the thoughts that "had cried out to be written down" the other night, when he received the phone call.

He watched Peter intently, not because he expected to hear anything new or perhaps even unpleasant about himself, but because he was fascinated by these concise, perfectly-honed sentences and this whole, seemingly spontaneous, performance. As he articulated each sentence, Peter would stare absent-mindedly into a distant corner of the room, paying him only fleeting attention when he paused. Subconsciously he realised that it wasn't for his sake that Peter had come, not at all; he'd come because he considered it his duty to his wife: she had helped him out quite a few times in the past, so he had reason to feel obliged to her. He recalled how once, when Peter was about to be torn to shreds by one of those campaigns in the fifties, she stood up for him and defended him fiercely, something many people had held against her for a long time, and now basic decency demanded that he should deliver a brief yet, at the same time, completely private eulogy, face to face; but there was also another reason why he had to come to deliver it in person now, namely so that one day he could note in his memoirs that not only had he thought of it at the time but that he had delivered it, too.

Peter finished and he didn't know how to respond. He kept nodding in agreement and said in a quiet voice, as if moved: "Yes." Peter was silent, as if inwardly reciting the Lord's Prayer. He likewise remained silent until he realised he too ought to say something, express his appreciation; after all, Peter was also a playwright and expected applause. So he came up with the sentence: "No one has said a word about her since it happened." He realised immediately that everyone he'd come across over the past few days had said something about her, starting with the people who had come the first night. Peter took a deep breath and exhaled through his nose. He always did this when he was tense, when he was about to make a contribution to a discussion of one of his books, or when he was seething inside, about to explode. Now, too, he inhaled deeply, thoroughly, meditatively, as if sucking all the words he'd said about his wife back from the ether where they were still floating, and burying them in his memory.

The first part of his performance was apparently over, for he got up, straightened his waistcoat and began pacing up and down. That was another thing he did every time he came to visit, on those three or four occasions a year, and whenever he began pacing up and down the room, with those long steps and breathing heavily, it meant he was concentrating on something and collecting his thoughts. It was a stage transition to the next act, he thought. Finally, Peter came to a stop by his side, his head towering high above his, and all he could hear were the words: "So what you should do now is sit down on your backside and write, write, write."

Study, study, study*. A great piece of advice, brilliant, thank you so much: the minute he comes home from the funeral he should sit down on his backside and start writing. He was mildly irritated, forgetting this was the kind of thing people in similar situations were usually told: you must find something else to focus on.

In his case, that meant writing, writing, writing. Actually, Peter had already told him something like that before, a few years after the war, after a play of his had opened. They were in a restaurant, with Peter's young, smart and sophisticated wife by his side. Peter was charitably inclined towards him as he'd written a piece for the theatre programme about his new play which opened that night. On that occasion Peter started chastising him, sounding like a kind teacher: "Some people regard you as our best theatre critic and also quite a decent literary critic, but in my eyes you'll never be a proper theatre critic unless you turn up at every opening night, and you won't be a literary critic unless you write something about every single, at least moderately significant, book by one of our Slovak writers – certainly not as long as you write only when you feel like it." That was some twenty-five years ago, yet he had gone on reviewing new plays only when he felt like it, and books by Slovak authors only if he happened to come across them, because in addition to this, he was also writing about film and, for a time, while on the staff of a daily, also about foreign affairs; he'd also written the odd piece of reportage, even priding himself on some of that work – in fact, not so long ago he wondered if all these writings, if collected, might not make quite a decent book – and, on top of all that, in the past ten years he'd rather enjoyed reflecting with some sophistication on current affairs, citing various thinkers, some of whom he'd actually read, as well as spending a lot of time sitting and drinking in cafés and wine bars and pubs, or just wandering the streets sober, and in all these years the one thing he had never managed to do was precisely what Peter had demanded of him twenty-five years ago and what he was also recommending now: sit on his backside, sit on his backside, sit on his backside. And write and write and write, non-stop, ad infinitum, like a machine. Like Peter. All Peter ever did was write – short stories, feuilletons, novels, triple-decker novels, and plays in between… his biography consisted of his bibliography. Peter had erected a pyramid of paper as a memorial to himself, as someone who disliked him once said, and there was no shortage of those who disliked him, sometimes for rather obscure reasons – not just because he kept sitting on his backside writing, although that was certainly one of the reasons. From time to time, Peter would permit himself to take a mistress, provided she didn't take up too much of his time. So it was quite logical that for the past twenty-five years Peter had regarded him as a shirker, an undisciplined sloth, an aimless dabbler. And he did have a point. His wife had also felt a little like that about him and had wanted to bring some order into his life. But now, in his present situation, he really saw no point in sitting on his backside and writing and writing and writing, and therefore turned to Peter with a weary question:

"And what do you propose I should be writing? And what for?"

"What for?" Peter's irritated voice rang out above his head. Now his visitor was sitting in the armchair again, repeating: "What for, you're asking me, of all people?" He was so upset that his voice actually trembled. Drumming on the table with the fingers of one hand he began to list everything he'd done lately, tossing a new card on the table with each tap: he'd revised his first collection of short stories, originally published after the war… he gave Peter an astonished look, for this was a mélange of wishy-washy metaphors over six hundred pages in length, yet Peter still valued it highly enough to be putting all that work into it now… Then there was the play he'd written in the early fifties … again, he gave him a baffled look … Peter mentioned the play's title…. oh yes, he knew which play he had in mind: there had been something elegant about the way he'd managed to come to terms with socialist realism for the first time… but that was then, why on earth would he want to tinker with it now… However, Peter kept his trump card to the end: he'd recently written a new book of short stories set during the war and the Uprising. He and his wife had discussed it at the time, wondering whether he might choose a different subject this time… And right now he was writing some humorous sketches about his school friends in the city where he used to live. He had to admit it was a remarkable achievement, purely in terms of the sheer volume of work, and Peter concluded with triumphant theatricality: "I could also ask myself, what did I do all of this for? I did it so that I have something 'for the drawer'. But one day I'll take it out of that drawer, or someone else will." He sounded proud. Unable to hold Peter's stare, he lowered his gaze and let his head sink deep into his shoulders. No, he wasn't sitting despondently in an armchair, he was actually lying on the floor, limp after a professional knock-out.

Later, whenever he recalled this visit, he realised that the whole time Peter was listing all the things he'd written "for the drawer", he'd been thinking of Peter's wife, who had lately taken to visiting them on her own from time to time and who still admired him immensely even though after all that time she may well have begun to resent his affairs. She had revealed a number of intimate titbits of family information, mentioning, for example, that every now and then Peter made phone calls to a certain very, very, highly-placed personage in Prague – but of course, nobody was to know about it as that might spoil everything; she was certain the two of them wouldn't say a word about it – and that this highly-placed person had promised to sort things out for him. He and his wife had also known Highly-Placed at one time, but the latter stopped acknowledging him in 1968 even before he became Highly-Placed, by which time he already considered his wife a shady character, some kind of a she-devil, a right-wing opportunist female Satan, but even had she remained in his good books they would have been unlikely to phone him in his current lofty tower. Peter was presenting himself as a shining example but he was only pretending to be writing for the drawer; in fact, day after day he waited impatiently for Highly-Placed to issue an order and as soon as that happened he'd be prepared to submit to a publisher the revised versions of his weighty old doorstoppers, offer another publisher the manuscript of his new novel set during the war and the Uprising, to take the humorous sketches of his school days to the children's publishing house, and the revamped version of his dusted-off early socialist realist works to the theatre, and everyone would be astonished to discover that he hadn't lost hope and that he had kept writing diligently in spite of the prospect of everything remaining in the drawer. But he didn't have Peter's prospects and he couldn't care less about what would happen fifteen or twenty years from now.

He continued to maintain a contrite expression on his face. Peter, who felt he had reason to be satisfied with the impact of the moderately indignant lecture he'd just delivered, stood up again and started pacing up and down the room, returning to his first question: "And you need me to come and tell you what you should do? You've been writing reviews for nearly thirty years. You've also written a couple of quite decent critical studies of some authors and of a few individual works…" – Peter even proceeded to list a few although he had himself forgotten some of them, consigning them to a past that was alien to him now. "Just pick an author, Slovak or foreign, it doesn't matter, study his work, get hold of everything written about him, and write a decent monograph. And then write another."

That's how easy it was. Irritated by Peter's doubtless sensible advice he was, however, unable to restrain himself: "But I don't feel like writing that sort of stuff anymore. The sort of thing I've written before. That's all water under the bridge. I don't like it anymore. And I'm not interested in it."

"Don't be silly!" This time Peter's anger was quite genuine. "Do you think you're the only one in the world to whom this sort of thing has happened? Not so long ago it might have been a little more difficult for me to come to terms with what happened," – he found himself nodding willy-nilly, compelled to show his agreement – "For a while I also thought I was finished, that it was all over and I'd never write again. It took me some time to get over it, but I did." Yes, he was right, it took him some time, but he did get over it. Peter's son had committed suicide shortly before his school-leaving exam. Initially, Peter had been paralysed by grief but he had the disposition of a conscientious journeyman, one who always ends up returning to his trade after a while, and so he had gone back to writing. But he was not like Peter, not a conscientious journeyman. He just wasn't that keen on work. Perhaps he was a layabout, pulled in too many directions, perhaps he didn't like himself enough and that's why he succumbed to something one could easily succumb to in these cases: he had become alienated, so to speak, from himself, from the person he had once been, and from what he used to do. Something inside him had cracked a long time ago and his wife was the only one who had noticed but even she was not sure what was going on inside him – and neither was he. There was no point telling Peter something he himself wasn't able to articulate and explain properly, so he pretended to be lost in thought for a while and then, without knowing quite what he was about to say, he just blurted out the first thing that came into his head: "Except perhaps something quite different from the earlier stuff... some fiction, for instance."

As soon as he uttered these words he was ashamed, writing even a single page of fiction being the last thing he'd ever fancied doing. He was embarrassed to have blurted out such nonsense.

Naturally, Peter latched on to it. "What? Fiction?" And then he started picking at him with a sneer: "I see, so you do have a story in your head, do you? So what's it going to be, a short story, a novel?"

"No, I've got nothing in my head. I was just babbling. It was just an example."

"Thank God for that. Look, you've been blessed with a brilliant analytical brain. You're good at analysing literature. You've proved it any number of times. That's your profession. And now that you can't spread yourself thin anymore, as you've done all your life, you can at last concentrate on one thing and you can really give it your all."

He didn't say a word. There was no point telling Peter what he didn't feel like talking about. For Peter, life was a straight line, just like in his books. So he chose to stay silent.

"OK, I won't bother you with that any longer," Peter was obviously about to move on to his next point because he was once again pacing the room determinedly, "but please don't get upset about one more thing that I have to say to you." As always, as in every debate, he'd planned it all out in advance, points one, two, three. It was now the turn of point three. Peter sat down again and nervously started drumming his fingers on the table, as if feeling shy and fidgety, as obviously something unpleasant was about to follow. "Why would I get upset: out with it," he encouraged him. And so Peter started on point three: "You know what I'd been through and believe you me, it was quite difficult for me, too." He believed Peter.

"And I know very well how you feel... This sort of thing always takes it out of you. It's hard to get back on your feet. But you have to get over it. And sometimes that might involve some alcohol, obviously... except that just now you ought to be extra careful."

Why just now? Because there wasn't anyone to keep tabs on him, because there wasn't anyone to consider as he went staggering from pub to pub in a semi-conscious haze, without the thought at the back of his mind that someone was waiting for him at home? Or did he need to be extra careful so that people wouldn't say he could now finally get pissed to his heart's content because he was free, that he could do whatever he liked now that he was rid of his wife?

He said: "Yes, I know. It's occurred to me too." For it really had occurred to him that people might start saying: he must be so happy to be free to get pissed to his heart's content.

Having ticked off point three, Peter got up. As he put on his coat he apologised and explained why he wouldn't be able to come to the funeral: "It's not because I'd have to take a train in the morning and then take a train back in the evening, that's not what it's about." He nodded, for he knew what it was about. Peter could drop in to see him in order to, first, deliver his eulogy, second, to tell him what he ought to be doing, and third, to warn him not to start drinking brazenly. What he couldn't afford to do was attend his wife's funeral where quite a few people might see him. He could not go to Zora's funeral one day and ring Highly-Placed the next. That might ruin everything. "I have to go to the office every day and there's a meeting on the very day of the funeral." He knew Peter didn't have to go to work every day; he'd been given permission to work from home two or three days a week. Shaking Peter's hand he said approvingly: "Of course, you've got a job." And he thanked him for coming: he said he imagined that very few of those in our – he meant writers' – circles would dare turn up here. He didn't want to demean his wife to the point of admitting: you will probably be the only one from those circles to turn up here.

He stood at the open door for a while absent-mindedly and waited for the lift to come to a stop downstairs. Then he walked over to the kitchen window and positioned himself so that he couldn't be seen from below. He wanted to know if Peter had come by car, in which case he would continue down to the city, or if he'd come one foot, in which case he would go back home.

He sat down on the sofa again. He still saw Peter sitting before him, only now more as a shadow, or rather as something translucent. He was telling him again: "And sometimes it might involve some alcohol…" He was speaking from personal experience. He remembered well that in Peter's case some alcohol had been involved. He and his wife had gone to see him five or six days after they heard the news about his son. They knew he had many visitors and decided to delay their visit; he'd rung Peter and thought his voice sounded quite different, aged yet almost shrill. When they showed up they found him sitting in his room as if turned to stone, throughout the time they spent there, almost five hours, he did not get up once to pace up and down the room as was his habit. This is really beyond what a human being can endure, his wife had told him after they had heard the news. Peter said very little, speaking in this altered voice all the time, and then they all sat in silence for a long time. Every now and then he would take a sip from the glass of Cinzano before him. Peter's wife, who had also never used to drink before and for whom this must have been just as much of a disaster, would down each glass in a single gulp, as if she'd been guzzling alcohol all her life, and when the bottle was empty she went to fetch another. He had kept pace with her and the first thing his wife said to him, annoyed, once they emerged into the clear night – they were still living down in the city centre – was that he didn't need to grab the opportunity with both hands and knock all that Cinzano back; he had no reason to, after all. Peter had actually not drunk anything in all that time, he just kept raising the glass to his lips. It seemed to him as if Peter had decided that in his situation he was expected to drink some alcohol when other people were around, he who'd prided himself on being a teetotaller; it was a kind of protocol, a symbolic gesture showing that he was having a breakdown. Everything else about him had been authentic, the way he sat there, turned to stone, the altered, shrill voice and this was the only act he had put on, apparently believing it was appropriate in this situation. And that is why he had now told him: some alcohol might be inevitable…

There was one other thing he suddenly remembered from that visit years ago. Peter had said, in a disjointed way, and kept coming back to the point, that over the past few days it was as if he had seen himself in the mirror for the first time, only to realise that everything he'd written had been worthless. A mountain of paper… Scrap paper… Naturally, he and his wife had tried to convince him it was not the case… Peter finally conceded: if he were to write again, he would start from scratch, from a completely different perspective. He remembered his wife telling him when they came home that that might be the only positive thing to come out of this tragedy, because if that didn't shake him up, he would never change. Some time later Peter published a collection of short stories; his wife had read it eagerly and reported: it seems he didn't really look into the mirror, or maybe he did, but then forgot what he'd seen.

On the other hand, he thought, he had to give it to Peter that he had phrased this reminder... elegantly, as one gentleman to another... "it may involve some alcohol..." Except that all his adult life had involved some alcohol: he had no need of special situations or occasions: that was precisely his problem. As for the rest of the advice Peter had offered... none of it was particularly original, he could shove it... into his drawer. And anyway, he failed to answer his question as to why he should sit down on his backside and write something. But thinking of Peter, he thought of at least one possible answer: in order to be someone. Because, obviously, that was what really mattered: to be someone. When Peter rewrote something he had published in the past, or wrote something new, he could be pleased with himself: I am someone, not one of those countless nobodies, I have left a mark... He, on the other hand, had been quite happy to live a secluded life just with his wife for the past two or three years. Being an anonymous zero. Zora needed him, and that was enough for him. One day, about a year ago, she had said to him: I have completed my life's work, and that was enough, she felt, even though in the end she too had been reduced to an anonymous zero. And although he couldn't really say that he had done his life's work, he had reached a certain point – he didn't know why, he just knew that at some point something had happened to him and he no longer cared about being someone.

He couldn't really claim to have completed his life's work: he was anything but satisfied with his life, having dabbled in all kinds of things that had happened to take his fancy at a particular time or that he had to do in order to earn his monthly salary. He'd spent his life messing about. But at least he could contend that he had lived for half a century. And that there was always something happening in his life. Perhaps the only worthwhile thing in his life was indeed the fact that he had actually lived for fifty years. But from now on he would have to find a way of killing time, of filling the void, all by himself.

But the one thing he wouldn't do was sit down on his backside and write, he was quite certain of that. Produce analyses, or perhaps case studies. He ought to try to find a way of making this clear to an imaginary Peter whom he now saw sitting before him, motionless. It was only right and proper of Peter to come to see him, and so it would be right and proper for him to explain why his advice on how to live was no use to him. He felt like talking but didn't know what to say.

He turned his eyes away from the imaginary Peter and towards the window, as if expecting some revelation from there. And the revelation did come: he would pop out for a bottle of wine, have a drink and that would get his brain going.

He quickly put on his winter coat and clutching a shopping bag he bounded down the stairs and dashed down the street as if on wings, turning into a wide boulevard lined with Jugendstil houses on one side and on the other the Grassalkovich Palais with its enormous park that had been open to ordinary folk before the victory of the working classes. For most of his life, this street had been named after Štefánik* and only once the historians of the new era of humankind discovered that this national hero was an ordinary French spy was it renamed The Street of the Defenders of the Peace – a highly appropriate name under Stalin, since in those days the entire peace camp was engaged in fighting for peace on all fronts, by labouring in the factories and in the fields, with every show trial a slap in the face of the warmongers, every individual hanged another slap in the face of the warmongers, every prisoner slaving in uranium mines yet another slap in the face of the warmongers, and when he, and his wife, and many others were banned from publishing, that too was undoubtedly a further slap in the face of the warmongers. On the corner, at the end of the street closest to the city centre, stood Café Štefánka, normally the nearest place he could get a bottle of wine, but he might run into someone he knew there... yes of course, the poet E. B. Lukáč could be seen there every afternoon, old but still sprightly, a Lutheran pastor in his youth who had once demanded the expulsion of all unworthy members from the Union of Slovak Writers included in a list supplied from on high. A telegram from Lukáč had arrived as early as the day before yesterday – he was the first to send his condolences – and he would be there today as well, surrounded as always by an entourage of young admirers. Respected and incorruptible, a man of integrity who had never joined the communist party, he would surely give him a wave, repeat his condolences and invite him to join him at the table... and that was why he was now walking in the opposite direction towards the Dax, even though it was a little further; the Dax went by a different name now but to him it would always be the Dax, where the chances of being spotted by someone he knew were minimal because they would all be at the the Writers' Club across the road.

The Dax was back in full swing after Christmas Day when everything was closed; the place was heaving with people and shrouded in thick bluish smoke. He had to settle for a 0.75 bottle, as they didn't have one-litre ones, but three-quarters of a litre was enough, he would have just a small drink now, to get his juices going, and leave the rest until the evening when Agneša had promised to come round with the second eulogy. In a way he was grateful to Peter for filling up his afternoon; in fact, every one of these last few days since it had happened, had been quite successful in a way, as he'd had things to organise all the time, people to see, dashing around making arrangements here and sorting things out there, and tomorrow he would go to Martin... the funeral was the day after tomorrow… that would be the last day he'd have something to do. Two more full days and then he would be free to lock himself in his flat like a hermit, leaving only at lunchtime to grab something to eat or pop out to the supermarket for a bottle of something, and should he start missing the world, he would dive into a pub where no one knew him, assuming he wasn't too drunk to give a damn. But just now time had not yet come to a standstill, the imaginary Peter was still waiting for him at home and he had something to tell him, though what that something was, he wasn't quite sure himself.

And sure enough, there he was, sitting in the armchair, a motionless and shadowy figure, ready to listen and to do nothing but listen, but he first had to go to the kitchen, open the bottle and pour himself a glass. He knocked it back, poured himself some more, and then sat down facing Peter. He felt his eyes upon him while, at the same time, he could feel the wine making his body sway gently back and forth and relax, but in his head nothing stirred and all he could hear was some static. He went back to the kitchen, topped up his glass, and as he was returning to the imaginary Peter with his glass of wine, it suddenly dawned on him what his sweeping monologue should focus on – for he still had plenty of time that he needed to fill with some incisive ruminations, so he launched straight into it:

"Now, let me tell you what I actually wanted to tell you, why I'm not going to write any critical studies or analyses or any other kinds of clever stuff." And now, without further ado, he thought, get straight to the point: "To begin with, let me say something that will sound quite stupid and awfully banal, but there's no way around it, it's a fact. The main problem is that we were born at the wrong time. What I mean is that as a result of when we were born, we kept finding ourselves in the most awful historical situations of every kind. At least we, the people in our generation. Don't laugh, I know this sounds very crude," he admonished Peter, who was not laughing at all, "but if you look at the history of anything, you can detect major and minor periods, times when things flourish, as well as times that in astronomers' terms are black holes. Shakespeare was a genius, as was Marlowe and a few of his predecessors and contemporaries, but after this flowering the Puritans suddenly came and bang – a black hole. As for us, we've done nothing but scrabble about from one black hole to another. By the time I graduated from *gymnázium* the war had started and I couldn't go to university, but that's all ancient history now; I started writing soon after that anyway, most of it got published, sometimes under a pseudonym, sometimes under my own name, but otherwise I just drifted about until the end of the war, living from one day to the next in a state of uncertainty that was quite exciting, but that, too, is another story. There's something else I wanted to tell you about those days: Mikuláš Bakoš, one of my literature teachers in my final year of *gymnázium*, grew very fond of me because I was the only one who found books riveting and the only one in class who didn't roar with laughter when he read out surrealist poetry to us – that was what he liked most and preferred it to sticking to the curriculum. And so I continued to see him at his home after I graduated. Being a theoretician, he was the leading light of the local surrealists, our very own André Breton, and besides he was the only Slovak structuralist, having imported the entire Prague linguistic circle to Bratislava both physically and intellectually. When I visited him, whatever we talked about, whether it was a new book or the latest issue of *Elán*, the literary monthly which was printed on glossy paper, it would be a kind of tutorial that taught me how to approach a particular book or article or review from the structuralist perspective. And of course, he made me read Mukařovský as well as Jakobson and Shklovsky and other Russians linguists from the 1920s, I forget some of the names. He was truly a fanatical devotee of his faith. And so it was quite natural that, whenever I managed to stop messing about and rise to intellectual heights, I would always have structuralism buzzing around my head. Nevertheless, even though I read all kinds of things in those days, certainly more than at any other time in my life, even surrealist poetry by Slovak authors, some of which I reviewed at the instigation of this fanatic, though I couldn't really make head or tail of them, my first love was the cinema – I would go and see every movie, irrespective of its quality. So no wonder that one day I came to the following conclusion: if there was a structuralist theory of literature, a structuralist theory of film must also be possible. And having been so inspired, I felt I was qualified to create it. I wrote it impetuously, in a fragmented way, skipping from one topic to the next, and the whole thing must have been completely amateurish, but I lived and breathed it. And I may have made a valid point or two, arguing for example against renowned theorists of the day who still viewed the talkies as the art of moving pictures, whereas I had made the discovery that film was really visual and epic narrative, thus resolving the relationship between word and image in film. Now, this was during the war, on the whole not a particularly productive period in Europe, with everyone around me, too, living from one day to the next, but then came the day that the war was at an end and we had peace and freedom and political parties and democracies. I forgot about my magnum opus, never adding a single sentence to it. *Citizen Kane* and *Ivan the Terrible* hit our screens, but I had developed my theory on the basis of films shown during the war, most of them trash, and I realised that I would have had to rework my theory, modify it, and besides, I was sure that someone in some other part of the world must have come up with the same idea long ago, most likely at some American university, and that this person would have had the expertise and erudition to write it up. So I thought of that opus of mine as a closed chapter. A new world, a new life had dawned after all: there were so many things that needed

writing about and it all came gushing out of me like a suddenly unblocked geyser. Admittedly, all of it just served the
needs of the day. But at that time everyone lived for the needs
of the day. We had all the prerequisites, and yet there was no
blossoming, those years bequeathed nothing of significance
to the future. We had freedom, but sterility had set in. That
historical situation was also derailed, in a way. It was then
that people first became dull-witted, albeit not in the same
way as later; perhaps this was because everyone likes a win-
ner and even though we all dutifully repeated the mantra
about having endured a great deal of suffering, which had
become a new national virtue, and all the Czechs and Slovaks
felt they were winners, although in fact no one had truly
come to terms with the countless horrors and privations that
had ravaged this continent through the endless years of war.
In our minds it had all turned into an abstraction, into the
victory we deserved, and that was all. While people continued
to starve to death and be brutally slaughtered all over the
continent, including in this country, although buildings in our
country survived intact, our world was broken and nothing
remained of what had existed before the war. But soon a new
era dawned, a new era for mankind, the most glorious period
in our history. And since there were many who would not
have realised of their own accord that this historic turning
point had opened up to them the vista of a wonderful future
and that they were finally living in a country where today
already meant tomorrow, everyone, just to be on the safe side,
had to be subjected to psychiatric treatment, stuffed to the
gills with tried and tested Soviet injections and pills administered to patients in hospital before surgery – downers, as
the medical profession calls them. After a while I, too, recognised that I had been a shilly-shallying intellectual and that
the driving forces, which determine everything all the way
unto the innermost recesses of human lives with an apoca-
lyptic inevitability, demand that all intellectuals, like the

halfwits in a psychiatric ward, endlessly repeat a few basic magic formulae until the final, seventh and most secret chamber opens up before them. And so I, too, spent a couple of years completely doped up, staggering around as if in a trance, until yet another series of arrests and the run-up to the greatest show trial of them all* finally awakened something in my brain – this was the time when Mňačko and I would go for a stroll around the park almost daily, trying to decipher, in whispers, what kind of world we were living in. That was when I realised that I had stumbled into yet another stupid historical situation. Later I got hold of some Polish newspapers and was astonished to read, in black and white, everything I had only intuited, fearfully, like a sleepwalker. But people in our country took a very long time to awaken from the trance and once their brains started to tick over again, they learned, in a groping, tentative way, only a fraction of what I had read in the Polish papers years earlier. And even when everyone, myself included, started opening their mouths, we were, as ever, a nation of epigones who discovered America long after Columbus. As time went by, I got hold of some books and journals from the West: not everything was brilliant but again I was astonished to learn that everywhere else normal civilisation had carried on quite happily ever since the war and gradually we started to discover what other Columbuses in the West had discovered before us. It wasn't until our brains were thoroughly cleansed and we became fully functional again that we suddenly understood that instead of drawing on what happened right after the war, we should be drawing on what we had before 1938 and all of a sudden, there was an explosion of great books and great films, we started to feel equal to the rest of the world, and prepared to return to civilisation – but just at that point the Soviet tanks rolled in, ushering in yet another stupid historical situation. Widespread psychiatric treatment was again the order of the day, Soviet injections and local downers were being dispensed, and it didn't matter that people had become resistant and were just pretending, they did it with so much conviction that they convinced even themselves and soon could no longer remember that only recently they had lived in a normal, civilised world, and in their resignation they settled down again somewhere on a Galapagos Island amongst prehistoric dinosaurs. This time I didn't have to convince myself that I was a shilly-shallying intellectual, injections and downers were not offered to individuals whose existence was tolerated only as a kind of living "dead souls", who were not wanted on the Galapagos amongst the dinosaurs and were banned from everywhere. And this situation would last until some day, who knows when, ten-fifteen years from now something nearby would stir again, the Poles would reawaken, maybe the Hungarians too, whereas in this country everyone would continue to snore away. And now imagine that right at the onset of this latest historical situation, whose end is nowhere in sight, here I am sitting on my backside and writing something addressed to those in a future that is totally uknown to me… a future that will undoubtedly arrive at some point in eternity, making the people in this country, too, awaken, rub their eyes, look around, re-acquaint themselves with normal civilisation, and at that point some person or persons unknown will unearth those sheets of paper I typed up a long time ago, browse through them, and exclaim with surprise and admiration: just look at all the work and effort that the wretched guy had poured into it but it's now all totally out of date, an antique, of no interest whatsoever, and this person or persons unknown will take it all and deposit it in some warehouse of ancient manuscripts. No, thank you. Writing one provincial theory of film is quite enough for me. So forgive me, this is the reason I blurted out that if I ever write something again, it would have to be something quite different, some work of fiction. Something that could be written anywhere, including on the Galapagos, in the solitude of time and space. Fiction, poetry... made-up stories. However, I'm no good at writing fiction, poetry or made-up stories, and that is why I won't sit down on my backside.

Only now did he notice that Peter, opposite him, had become so shadowy that he must have vanished completely without him noticing. He must have taken offence at something in his long monologue. Peter, too, opposed radical psychiatric treatment but he went on swallowing a reasonable dose of pills, self-prescribing them with caution: he needed them because they made it easier for him to write his short stories, his long novels consisting of several volumes as well as humorous sketches, the odd play, poetry for children and opera librettos. He wished Highly-Placed would sort things out for Peter soon. So that he got his wish and was happy.

But what about the professor, he thought, a scintilla of doubt creeping into his brain, the professor he'd gone to see yesterday and who was going to give the eulogy tomorrow; he was now studying Dante and the heavy tomes he'd brought back from Paris so that he could later sit down on his backside and write – just as Peter had advised him. After giving it some thought he decided that the similarity was purely coincidental. The professor was older than him, from another generation, was able to get a university degree, literature had always been the only centre of his universe and the yardstick by which he had measured every regime, detesting every regime that bullied literature. He had never allowed himself to be injected or stuffed with pills, and had as a result been fired from his job at the university, but was allowed to return to teaching after many years, travel to Paris last summer, and although he nearly starved to death, he came home with a suitcase full of books on Dante, and his library now had everything ever written about Dante by neostructuralists and poststructuralists and semioticians, social anthropologists and esoteric essayists and historians of the Annales School in Paris, and he was living among his books from the civilised world rather than here on the Galapagos, and would draw on these resources to write something and have it published in six months or twelve, depending on the production schedule. Not in fifteen or twenty years, or more. The professor wasn't writing for distant, future generations.

He was the professor's opposite in every respect. He lacked any kind of focus. He was an amateur dabbler. He had squandered his life. Nonsense, that wasn't quite true either. He had spent a considerable part of his life sitting on his backside and writing. He had often been inspired. And sometimes his work was even of a decent standard. He had written a number of things he had no need to be ashamed of. He just couldn't find his place in the world. His wife had once reproached him for keeping his distance from everything and perhaps that was what made him look for some direction. Perhaps that was a kind of a turning point for him, but he needed a little more time to figure himself out. But it was too late... Oh well, yet again it was the times that were to blame for everything. Obviously, one didn't live in a vacuum. He had certainly felt the full, brutal impact of the times he lived in. On occasion the times even help a minor talent to flourish, while on the other hand they can deform a genius. His talent was somewhere in between, and he'd been unlucky with those historical circumstances.

Having said that, he had squandered much of his life as well. And so what? Was the number of lines he'd written the only measure of his life? Or the number of typewriter ribbons he'd used up, the quantity of printers' ink used up for his publications? And what if he had squandered even more of his life: never mind, the totality of one's life didn't amount to the aggregate of one's output, whether or not it had achieved anything. For decades he had been a witness to something that was subject to continuous change. For decades he had been this slightly crazy outsider who preferred to stand on the shore gazing at the water, watching its ebb and flow, its changing colours and and its varying degrees of murkiness, seeing the waves rise heavenward before returning to a limpid calmness. He had lived. And it had been a variegated life. What did it matter that very little of what he'd been through left pleasant memories, what did it matter that most of it had been ugly, repellent, and – most often – pathetically shallow? There had been an awful lot of it over all those years, an entire ocean. And whenever and wherever he cast his net, he always managed to catch something. His memory was his ocean. And that would never change.

He remained sitting in his armchair, his head empty of thoughts. Then he glanced at his watch. Agneša was due tonight and he may have to go over some of the text with her before he could finish in peace and quiet the bottle of wine that was awaiting him in the kitchen. Maybe he should use this time to pack his bag for tomorrow's trip.

He got up, found a suitcase in a wardrobe in the hallway and packed his things. First the clothes he was wearing at his sister-in-law's on Christmas Eve – the black suit, white shirt, black tie, black socks, black shoes. Next the two records with Janáček's Moravian or Lachian songs, some of which would be played at the funeral, at the start, in the intervals, and at the end, while the coffin was carried out. He made sure he had the piece of paper where he had noted which sections of the two records should be played and in what order. His sleeping pills, another thing he mustn't forget. He went into the kitchen and wrapped a few in a napkin. And a tranquilliser for good measure. He wasn't going to take a book to read on the train. Or his slippers. He'd go straight to the hotel in the evening, go to bed and in the morning he would get up and get dressed, no need for slippers. But he made himself a note: shaving things. Tomorrow morning he'd shave at home and the next morning in the hotel. Oh, and the paperwork from the funeral parlour. And the money, which he had fortunately taken out of his pocket last night: he'd need all of it, not just for the train fare and the hotel, but also for any extra payments at the funeral parlour, and there might be other expenses as well. He surveyed the contents of the suitcase. Of course, he'd forgotten his pyjamas. This had happened to him at least twice before, forgetting to pack his pyjamas, so to be on the safe side, he went over to the linen cupboard straight away and packed a clean pair, in case he forgot about it again in the morning. Was that all? Yes, that was all. The small black suitcase was still half empty.

He went back to the living room which had gone dark a long time ago but he hadn't switched on the light while he was talking to the imaginary Peter. He leaned back in the armchair, stretched out his legs and waited.

Agneša arrived quite early actually, soon after seven, or perhaps it was already eight. On the doorstep behind her stood a tall, well-built man in a fur hat which made him look even taller. "Look who I've brought you," Agneša announced, as if she had come with his best friend, except that he had no best friend. He had met Roman, a former journalist, a hundred times, they would always say hello to each other and exchange a few words. For a few years Roman had been on the staff of *Kultúrny život*, had left before the journal was banned and gone to work for the TV. He hadn't seen him for years now, but Roman shook his hand as if they had met just the other day, conveying his condolences fervently, at the top of his voice and with a cheerful smile, as if he was pleased to see him again and congratulating him on his birthday, "I have brought him along specially," said Agneša. He pointed to the hangers for their coats, "no, we'll be on our way very soon, you'll see why," Roman said with a hint of mystery, as Agneša headed for the living room as she knew her way around the place. He had left the kitchen door open and now he noticed that she glanced that way: in the glare of the neon light from the street the bottle of wine stood out on the table: what an idiot I am, he thought: I knew there was someone coming, I should have put it away. But Agneša was already opening the living room door, Roman followed suit, and didn't notice anything. She stopped under one of the ceiling shades and apologised for being slightly late, but she had to go and see Roman first. "It's all done though," she announced triumphantly, taking a few folded sheets of paper from her handbag and handing them to him. She asked him to read it and tell her what he thought.

He offered them a seat and was about to settle in his armchair with the papers, but Roman said that the two of them had been sitting for long enough. "It'll be better if we don't sit down, you'll see." He couldn't see why it would be better that way and thought Roman must have had a drink or two. He started to read without sitting down.

The beginning was fine, stating, just as he'd required, that something needed to be said about the last three years of her life, "This is what I would like to speak about as I have known her only during those three years," the girl would say, and then it continued along the lines of what he'd told Agneša off the top of his head, what he'd memorised, not word for word but in the same style, then came a passage he wasn't very happy with but it wasn't too bad; the next bit was fine again, ah, here is something she has added but it fits in quite well, then another bit that was fine and then again he thought, hm, I would have worded this slightly differently, and he started to worry whether she would keep it up to the end. Yes, this bit was just what he had in mind, but then there was something again that wasn't quite right, he pressed his lips together and screwed up his eyes, and then it was fine again, then not so good and again, another good stretch... the whole thing wasn't quite what he'd envisaged, but then again, she couldn't have written exactly what he'd wanted, as he'd given her only a brief outline after all, the gist: it should include this, that and the other, and it was all there, only in her own words, that was probably what bothered him a little. So he looked up from the final sheet and said: "Yes, I think that'll do. Everything that should be in it is there."

Roman chipped in straight away, as if on cue, disagreeing: "Come on, old chap, I know what you're really thinking, you think it will do but it's not really up to scratch." Standing close to him, Roman pointed with his finger to three lines almost at the end of the first page – now he understood why it was more convenient to remain standing: Roman was nearly a head taller than he was and could see the text and point out individual lines, underline individual sentences with a finger while the manuscript remained in his hand. "See, this bit is too casual, this won't do in a eulogy," he said, taking the first page from his hands, pointing with his finger and saying, "or this"… "or this here…", and he took another page from his hand, "and this bit here, I couldn't believe it, it's far too light-hearted, as if she was writing a birthday card for a friend"… he felt quite embarrassed to hear him put Agneša down like that, but she just stood there smiling happily, pleased with the clever idea she'd had… "and this… just take a look at this sentence, an ordinary twenty-something working-class girl would never say that; it sounds too intellectual." He pulled a face and pointed to another line, "… or this", and then he picked up the last two sheets and without pointing at particular lines just offered a summary: "She's made it sound as casually sophisticated as if she were writing a feuilleton for that paper of hers. It needs to be raised to a completely different level, licked into shape so that it sounds solemn and dignified." Although he was commenting on style, his voice filled the room as if he were a village lad coltishly calling out to his sweetheart raking hay on a hill half a kilometre away. No, not a lad, he was more of a somewhat care-worn manual labourer charging with fellow striking protesters with fists raised at a line of policemen, shouting: "We want bread, we want justice!" Not that long ago there would be a scene like that in virtually every Slovak film. He was basically the kind of fellow who, after a few drinks, was liable to get up and launch into the folksong "Three times they chased me... and three times they will hang me," and sing it exactly as it ought to be sung. He was the outlaw type. And true enough, in 1968 he had produced television reports on political outlaws who would hold people up and who ended on the gallows.

But the outlaw went on: "I've told her already," he said looking down at Agneša who was the shortest of them all, barely coming up to Roman's shoulders. "So here's the deal: I'll take it home, rewrite it tonight and bring it over tomorrow morning at nine. It will be so good you won't have to change anything, not even a comma. Agreed?"

He agreed, of course. "Well, wasn't that a good idea of mine?" Agneša asked. This was the first time she smiled at him in a while, since her husband had been arrested if not longer. "Yes, brilliant," he said, but Agneša had already turned to Roman: "So, let me show you around here." "What for?" Roman asked, genuinely indignant. "It says it all here." – "But if you are to rewrite it in your own words, you should have seen the place for yourself," she said, reminding him of some basic principles of professional journalism.

The four best paintings they owned hung on the wall above his wife's desk. Playing the role of the guide, Agneša pointed to each picture and named the painter. He sneaked out to the kitchen to put the bottle of wine in the fridge and the glass in the sink. On his return he found them standing by the coffee table next to the bookcase where the tiny pots of cacti were lined up. It reminded him that he'd completely forgotten to water the plants today.

As they moved over to his wife's room, he turned the light on for them. They would, of course, immediately notice the painting he disliked but hadn't yet taken down. He heard her giving the painter's name and to prevent Roman from looking too closely at the powdered, mask-like face of the artist's

Beatrice, he joined their conversation, explaining the view it depicted and which way it was facing. "Aaah, I see," Roman intoned happily, immediately giving the name of the village visible at the bottom of the painting, in the last rays of the setting sun. Just as he expected, all of these laddish outlaw characters came from a village on this, or the far, side of those mountains. So now he lingered in front of the painting for a while, admiring it.

Alongside the large window in his wife's room that opened into the garden hung two broad folds of linen or canvas with red embroidery. "These were her mother's, she collected folk craft of this kind," he said. Two small pieces of embroidery, framed and under glass like paintings, hung on the door. There were two more tables with flower pots of various sizes. And huge ones in the corners of the room.

They went back to the living room and moved on to the kitchen. Five framed lithographs from the previous century hung on the narrow wall above the bench. His wife had them framed together, separated by wooden dividers. They showed young lads and strapping lasses in folk costume. Their figures and faces were actually not rendered in detail, unlike the folk costumes from the various regions of the country they were wearing. For some reason, in those days this kind of thing was thought to instil national pride. "Now, this is really precious," said Roman with admiration and Agneša drew his attention to some old ceramic plates. Roman fixed on the one with a a bird and a pattern of branches and read in out in astonishment: "A little birdie sang in a mountain pine… why is *ptáča*, birdie, spelled with a p, not a v?" – "Perhaps it's in Western Slovak dialect."

Agneša led the way to his room. But that had only contemporary art, a coloured drawing in India ink by a famous contemporary Chinese painter, which had no connection to the funeral, and there was another small table with plants. They returned to the hallway.

Agneša asked Roman to turn around and face the mirror. "Everyone just passes by, but you must take a look at all these things." By the side of the mirror, in several rows from top to bottom, hung various small ceramic plates. Roman dutifully ran his eyes up and down them three times and declared: "Well, I'm really glad I saw all this. So we'll be off now and I'll come back tomorrow at nine," he said offering his hand. But Agneša chided him: "Hold on a minute, you haven't seen the garden yet." – "Oh please, it's gone dark, what is there to see?" "You'll get a general impression at least." He fetched a torch, went down with them, and led them out into the garden.

It was pitch dark. What moonlight there remained was obscured by thick clouds; snow was falling. "It's snowing," he said, surprised and almost pleased by this change. They had not yet had any proper snow this winter. "Haven't you noticed?" Agneša asked, "it's been snowing for at least an hour."

He wasn't sure which way to point the torch, as it illuminated only a narrow circle a few steps ahead, but Agneša took it from his hand, found a narrow path up the slope and, to prove that it was worth going down to the garden in the dark, kept talking: about the crocuses that grew down below as well as the extensive patches of a particular moss, and higher up there were daisies and… all kinds of shrubs even further up, and right at the top Zora had planted a few young trees but only one had survived, and as Agneša talked she pointed the light the way she went and then swung it round behind her so that Roman could follow in her footsteps. When they got back to the house Roman said: "I saw absolutely nothing." "But you did see that the whole garden is on a slope," Agneša pointed out. Shining the torch three or four steps behind her again she added: "And she had to clear all this ground." Although it was obvious that he couldn't see the area Zora had had to clear, Roman said: "Oh yes, I have a better idea now." "There, so it was worth taking a look at the garden," Agneša concluded and gave him the torch back.

Once they were indoors, Roman offered his hand again. "We're not going back with you. I'm sure you'll understand, I've got to write it up." He walked them to the front yard even though he was in his slippers, and kept saying how pleased he was… They parted ways at Agneša's car.

He turned off the kitchen light and leant on the window frame. He watched with delight as the snowflakes floated in the air. There were not many of them and they seemed frostbitten, fluttering to and fro in the air as if dancing, each snowflake doing its own dance. Then he looked down into the courtyard, thinking his two visitors were about to come out and get into their car. But of course, the car was long gone.

How strange, he thought, they spoke like old friends: Roman addressed him by the diminutive form of his first name – they were indeed on first name terms – and their conversations had always been very friendly, and yet he couldn't recall a specific time or place where they had actually had a conversation. He would often drop in at *Kultúrny život* when Roman was working on the journal's reportage desk and he himself had stopped writing reportage by then, but they would just exchange a few words. Sometimes one of them might have joined a table in a café where the other was sitting with a few colleagues… Only one clear memory remained: the two of them at a table with someone else, at closing time, with nowhere else being open in town, and Roman declaring: "I know where to go, I'll get a cab," and while they waited, he explained that out of the city, just beyond the third village, there was a spa with a restaurant that stayed open till four in the morning. He was puzzled and objected that the taxi ride would cost a fortune, and Roman generously admitted "Well, yes, it's about thirty kilometres," except that when they got there, not only was the restaurant closed but there was also a sign which said that the spa had shut down long ago, so they had to go back with Roman having to fork out two or three hundred crowns for the cab. He was left to scurry back to his flat, which took him another forty-five minutes, because Roman told the driver to take them to where he lived... Later, when he was no longer such a stranger to taking cabs, he realised he could have stayed in the taxi and asked the driver to take him home... it wouldn't have cost him more than ten crowns. But back then, taxis were as exotic to him as a zeppelin. It must have happened a very long time ago, sometime after the victory of the working classes, in the days when all bars and restaurants had to close at midnight: that, too was somehow linked to the victory of the working classes. And the spa next to that village never reopened, at least as far as he knew... But he couldn't recall any other occasion when he was with Roman... He had dozens of acquaintances like this, people he was on first name terms with, but with whom he had nothing in common. Although in this case there was a more personal element to being on first name terms: he had always enjoyed Roman's reportage, which had nothing to do with politics and didn't, therefore, have to include empty clichés. Roman tended to write about quite ordinary people, while Roman himself probably appreciated his expertise in the arts.

He now had to ring the girl. He should have done that as soon as his two visitors had left. She was sitting at home and had probably been waiting for hours, as he promised to come in the early evening. Now it was quite late... He rang her neighbours. They said they would go over and get her to ring him back in five minutes. When she phoned, he apologised in a faltering voice: he was really sorry but his friend had brought the text round later than promised and they'd been working on it until now. The friend had now gone home to rework a few passages and would bring it over in the morning, so could she come over soon after nine.... he was really, truly sorry... Oh, in that case she'd have to ring her boss and say she had to go to the doctor's... yes, he understood, and he was sorry that things had got more complicated...

And now he had to ring his brother. He should be the one to tell Pavol that he would take the train tomorrow. And that someone would ring with the information on the departure of the coach… He also mentioned that perhaps it wasn't necessary for his daughter… But it was to no avail, apparently both his wife and daughter had to be there… His brother had nothing more to say to him; it was, as always, a brief conversation.

He returned to the kitchen, cast a fleeting glance at the freezing snowflakes, took the unfinished bottle of wine out of the fridge, got himself a glass and went to his room.

Now he could savour the wine at leisure, without having to explain to Peter why he wasn't going to sit down on his backside and write, he wasn't going to point the finger at himself and bring charges against himself either; a couple of glasses of wine would lull him into a drowsy equanimity. Nor did he have to worry about Roman and whether he'd come with the revised text tomorrow. He had his journalist's honour, and that included keeping to deadlines. So that was another thing he'd sorted out. He had dealt with everything necessary. He could be pleased with himself.

But no sooner did that occur to him when he felt a vague sense of unease welling up within him. He knew it wasn't because of the journey tomorrow. He'd board the train and then get off; he'd have things to see to tomorrow and the following morning, and then it would be time for the funeral. In fact, it wasn't unease that he felt, but rather a kind of melancholy. Thinking of tomorrow's train journey to Martin reminded him that this evening marked the end of a distinct period of his life. The period that began the evening he received that phone call. No, actually, it included the time he had gone to see his wife in hospital and had already been told the name of her illness. And that, in turn, was preceded by the period when his wife started to feel ill and stopped going out, afflicted by some strange flu, and reacted quite indifferently to the news that he'd probably survived a heart attack. In fact, it was only now that the part of his life he'd spent with his wife in this flat as well as the earlier years in his old flat in the centre of town was coming to an end. The part of his life that he'd been with her. Not because she would not be truly dead for him until she was laid to rest in the family vault. It was because, ever since the phone call from the hospital and throughout the days that followed, he was constantly busy doing things that related to her; she continued to shape his life, just as in the two weeks when he was thinking about his next hospital visit, going to the University Library to take out some books for her, having to remember to buy her a bottle of Coca-Cola and some stewed fruit, pick up her pyjamas from the express laundry... or all the years before that, when he would think about things she shouldn't find out about, that he had to keep secret from her, while coming up with something else to write to her about or tell her on the phone, although for many years they didn't have a phone... or send her a few more pages of his literal translation to look over. For the moment, his life was still ruled by her presence or absence, she still existed for him, his obligations to her still giving his life some kind of purpose. He could not yet just sit down on his backside and write something, or not do anything at all, he was still living in a point in time that was not empty and she was the one giving this point in time its content. But once he returned to his flat from Martin, everything would be different, there would be nothing more to organise, he would be adrift in an ocean of empty time, drowning in that ocean of empty time, whereas today he was still, in some respects, living his life of old, and tonight was the last time he would be sitting here in this flat at the close of a day that had been suffused with her presence... That was why this melancholy that he was feeling really made no sense, as he had to concede, since he was clearly trying to delude himself into thinking that something had not yet come to an end, though at the same time, it was justified to the extent that there were two more days, tomorrow and the next day, that would be suffused with her presence, even if not here, in this city.

And as he pictured himself in Martin making all the arrangements to do with her, it occurred to him that he had completely forgotten about the keys to her parents' house, where they still had a room and a kitchen and where his sister-in-law, who was already there, was making preparations for the funeral wake. It hadn't occurred to him because on their visits to Martin the keys to the house had been her responsibility.

He could take his sleeping pill now. The pills were already packed but he'd left one for tonight in the kitchen. As he stood there washing it down with a glass of water, he remembered that the girl and Roman were coming at nine and that he should be ready to leave for the station by then. He was sure he would wake up in time, but he knew he would sleep more soundly if he set the alarm now.

It was now past nine o'clock: the girl who was to deliver the second eulogy had come a little early and while they were waiting for Roman, he repeated what he had said on the phone yesterday, that he and his friend had looked through the text last night and decided that he should revise a few passages and come at nine today and that was why he had asked her, too, to come at this time. He apologised for making her late for work this morning; he told her about the coach again and the girl kept nodding without saying anything and just looked awkward and sad. He couldn't think of anything more to say – he'd just mumble a few words and fall silent, then say a few words again. She didn't want any coffee, so he said he'd go and make himself some, even though he'd already had one cup.

He put the kettle on in the kitchen and repeated to himself: surely it's a matter of journalistic honour for Roman, journalistic ethics must run in his blood, and the first article in the journalist's code of honour is to meet a promised deadline. At the same time, however, he was aware that the whole thing about journalistic ethics and the first article of its code of honour was just something he'd dreamt up last night: he'd never before formulated anything like that in his head, though admittedly, on the few occasions when he had put off writing an article and gone on a bender the night before the deadline and come home late, he would ask his mother to wake him up and would get down to writing at six in the morning, if need be. But for some reason he was certain that Roman would come, that he would keep his word, even though he was running late – not very late but for him every minute counted just now. Another thing occurred to him and he went back to the living room, jotted down Soňa's phone number and told the girl to give her a ring if she hadn't heard about the coach to Martin by tonight.

The doorbell rang just as he was bringing the coffee into the living room where the girl was sitting. He opened the door and waited for the lift to come up. Roman started apologising even before he came in – there had been some family problems, – but he didn't really take his explanation in, all that mattered was that he had come. "Let me take your coat," he offered but Roman wouldn't take his coat off, "No, I'm in a real hurry," he just wanted to drop off the text. He ushered him into the living room and introduced him to the girl. Roman sized her up with the brief glance of an experienced reporter, found her to be just as he had imagined, then took out a bunch of papers, – "you can read it all later" he said –, for the moment he wanted him to check only one passage on one page, another on the next, and a third on yet another, and also the final part: those were sections he had completely rewritten, elsewhere he had made just minor revisions, so he picked up those few sheets without sitting down, with Roman towering above him as he pointed out the passages he was to read. He quickly ran his eyes over the text and saw that it now read more smoothly, more powerfully, and did seem to be closer to what he had in mind – indeed, it was more or less what he had in mind. "Yes, this is more how I imagined it," he said after reading the final lines. "Right then," Roman said with a nod; he had to go, and shook the girl's hand, said something to him, and before he knew it was out of the door and in the lift.

Back in the living room he sat down, picked up the papers and started reading the first page, – "I'll let you read it in a minute," he said to the girl – he was now reading more slowly, with greater concentration, as this was the final version and no further changes could be made. When he finished the first page he passed it on to the girl, took a sip of coffee, and continued reading. He couldn't remember the exact wording he came up with when he had woken up in the middle of the night, or how he had repeated it to himself the following morning as he walked up and down in the living room and kept reciting it to himself until it was time for him to go and see Agneša and present her with what he had in his head, though not verbatim, quoting only some of his original sentences, giving her a version distilled into a few keywords, catchphrases… this is what it should say, and… something along the lines of… this is roughly how it might go… No, Agneša wasn't familiar with his original version, she had to flesh out what he had presented to her, probably not to a high literary standard; he was on edge and the longer he spoke, the more on edge and the more terse he was. Now he remembered only those keywords and catchphrases, though he did retain a vague sense of what it ought to be like overall, and told himself, yes, that's right, this is it, as he passed the second and the third sheets over to the girl. Roman had really revised it in such a way that she could have been the author, he had nailed the simple style. When he finished reading the last page and saw that the girl had also finished, he asked: "What do you think, is it any good?" although what he really wanted to ask was if it was written in a way that she might have written it, but the girl just said; "Yes, it's very good", as if she had read something she liked but that had nothing to do with her. He also thought that it was really good now. "I think we should be going," the girl reminded him; he looked at his watch and saw she was right, it was time to go.

His suitcase was ready in the hallway – in the morning he also took some rolls that Soňa had given him yesterday for the journey, just enough for lunch on the train. Thrust under the door to the building he found more large envelopes, telegrams, perhaps some letters sent express which he picked up and stuffed into his letter box, to look at when he got back and read at leisure, as he would have nothing else to do anyway. As they walked down the street, he remembered another thing to tell her: if there was anything in the text she didn't like or thought she wouldn't have put that way, or even if there was something she just didn't feel comfortable with, she could just leave out the odd sentence… or even cross out an entire passage… it was entirely up to her… He also said that before reading it out at the event, it would be a good idea to look it over two or three times to familiarise herself with it, so she'd know roughly where to pause and so that it wouldn't sound as if this was the first time she was reading it… but she knew that, of course, it went without saying… They reached the bus stop at the crossroads with Malinovského Street, at the other end of which she would change to a tram that would take her all the way to the optical instrument factory, and her bus came quite quickly. For him it was only one stop to the railway station but he waited for a tram, since he didn't feel like walking with the suitcase in the cold drizzle. His train would be at the platform by now and he wanted to find a seat as soon as possible. He bought a first class ticket and found an empty compartment.

Soon the train started to move and he stood up, out of habit, and went out into the corridor to take a look at the city below – the station was built at the edge of the city, towering above it at the level where the vineyards began – and the first thing he saw through the fine drizzle was a maze of tiny family houses and beyond them the broad outline of Malinovského Street, the highrise buildings at the bottom of the street where Jozef B lived, his colleague in his last job who had turned up that first evening with his wife and Viera H – while just behind the highrises descending rows of three-storey 1950s tenements were visible – his brother had once lived in the top row of these – while right behind them loomed the grandiose white-walled compound of the secret police. From his vantage point he could see the inner courtyard and the bars on the small prison windows. He wondered who was kept behind those bars, now that not so many people were being locked up for political reasons and ordinary criminals were held in the old detention centre behind the police headquarters known as "At the Sign of the Two Lions" in the the city centre – then came more highrises and the road leading out of town, behind which he could clearly see the Stollwerck sweet factory that he had to pass before turning towards the small family house where the girl lived. Next came a lightly built-up area that went right up to Dynamite Nobel, now known as Juraj Dimitrov Chemical Works or CHZJD, where the terminus of tram C used to be in the days before tramlines had numbers: when he was growing up, he would often take the tram with his parents to the terminus, then walk on to the next village through the hills and vineyards before taking a train back. He generally returned to his seat at the point where the city once ended, but now he remained standing there looking at the brand new highrises and the smaller factories beneath them: the tramline now went all the way out here and even further, to the next village. That was a good moment for returning to his seat. The train had now moved away from the vineyards and he could make out the ridge of the Lesser Carpathians – how many times had he walked through these woods when his father was still alive, and in their early years with his wife, too, – though only in their early years, until she confessed that she didn't like the Lesser Carpathians, didn't consider them proper mountains. He'd done his share of mountain hiking with her elsewhere, every time they visited her parents' home town, which was surrounded by mountains – it must be snowing there if it's drizzling here, he thought – as well as in the Tatras, both the High and Lower. Soon the first village after the city would appear, he'd wait a moment until they also left this village behind, and there they were: the concrete anti-tank bunkers where he'd spent two or three days digging trenches shortly before the end of the war. He went back to his seat. The train began to leave the slopes of the Lesser Carpathians, nearly all their peaks the same height, the ridge forming a single continuous line. It was true: these really weren't proper mountains. He looked at their ridge in the distance, then there was one more thing he waited for, a tiny deserted station without any houses by it, which the train now whizzed past, the only people who sometimes alighted here were those about to take the dirt road to Modra, the town at the foot of the Lesser Carpathians. It was from here that he once set out with his mother and brother on their biggest camping expedition. In those days they still lived in a small house in the workers' district at the edge of the city, where in summer he and his brother would often pitch their tent and live in the world of the Wild West or the trappers, well hidden from the people in the street. And it was from this little station that they trudged through Modra carrying their tent to one of the few chalets in the Lesser Carpathians. They forgot to pack a blanket and since they couldn't sleep on the grass, they spent the night sitting on their folded-up tent. As their mother was useless at organising outings, all that was left after their father died were their beloved boat trips to Devín. The train had now moved far away from the Lesser Carpathians and he stared out of the window apathetically, as if watching a film he wasn't interested in, while still registering the landscape as it rapidly passed by, instantly forgetting the flashing images.

At some point in the late 1950s they bought a car and for a few years they would drive to Martin along what turned out to be the least convenient route, via Trenčín and Žilina, the way the train went. In the summer of 1969, they once again drove along this route, he no longer remembered why, but it was after normalisation had entered its aggressive phase and the elimination of right-wing elements was in full swing – after Trnava the road ran parallel to the railway line almost the whole way – and on the approach to Trnava, on the town's outskirts, with its old factories and small houses, slogans daubed in lime on the road surfaces screamed "No to Zionists in the Government and the Party!", followed by more in the same vein, right up to "Death to Zionists!", and on leaving Trnava they saw the same calls to arms daubed on the tarmac. In no other town they had passed had the normalisers painted any slogans against counterrevolutionaries: only this town was on a war footing, aiming its main line of fire at Zionists and calling on drivers to oust them from the government, the party or, if need be, from life...

He had always found this route tiring, what with the frequent and long waits at railway crossings and the growing number of private cars and lorries. He couldn't remember a single drive via Trenčín and Žilina: these trips had left no trace in his memory, it was as if they had never happened. Over the last two weeks, while she had lain in hospital, as well as during these last six days lying in a metal container at the Institute of Pathology, during the hours he spent sitting in his armchair or lying in bed tormenting himself with belated self-accusations, bringing charges against himself and beating himself up, whenever he got exhausted by these activities, he tried to summon up other kinds of memories of their years together, for surely there had been other things, and in fact other things had been the backbone of all those years, and he would recall various events, but in the end, as if by some automatic mechanism, he would always revert to the memory of the two of them in the car on their way to Martin, to her parents' home, not along this route, the way the train went, but via a completely different road that someone had recommended, through Nitra, Svätý Beňadik and Kremnica and from there on to Martin. This other route was perhaps twenty kilometres longer but the roads were less busy and the countryside more varied: in a word, it was much more pleasant. It was only from the point where the road from Nitra became narrower, descending via steep bends down to the river at Svätý Beňadik that the film of the journey would start rolling in his head. He would play it slowly and a little at a time; by now he knew it almost by heart, and the film would always get stuck once they passed Mošovce, as from then on his wife was inside the world of her parental home. They had always been happy in the car, comfortable, just the two of them, insulated from the rest of the world, insulated from everyone else as securely as a car is from lightning.

At Vrútky he got off the train, walked over to the bus stop in the little square outside the railway station and put his suitcase down, as he knew he'd have to wait here for a while. Some eighteen years ago, when he first started to visit his wife in Martin, there was no bus, only a local or express train to town, just one stop away from Martin and he would wait for it on the covered platform or, in bad weather or in winter, in the musty and smoke-filled third-class waiting room, the only one there was. Once, waiting for a train, it struck him that stations like these and the people milling about in them with their luggage, were almost completely absent from the literature that also used to be his literature before he was excluded from it, while in writing by Czech authors such stations, complete with their staff and the travellers they served, were actually a literary topos, featuring as frequently as did the mountain shepherd with his hut and sheep in Slovak literature: these were all symbolic of the Slovak nation, whereas the station master and the station staff, the linesman, or even the station master's wife in the works of the likes of Čapek or Hrabal, or in various Czech films were, to a degree, identical with the people getting on and off the trains or waiting for them – this was life in a nutshell: the arrival of the train being the beginning of something, its departure the end of something, and the people getting on and off and waiting, as well as the station master and the station staff, were all living, breathing people, whereas Slovak writers, even when they wrote about themselves in the third person, depicted a member of the intelligentsia or an intellectual as a sad figure with a sad fate, and regarded themselves as something of a symbol. Back then he thought that this might make a good subject for a feuilleton – years ago, early in his career, he greatly enjoyed writing feuilletons and thought he would be writing them all his life, he'd even written a feuilleton explaining what a feuilleton was, likening it to an elderly gentleman with a walking stick who, having nothing to do, spends his time wandering the city streets, looking around, noticing everything and smiling under his moustache... But he had never written his railway feuilleton... so many times in the past he had told himself that he ought to write this or that and then ended up writing something completely different, which was much less enjoyable but of greater social import.

In later years, when Martin was no longer merely a notable cultural centre boasting a major cultural institution and glorious traditions, especially in terms of literature, but had also become the seat of a huge newly-built heavy industry plant, a bus line was laid on for the workers from the surrounding villages, and in recent years buses ran almost as frequently as in the city.

It was drizzling, just like in Bratislava, maybe slightly more, although he had expected that when he got off the train the square outside the station would be dotted with little heaps of snow. In winter, when it was raining in Bratislava, here it would always be snowing, as Martin was surrounded by mountains. Before travelling there in winter or in early spring, Zora would remind him time and again that he should pack some warm clothes, as there was a mountain climate here, but this time the climate was just the same as in Bratislava. Meanwhile the bus had come, he got on and found a seat. The bus stood there throbbing away, shaking and vibrating feverishly, as the drivers never turned the engine off at the terminus, even if the bus waited there for ten minutes, so at least here everything was the same as ever. The bus windows, splashed by the rain, were streaked with black mud. In Martin itself as well as between the villages and in the foothills, on every route the buses would regularly sink into potholes filled with dirty water, the kind he always tried to avoid as a driver, and the buses and lorries coming in the opposite direction were equally liable to sink into potholes and drench each others' windows in mud that was sometimes quite thick. Only on reaching the new concrete sliproad towards the dual carriageway would the bus glide on smoothly and gracefully, and a view would open up of a housing estate that seemed more airy, as if it had been built to a better architectural design than many in the metropolis. He felt there was something magical about this housing estate: in summer, whenever they returned from a hike or a visit to the Kollárs near the Polish border, after two hours of driving past nothing but lonely, abandoned and not especially memorable and poorly-lit villages, as they approached Martin, out of the dark of the night, this mirage would emerge and light up the blue emptiness like a sea of fairground lights or a miniature Las Vegas, with its yellow arc lights blazing above the wide road that crossed the housing estate and illuminating the side streets between the box-like buildings, and with the neon lighting above the shops, as well as, despite the late hour, the odd window with a somewhat dimmer light still on, sky-high, somewhere on the twelfth floor… in those days, having left behind the darkness of the villages in the foothills and of the constantly winding roads, the housing estate with its mesmerising lights emerging before them would take their breath away… but this would soon be just a memory, as in future he was unlikely ever to drive back to Martin from any trips further afield, or from visiting the Kollárs near the Polish border.

He wondered why Zora seemed to need this kind of spectacle less than he did. Maybe she was able to live just by herself. And being older and probably wiser – wiser may not be the right word – and therefore probably so self-contained. He, on the other hand, perhaps lacked substance. He needed at least a little bit of sparkle and effervesence around him.

Though as a matter fact, when she was on the cusp of adulthood and began to write and translate, that is – to put it somewhat grandly – during her formative years, she had been surrounded by more people than he had in the same period of his life. People who shared her interests and with whom she could talk about anything. And many of these people were regular visitors to her parents' house, as their group photos showed. But in 1939, soon after his city, Bratislava, was elevated to the status of the capital of an independent state, most of these people had left Martin one after the other, to teach at the capital's universities, or take up positions in various agencies and ministries, at newspapers and journals. And those who didn't leave then, left after the war. The small town had turned into a backwater. Matica slovenská, the venerable cultural institution founded in Martin in the nineteenth century remained, and even expanded, with a huge new, ultramodern headquarters being built somewhere on the town's outskirts, or at least so he had heard, but it was drained of any living content. It no longer had its own publishing arm, it had stopped publishing journals and started to collect all manner of stuff instead: embroidery, lace, pottery, anything that could be deemed ancient folk art; the manuscripts and archives of dead writers; portraits and old books it could sell abroad for hard currency; and it churned out bibliographies of every kind; but these were activities more appropriate to a museum than a dynamic, living organism. Similarly, the town's central square was now a listed space, which was why it had become so ugly and sad. And the people she still knew in this town all lived in the past, with no interest in the present; they avoided her and wanted nothing to do with her, while by contrast all she was interested in was the present.

He got off in the centre of town, at the point where the main street became the main square. Admittedly, the square wasn't a square in the literal sense of the word; rather, what the city planners had originally envisaged was a boulevard, a wide belt of land offering peace and rest for the eyes between two busy streets, with the odd tree planted here and there, and indeed – particularly on Saturday mornings, when it was full of shoppers hurrying from store to store – groups of older men would hang around here, as would younger men from the working-classes as well as Gypsies, taking up all the benches, and yet others who stood around reading newspapers, especially in 1968, when folk were eager to read the papers, since in the middle of this park of sorts stood the city's biggest newsagent. Nevertheless, this was only a half-hearted attempt at a boulevard, because at the far end of the rectangle there was just a narrow one-way street, almost free of traffic. The other reason why this was considered the very centre of town was that a wide street leading to the railway station started at right angles to the square, while on the corner facing the park stood what used to be the only hotel in town with assembly rooms opposite, where in the nineteenth and early twentieth centuries balls "in the national spirit" and amateur theatre productions were held. That building was now home to a theatre: as both parts of Czechoslovakia had to have an army theatre, for the Czechs there was one in Prague, and for the Slovaks this one here in Martin. Shop after small shop lined the street, and the broad pavements were teeming with people. He walked carefully to make sure his suitcase didn't hit the knees of pedestrians coming the other way. He would in any case soon turn off into a side street.

He had decided well in advance that he would book into the newly-built hotel. One reason was that it was closer to his wife's house. Another, that he wanted to spend this night in the sterile atmosphere of a modern room, devoid of memories of the old days. The restaurant's expansive windows looked out onto a meadow where cows grazed in summer, and behind the meadow stretched fields of alfalfa, with a dirt road to the villages in the foothills. He was very familiar with the meadow in front of the hotel because that was where they had lunch for the last couple of years. After the death of his wife's mother, they had to find somewhere for lunch. His wife didn't cook then, and on the days when they didn't go for a hike or a drive, they usually ended up in this new hotel. They had never had any complaints, even though it was on the expensive side and they were often almost the only guests. Only on Saturdays and Sundays were most tables occupied by families who – as they picked up from their conversations – had travelled from as far away as the Czech Lands, mostly parents visiting their sons drafted into the army and based in the sizeable local garrison. That was another reason he made sure he reserved a room at the hotel: it was Christmas, after all, and besides, although it was rather unlikely, there might be tourists or skiers, as a short drive from town there was a hill rising to almost a thousand metres, which he found impressive; however, looking at the mountains from the bus now, he saw that neither this mountain, nor anywhere else at that altitude, was covered in snow.

His room was ready, yes, one night only; he picked up the key, took the lift up to the right floor, opened the door to the room and was very satisfied by how it looked: just as he had imagined it, a quite small hotel room, just like rooms in hotels in other towns he had stayed in, every piece of furniture exactly the same as everywhere else, nothing out of the ordinary or with any hint of cosiness or intimacy. He wanted to spend this night in a neutral space, somewhere purely functional that would not bring back any memories, anything that might prevent him from having a good night's sleep. He placed the suitcase on the stand and looked out of the window: from high up he saw the meadows in front of the hotel, the alfalfa field now the same colour as the meadows, the dirt road winding its way up the rolling landscape. They had taken this road many times when they wanted to get out of town quickly for a walk by the side of the road. Everything was as he had imagined, everything was the way it was meant to be.

Still wearing his coat he opened the bathroom door to check that everything was as it should be there as well. It was. There was even a bathtub. He hadn't taken a bath for years and he wouldn't even take a shower in the morning: he would probably be too tense. And a toilet, too, that he would make use of, though not immediately because, as the train approached the station where he would get off, about twelve minutes earlier – he knew exactly when the right moment came – it plunged into a tunnel, which was the cue for him to leave the compartment and look for the small room at the end of the corridor.

He closed the bathroom door and stood uncertainly in the middle of the room. It seemed a bit strange to turn on his heels straight away and leave the room to go downstairs, so he pulled up a chair and sat down, just for the sake of it. As he sat there for a while, just like that, looking at nothing in particular, the room seemed to speak to him: he listened to it for a moment, until he grasped what it was trying to convey. He turned his head slightly to the right and to the left as even a slight movement was enough to take in the whole room, and nodded: yes, that's right, no memories hanging anywhere on the walls, no memories treading on the rug, nervously or very quietly, no memories displayed on the table, no memories lying motionless on the bed, as if they were dead, no memories smiling at him from the suitcase stand, no reminiscences suspended from the ceiling all the way down to the floor like giant spiders, no memories hovering invisibly in the air: he detected no spectral presence around here, not a single memory lingering under the lamp on the small desk either – he just had to avoid looking out of the window. But the room itself was perfectly decontaminated, wiped clean of any memories. He was comfortable sitting here in a kind of vacuum, like someone who had checked into a small hotel room, leaving behind his memories and everything that had happened before, and who would emerge from here into a new, decontaminated life.

But the feeling didn't last long. He had to return to the life which he had been living for the past week, with things to see to, and that would again trigger his wretched memories.

He got up, pushed the chair back under the desk, picked up his hat which he had left on the suitcase, went out of the room and soon also out of the hotel.

He returned to the main square, walked to the end where it continued along an even shabbier street – from which a turning led to the cemetery – lined with single-storey houses where peasants used to live, with cowsheds and pigsties at the back. After the new housing estate for the workers in the heavy industry factory was built, most of the old owners and tenants moved out and Gypsies moved into the flats they had vacated. Her parents' house with its garden remained an oasis surrounded by feral ex-nomads and the pub a few steps on had also turned into a Gypsy pub, with no curtains on the door or windows, almost empty at this time of day. At the point where this downmarket street took a turn towards what used to be the main road out of town there stood a large iron double gate and beyond it a garden with a single-storey house in it. There was a smaller house at the far end, with another large garden beyond. Her parents' residence.

The heavy iron door had been left ajar, as his sister-in-law who had arrived a day early was expecting him; otherwise everything else was kept carefully locked up, which didn't prevent young rascals from climbing over the iron fence at the front of the house, or the wooden fence at the back. The gate closed behind him with a creak. The long single-storey house seemed neglected and run-down: that was the first thing Zora had said whenever they had arrived in recent years for a few days or weeks in summer, it all looks so neglected and run-down here, she would say ruefully: the one room and the kitchen, the only parts of the house not let out to lodgers were at the far end of the house. As the gate wasn't locked, he wasn't surprised to find the door to the house also standing open. Inside a wave of cold air emanating from the stone floor and the airless hallway swept over him, and as he opened the door he was struck by the chilly odour of the damp walls. He went up to the window at the front of the room, and found, as he did every time upon arrival, that the wall was sodden with damp all the way up to the bottom of the window frame. The wall remained damp even when his wife spent all winter here, though then the place was well heated and so the damp would barely be felt. Many years ago, the first time he walked into this room, it rang with the sound of women's voices, and the cosy, all-embracing warmth of the large tiled stove wafted towards him. Back then this was her room, serving as both study and bedroom, and nothing in it changed after he started coming here, except that his wife would work in her parents' part of the house, in the drawing room. The massive long bookcase made in Prague, perhaps the most beautiful piece of furniture in the whole house, was now in their flat in the city, taking up the entire shorter wall of their living room, and its place here was now taken by a pile of something covered with a dark old blanket – bedding for two piled on top of mattresses and a bedframe, where his wife used to sleep in recent years when they came to stay, while he would sleep on the sofa. Apart from the bookcase they had taken only one other piece of furniture to Bratislava, the recamier where his wife used to read, semi-recumbent. In her final weeks, she lay there most of the day.

He opened the window and despite the chill of the December evening that he let in, he remained standing there, looking out into the garden. Not far from the house was the biggest tree – a cherry tree, laden with fruit in summer, now a dry and barren skeleton of dark wood. The garden seemed to have disappeared into the ground. It was once her mother's pride and joy, her life's work, she'd even won a few prizes for it in the nineteen twenties, for the fruit trees that once grew there that had since been cut down to make room for the encroaching housing estate. His wife stopped looking after the garden when her mother died; she couldn't have maintained it even if she had wanted to, as they made only occasional visits between spring and autumn, and there wouldn't have been any point anyway with Gypsies living all around.

"The roses have blossomed in front of my window, all flaming red, I can't take my eyes off the long, luxuriant flowerbed" – this was more or less what Zora would write to him every year when staying at her parents' house. She would often add that whenever she felt tired, she would go for a stroll in the garden, where in addition to the roses there were also dahlias, cinerarias and God know what other botanical names she would list in each letter at least once a year. The splendour! The colours!

Year after year he would read letters of this kind, doing his best to visualize the splendid colours but only because he felt an obligation to do so since, except for the roses, he had no idea what colours he should be conjuring up, and, in fact, reading these letters always brought on in him a kind of soundless fury. He knew even without reading a letter like this that to her this place felt like paradise, it was so wonderful there, with her mother and in the garden, whereas in Bratislava she would have to endure the foul smells and the noise and if she looked up from her work and out of the window, all she would see would be the top of the façade and the sloping roof of a building that was at least half a century old. The building had been reduced to rubble in one of the final air raids at the end of the war, and even though it was renovated in the fifties, it remained ugly and shabby-looking. An ever-increasing number of cars could be heard from the street below with the advance of the dynamic socialist evolution, largely thanks to the working classes and their vanguard, the communist party, and although the street was narrow, there would always be someone parking a car or starting an engine, because the building across the street housed quite a few offices and most of the people who worked there now owned a car. He could understand that she preferred a room that afforded a view of a rich bed of roses, he accepted all that, and yet he would have preferred if things had been different and if she'd been with him in Bratislava, in one of the rooms of their old flat in the city centre, with the view of the top of the sloping roof of an ugly tenement. They would have been together all the time, living a more normal life, with his life, in particular, being more normal.

He couldn't care less about the garden, and the fruit trees filled him with horror. Each year he tried to drum into his head when the cherries would be ripening, but over the winter he always managed to forget and he ended up in Martin again just as the cherry season began. For as long as the cherries were on the tree, the whole house was aflutter. The branches of the cherry tree he now saw from the window formed a kind of dome above the fence, its canopy tantalisingly shrouding thousands of red fruit. And even when the cherry tree was almost the only one left in the garden, it was used by boys from the neighbourhood in something like a rite of passage that involved scrambling over the wooden fence, climbing the tree, picking some cherries, eating some and bagging some, then climbing back over the fence. Apparently, this was a long-standing tradition: his friend Mňačko, who had lived in Martin as a child, confessed to his wife when he was already a well-known writer, that some thirty years earlier he had been one of the boys who scrambled over the fence to pick the ripe cherries. This sport had been practised mostly by boys of fourteen to sixteen, but sometimes a few younger ones might join in, treating this as a kind of initiation ritual – and with the growing emancipation of women, girls about that age also started climbing over the fence. One Sunday, in broad daylight, his wife came across one such girl, decently dressed, probably from a good family, and made her climb down and invited her into the house. Between sobs the girl admitted that she had done it because she had been egged on by her girlfriends, who were waiting on the other side of the fence. His wife had to comfort the girl and tell her that nothing terrible had happened, and sent her home with a big punnet of cherries as a consolation prize. That was easy. But later, in the 1960s, not even the presence of his wife or her mother was enough to deter them. In well-planned raids they would come and pounce in a group, completely ignoring the pleas of the two imploring women, and his wife's shouting "Janko! Janko!" to get him to come, because they must have known they had nothing to fear. And he was furious, for even if it was just one boy who had climbed the tree, that boy would have the upper hand, just like when he was growing up, he had always been the one to get a thrashing when he tried to stand up for himself. He knew his limitations and, besides, he knew that he was a coward. All he could do was yell at those up in the tree and offer some rational-sounding advice – such as telling them to come when no one would see them – but that was utterly stupid too, since for them this was the main attraction of the whole enterprise: there was this garden with two middle-aged women and a man who yelled at them but none of whom dared to take them on. So younger boys as well as older brats would perch on the fence watching the noisy spectacle, until he got fed up with the pointless stress and went back to this room, where he was now standing by the window, seething within, feeling powerless, humiliated by seeing the law of the jungle at work and being taken for granted… That was why he hated these most beautiful weeks of the year between spring and early summer, when the ripening cherries unleashed that annual mayhem.

There had been a slight improvement in the past few years. Now that there were Gypsies living in the neighbourhood, they eliminated the problem neatly and painlessly. They too would scramble over the fence, but they did so when no one was watching, after midnight perhaps, or at dawn. And they didn't try to show off, had no need to prove to themselves or anyone else what tough guys they were… they didn't – pardon the expression – give a shit about any of the things that were so important to the *gadjos**. Presumably they climbed over the fence with large baskets, treating the whole business as a commercial venture, their only goal being to pick as many cherries as possible, and so once the cherries were ripe, the trees were picked clean within a day or two… They ate some of the haul themselves and probably sold the rest quietly in small batches. Problem solved.

In recent years, what they minded was not the fact that the cherries disappeared so quickly, but that thieves would now climb over the fence in the moonlight or with the first rays of the sun to pick not only cherries but also flowers. Zora would take an afternoon or evening stroll in the garden and inform him that the dahlias, or whatever, would be in blossom tomorrow, but when she went to take a look the next morning, the flowers would be gone. They would go to bed with the dreadful feeling that someone might be out there, walking the length of the garden, almost right under their window, so they would draw the blinds as early as possible so they didn't have to see the garden though it was lit quite well by the lamps in the street. That was also why they never took a walk in the garden after dark. When he set up the deckchair, he would no longer sit in the shade of the tree but positioned it in such a way that he was shielded by the house. And yet, as he reclined there reading, he often heard thudding from the far end of the garden: he knew it was the youngsters smashing the wooden slats in the fence to force their way into the garden – not for mercenary reasons, but just to hide in the weeds behind the fence and shout from there to those on the other side.

In the end they had to summon old Mr Skoričanský, an old-school jack-of-all-trades who could fix leaky gutters, dripping water taps, a blocked toilet or dislodged or damaged rooftiles. Mr Skoričanský arrived on his bike with new slats, fixed the fence, collected his fee, and then joined them for a moment on the bench in front of the house to sip some slivovitz, out of a bottle they kept in the kitchen cupboard specially for him; after each repair job he would get a few drinks – and since he'd been called to fix the fence broken by the Gypsies, Mr Skoričanský would pronounce unforgiving judgement on them which, like any talk of this kind, invariably made him bristle, even though he conceded that living with or near Gypsies had its problems.

They didn't mug people, rob flats and kill their owners if they happened to turn up unexpectedly; they didn't commit any major crimes commonly committed by the *gadjos*; their offences were mostly trifling, and they would have forgiven them the baskets full of cherries too, if only they hadn't been robbed of the feeling of privacy in this house and garden, something they used to take for granted; if they hadn't in-stilled in them a neurotic fear, the sense that someone was always lurking there, watching them and on the alert, and that the two of them were actually in their way.

He sat down in the armchair, only to get up immediately when he saw it whip up a cloud of dust. He started taking out armfuls of the old newspapers, journals, books, blankets and cushions that were spread out on the sofa. Everything on the big rectangular table where she used to have her typewriter and her papers, as well as on the smaller round table by the sofa and the armchair where he used to sit, everything was just as they had left it when they stopped here last summer, exceptionally for only two or three days. He carried the news-papers, books and blankets out into the hallway and stuffed them into the wardrobe where they kept old clothes. He didn't feel like dusting anything. He didn't even go into the kitchen.

This was what he expected to find in this room; he knew he would have to put the tiled stove on and do some dusting: that was why he had booked a room in a hotel. Though in fact he would have booked a room in a hotel even if this room had been waiting for him all clean and warm.

He went out and knocked on the door of the small house opposite. In recent years his sister-in-law always spent several of the summer months as well as a few days around All Saints' Day here. His wife told him that before and during the war, she used to have a paediatric practice and see her patients in this little house. She and her husband Fedor, his wife's brother, and their daughter Jelka, his wife's niece, had once shared the long single-storey house with Zora and her parents, living in the three rooms looking out onto the street. Fedor died in February 1948, a few weeks before he would quite certainly have been arrested as a high-ranking government official and member of the Democratic party.

His sister-in-law was at home and asked him to come in; she had two small rooms and a kitchen. He told her he had just arrived and had emptied the room of everything that was lying around but wasn't sure what to do with all the bedding. She had already thought of that and found a solution. A friend of hers would come first thing in the morning and the two of them would tidy up the room and prepare refreshments. It would be nice if he could go to the shops and bring a few bottles of wine and some beer. She would get everything else. He said he would, of course, reimburse her for everything afterwards, but he'd better be going now as the shops would be closing soon.

Under the eaves of her house stood a pram which she had used when gardening. He checked if it was still usable and thought that it might double up as shopping trolley; and set out with it to the bottom end of the square where the nearest supermarket was. He took two shopping baskets, having calculated that there would be at least thirty people, including some locals, so he needed at least ten bottles of beer and ten of wine, or maybe a dozen of each; he also bought a loaf of bread. Everything fitted comfortably into the pram.

One half of the heavy iron gate was still ajar, and as he steered the pram towards the wide path that ran alongside the house, he noticed a dog kennel with a wolfhound chained to it, and a man smoking a cigarette standing by the veranda jutting out from the middle of the house, its lower part made of wood, the upper part of glass. The man was standing in front of a door that opened directly into the two middle rooms, the former living room, the largest room in the house, and her parents' bedroom and bathroom. He was their tenant, a policeman who was renting these two rooms with his wife and young child. As he passed him, the tenant said only hello and he returned the greeting. He thought it was quite strange: he hadn't been here since the summer – six months ago – and as the man must have known from his sister-in-law why he was here, it would have been natural for him to say a few words.

He knocked on the door of the little house and his sister-in-law asked him to take everything into the kitchen of the house opposite. He did so, closed the windows, locked up, and told his sister-in-law that he would drop in again tomorrow morning and that he would, of course, pay her back for everything she bought.

Before he left, he asked if the dog that didn't even bark at him was always there, chained to its kennel. "That's the only way. The tenant takes it for a walk every day, but the rest of the time it has to be chained up." He was incredulous: "But surely…" Guessing what his objection might be, his sister-in-law explained, somewhat gruffly and laconically: "I couldn't take it anymore, you see. The dog kept running around the garden, among all the shrubs and flowers, digging up everything I planted" – she had a small vegetable patch there – "I had to ask him – the tenant – to keep it chained up."

He understood. They exchanged a few words, some small talk, none of it leaving any trace in his memory…

He went out of the gate and saw the outline of the highest mountain looming above the town, and a tiny light shining just below its summit. It was a chalet they had hiked up to on his first visit here, with him in his ordinary flat shoes that got soaked through. Since then a partly tarmacked road had been built all the way up; he lost count of how many times this last summer they had driven up that road, higher up than the chalet, and sat on the ground amongst the mountain pines, each of them with something to read: he was reading the collected stories of Thomas Mann among the mountain pines and the mountain seemed to mock him, everything mocked him, or rather, not him but his wife. He was like someone whose sunburnt skin reacts to everything hypersensitively.

The first tenants hadn't given them any trouble.

In the spring of 1970, before she cleared out her parents' house and had the furniture delivered to their new flat in Bratislava, Zora had reached an agreement with the town authorities or with Matica that the two rooms nearest to the street would be turned into a museum commemorating her uncle*, the renowned writer Janko Jesenský, who was born in this house. She was going to keep for herself the room at the other end of the house, with its window to the garden and the kitchen. The two middle rooms were to be rented out: the enormous former reception room, or parlour as they used to call it, and a smaller one, her parents' bedroom, with an en-suite bathroom. Someone suggested some nuns as possible tenants, and his wife sent word that she had no problem with nuns, so they came and introduced themselves and moved in at once. They were quiet, unassuming, unobtrusive, almost invisible. As far as the authorities were concerned, however, they were pretty visible and anything but unobtrusive: they would go around all day long visiting people, especially looking after children and the sick, they must have talked to them, quite certainly about God and things like that, matters of great importance to nuns.

And as part of the quest to obliterate the assorted vestiges of counterrevolutionary liberalism, one day it was the turn of the nuns in his wife's parents' home: they were piled onto a lorry with all their goods and chattels and taken away – as they had been once before, in the early 1950s, under Stalinism – for "retraining" in some remote convent in Bohemia.

It was autumn when the nuns were taken away and his sister-in-law was still in her little house, where she had spent all summer. She wrote to Zora saying that the most important thing was to find a tenant who had a dog. She may have had a point. Soon after that she told them in another letter that she had found quite the ideal tenant: he had a dog, a wolfhound, and was a policeman. The dog would guard the garden and the Gypsies would be scared off by the policeman. A more perfect tenant would be hard to find.

The idea of renting her parental house to a policeman struck his wife as so absurd that she couldn't bring herself to write back and explain to her sister-in-law – who had apparently not been reading the papers – about her history with the police, which had brought all her public activities to a permanent end, as well as making her a person whose name could no longer appear in print or be uttered in public.

Early in 1969 his wife wrote an article for the final issue of the Prague paper *Listy* about the first major crackdown by the Slovak police in Bratislava after people went out to the streets to celebrate the victory of the Czechoslovak ice hockey team against the Soviets.* The target of her criticism was not so much the two blows with a truncheon to her head, the first of which knocked her to the ground and the second of which was administered as soon as she hit the pavement, but rather the violation of basic standards of policing: no sooner had the police leapt out of the lorries that had brought them, they began beating people up without asking the crowd to disperse.

The police spokesperson published a sarcastic reponse in *Pravda* under his own name, calling her a political prostitute. In an organised follow-up the post started to deliver abusive and demeaning letters from regional police headquarters up and down the country almost on a daily basis, which never failed to call her a political prostitute or a political whore.

The letters made her very depressed. He had assumed and still believed that this stemmed from her profound sense of shame for having for many years associated with this nasty pack that included the writers of these letters, and that she had believed in the fantasy that anyone belonging to this nasty pack, who lacked all moral scruple, might have been genuinely striving for certain ideals. Whereas she had been striving for ideals all her life.

So now, every time they came back from a day trip or shopping late in the afternoon and passed the veranda, they would find three or four policemen sitting there in their shirt-sleeves, their uniform jackets flung across chairs, a bottle on the table, playing cards. One day their friend Darka, the one he was going to see tonight and whom he had asked to book the hotel, came over and said, quite shocked: "Well done, you! You've turned the house into a policemen's retreat!"

Darka, a relative of his wife, an ophthalmologist who had been a regular visitor to this house since she was a girl, couldn't stand the police. He knew from Zora that in her student days Darka had a great love, an engineer, whom she was planning to marry after graduating. But nothing came of their plans. He was arrested and charged with subversion. By the time people were being rehabilitated and he was released, years of hard labour in uranium mines and other privations had turned him into a wreck and he died quite soon after. That is why she couldn't hide her distaste at finding that the house she had been visiting all her life, had been transformed into a policemen's retreat. She had later married an actor with the Army Theatre in Martin.

He shut the heavy iron gate behind him and headed straight for Darka's house, where he was expected for dinner.

When he and Zora had visited this couple in the past – the only people in this town they still saw regularly – his wife had been the one who did most of the talking. She liked to talk, had a lively, dramatic way of speaking, never omitting any detail yet without losing the thread or indulging in unnecessary digressions: in a word, she was a gifted storyteller. She told their hosts what went on in the big wide world, that is to say, in Bratislava and Prague. About the discord among writers and also about arguments that raged between people much more important than a few writers in Prague.

What she told them was – to put it romantically– how the old world was collapsing. Darka hung on her every world, because her most ardent wish was for the world she lived in to be different. And although her husband cared more about being cast in a better role in the next play, he went along with his wife and their guest and the expression of full concentration on his face demonstrated that he was listening intently.

The long square he had to pass on his way to their house was completely deserted at this time of day. Only here and there could a sole figure be seen hurrying home. Before the housing estate was built, all the shops in town used to be concentrated in this square. During the month or so they spent here in summer, the only shop he would go to was the bookstore, where he was known as a regular. New books tended to appear in the summer months and he had to get hold of them here as they would sell out by the time he returned to Bratislava. The bookshop was small, as were all the shops in this square, except for a large supermarket built on the corner of the street leading to the railway station. Next to the supermarket was a cinema, the Moskva.

At the end of the square he turned into a poorly-lit street and then, one block further on, there was a large block of flats built in the early 1950s.

Darka opened the door and after a few words in a faint voice, she added: "This all sounds so hackneyed. I don't know how to put it, but I speak from the heart. You know how much I loved her."

She genuinely did. Suddenly he realised that he ought to be grateful to her. When his wife's father died and her mother was left alone whenever Zora came to stay with him in Bratislava for a week or two, Darka would often drop in on Zora's mother after work and keep her company for an hour or so; sometimes she would go every day, just so that the old lady wouldn't be alone in the house all the time. He was rather moved when he thought of it. Darka's husband shook his hand, looked him in the eye, and gave an almost military shake of his head, in an expression that combined commiseration and supportiveness. Darka asked when he had arrived and when he told her which train he'd come on, she declared: "I see, so you haven't had lunch. Do take a seat and I'll serve dinner right away."

Over dinner he told them about all the arrangments he'd had to make this past week. How fortunate it was that Dr Felix had agreed to deliver a eulogy without giving it a second thought. He also mentioned there would be another speech, though not that he had someone else write it on the girl's behalf, or that yet another person had rewritten it. Darka asked, quite casually, if it was going to be a church funeral. "No," he said tersely. Apparently, the old Martin families had decided that it should be a church funeral, in keeping with family tradition. To make it clear that he didn't really have a choice, he said: "But she left the church some twenty-five years ago. And just because she left the party doesn't mean that she joined the church." They didn't labour the point. Then he mentioned the death mask. At least that was something the old families might give him credit for.

All through dinner he kept thinking that once the meal was over, they would settle into comfortable armchairs and he would have to give them a full account. Yet again. He knew it almost by heart. But then he suddenly remembered that it was only one day to the funeral and after that he would probably never give this account to anyone. The people in Bratislava all knew more or less how it happened, so there would be no one there to tell, and even if someone asked him about it, he could sum it up in a couple of sentences.

In the end, he gave a completely different account, and instead of explaining how it could have happened so suddenly and what went on at the hospital, as he had to all those people who had turned up in their flat on that first evening, one after another, he started right at the very beginning, at the point to which he had traced it over the past few days: from their last summer vacation earlier this year, how she felt poorly all of a sudden even though there wasn't anything really wrong with her, which was why their departure to the cottage was delayed by a few days, how she had bouts of lethargy and ill-temper that did, however, pass, and how nothing suggested that she might be ill, until she started to feel unwell sometime in mid-November, or even earlier, and assumed it was flu, how a neurologist friend who had been at his birthday party suspected that something was amiss and sent her for an examination to the relevant department, how the doctor gave her one of those blood tests which showed what was wrong, how a bed at the hospital very soon became available and she was put on a drip on the very first day, but kept feeling worse, though the doctor warned him when he disclosed the diagnosis that "your wife will feel worse at first" and, indeed, she was completely exhausted, but she did sometimes get over the fatigue and on two occasions she asked him to get her particular books from the University Library, thick novels – she did a lot of reading – but though she didn't want visitors, it so happened that someone came to see her on that last day, that the consultant congratulated him on the results of the blood test, they were much better than could have been expected in just two weeks, and how at that time her main preoccupation was Christmas Eve and wondering if she should get herself discharged, but in the end she preferred to stay in hospital, he was just supposed to organise the carp for Christmas Eve, that was the very last assignment she gave him, and then, about an hour after he left, it happened.

He delivered something akin to his own eulogy. Right now he was unable to say anything else about her apart from this witness testimony.

Darka asked whether she had been aware of the prognosis.

"I don't know. Maybe she was, towards the end. Or perhaps she knew that things were bad but not quite how bad."

"That's why I asked," Darka went on, "because I know that she wasn't religious in the church-going sense, but I think, in fact I am sure, that she did believe in God, and knowing how things were with her..."

He didn't think she believed in God: why would she have kept that secret from him? And even if she did know how bad things were with her, she was too realistic and unselfish to believe in any kind of transcendence and afterlife. It was more likely that she thought that it was a good idea to write down the passwords for the savings books and that she wondered how he would manage; but on the other hand, she might have thought that he was still relatively young and would get over it. The only "transdencental" thing she may have thought of were her parents, her late brother and niece. Belief in one's ancestors, one's loved ones, is more ancient than faith in God.

"Perhaps," he said, when Darka finished. "I really can't comment on that."

"But isn't it horrible," said her husband Jozef S, venting his indignation, "not a word in any of the papers, not even a couple of lines!" How many times had he heard that over the past few days? "Would it have hurt them to print a very brief notice, three lines would have been enough, that such and such has happened? Why do they need to keep it a secret?"

"Actually, they're not really keeping it a secret," said Darka, and smiled for the first time. She mentioned Matica, which was based in this town, and the approximate number of people it employed. "Well, this morning they all found a memo on their desk which recommended that they do not attend the funeral tomorrow. The same memo was sent to every schoolteacher. I first heard about it from someone in my surgery, and then from a teacher I bumped into on my way home. Word gets around fast in a small town like this."

"So I expect to see this memo displayed on the noticeboard at the theatre," said the actor.

He was flabbergasted. He didn't care however many people didn't come to the funeral. What made him angry was that they were kicking up such a fuss about it, turning it into a scandal. That it couldn't be dealt with in a quiet, low-key way, as a simple funeral. He tensed up again. They were talking about something but he couldn't get this news out of his head. He got up and said he had to go.

"Don't worry, we'll be there," said Darka, "even if every doctor was sent the memo as well."

As he headed back towards the square along the dimly lit street, he was still feeling angry and tense. "These bastards, they have to stick their nose into everything," he said to himself out loud three or four times, venting his frustration.

The square was lit by fluorescent lamps and the silence was so overwhelming that he thought it augured snowfall.

Just then he remembered the tenant standing by the veranda, smoking and saying no more than "Hello" when he passed him on his way in and nothing but "Goodbye" on his way out. Now he knew why the man wouldn't talk to him. The police must also have received a memo about the funeral, with some additional instructions. This was the first time that the policeman-tenant had discovered what kind of character he'd had as his landlady. He should never have got involved with this kind of person. And he, her husband, was of the same ilk. That was why he didn't say anything.

People came streaming into the square from a side street in small groups. The last show in the Moskva cinema was over. Just as well he had stayed so long. He could go straight to bed now.

He wondered if he should take half a tranquillizer or a whole tablet in addition to the sleeping pill. He'd take a whole tablet, he decided. He needed his sleep.

Having thoroughly knocked himself out, he slept through this night, too, waking up only once from a chaotic dream about his wife; but then his dreams were often chaotic.

He had breakfast, put on his coat, opened his suitcase and found the receipts from the funeral parlour in Bratislava and the two LPs. The funeral parlour was not far from the hotel, the only thing that was far away here was the housing estate, but that had no municipal enterprises or offices. He knew exactly where the local funeral parlour was, as he'd been there two years ago to arrange the funeral of his wife's niece.

In Bratislava the waiting room of the funeral parlour was furnished almost like a private living room, with small armchairs; here in Martin it was just an office with a counter dividing it in two. Standing at the counter instantly made him feel like a client in some office, made to wait and expected to be grateful to have his business dealt with, rather than a paying customer.

A middle-aged gentleman appeared on the other side of the counter, thin and quite tall, immaculately dressed and with a tiny moustache. He gave him his name, said which funeral he had come about and asked about the consignment from Bratislava. With the aloof expression of a government official, the employee confirmed that the hearse had arrived. Using these words.

He placed the two LPs on the counter and explained that he would like some passages from these to be played during the funeral; it was all written down here, he said, placing the piece of paper on the records, and adding that he would like to specify the order he wanted the individual extracts to be played in the course of the funeral.

"The funeral can't go ahead as yet," the employee informed him in an official tone. He gave him a bewildered look. The employee continued stiffly: "We had a call from the National

Committee. You need to go to the Department of Interior Affairs. Once they phone through their approval, the funeral can go ahead as scheduled."

He stared at him wide-eyed. "But why?" The employee shrugged. "I don't know. You'd better go there straight away and come back later."

He left the funeral parlour utterly flabbergasted. The Interior Affairs Department of the National Committee - but that was the secret police! The very words filled him with horror. The secret police brought only one image to mind: they would make him sit on the other side of a desk, bombard him with questions trying to prove something, insisting that he did know, must have known, had to know what this or that person had said, and didn't he himself say this thing or that, they had a witness who could testify to it, and they would pretend they knew everything even though they knew nothing and would blow everything out of all proportion, but it would drag on for hours, until he was so exhausted that he would say something that would be of some use to them.

To delay his visit to the National Committee's Department of Interior Affairs he decided to stop by his sister-in-law's and inform her of this development. She might have an idea of why he was supposed to go there. His wife's parents' home was less than five minutes' walk from the funeral parlour. He again found one of the heavy iron gates ajar. The courtyard as well as the garden at the back looked somewhat more inviting now that the sun was shining and it was a clear day without any mist.

Without any thoughts in his head he went to the room where he thought his sister-in-law would be. It had already been tidied up, the bedding taken out, the bottles he brought yesterday laid out alongside several trays. The door was wide open and fresh air was streaming in, the dampness of yesterday was gone, with the tall, tiled stove giving out a pleasant, soothing warmth.

He went out into the courtyard again and just as he was about to knock on his sister-in-law's door, out she came carrying a tray of canapés. The preparations for the funeral wake seemed to be keeping her fully occupied. He told her that he'd been to the funeral parlour and was told that the funeral couldn't take place until he went to the National Committtee's Interior Affairs Department. While he was talking, his sister-in-law's friend came out of the door also carrying a tray; he said hello, his sister-in-law said something to her, her friend said something in response, things to do with the preparations; he realised that his sister-in-law had been only half-listening to him and had neither the time nor the room in her head to think of anything else and gave a brief response along the lines of: why didn't he go and have a word with them, it couldn't possibly take long, the request didn't strike her as unusual or outrageous, and before he knew it, she was off with the tray of canapés, apparently to indicate that she had her hands full preparing the refreshments and would appreciate it if he looked after his affairs himself.

Closing the heavy iron gate behind him he felt the first wave of panic subside. Stuff and nonsense, they had no grounds for investigating him today. They must have received an order, similar to the memos that had been sent out. They had to meddle, they simply had to put their oar into everything, the bastards.

He crossed the little park, passed the cafeteria that served mostly as a pub, where even at this time of day a few men were hanging around outside with their beer bottles. The National Committee was a little further on, in the middle of the square.

He looked at the noticeboard to see where the Department of Interior Affairs was located, walked up to the first floor and knocked on a door but there was no one there except for a secretary behind a desk. He gave his name and before he had time to add that he came about the funeral, the secretary interrupted him: "Ah, so there you are. We've had a call from the funeral parlour, they told us you're on your way. Just a moment." She went over to another room, announced him and ushered him in.

In a large, rather empty room, a shabbily dressed official sat behind a desk close to the window studying a file on the desk in front of him. Next to him, to the side of the desk, there was another, chubbier man in clothes that were even shabbier and ill-fitting, with the fat face of a butcher or a rough brawler in a pub. One quick glance was enough for him to register that neither of them were as well groomed and sophisticated as those he had to deal with in the Bratislava office of the secret police.

He introduced himself and said he'd come about the funeral. The man behind the desk asked: "So you're the husband?" – "Yes, I'm the husband." "Got your ID?" He gave him his ID, the man flipped through it, found the page in which the register office had recorded his wife's death, and returned it. "We just need to clarify a few details," said the man with the butcher's face. "Yes, just some minor details," the man at the desk echoed, and glanced at the file. Then he started firing off questions at him.

"Will it be a civil funeral?" – "Who will be giving the eulogy?" – "Who's that?" – "And who had asked him to do that?" – "Why was it your wife's relative and not you in person?"

He said that on the first evening after his wife died, some friends had come to see him, and in the course of discussing who might give the eulogy, a relative of his wife's suggested the name of professor Dr Felix. The relative made the call and told them that the professor had agreed.

"So you approached him in your private capacity, not through or on behalf of the Writers' Union?"

No, the relative made the call in his private capacity. The Writers' Union knew nothing about it at the time, nor had he informed them since. "She was no longer a member of the Writers' Union," he added by way of explanation.

"And what will the eulogy be about?"

"I don't know."

"What do you mean, you don't know? You haven't spoken to him at all?"

"I gave him a list of the books my wife has translated. And some biographical information in case he needed it. When someone is asked to deliver a eulogy, a family member always provides them with some details."

"So you have absolutely no idea what the eulogy will be about?"

"I suppose it will be about her being a translator." He remembered one other thing. "Dr Felix is the head of the Translators' Section of the Writers' Union after all. He is, or at least he used to be; actually, I think he still is."

"So is he going to speak officially in his capacity as the head of that Section?"

"No, my wife's relative asked him because they know each other. And he agreed to give the eulogy because he knew her. As a translator and also privately."

"In what way, privately? Were they friends? Did they meet often?"

"No, not at all. But she had known him for quite a long time, from the publishing house and his work in the Translators' Section. He knew her primarily as a translator. He himself has been a translator for some thirty years, so he must know quite a lot about her."

"So he's going to talk about her primarily as a translator?"

"Presumably. After all, she had been mainly a translator. But I could hardly ask him to show me his eulogy in advance, could I, what for – to censor it? Who would do such a thing? "

They couldn't say that anyone ever did that, so the official just nodded. "Very well." He seemed to have ticked his first box. Then he went on: "Who else is going to speak?"

(372)

"A friend of hers, a young girl, or young woman, rather, as she is in her twenties. Works in the optical instrument factory. She knew my wife only in the last three years of her life, but they had become very close."

"Close in what sense? And how come, if she works in the optical instrument factory? Was she a translator before, or what?"

"Oh, no." The man was probably thinking of the time before 1968. So he told them how his wife's niece was killed in a hiking accident in the Tatras two years ago. And the sister of this worker in the optical instrument factory, a friend of his wife's niece, was killed in the same accident. After that, the girl came to see his wife quite often, with one or other of her girlfriends.

"Did you ask her to give this speech? Or was it her idea?"

"I asked her."

"Why?"

Why… He gave it some thought. "My wife was very fond of her. And also because of everything that had happened. She was someone who knew my wife only in her private capacity, not as a translator." Finally, he managed to put it succinctly: "I wanted someone to offer a purely personal reminiscence."

This point seemed to be exhausted. "Who else is going to make a speech?"

No one. At least, no one he was aware of.

He thought that now it really was over. But then the man with ill-fitting clothes and the butcher's face took over.

"We've had a call from the funeral parlour. They told us that you have brought some records. What did you bring those records for?"

He started to talk about his wife's niece again. Her funeral had taken place two years ago. On that occasion his wife had also chosen two records, from which extracts had been played at the funeral. Her niece loved listening to music and

(373)

his wife wanted the sort of music she had liked to be played at the funeral. He went into further detail, hoping that the more he talked the fewer questions they would ask, because they would get fed up. What did it matter what kinds of records would be played at the funeral?

But Butcher Mug wasn't so easily satisfied.

"But what records?" – "They have plenty of records at the House of Mourning. You can have Dvořák, Tchaikovsky, anything you wish."

"So why can't they play some of the Janáček records I've brought?"

"Mourners must pick from what is available at the House of Mourning. There's Bach and Beethoven, too."

The official behind the desk suggested that he go to the House of Mourning to see what records they had.

This was no longer an interrogation, a sequence of questions and answers, it turned into an argument. Why did it have to be Janáček and not someone else? But why not Janáček? Because it was unusual… But two years ago my wife did… Well, maybe she did, but today it's easier this way for the House of Mourning.

But why on earth were they having this argument at the Interior Affairs Department of the National Committee? It was beyond him but he was clear that he had to find a different way of making his point. The same point but phrased differently. He gave it a try:

"My wife studied the piano at the conservatoire, you see. And because of that her taste in music was quite distinctive. So when she listened to records, she obviously preferred the pieces for solo piano."

The effect was surprising, even though he wasn't telling the truth. His wife liked to listen to piano music just as much as to orchestral works.

The two men asked almost simultaneously: "Oh, so it's just piano music?"

"Yes, only the piano. And the other record, the Moravian songs, is for solo female voice."

For some reason, this made them throw in the towel. "All right, then. You can go to the funeral parlour. We'll give them a ring in the meantime to let them know that the funeral has permission to go ahead."

Once he was out in the street again, he thought, you mean you could have prohibited it, you morons? But he was no longer fuming about their meddling in everything, no longer asking himself, why do you have to meddle in everything, you bastards? He had accepted it as inevitable that they had to meddle in everything, as part and parcel of everyday life. But he managed to handle it, to overcome this particular obstacle.

This time the funeral director treated him like a customer, in an obliging and accommodating manner. He looked at the piece of paper and listened to his explanation of which sections on the two LPs should be played and in what order. Then he said:

"We'll go over it one more time in the House of Mourning before we begin, to make sure nothing goes wrong. I will be there just before three, you'll find me by the door on the right, at the top of the hall. You should come with the people who will deliver a eulogy and I will take them to a room where they can wait before going on stage.

"Right, then, see you there just before three," he said and made to leave, but the man behind the counter made a long, awkward face like a shop assistant who had some unpleasant news for a customer, for example that the goods couldn't be delivered immediately.

"Erm, there's one more thing," he said. "The burial will be into the family vault, which means I can't use our gravediggers." By using this official turn of phrase he wanted to make the point that there wasn't a grave to be dug. "It means that a few stone slabs will have to be lifted and then put back in place. This is not part of our gravediggers' job description;

and in addition, the blocks might get damaged while being lifted out or moved back. I will have to hire the men we use when we deal with vaults of this kind. Or you can hire someone yourself."

He said that of course the funeral parlour should hire them, that was the only option. "But that will be an additional cost, on top of the original quote."– "I see. I will cover the difference." – "Will you pay now or should we send you the bill?" – I might as well pay straight away." He had brought some extra cash just in case. The man behind the counter took a large notepad, filled out his name, address, the job to be done, and the cost. He was rather taken aback by the amount but didn't ask any further questions, impatient to get it over with.

It was time to go back to the hotel. With a bit of luck, there was nothing else left to organise. He just couldn't understand why they made such a song and dance about the records he had brought and why they tried so hard to make him choose from the music they had at the House of Mourning. It was quite beyond him.

Back at the hotel, as he walked to the lift after picking up his key at reception, he looked towards the restaurant. Many of the tables were occupied by people he knew. So the coach had arrived. And they were having lunch.

It would have been nice to have a little lie-down in his room, as he was still quite agitated and angry after what happened at the National Committee. But in the event he just had a quick wash, put on a white shirt – the one he'd been wearing was now drenched in sweat, and got his black tie, black shoes and black suit out of the suitcase, got changed, popped a tranquillizer out of its blister pack and put it in his pocket, to take about half an hour before the funeral, then he packed his suitcase and sat down for a moment. He would now go downstairs and settle his bill. He would leave the suitcase at reception, collect it after lunch and take it to their room at her parents' house.

He was still feeling restless and on edge. And tired. No, there really was no time to lie down. He had to make an appearance. He would walk into the dining room and all eyes would be on him. And he would feel uneasy and self-conscious as he always did in any unusual situation.

He picked up his suitcase and the key to the room, took the lift down, paid his bill at reception and asked if he could leave his suitcase there while he had lunch. Then he entered the restaurant.

Everything was as he had expected. He immediately felt awkward and discomfited, since the room was full of people he knew, and he didn't know who to turn to first, who to say hello to or go over to, or which table to join. He spotted a woman sitting on her own, to one side from everyone else, and went up to her first, shook her hand and thanked her for coming: she was the only person from his block of flats to have come to the funeral, which was why she didn't know anyone; then he went over to the far end of the restaurant where his brother was sitting with his family and exchanged a couple of sentences with them. They didn't know anyone here either; as he turned to the other tables, wondering which table he could join, he heard someone calling him from a table where a group of women were having their lunch. The women – Viera, Ružena, Soňa, Marta, Ela and Hanka – all of them translators, had something to tell him. He went over to their table and one of them told him they had also prepared a eulogy on behalf of his wife's former students who had attended her university course on principles and challenges of translation. The speech would be delivered by Viera H although it was Ružena who wrote it, but she couldn't read it out herself as she still had a job at a publishing house (they had once visited her hoping she would agree to front one of Zora's translations but Ružena had taken on so much work herself that she wasn't able to help). He said he was delighted to hear this unexpected news, and explained to Viera that she should be at the House of Mourning before three. There wasn't room for him at this table but before he moved on, he thanked Soňa for organising the coach, apparently everything had gone without a hitch, the young man was very reliable, then he waved to the cousin sitting at a table with her family; they must have all driven from Nitra together. He noticed that there were only two people at the table with Dr Felix so he said hello and sat down with a grateful smile. Felix was in the middle of a lively conversation with Gabo, a relative of Felix's wife. There was a bottle of wine on the table, as on several others, though most people were drinking beer. He ordered something light that wouldn't take too long to eat, and a bottle of mineral water, although a glass or two of wine would have helped to calm his nerves. Felix was still immersed in his conversation with Gabo, who had unleashed a torrent of words: he gathered they were talking about the head of the publishing house where the professor had worked for a while, as had Zora. Her contract required her to spend only a few days a year in the office: she used to work from home and when she wasn't staying with him in Bratislava, she would copy-edit other translators' work at her parents' house. "What a shameless opportunist!" Gabo said, referring to the man's 1969 novel, whose protagonist, the head of a publishing house, was terrorised by cultural counterrevolutionaries in 1968 and had to struggle to resist the pressure they put him under. He knew the man and had heard about the novel Gabo was talking about. Felix asked a few more questions, but as he had meanwhile finished his lunch, he asked to be excused, because he had to talk to a few other people, but they barely took notice of him. He got up and noticed that only two people were sitting at one of the tables – Martin R, the blue-eyed doctor with the broad shoulders, and his wife Viera – so he went over and joined them.

The doctor, who was a personable and genial man, a little older than him, must have noticed his unease and nervousness, now compounded by a feeling of being lost here, as if he didn't belong, as if the people who arrived by coach had bonded during the journey, leaving him a straggler who had wandered in when everything was over. That was probably why Martin R asked whether he was staying at this hotel and wanted to know when was it built, as he hadn't seen it before, and also asked what he had been up to in the morning. He explained how he'd gone to the funeral parlour and encountered some idiotic problems there. But that's awful, what sort of problems, Viera R chipped in, but he said he'd rather not talk about it now; they had to get going soon anyway, as he remembered that his sister-in-law had spent all morning preparing refreshments for them all. Viera recalled the last time they had been to the house was about five years ago. "Four," he corrected her, "it's been four years since your last visit." Has it really, she said. "How come you remember it so well?" the doctor inquired. He explained, looking at the doctor's wife: "It was when I drove your father around these parts, two days in a row, remember; it was the last year we still had our little Renault." – "Oh yes, of course, silly me!" Viera gave a whoop that could be heard halfway through the restaurant; in fact, she always so loud that she could be heard at least at all the adjoining tables. "It was four years ago, of course, now I remember." At the mention of her father the events of the last few years must have fallen into place, as her father had died a year before. "I was sure that a man his size wouldn't fit into that matchbox of a car, but my father did manage to squeeze in and was sitting quite comfortably, and afterwards he kept telling us about all the places you'd taken him to, places he recognised and others that he'd forgotten."

Before long people around him started settling their bills, so he paid his, and Viera R announced in a spirited voice, this time deliberately loud enough for everyone to hear, that she was headed for the family home, for possibly this would be the last time that they would all visit it, and that then they would all go to the cemetery together. As people started to get up, he returned to his neighbour from Bratislava and invited her to join them, but she shook her head and said she'd rather take a walk around town, as it was her first time here – "but you won't see anything, there isn't really anything worth seeing here" – but no, she'd rather take a walk, so he went over to the table where his brother was sitting with his wife and daughter and asked them to join him, and then he collected his suitcase from reception and left the hotel.

He walked with his brother and his family, bringing up the rear. He asked how the coach journey had gone, how long it took and whether the coach was heated. He saw the whole crowd walking ahead and deep in lively conversation, taking up the entire width of the pavement. Only once they turned into the main street at the end of the square did they start bumping into people coming in the opposite direction and had to split up into smaller groups. The main street was noisy, as always at this time of the day until about five in the afternoon, with a continuous stream of buses and lorries and tractors, as well as private cars and coaches and vans with trailers, for this was not just the town's main street but also the arterial road across town. When they reached the end of the square, they continued up the bit of the road that was now a part of the Gypsy settlement, past the Gypsy pub; an older man and a young Gypsy couple stood outside and stared at them long and hard. He found it a bit embarrassing but also rather amusing, and felt a certain sense of satisfaction, as many of those ahead of him hadn't been to the house for years and would have remembered it as an idyllic, tranquil place, a manor house surrounded by small cottages in a quiet little town, so now they would see at least how much the place had changed. As they went through the half of the gate that had been left ajar, his eyes ran over the bric-a-brac their tenant had on display as if for sale; only the enormous old trees were as tall and majestic as they had always been, and the house didn't seem as woefully desolate as it did yesterday. He saw Viera R leading the way, talking loudly, and when his sister-in-law heard her voice, she came out of her little house, said hello to everyone, shook hands with those she knew and indicated they should all go into the house opposite.

He set his suitcase down in the hallway, invited his brother in and followed him and his wife and daughter into the room. It was nice and warm inside, the warmth emanating from the tall, greenish-blue tiled stove just as when they stayed here in wintertime: the room was once again cosy. At the back where her small desk once stood, a large rectangular table was laden with trays of canapés, while bottles and glasses were laid out on a smaller round table in front of the sofa and the leather armchair. Having taken a quick look at the people who had come in, some already seated, he went out again, and after passing his sister-in-law, who was deep in conversation with the doctor and his wife, Gabo and a few others who were once frequent visitors here, he knocked on the door of her little house and went in. As he expected, the two girls he hadn't seen at the restaurant were sitting here, the one who was going to deliver the speech wearing her usual clothes, a sporty grey jumper and a rather long skirt. He asked her about the speech: did she find anything to cross out or leave out, did she need to take something for stage fright, would she like to come and join everyone else: she just shook her head in response to each question or said no, so he asked her to be at the cemetery a few minutes before three, as he had to introduce all the speakers to the gentleman from the funeral parlour who would show them to a side room where they would wait their turn. Then he returned to the house opposite.

By now everyone was either standing around or had settled into chairs. He sat down on the edge of the recamier where Agneša was sitting, semi-recumbent; after a while the professor asked him what use had been made of the house, so

he explained that the front two rooms served as the Janko Jesenský literary museum, primarily for visiting school groups,
while the middle section had been let to a family of three –
this time he omitted to mention the fact that the head of the
family was a policeman – while he and his wife had kept the
kitchen and this room, which used to be her study. In fact,
many years ago, it used to be two separate rooms but they
had the door and a part of the wall knocked down, though
you could still see where the division had been.

A murmur of voices rose around him again; someone
opened a bottle of beer, and suddenly he heard Viera R's
voice: she was asking him about the problems he'd mentioned
in the restaurant that he didn't feel like talking about earlier: had they got the times mixed up and perhaps scheduled
another funeral for the same time, or what?

"Oh no, there was no mix-up. But for a moment it looked
as if there would be no funeral at three o'clock." He paused,
wondering if he should give her the whole story or keep it
brief, but was bombarded with astonished questions. "It all
started in the morning, when they told me at the funeral
parlour that the funeral couldn't be held and that I had to go
the Interior Affairs department at the National Committee to
ask for permission." There were gasps all round: since when
was the Interior Affairs Department responsible for giving
permission for funerals, and what would happen if they refused? Initially he was able to remain laconic, but once he
got to the grilling he was subjected to at the National Committee's Interior Affairs Department, and the questions about
the eulogy, and who would deliver it and at whose request,
was it you, in your private capacity, or someone else, it was
in a private capacity but related to this person's profession;
so what would the eulogy be about and have you read it, and
who else was going to speak and why that person, how did
that come about, who was she and what was she going to say.
And when it looked as if it was over – as he spoke he worked

himself up into the rage he had felt earlier, when he left the National Committee muttering to himself, "the bastards, why do they have to meddle in everything," – it was by no means over: then they got started on the music: the funeral parlour had rung them and said he had brought two LPs and wanted some extracts to be played during the ceremony, and what happened next seemed so absurd now that he was no longer able to keep it short and gave a blow-by-blow account: why he'd brought the records, how two years ago his wife had brought two records to her niece's funeral; but they could play Dvořák and Tchaikovsky, said the fellow with the butcher's mug and they started to haggle, there was also Bach or Beethoven; the secret policeman suggested that he go to the House of Mourning to see for himself what was available there and choose – now he could feel his face turning red: it had been a long time since he'd spoken for so long and so furiously, he was getting out of breath – and eventually it turned into a squabble: why Janáček, well because Janáček was what he wanted, but that was unusual, they said, and kept trying to get him to change his mind, as if those two records were in some way dangerous, some kind of explosive device, so eventually he told them that his wife had studied piano and therefore liked to listen to piano music, that she was particularly fond of it, and at that point they asked if the Janáček was just for the piano – by now he was barely coherent, so upset he could scarcely breathe and exhausted by all the talking, and then suddenly he recalled the moment it came to an end and burst out laughing before he even finished his account, like someone who is telling a joke and starts laughing before the punchline: he was almost hysterical and realised he was on the verge of losing it, but he managed to get a grip and finished: the minute he told them that they were just pieces for piano or piano and female voice, everything was suddenly fine, they said they would ring the funeral parlour to let them know the ceremony could go ahead and he was free to go, but he didn't understand any of it, why all this fuss about the music and why they suddenly said "all right"; he really and truly just didn't get it, not at all.

Silence reigned for a moment.

"They've probably never heard of Janáček, that's all there is to it," said the professor.

"Yes, I'm sure that's it," said Gabo, by way of confirmation. "And since they didn't know him from Adam, they thought it was risky."

"He might have been some kind of a counterrevolutionary," added Viera, almost laughing.

"Or it's someone who has been banned, and imagine they allowed his music to be played at the cemetery," said one of the translators, rounding out the hypothesis.

The hubbub of voices resumed and thanks to this apparently plausible explanation he eventually managed to push to the back of his mind the issue with the records that had so baffled him. He was well and truly exhausted by all the talking and when he lit a cigarette, he had a coughing fit. He stood up and glanced at the bottles set out on the table at the back but there was only beer and wine. He went into the kitchen, found a glass in a cupboard, rinsed it thoroughly, and had some water. Then he went to sit down again, hoping to pick up some of the conversations around him, but everyone was talking at once, the people sitting on the old sofa where the bedding had been piled up and others, who had pulled their chairs up to the sofa, as well as several standing around him, but all he could discern was a steady buzz. He stared at the floor and the bottom end of the tiled stove. Then he remembered something and went over to his brother. On their way from the hotel his brother suggested that the three of them didn't have to go back by coach, but could take the train with him.

His brother was sitting at the back of the room with his wife and daughter. He bent down to him and said he'd rather they took the coach back, as he was already very tired and was sure he would fall asleep on the train. He would prefer to be alone at this time.

He went back and sat down on the edge of the recamier and lit a cigarette. A quick glance at his watch told him that he wouldn't have to sit there much longer, as at around twenty to three he ought to leave this hubbub, where he felt completely superfluous anyway. He just sat there, resting.

All of a sudden he felt a hand on his shoulder. He looked up to see a gaunt figure with thinning white hair: it was Tóno Rybárik, whom he recognised although they had met only two or three times before. "The funeral begins in less than half an hour. Perhaps you should be there earlier. I'll give you a lift." He stood up, nodded and went out into the hallway, where he had left his coat. Rybárik and his wife also went out: they had thrown their coats over the chairs in the kitchen, like all the other guests. He seemed to remember that Tóno R had been a designer in a factory in Partizánske, while his wife, now also a pensioner, had worked in the factory workers' hostel. One of his wife's cousins – she was tall, powerfully built, and loud – he couldn't stand her when he first met her in this house but soon discovered that she was actually rather nice and good-natured.

There were two cars parked outside the gate: one had brought his wife's relatives from Nitra, the cousin from Bratislava, her sister, mother and her brother-in-law, who was the driver. They got into the other car: he said he wanted to sit in front, next to the driver. Tóno started the engine and said: "It comes to us all in the end". He nodded, with his spirits lifted now that he had left the crowded room behind, and said, almost bragging: "About a month ago the doctors said I'd had a heart attack. I never even knew." The car turned off the main road towards the cemetery. He noticed the policeman-tenant standing on the corner, as if on duty. The old gentleman at the wheel gave a melancholy smile. "Oh, the good old days of my first heart attack." And then fell silent.

They didn't pull up at the gate which he and his wife normally used when they went to the cemetery at All Saints', whether on foot or by car, with piles of wreaths and bouquets and flowers in pots, and it was often difficult to find a parking space there. He didn't know where they were going but soon the car stopped, at a car park that was new to him, just outside the newly extended part of the cemetery. They got out and he saw after a few steps that this end was very close to the House of Mourning. The path went slightly uphill and as they walked, a view of the old cemetery opened up before him, with his wife's family vault a little higher up beneath a big tree.

The House of Mourning was quiet and rather dark. It felt good to be in the dark, silent and empty hall but at the same time he wished it would fill up as soon as possible. And that it would start. The elderly couple who gave him a lift sat down in the third or fourth row. "Thank you for the lift," he whispered, as if they were in church, and headed for the front row, as he knew that was where he'd be sitting as family, indeed: next of kin. He could choose any seat in the front row. He opted for the end seat by the central aisle, of course.

He was glad he was able to pick his own seat, having once had a terrible experience here: he had palpitations and kept looking around in confusion, just because he had to sit in the middle of the front row, next to his wife. At that time he had a phobia about sitting in the middle of a row: at the theatre or the cinema he always wanted the seat at the end of a row. It must have been in October 1957, at the funeral of his wife's father Fedor, the second of the three Jesenský brothers. He had died quite suddenly: he had gone to the bedroom to take a headache pill and was found dead in his bed the next morning.

That was the first of three family funerals he had attended here, in October 1957, then came Zora's mother's in May 1967, and finally, two years ago, her niece's funeral. But those were church funerals, with the church in charge of everything, within an established framework that ensured the right atmosphere, and there was no need to organise a eulogy. His wife had in fact made a speech when Jelka died, but normally all you had to do was tell the minister what needed to be said and he would put it into set words and phrases and could be relied on to deliver it in the appropriate tone of voice. The way the church could stage a funeral saved so much effort: this alone made paying the church tithe worthwhile. But his wife had stopped paying her tithes long ago. He was obliged to take on the role of director even though the premiere would be taking place without a dress rehearsal.

He heard some rustling at the back, looked around and saw people enter and take their seats in the back rows. Those who had come by coach had not yet come, but looking at his watch he thought they would be there any minute. He got up and went to the front where there was a door, as the man at the funeral parlour told him to. He stopped before a raised stage which took up the front of the room: that was where the coffin lay – he saw it the minute he came in – and above the stage was an organ. He remembered there being some singing at each of those past funerals. The priest would say something, the mourners would stand up and sing, then sit down again, then get up and sing and sit down again. At the mention of Protestants, his mother always said that when she was growing up in Liberec there was a saying: the Protestants are a choir, they go to church for the singing, they get up and sing, sit down and stand up again and sing, then sit down again, then they sing again for a while. That's what a Protestant service is all about.

The funeral director emerged discreetly from a nearby door with the two LPs, and quietly checked if he had the order of the passages right. He informed the funeral director that there would now be three eulogies. The first would be by a man, the second by a tall, slightly older woman, the third by a younger woman. It wouldn't be hard to remember. They would be here any minute anyway.

The professor was already there. He made the introductions. The first eulogy. He turned around and saw the translators in one of the back rows. The one who was supposed to give the speech was standing at the end. He caught her eye and gently beckoned her to come over. The master of ceremonies told both to go into a side room and stay there until asked to come out. He spotted his sister-in-law approaching down the central aisle, followed by the two girls. She stopped at the front row and he was about to go over to her but then saw that the third speaker had pushed in front of his sister-in-law and was coming to the front. Once the girl reached them he introduced her to the emcee as the person who would be giving the third speech. His sister-in-law was still standing by the front row. He went down the narrow aisle between the podium and the benches and sat down in the last seat before the aisle, while his sister-in-law took the last seat on the opposite side. As he turned to look at her, he saw Agneša some three rows further back, while the cousin and her family took the seats in the front row next to him.

He cast a final glance back. The people who had arrived by coach were quickly taking their seats. Through a gap between them he saw Darka and her husband, with whom he'd had dinner last night. So everyone is here now, he thought. He heard the shuffling of many feet, then the odd single shuffle. The shuffling came from the feet of people who couldn't find a seat and had to stand at the back and were now slowly edging forward on both sides. The gentle shuffling of feet was actually all he could hear now. He was reminded of his childhood days, when his father used to get complimentary tickets as a journalist to every theatre production and would often take him along to his beloved operas. Once the audience had settled down in their seats, the orchestra would start tuning up. A meaningless jumble of sounds – this was before he knew the word cacophony – would suddenly stop when the conductor took to his dais. Now, too, the room fell silent, everyone was sitting or standing, except the conductor was nowhere to be seen. He wondered what was going on, as until just a minute ago he had seen to everything like a stage manager, he had taken the performers over to the emcee, the score was in hand as well as the LPs, so why the delay? What fresh problem could have come up, he fretted impatiently, as if it were his fault.

At his mother's funeral, too, he had fretted like this before the ceremony began. In the morning he'd been to the National Committee to hand over the eulogy which was to be delivered by one of their staff. A clerk asked if he wanted some poetry to be read, as they had some poems specially for the occasion and she could arrange for an actor to deliver them. He took a look at the poems, chose one from the turn of the century and said he knew people at the theatre, and rang the artistic director of the drama company, his former boss from his time as a dramaturg, who was one of their two best declaimers of poetry. The man promised to be at the cemetery by three o'clock. It was long past three, there was music playing, and everyone was standing around his mother's coffin. When he arrived at last, he quickly ran his eyes over the text and read out the poem. Impeccably.

Suddenly he gave a start. He got a real fright. He heard some noise coming from the loudspeakers, a sharp, shrill sound amplified extremely loud. Goodness gracious, what was going on? Were they doing it on purpose? How long would this go on? Then everything went quiet again. A few seconds passed and there was more noise from the speakers, more subdued this time, but soon after that, the first bars of piano music and a female voice rang out. Their stereo system was probably better than his, at home he did notice that the record was quite worn, but here it was much more obvious. However, the noise receded after the first few bars and only the piano and the female voice could be heard. He started fretting again, wondering if others, too, would hear what he heard in the piano and the female voice, the plaintive tune, so strange yet so much like folk song. As the piano and female voice continued to ring out steadily and mournfully, he hoped that perhaps what he heard in them was also heard by everyone else.

The piece finished and for a while nothing happened, until a side door opened and the professor came out onto the podium. He began in a lyrical tone, the way he had spoken to him in Bratislava, about the last time he had met Zora, last summer in the mountains near the Polish border, that it was symbolic that their encounter happened by a well which was believed to have some unusual properties that brought people from the nearby villages to draw water from it. He had a distinctive voice and spoke with an earnest dignity, pausing here and there, emphasising particular words and phrases. He speaks well, that's s good, it's as it should be, he thought. He offered just a series of impressions, which made it more personal and also more effective, although the outline of the person he was talking about remained blurred, as the professor didn't go into specifics or use any of the material he had prepared for him.

Once the professor had left by the side door, one of Janáček's Moravian songs rang out from the speakers. This was the one whose dissonant charm had always given him butterflies in the stomach. At the point where a female vibrato suddenly comes in on a high note he felt as if someone had stabbed him in the heart, something in his chest trembled and he almost let out a sob. He sat there all curled up within himself, forgetting about everyone else for a while, just listening to the music until it came to an end. Then he turned to look at the door, expecting the translator to emerge. But she did not.

He fixed his gaze on the door. The podium was empty, there was no music. He couldn't imagine what might be going on behind the door. They were aware that the professor had finished his speech, as after all he'd returned to the room from which the others were supposed to emerge. Yet no one did. This time he heard whispers behind him. Perhaps some people thought that there was only one speech and were now waiting for the gravediggers to take the coffin away. But no one came. It was like in a cinema, when a film reel snagged in the middle of a screening. Suddenly he noticed that Martin got up from a bench behind him, went up the steps to the podium and through the door at the back. He emerged a moment later, followed by Viera H, who was going to deliver the speech. He couldn't understand what was happening. Did Martin have to go and call her? Wouldn't she have come out of her own accord if he hadn't gone in to fetch her?

The woman on the podium spoke of the deceased as a translator who had helped to raise a whole new generation of students, in a specific, very specific way. She delivered the speech in a clear, distinct voice; she was pleasant to look at, she had retained an air of freshness and youthful charm, and her voice was quite mellifluous too; the only problem was that the actual text she was reading was too factual. After a few minutes he realised that this wasn't really a eulogy but series of reminiscences more suitable for a limited circle of translators in the Writers' Union. The longer he listened, the more his disappointment grew. Translators can't write, he thought. His wife had been an exception.

Another Moravian song could be heard, but his mind was still dwelling on the last speech. He felt like a dramaturg responsible for the repertory at the House of Mourning. Listening to the piano and the voice, he decided that even if many in the audience may have failed to grasp the full import of what had just been said about the deceased as a translator, they must nevertheless have been left with the impression that her work had been complex and difficult. In a way, the translator complemented the professor's lofty speech by making clear how much imagination and invention Zora's work required, but she had done so in a tedious, unimaginative way. But at least something about her professional career had been said.

It was now time for the girl to read the speech that he knew intimately. From the first words, spoken in a shy voice, it was clear that she was going to read the whole text too quietly and monotonously. Unwittingly he turned somewhat to the side, to where Agneša was sitting. She was looking at the girl on the podium and their eyes met briefly. He gave her an imperceptible smile and she, too, responded with the trace of a smile: it wasn't a waste of effort, their smiles said to each other.

The girl continued in a monotone, without raising her voice: the person who had now taken to the stage was someone who had never addressed a large group of people and therefore spoke indistinctly, unable to pause where needed, or to lay emphasis on a particular point. She seemed almost to be in a hurry to get the whole business over with as soon as possible. But this was what he'd had in mind. Here was someone quite anonymous, whose name no one knew – and would never know, since no report of the funeral would ever appear – here was this unknown person in a grey jumper and a skirt that was slightly too long, speaking about a woman who sought and found a purpose in the last years of her life in reading cookery books and in cooking, in reading books on gardening and rockeries, in clearing the ground, planting shrubs and building a rockery, in going to markets to buy flowers to plant, by watering the garden – in short, in living a completely ordinary life. She kept coming up with fresh ideas for the flat, the first one she had personally furnished in her life. He noticed one of the relative in the front row gingerly taking out a handkerchief and dabbing at her eyes. He heard women behind him sniffling: sounds of emotion. Perhaps some in the audience could detect in these undemanding personal reminiscences an allusion to the undoing of the person it concerned; and perhaps some felt closer to the deceased not when she was creating works of art but living the same ordinary life as everyone else. It had not, after all, been pointless to include this speech, he thought with some satisfaction. In fact, the monotonous delivery reflected the weariness of those years that the speech was all about.

Now solo piano music sounded from the speakers and after a while four men came down the central aisle, positioned themselves around the coffin, placed two straps underneath it and raised it. They began slowly to walk off. His heart was pounding again. Until this point he'd been merely watching, observing the whole process in the manner of a stage manager, a dramaturg; but now he too would have to mount the stage. After the men carrying the coffin passed him, he stood up and followed them. His sister-in-law at the end of the bench also rose and walked beside him. Her closest relative, even though she hadn't been to see her in hospital once during her last two weeks. He sensed that his wife's cousins and their families had joined the mourners, followed by those who had come by coach. They emerged into the light of day but the sun had sunk somewhere below the horizon. He noticed that quite a few people were standing outside. Had they heard anything of what had been said within? They went down the gentle slope towards the old part of the cemetery, and then through the old cemetery itself, until the men carrying the coffin came to a halt before a vault not far from the main gate, further down the hill. This spot – one might justly call it prestigious – had been chosen for the writer Janko Jesenský soon after the war and was later expanded to accommodate the whole family.

He could see people standing around the tomb, as well as a long row of people stretching all the way down to the cemetery entrance. He had thought that everyone would fit easily into the House of Mourning and it made him feel almost uncomfortable that so many eyes were now fixed on the coffin, and quite certainly also on him.

The gravediggers lowered the coffin onto the ground. The people behind him fanned out in a semi-circle around the tomb, and three men in overalls and with some tools appeared. Their first attempt at lifting the first of three stone slabs from the vault was unsuccessful: they tried to insert the tools this way and that, but couldn't shift the slab. Raising their voices, they made suggestions to each other about how to proceed, and eventually they managed to lift the first slab and drag it to one side. Now, even without any tools, they had no trouble easing out the middle slab as well as the one at the other end, as they could now use their hands on one side to lift them.

The sound of bells tolling had been coming from the speakers in the House of Mourning for a while now. He thought that the bells sounded more powerful at his mother's funeral, as there were speakers among the graves as well. It was the turn of the gravediggers again: they lifted the coffin by the straps, held it above the vault and started to slowly lower it. There was room for two coffins there, he calculated in his head, her brother, father and mother were in the bottom row, above them was her niece, and now his wife, and the last place would be left for his sister-in-law. She attached so much importance to being buried here, next to her daughter and husband, he thought. As far as he was concerned, he couldn't care less where he ended up being buried. Suddenly, however, he saw that the gravediggers didn't balance the coffin properly, its lower edge was tilting downwards – if they let it slip off the straps now, its weight would pull it down, the front of the coffin would slide down onto the stone slabs covering the bottom graves, he would hear the cracking of chipped wood – but the grave-diggers, amid constant shouting, managed to re-balance the coffin and began lowering it very slowly. He breathed a sigh of relief when he heard a knock as it landed without a scratch, and the gravediggers immediately hauled the straps out from under it. Now the three men in overalls got to work on the vault, without using tools this time, except that whenever they were about to lift one of the slabs, they yelled to each other like removals men lifting a heavy piece of furniture, and before long the three stones were back in place and the vault was closed again. The gravediggers brought four wreaths and laid them on the tomb; he hadn't noticed them before as they had lain before the podium, in front of the coffin, thinking they were a fixture of the room, so he hadn't even glanced at the ribbons to read what was written on them – oh my God, he thought, he hadn't ordered a wreath! How could that have happened? He stared at the wreaths as if he had lost his mind, until it dawned on him that a wreath in his and his sister-in-law's name was included in what he had ordered and paid for at the funeral parlour back in Bratislava, so everything was all right after all; the third wreath was probably from the translators, and the fourth from the families of the cousin in Bratislava and her sister in Nitra; some people had also brought bouquets to the vault. The tolling of bells from the speakers stopped and in the sudden silence he heard only a sort of amplified sound of movement as people swarmed all around him, and he was astonished to realise that it was actually all over. The programme had run its course. Suddenly he stood there helpless: what was he to do now? Up to this point he had planned, arranged and organised everything that happened here but now the curtain had gone down and he hadn't planned anything from this point onwards. Was anything else expected of him?

As he looked around uncertainly, Luda Škultéty approached him. He recognised her, as he and his wife had been to see her a year ago about a translation; she too had been a translator for many years and still worked at Matica; he knew she had been his wife's childhood friend, and a few years older than her. Luda agreed to front that particular translation, but by the time his wife thought of asking her the publishing house had given it to someone else.

Luda – scion of another ancient and illustrious family that schoolchildren are taught about – told him as they parted: "We all got a memo advising us not to attend the funeral, but I came anyway." She sounded a little proud of herself and rightly so; she had rejected the advice, disobeyed the memo and, since she mentioned it to him, she probably saw no one else at the funeral who had shown similar courage.

A tall, though stooping elderly man came up to him. He had tears in his eyes. He was once, many years ago, a frequent visitor to her parents' home and would chat with her mother about the old days and what those from the old days were up to, those who were still alive that is. He also once worked at Matica but had long ago retired. He held out his hand and started to speak but stopped mid-sentence, his whole body overwhelmed by tears. After shaking his hand feebly with his own trembling hand, he took a step back. This was how he himself should be weeping, he thought, and felt another pang of guilt.

He cast another, surreptitious glance at the old man, who now stood on the incline next to the vault, still in tears. He recalled photos his wife had shown him from the old days, when young people used to come to the house and there had been a very joyful atmosphere: the old man was there in all of them. He is not weeping only for Zora, he thought. He is weeping for her brother, his friend and contemporary, he is weeping for her father and mother, the whole family that had died out, all of whom now lay buried in this vault; a piece of history that he too had lived through had just been buried, the world of his youth had been lowered into the vault, a chapter in the cultural history of this small nation, to which he, too, had wanted to contribute had now closed: she had been the last one still standing but now she too was gone.

Now Darka S and her husband stood before him. They both wore black and Darka had a veil over her face. How tiny she looked next to her husband. He must promise he would still come and visit them from time to time. And the actor said, in a quiet but clear voice: "It was a dignified funeral, as she deserved."

Now it was the turn of a tall, somewhat mannish woman, ramrod straight and with a long thin face, to hold her hand out to him. She wasn't the scion of an old family but had taught literature at the *gymnázium* for many years. Whenever they bumped into her in the street, his wife would avoid getting into a conversation, although they were once good friends. Later Zora explained: "When we were getting married, there was no one who badmouthed you more or spread more stupid gossip about you than that woman." But after the Russians invaded, his wife went to see her a few times, bringing things to read that circulated at the time, foreign journals with Sakharov's long memorandum*, as well as articles analysing why it all ended in such abject failure. And she came now, even though she too had received the memo. He got a bit cross, however, when she ended by saying: "I wish we had sung something for her, perhaps 'Hey, Slovaks'*" He smiled weakly and thought how lucky it was that no one else had come up with this idea. 'Hey, Slovaks', or the Internationale, or some other symbol-laden song.

He stood all by himself again, clutching his hat and staring at the vault. So this part of the proceedings was apparently now over for him too. A little further up a group of people surrounded Martin R, whose wife Viera was also a descendant of the Jesenský clan and some people here had known her father Vlado, the youngest of the three Jesenský brothers. He was sure that another group huddled around his sister-in-law and his wife's two cousins, indeed everyone here, knew many other people, except for him: no one knew him anymore, no one came up to offer their condolences.

After a while Tóno R turned up at his side and quietly suggested that it might be time to leave; he nodded and looked back one last time, to see a long line of people still stretching all the way to the lower cemetery gate, standing among the graves, by the tombs and down below around the gate, even though there was nothing happening anymore, as if waiting for something; the long queue stretching away to the gate reminded him of a line of pilgrims. He turned around and followed Tóno to the car park, almost all the way to the House of Mourning, where the people who had come by coach were standing. They were no longer offering their condolences, as he had seen everyone earlier or at lunch, but then who were all those folk he didn't know in the line all the way from the vault to the gate and among the tombs? Presumably they attended every funeral, or maybe they didn't attend every funeral but came now because the last member of a family that had been an integral part of Martin had died, a family that had lived here for well over a hundred years, in what had originally been a farmer's house – although by then the farmer, his wife's grandfather*, who was also a lawyer, may still have kept cows and pigs, but he was already dabbling in politics and as a result lost his fields after running up debts standing for election to the parliament in Pest and failing to be elected. Others in the crowd will have come because they knew that some sort of notable figure was being buried, although most of those who knew it was happening, the nationalist 'Hey Slovaks', had stayed at home.

There were about eight cars in the car park. So they were not the only ones who had come by car. Two of the cars were official. Who knows how many more cars were parked in front of the old cemetery gate. To the best of his recollection, that was where people usually parked.

This time he asked Boža to sit in front. Tóno started the engine and as the car began to move, he said: "You will find things difficult now for a while when you're back home." He thought about that: difficult, that was one way of putting it, but it was not quite the right word. Difficult – what did that even mean? When they came to the crossroads by the main gate to the old cemetery, he noticed his policeman-tenant standing there. Nothingy, that was the word, from now on things would be sort of nothingy. But that would have sounded stupid. So he said: "Especially when one has nothing to do all day."

Boža asked: "By the way, how many years were you together?" He did a quick calculation in his head, just to check: "Eighteen." As he uttered the last word, he choked up, and if he'd had to say anything more he would have burst into tears. What's going on? It's not as if this was news to him. Yes, eighteen years was a long time, but many people had been together for far longer, so why should it be such a big deal? Yes, it has been eighteen years, and now she has left him, all of a sudden. He could no longer walk properly on his own two feet, he would just stagger about from now on. She shouldn't have left him here. He never asked for that. He felt so sorry for himself that he was tearing up.

But by the time they reached the iron gate and got out of the car, he managed to get a grip.

As they walked down the wide path by the long house, a small woman, as round as a ball, in a peasant-style black dress, came out of the sister-in-law's little house. She stretched out both her arms in their direction as if to welcome them. His sister-in-law had asked her to stay and look after the house. She shook hands with everyone and lamented that she wasn't able to attend the funeral. She was from a nearby village where his sister-in-law often visited her in summer, and despite her extraordinary bulk, accompanied her on day-long hikes. He and his wife had also visited her a few times. Blatnica, her village, was at the entrance to a valley some ten kilometres long and you could drive through it on a narrow, winding road. She advised them about where to find the most beautiful spots in the valley. Last year, when they spent nearly two months here because they no longer had a place to stay in the Tatras, they would often came to this valley for the day, pitch a tent, and read, or sometimes climb the hill. The woman asked how the funeral had gone.

He knew that Boža would give her a detailed report. He excused himself and said he needed a little rest.

He went back to the empty room and sat down at the large rectangular table and surveyed the trays of canapés and the bottles of beer and wine. Never in the past eighteen years had he ever seen so many bottles in this room. Nor had as many people ever been here as there would be now. There was quite a large gathering when Zora's father died, but the people mostly stayed in the reception room and on the veranda. But even then, there probably hadn't been so many bottles of wine and beer. They weren't the celebrating kind, not even after their wedding, but in any case they were married in Bratislava and she had kept it secret from her parents, although they did find out eventually of course, and once her parents had come to terms with what was now a fact of life and he was allowed to enter this house again, there were still no celebrations. The only celebrations that took place were on birthdays, at Christmas and Easter, and on those occasions a tiny shot glass would be placed by everyone's plate with just a few drops in it, from a bottle kept in the Moroccan Art-Nouveau sideboard that now bulged out in all its glorious ugliness in his sister-in-law's flat one floor below theirs; a single bottle of greenish or whitish alcohol would always last for at least a couple of years. And wine? Had wine ever been served on these occasions? He couldn't recall. Actually, yes, fruit wine, usually made from apples, produced by her father: everyone was offered a glassful after a meal; it went straight to one's head like strong alcohol and there were tales from the old days of people who had drunk too much and could barely stand on their feet.

People gradually started to trickle back. He went over to his sister-in-law's house to ask someone to make him a cup of coffee. The two girls were already sitting there so first he thanked the one who delivered the speech: it was just right, so free of any frills, and after praising her he added, looking at both of them: "You must be quite relieved that it's over," and her friend said, "Well, yes, it's not the kind of thing she does every day." He asked her for the text and stuffed it into his pocket. Then he asked his sister-in-law for a cup of coffee. Why, she was going to make coffee for everyone, he just had to wait a little, she said, mildly annoyed. Yes, but he had to go earlier, he had a train to catch, that was why he was asking.

He went back to the house opposite and stopped in front of the door. A whitewashed bench that stood here by the wall had already been there eighteen years ago, when he first came here. How many times over those eighteen years did he leave the house and sit there when he was feeling down or bored, thinking that he would much rather be at home, that he had overstayed his welcome. He would sit there for half an hour, or even a whole hour, and if a cat passed by – because there had always been cats around here, descendants of an original mother cat – he would pick it up, put it in his lap and pet it. Or he would come and sit out here when visitors he didn't know came to the house, or when something had hurt his feelings and he had to slowly get over his sense of resentment. The bench provided a kind of privacy, a place to which he could withdraw from the house. And sometimes he and Zora would sit there in the early evening, exchanging a word now and then, and once his wife remarked: "We're sitting here like an old couple."

He saw the professor coming back with a group of friends. When they took their coats off, he went over to thank the professor. "I've already told you that it was an honour," Felix said, indicating that the topic was closed. They went back to the room together. Still in the doorway, he asked: "What happened after your speech, why was there such long pause with nothing happening?" – "Oh, that was quite a brouha-ha," Felix said, "or rather not a brouhaha, it was incredible, outrageous." He wanted to know what had happened. "I've already told the story on the way here," the professor said but someone shouted from the room: "Just tell it again, it's not the last time you will have to tell it."

It turned out that when the professor first went into the side room, he was approached by a fat, stocky fellow, not nice at all – aha, he thought, that was the fellow with the butcher's mug who had sat by the desk – he flashed his secret police ID and wanted to know what he was going to talk about. That's none of your business, the professor told him, you'll hear it in a minute anyway, but the man said he just wanted to know what he would focus on. You'll hear in a minute, he repeated, but the fellow kept insisting, so he did say something, but by then it was time for him to give the speech, so that was the end of Act One. When he returned to the room after delivering his eulogy, the man came up to him again and asked him to hand it over. "Certainly not," the professor told him, but the man insisted that he had the right to ask for it. So the profes-sor said that if his agency made a request, he would send it to them, but he wouldn't hand it over now. "What do you mean, you won't hand it to me?" "I just won't, and that's that. I'm not giving it to you, end of story." At that point the man tried to wrench the speech out of his hand but that really went too far, so he grabbed it back, put it in his pocket and said, in a rage: "Who do you think you are? This is outrageous. I will complain to the relevant authorities." The fat man realised that he wasn't going to get the speech and resorted to threats: just wait and see what happens, so he told him, "Very well, I'll see what I'll see," at which the chap exploded again and shouted that he was acting in an official capacity, so he told him, "all right, so why don't you behave as appropriate to someone acting in an official capacity?", but the fat man kept

(402)

threatening him, claimed he was prevented from carrying out an official act, whereupon he told him to go and get stuffed. The fat man started shouting but just then Martin came in and asked what was going on and why the proceedings had stopped, why was the next speaker not taking the stage, and that's when the man finally left him in peace and sat down on a bench in the side room, giving him dirty looks.

Someone said, almost in disbelief, "But that's absurd, totally absurd," and someone else chipped in with a sarcastic explanation, "Oh well, they've brought back censorship and now they think they have to censor everyone who wants to open their mouth in public." Soňa shouted: "Isn't that just typical of the Husák regime?" He saw that in her fury she had gone all red in the face and kept shouting: "This is the very essence of the Husák regime." There was a moment's silence and then his sister-in-law brought him his cup of coffee, someone gave the professor a glass of wine and said he needed to wash it away. The professor downed the glass in a single gulp and concluded: "They can kiss my arse, if you'll pardon the expression." Suddenly, a hubbub of voices arose again, the professor went over to one of the groups, while he went back and sat down on the edge of the recamier.

As he slowly sipped his coffee something suddenly struck him as quite amusing. It was the way everyone fell silent as soon as Soňa, ever the radical, spoke of "the Husák regime". If she had said the communist regime, everyone would have agreed with her – those expelled from the party as well as those who were still members but were fed up with the communists, those who had always been opposed to communism, as well as those who were fed up with everything. But bringing Husák into it was a different matter; Husák was a Slovak and he had reached the highest position in the country, higher than everyone, including the Czechs; he knew what he was doing and would figure it all out, find a way of dragging the cart out of the mud; he was the only one who could manage to do it. There may have been three or four people here who didn't think so, but for everyone else, criticising Husák was crossing a line. How often did Zora clash with many of these people on this issue, how often did she try to make them open their eyes… but they would just give her pitying looks whenever the subject came up. All her talking and arguing had been in vain. She should have recognised long ago, in 1968, that everyone she knew, as well as her readers whom she didn't know, all her compatriots – well, maybe not every single one of them, but a majority – had found their Messiah: this kind of faith was not to be disproved. Had she recognised that, she might have had a state funeral today. But what use would that have been to her, he thought? Was there anything more futile than trying to convince someone of something, given that everyone had their own opinions and their own grounds for it? This occurred to him because he himself had all his life, ever since his *gymnázium* days, tried to convince his classmates of all kinds of things and after the war used to bend his friends' ears about all kinds of things. He would have been better off fishing instead of wasting his time.

As he was finishing his coffee he heard someone at the back say that the police had closed off one of the roads to the cemetery. He remembered their policeman-tenant positioned throughout at the crossroads by the gate of the old cemetery. Well, of course, they too must have received a memo, their instructions, a warning, an order.

He glanced around the room. The bottles of wine and beer were open, people were tucking into the canapés. The funeral wake was in full swing. Now he, too, could go up to the small round table at the back and pour himself a glass of wine. And then another. He was now entitled to do so and everyone would accept that. But afterwards he'd have to sit on the train for hours tormented by the thought that there wasn't a single bottle of wine anywhere on that train and he couldn't have another drink. He could start hitting the bottle here, he was within his rights to do so, they would all grant that, but he wanted to go back by train, not on the coach with everyone else. He wanted to be alone.

He went over to the group of translators and asked the one who had delivered the speech if he could have the manuscript as a keepsake. But of course, we've made copies. "Wasn't it a bit too heavy, though?" a translator asked. Oh no, it wasn't, he assured her, and if even if it had been, what really mattered was that it had been said. And it wasn't all that learned anyway. He no longer cared what he was saying. Then he went to find his brother and his family, who were sitting apart from everyone else. He said goodbye to them as well, since he was about to go.

He went from one group to the next, saying a few words here and there, asking the odd question, listening to scraps of conversation, and then started to say his goodbyes: he felt superfluous here, nobody needed him, and whichever group he might have joined, they would have felt uncomfortable because they would have to be considerate to him. There was nothing more for him to do here. And he had a train to catch. He shook hands with a few people quietly, since he couldn't say goodbye to everyone, waved to his brother once more, crept out into the hallway, put on his coat, said thank you to his sister-in-law, picked up his suitcase, and left the house.

He closed the heavy iron gate behind him, walked past a hovel which was now home to several Gypsy families – he knew some of the children and old men and women who used to hang around outside the gate all day long in summer – then turned around the corner to a fork in the arterial road leading out of town where the bus stopped. He found his bus on the timetable, as all the local buses stopped here, and seeing that it was due in about ten minutes, he put his suitcase down even though there was mud on the pavement.

It was late afternoon, the sun lying low behind the clouds, with cars and tractors, lorries and buses and coaches flowing in both directions in an endless stream, through puddles and pools of water that splashed every which way. The hills above town loomed grey and the long straight road from which the bus would emerge and which led out of town was even more unattractive than usual. This part of town had always been particularly ugly even though there was a hospital right across the street set amidst lots of greenery and a lawn. This, too, used to be part of his life, the wait for the bus that would take him to the station, or the drive along this road on their way for a day trip, but now it was part of his life no longer: he stood there as a tourist who had no idea if or when he would ever return to this place and whether he would ever set eyes on this gloomy and shabby part of the country again.

When he didn't come by car, his wife would usually see him off, taking the bus and going all way to the station with him. Nevertheless he was usually, although not always, glad to wait for a bus and happy that a train would take him to the city, back to the winding tracks along which his normal life meandered. But because of his wife, he usually spent more time in this place than he would have done of his own free will.

But he was usually also quite happy to come to Martin and to spend a few days, often a week or more, in her parents' home. Being here was a comfort and for a few days he would feel his lungs fill with tranquillity. Everything that he found annoying about the city seemed very far away. The hills were within easy reach. And quite often it felt cosy in her house, almost as in a sanatorium. He had his peace and quiet. Though he couldn't stand the peace and quiet for very long, he did initially find it soothing. This was somewhere he could escape from the city. What a shame that after a while all that peace and quiet that began behind that iron gate would start to get on his nerves. He couldn't help feeling there was something waiting for him back in the city. While his mother was still alive, she would be waiting for him, but otherwise there was nothing for him to hurry back to. And now all that was left here was one partly furnished room to which he no longer had any reason to return.

He boarded the bus. The square was teeming with people out shopping. Beyond the square lay another ugly street with the only imposing building being the greyish-black two-storey post office, the former courthouse under the old Hungarian Kingdom. And then there opened up a view of the housing estate's highrises, with crowds of people likewise on their way to the shops. Beyond the housing estate there was only a short stretch of fields before the next village that merged with Vrútky, the railway junction from where trains from Bratislava and also from Prague continued to the Tatras and further east, towards the Soviet border and Moscow.

As he watched the fields pass by and as the first houses of the village became visible from the windows of the bus, it suddenly occurred to him that for the entire duration of the funeral, an hour or more, he hadn't thought of her face at all, nor had it appeared to him earlier, while he was making the arrangements, he was merely registering what was being said about her and appraising it; when the girl read her speech, he listened out in every sentence for at least some trace of his own voice and how it sounded the first time when he delivered the speech, somewhat haltingly, to Agneša. All kinds of things occurred to him but never her face and guiltily he now recalled it as it had looked in the hospital when he was summoned late at night, the nurse having tied a white band under her chin and around the crown of her head. No, this wasn't how he wanted to remember her face, nor did he want to see it the way it looked during the last few days and weeks at home, reclining on the chaise longue, expressionless, somewhat puffy, tired, taciturn… no, this was not what he had in mind when he felt guilty about not seeing her face, and maybe because during the funeral he had to look at Viera H for some ten minutes as she stood on the podium delivering her eulogy, he now remembered one afternoon at a café with Viera and someone else: it was after three in the afternoon and he hadn't been home since the morning and that's when he saw her standing there, in another part of the café, scouring the room, so he got up and said he had to go, he went up to her and saw that her face was tense, her jaw tightly clenched as always when she was angry and power-less. No, that was not a face he wanted to see either, it was as if he were browsing through a photo album: at the beginning her face was smiling and much more youthful as she came towards him – this would have been about the third time they met, he had been waiting for her outside Café Štefánka, on the corner of Palisády and Suché mýto, he saw her from afar in her brown leather jacket, there was something fresh-faced and elated about her, they had arranged to go for a little af-ternoon hike, took a bus from the stop at Štefánka to Koliba Hill, and from there they would walk up to Kamzík and down to Červený most… but that had been a very long time ago, before they were married, over eighteen years ago. And he thought that the reason why he couldn't conjure up her face was that it wasn't a single face but hundreds of faces over the years, entire albums that he could browse through, but if he picked out any one of her faces it would be only a stone statue rather than her face in a particular situation and thus a face that had reflected something of her. He found it impossible to pick out just one face from these albums because his mind would keep scrolling through all her other faces, the faces stored in his memory.

Having got off the bus in front of the railway station, he went straight to the platform for some fresh air, and when he looked up at the high peak behind the station it was no longer grey and he could see only a thick blue outline as dusk was falling, and he went back inside to hide from the chill of the evening. He had nearly half an hour to kill before his train was due; he knew the train timetable by heart as this was usually the way he went home when he didn't drive. He opened the waiting room door but was instantly hit by its stale, cold and damp air, so he closed the door and sat down on a bench in the big ticket hall, and as he sat there amid the hustle and bustle of people coming up to the ticket counters and listening to their footsteps clacking on the floor, he wondered how much longer the mourners would stay at the house chatting, eating snacks, drinking wine or beer, perhaps till six, or seven, or eight, it would make no difference to the coach driver as he'd have to drive in the dark anyway. He enjoyed the sound of the footsteps more than that of people talking, and now he no longer had to watch himself either and wonder who he should talk to and what to say. It felt a bit like after an opening night at the theatre in his dramaturg days, when the curtain came down on a show he had worked on: when it was a triumph, the tension inside him abated and he would feel an easeful tiredness coursing through his body; if, on the other hand, he couldn't tell from the perfunctory polite applause after the final curtain whether the production was a flop, that felt different too; but this time everything had worked out, the performance had been a success, he recalled Tóno coming up to him and saying it was time to go and offering to give him a lift back, he remembered looking back one more time and seeing a long line of people stretching from the vault all the way to the old cemetery gate, people even standing outside, filling almost the entire width of the gate and the long queue from the gate reminding him of a line of pilgrims, yes, that was how he remembered that moment, exactly like that. But wait a minute, how was that possible, he suddenly wondered, in the ticket hall that had meanwhile gone dark, the bright lights at the counters flickering on; that was hard to believe, could he really have remembered that moment in this way? After all, he couldn't have seen all the way to the end of the cemetery, his imagination must have hijacked his true perception and given it a workover, surely this couldn't be the real, genuine memory, the family vault was not all that far from the old gate and the path to the vault went up a slope that was only moderate, so how could he have seen a long line of people along that short stretch between the gate and the family vault, how could it possibly have reminded him of a long line of pilgrims? This was just his imagination playing a trick on him, already at work concocting legends: maybe, just maybe, if he had been looking down from a higher vantage point, after walking up to the House of Mourning with Tóno and before turning towards the car park... but he was quite sure that he had followed in the other man's footsteps, head down and looking at the ground, as he didn't want to see any familiar faces, and the only time he looked back at the gate was when he stood at the vault; he must have seen something that wasn't there, or perhaps he did see what was down there at the time, but now, as he tried to recall it, he had already formed his own image of it, but at the same time he knew that from now on, whenever he would recall that moment, in his mind's eye he would see not what had really taken place, but only what his imagination had conjured up. And he would continue to live in the world of memories, but they would be legends, some more beautiful, some less, and the sense that he was bringing a bit of the past back to life would be nothing but a delusion.

There was an announcement that his is train was due, so he went to wait for it on the platform. He would find an empty compartment, where it would be nice and quiet, and the steady rhythm of the turning wheels would help him sit back and relax, he would look out of the window at a landscape that was familiar to him and later just imagine it under the cover of darkness. Or he would just stare into the dark.

He boarded the train and sat down in an empty compartment, and when the train started moving and he looked out of the window at the landscape he knew so well, he didn't feel sad or mournful; he just felt as if it had been only yesterday that he got the call from the hospital telling him to come, as if it had been only yesterday that he drove to the hospital with the cousin who started packing his wife's belongings while he looked at the nurse as she closed his wife's open mouth with a white band. And the past seven days, when he constantly had to organise things, discuss funeral arrangements, see various people, when there was still something ahead of him, something to do, those seven days seemed to him like a single long, extremely long day, in the course of which he met lots of people and was constantly running from pillar to post. He knew that from now on he would have his peace and quiet. From now on he would meet hardly anyone, there would be nothing to organise or plan, nothing to arrange, no particular goal to follow. It would be the beginning of days that for him would be devoid of purpose or meaning.

When he got off the train soon after nine o'clock and reached the station building via the underpass, he headed – as planned – to the far end of the station to buy a bottle of wine from the restaurant at the station.

Outside the station he hailed a cab to take him home.

He was entitled to hold his own, private funeral wake. Everyone else was now on the coach, no one would ring, no one would drop by, he didn't really exist as far as anyone else was concerned. He could get through his bottle of wine quietly and at his leisure.

Next morning hunger drove him out of bed. Last night's dinner had consisted of the bottle of wine; there was no food at home even before he set out for the journey. He got dressed and went to buy some bread, butter, and cheese in a small shop open only for morning goods, came home, had his breakfast and sat down to do the only job he had left. When he got out of the cab last night, he found his letter box was full. Fewer telegrams now, mostly letters. He divided them into piles: those addressed to himself, those to his sister-in-law, and those to Viera and Martin, and to the cousin.

He started with the letters in his own pile, reading each one two or three times. Most letters, even if no longer than five lines long, conjured up the image of their writer. Some made him smile. Some addressed him directly while others were in the style of a "reflection", offering an assessment of Zora and highlighting what the writer thought was most important. Some of the letters made him get up, walk up and down the room, and let himself be moved by their content, others brought only the writer to mind. After starting with some hackneyed phrase, each writer in their own way stuck their head above the parapet of convention. And every one of those heads was familiar, spouting the same sort of stuff it had said to him before, and by which he was able to recognise it. Basically, the written word makes people reveal their true colours, show themselves for who they are.

At eleven thirty he took the lift down and collected that day's mail. There were only letters this time: he sorted them out; some were for him.

He sat down in his armchair reflecting on the people who had written to him. They were mostly those he had had dealings with over the past fifteen years or so. At the institute of the Academy where he had worked for years before he got fired, at *Kultúrny život*, the weekly to whose editorial office he used to bring his articles or just drop in for a chat, and also a few people from publishing houses. To him they read like farewell letters. Neither he nor they were in the habit of writing postcards from their holidays or Christmas cards. With a prescient certainty he knew that he would never have anything to do with any of them; he would never work at the Institute, even if after a while some of those who'd been fired might be rehired; he would never go to the editorial office where he'd stopped working three years ago, soon after the Russian invasion; he would never again go to a publishing house to hand in a translation, let alone a book he had written, or even just a reader's report on some German or English novel, nor would he sit there with a copy editor going through page after page of their comments on his manuscript. Yes, he would certainly bump into some of them in the street. They would exchange a "how are you?" and some small talk, and then part ways. Then there were some of those who'd been on the coach whom he would definitely go and see from time to time. But contact with them would be only occasional. It would be difficult to start a lively, even if just casual conversation about all manner of things with someone who is not busy doing something, who carries a void inside him, and who agonises only over himself and doesn't know what to do with that self. Things had been different when he went to see people with Zora: she had an easy manner that he was lacking, people enjoyed her company because she was good at listening and engaging with them, whereas he had always, willy-nilly, kept a certain distance from others, and was increasingly turning into an antisocial dullard.

It was past twelve-thirty, high time for lunch. From the day he had taken his wife to hospital, his daily routine had two fixed points: going for lunch between twelve and one, and visiting his wife in hospital at around four o'clock. Now there was just one fixed point left in his routine. The cousin was no longer in the canteen. He ate his lunch and walked up to her small office on the first floor at the back of the building. The door had been left open, she must have expected him to drop in. He sat down and waited.

When she came, he told her about his train journey home and about the morning spent reading the letters and telegrams that had arrived; he had sorted them out, some were for her. But first and foremost, he wanted to know how the coach journey had gone.

They had stayed till almost six; the journey was fine, there wasn't much traffic, and they were in Bratislava by ten. People continued talking about the funeral, saying how good the various speeches were, how well they complemented each other.

"But there's something I really have to tell you, I don't even know whether it's funny or sad: shortly before lunch I had a call from my cousin Lýdia who works at the Literary Foundation. She said that the secret police had turned up at the Writers' Union in the morning. They wanted to know if the Union had asked someone to give a eulogy. They were mainly interested in Professor Felix and whether it was the Union that had approached him, and also if they had been involved in any of the funeral arrangements. They discussed it with two of the Union's secretaries, then asked someone else a few questions, but everyone kept repeating, no, they hadn't approached anyone, they had nothing to do with it, answered no to every question, no, no, no, until the men eventually left. They got quite a fright and thought that the secret police might come back."

"Those people really have no reason to be frightened. They can say with a clear conscience that they hadn't even heard that she died. Certainly not from me, I didn't send them a death notice. They hadn't read about it in the paper; her death was of no concern to them, as she was no longer a member of the Union. But I'm glad those namby-pambies in the Writers' Union got a bit of a fright anyway."

"Oh, and there was this one rather awkward thing that happened on the coach. The young man who had organised the trip and made the arrangements with the driver, got up all of a sudden and started collecting money. People were taken by surprise, everyone thought you'd paid for the coach, and some actually said something to that effect."

Of course he was going to pay for the coach: he assumed they would send him a bill. Perhaps he should have left some money with Soňa and Edo when they promised to organise it. The idea simply hadn't occurred to him.

The cousin wondered what could be done now to put things right. But he didn't wish to revisit anything to do with these past seven days. As she remained silent, he said defiantly: "If someone thinks she wasn't worth it, too bad. Let them be offended. I don't give a damn."

Two months later he received a summons from the police as a witness. Not the secret police, but then again, they had been known to summon people to the Lost Property Agency where they also had offices. (Back in the 1950s they could set up an office wherever they liked, and for all he knew, they may have revived the practice.) He was supposed to go there the day after tomorrow but rather than waste his next day agonising over what it was about, he decided to go the next day.

It was the ordinary police. The policeman accepted his excuse (that he was about to go away) and agreed to talk to him straight away, found his file without further ado, unnecessary secrecy or chit-chat, and explained that the funeral parlour in Martin was under investigation: they had been overcharging, tampering with receipts and pocketing some of the money. A receipt with his signature had been found among the papers in their office. He remembered the three extra men they needed to hire to open the sealed family vault and to reseal it after the coffin had been placed inside. He had to pay for this, about a hundred and fifty crowns. "The receipt says one hundred and seventy." Oh yes, that was how much he had paid, he agreed, and the policeman let his colleagues in Martin know that his bill hadn't been tampered with.

Back at home he found the receipt from Martin in his desk. He had actually paid three hundred and twenty crowns. So this receipt had also been tampered with. He'd been cheated twice: first by being overcharged and then with a fake receipt, which he now validated. He was annoyed, but not enough to go back to the police; he was glad to draw a line under the matter. What annoyed him much more was that he had deceived himself. He didn't want to lie to the official and yet didn't tell him the truth. If he hadn't seen the receipt, he would have recalled a different amount whenever he'd been asked. His own memory had deceived him.

He stayed at his desk. It had been months since he had done any work, months since he had used the typewriter: he used it only as somewhere to keep letters, bills, everything that shouldn't be thrown away. The other day, as he thought back on the funeral, a small detail floated to the surface of his conciousness: in all his recollections up until now he saw himself sitting on the edge of the recamier as he told the guests about being summoned and questioned, and the argument about the LPs. But in fact the recamier was here in their flat in Bratislava; they had brought it over along with some other furniture from the house in Martin three years ago, so he couldn't have sat on its edge during the wake – his memory was like a sieve, making things up or changing details of things he was trying to recollect. He was annoyed, because just as the people in Martin had tampered with his bills, there was something inside him that was manipulating his own recollections.

1.

I have just returned from Martin. This was the first time I'd been back since my wife's funeral on December 28 last year (1972). I had to make that last visit in order to have the house surveyed, see to various minor matters, and to scour the place one last time for things that hadn't seemed particularly valuable before, such as old letters or documents, because Zora had either kept all the information contained in them in her head or else had long forgotten it all as unnecessary and relating to a long lost past and so she had felt no urgent need to bring such items to Bratislava. But now they were the only traces that remained.

I had been pondering the trip for some time, and then took off on the spur of the moment, as if driven by some manic impulse to flee from our flat in Bratislava for a few days and get away from all those things you can't really get away from, things you have to chew on, digest, leave to be processed by the passage of time. I flung a few things into a bag and got into the car. I knew I would find the drive diffi-cult: I would have to drive past the same scenery that kept flashing through my head in the first weeks of the New Year, only this time in reality and on my own. There was one thing I hadn't counted on: several sections of the road between Bratislava and Martin had been under repair, or were being widened, for years on end. Over the years we had followed the progress of the works together: for instance, soon after the exit for Žiar nad Hronom, in the direction of Kremnica, a stretch of the new wide concrete road had been completed though the next stretch still had a temporary surface so I had to drive carefully as the asphalt was uneven, the odd rectangle mysteriously left unfilled and waiting to be patched up; then, just before Kremnica, you had to turn off the new road, rejoin the old one, and drive down a long village high street. But now the entire road was completed and there was a permanent surface and no diversions. Each time I passed one of these stretches I felt this was unfair to her: she didn't get a chance to see the completion of the roadworks whose progress we'd been following at roughly six-monthly intervals over the years. The completed sections of the road almost brought tears to my eyes.

The things I'd packed included some underwear and a spare suit, my shaving kit and a few books: basically, all the things I always took with me. But as I pulled up outside the gate of the family house in Martin I realised I hadn't brought something I'd never had to think of before, something that had never been my responsibility, which is why it hadn't crossed my mind on this occasion: the keys to the gate and the house.

Ever since I could remember, there was no bell at the gate. Maybe this was because kids from the neighbourhood might have played tricks: rung the bell, run away, and relished the spectacle of someone having to walk the hundred metres or so from the house to the gate only to find no one there. For some time, the gate had been left open for a few hours a day. And it would be open when visitors were expected. Later, when the locals began to move out of the nearby houses to the new big housing estate and Gypsies moved in, the gate would be kept locked at all times.

Two rooms had recently been let to a tenant, a middle-aged woman I had yet to meet. I walked around the house to where the windows opened onto a narrow alleyway and tapped on her windows but couldn't see or hear anything through the thick layer of dust and dirt. I tapped again, waited, but still there was no response. I walked back to the gate where I had parked but no one came out the house. The smaller house at the other end of the yard belonged to my sister-in-law. It had been her surgery until she moved to Bratislava two years ago, at the same time and into the same apartment block where I lived with my wife. She often went back to Martin, and was here right now, but all her windows opened onto the back yard and I had no way of accessing them. Someone fitter could have climbed over the fence. But not only was I not fit, I was tired and thirsty after hours of driving, and rather unnerved by the fact that I'd forgotten my keys. And on top of everything else, the silence that greeted me chilled me to the bone.

I turned on my heels and headed for the centre of town telling myself: "I'll just go and sit somewhere for a while, the tenant is bound to be back soon. She's quite elderly and likely to spend most of her time at home."

Down the road from the house there was a pub. As usual during the day, it was half-empty, just a few Gypsies huddled round a couple of tables. I continued towards the town centre where I knew every house; most of the small shops were gone by now; the large radio store was a little further down the road. I would always stop to look at its display even though they always had the same radios on show, but when I came to stay for a few weeks it was the only thing in town worth looking at. Just a few steps away was a square with a small park in the middle; this was the main square in the historic centre and here, too, I knew every shop – a watchmaker's, a souvenir shop, a fabric store, a bookshop, a leather goods store, a clothes shop, a store selling glass and china, and another pub that was always crowded. But everything seemed so alien now, I could easily have found myself stranded in any old small and ugly town for a couple of days. I went to a pub on the far side of the main square, ordered a beer and sat down at a table that had seen better days. It was early in the afternoon, the spring sun was still quite weak, and I felt thirsty but also cold. I didn't enjoy the beer – the mere fact that I was sitting here, that I was here right now, suddenly seemed to make no sense – so after slowly finishing it off, I went back to 29 Kollárova Street. My car was still parked outside the gate, nothing stirred in the garden: I hoped some-one might have spotted my car and would be waiting for me.

I went around the corner again and started banging on the tenant's windows, more vigorously this time, but still nobody answered. At a loss, I returned to the gate. Soon an elderly woman, apparently the tenant, shuffled out of the house and unlocked the gate. I told her who I was and explained that I'd forgotten my keys. Without further ado she launched into a diatribe, as if this was the moment she'd been waiting for: how she'd swept the yard and the area in front of the gate regularly, how she'd once even cleaned all the windows on the outside, including the rooms that were not in use, how well she was caring for the family vault, cleaning and sweeping up at the cemetery, too; she went on and on about how useful she'd been. She then mentioned that she usually brought her lunch from a place locally known as "Chairs", a former furniture factory, and that she'd heard me knocking earlier but it took her a while to get ready and by the time she reached the gate she found nobody there.

She was rather strange, this old woman, and as I listened to her I noticed that no sooner had she finished rattling on about something, she would say the same thing again, not just for a second but also for a third time, partly for emphasis but also out of the feeble-mindedness of old age. I interrupt-ed her torrent of words by pushing the metal gate open, getting into my car, starting the engine and driving in. Then I knocked on my sister-in-law's door. It turned out that she, too, had been home all along. She couldn't understand how I could have forgotten the keys because that was not some-thing she would ever do. She lent me a spare set and I was now able to open up the house as well.

The kitchen was shrouded in gloom. The small window, typical of village houses – this had once been a farmer's house – used to have a curtain to stop people seeing in from the alley. There once used to be a thin net curtain for the day and thicker drapes for drawing in the evenings after the lights were turned on. Now there remained only the thick curtain, which let in hardly any light. The key to the main room was in its usual place, on top of a wardrobe in the long corridor running from the kitchen almost all the way to the far end of the house, known in the family as *pitvor*.

The first thing that struck me as I entered our room next to the kitchen was the smell of dust that had settled on everything, mixed with the odour of the rough walls where the damp would rise whenever there wasn't much sunshine in the summer or the house was left unheated.

I turned on the storage heaters in the kitchen and the bedroom and sat down in a cosy leather armchair, the last remaining item of old furniture, part of a suite. This was my routine: in the old days, exhausted by the long drive, I would sit down in this armchair or, on warm days, on a bench in front of the house. Meanwhile Zora would go to the shed to fetch some kindling and start the fire in the tiled stove, which would heat up the room quickly. Then she would put the kettle on for coffee and at the same time start dusting and sweeping; she would then put fresh covers on the pillows and the down duvets. And while she was at work inside the house, I would sit in the armchair or on the bench in front of the house with my cup of coffee, resting.

In fact, this was one of the reasons I'd been putting off this trip: I was worried that after getting here I would have to get rid of the dust whose smell permeated the whole place, sweep the floor, fetch some kindling, light the fire in the tiled stove and change the sheets for the night. Now, as I sat in the armchair, I realised I didn't have to do any of this: it wasn't all that cold and the room would warm up soon enough, I would get used to the musty smell of dust and damp before too long; there was no particular need to sweep the floor and I couldn't put fresh sheets on the pillows and the duvet because I had left the bedding at home – like the keys, this had never been my responsibility.

After a while, long after I finished my coffee, the only part of the old routine I stuck to, I went over to the small garden house for a chat with my sister-in-law, because that was what was expected of me. She gave me the latest on the state of the house and the elderly tenant who was supposed to look after the vault but didn't do her job properly; there was no point raising this with her, however, as the old woman simply wasn't up to looking after anything; my sister-in-law finished with what seemed a genuine offer to let her know if I ever needed anything, to treat her as if she were my own sister. I was rather taken aback since our relationship had always been courteous but formal, without a hint of sibling closeness.

However, her report on the vault and the state it was in reminded me that I should visit the cemetery. I've never been in the habit of going to cemeteries, to visit the graves of my loved ones – this form of paying my respects was alien to me. After my father died, my mother and I soon stopped visiting his grave; later I would go to my mother's grave about twice a year because it tended to get covered in fallen leaves and overgrown with grass, but otherwise it was mainly my brother and his family who looked after it. Here in Martin, a very traditional old town, looking after the graves or vaults was as important to a select circle of families as keeping the parlour in their home tidy; the upkeep of the graves, too, had to conform to certain standards, since schoolchildren were often taken to a particular section of the old cemetery, though the locals also kept a watchful eye on how family members looked after individual graves, and there was fierce competition over decorating them with bouquets, wreaths, flowers, spruce branches, candles and, on All Saints' Day, old-fashioned lanterns.

I had accompanied my wife on her visits to her family vault countless times. Sometimes her mother had sent her, sometimes Zora felt the vault needed attending to; I would

carry the wilted flowers and bouquets to the cemetery rubbish heap, pour the musty water out of the vases and glass
containers and refill them with fresh water from the cemetery
tap, while she would see to the vases and remove any dead
flowers. My own father's grave had become as overgrown as
the cemetery where he was buried; while my mother lay in
the vast city graveyard in Bratislava, close to a concrete water
tower that tended to leak, leaving her grave and everything
around it permanently sodden. But this time I hadn't come to
the family vault because I had to accompany Zora, but rather
because of her, since she now lay buried here. To my surprise
I felt a lump rising in my throat.

Back in town I bought some rolls, ewe's cheese and butter
as well as a small bottle of brandy, and forced the food down
in slow gulps in the kitchen, which was no longer gloomy.
I knew I would have the same things for breakfast the next
day as well and, if I stayed another day or two, I would
eat a similar meal in the evenings. By now I realised that
I couldn't stand it here much longer, that I wouldn't open
a single one of the pile of books I'd brought in my suitcase
because, although being here felt like being on a desert island, that was precisely why I wouldn't be able to concentrate
on anything; apart maybe from knocking back a small bottle
of brandy every night, which would be enough to set my imagination free and let me experience what they call a rich and
eventful emotional life.

As expected, the storeroom was ankle-deep in papers we
had tossed there when we emptied the larger part of the
house two years ago, and a shelf running the length of the
wall was also piled high with papers.

I began moving the papers into the room. I decided to start
by sorting them into three broad categories: those I would
simply throw out; the manuscripts of her translations, which
I would keep; and miscellaneous papers I would take back
home to look through later.

And so I spent the whole evening, well into the small hours – sustained by the brandy which I deployed in moderation – reaching down to the floor for papers, sorting them into three piles, until my back began to ache from repeatedly lifting small piles onto my knees and nearer to my eyes, and replacing them on the carpet once they were sorted.

The next morning the tenant knocked and shouted through the door that there was something she needed to discuss with me; she'd been waiting for this opportunity for months. I shouted back that I would go over to see her as soon as I was dressed and had had something to eat.

Again I forced down some rolls with butter and cheese, followed by some instant coffee as I thought about what lay ahead: not so much the conversation – my sister-in-law had prepared me for that – but what I was about to see. I could imagine what the two rooms she was using – formerly my wife's parents' bedroom and their dining-room-cum-parlour – might look like by extrapolating from the state of the toilet: the toilet seat lid fell off as soon as I tried to lift it, the flush had been turned off and a ventilator in the ceiling had been opened or rather, removed, with the effect that when you used the toilet, water would drip on your head from above at short but regular intervals; sheets of newspaper of various sizes lay scattered on the floor for occasional use, and since some water would always spill out when the toilet was flushed with a bucket, two wooden planks offered protection from the wet stone floor. Out in the yard there was also an outhouse we had used in later years.

To reach the tenant's part of the house at the far end of the corridor, I first had to pass by the toilet and the bathroom. The bathroom had been transformed into a kitchen and the bath into a kitchen cupboard where pots and pans and various kitchen utensils had been tossed willy-nilly. There was a small stove from which a pipe led to the huge cast-iron stove in the bathroom. I knocked and entered what used to be the bedroom and had been left almost empty, except for another small stove in the corner and all sorts of junk, as well as some kitchen stuff, scattered on the floor. The door leading to the former dining room and reception room was open, the assorted odds and ends in it emphasising its bleakness. The floors were bare, not a scrap of carpet, lino or anything of the kind to be seen anywhere, and the parquet floor had turned black and was covered with all kinds of spillage and encrusted with dirt. The windows were covered with the old sheer net curtains, which was why – as she had mentioned in passing – she never turned on the light after dark to stop people from being able to peer in.

We remained standing while we talked, since there was only one chair in the room. The tenant started by repeating her rant from the day before: how busy the place kept her and how much work looking after the house involved. After delivering a long peroration on her immense usefulness she finally got to the point: the rent was too high given how much work she was doing; she had already raised the matter with the housing department and I was sure to hear from them soon, but meanwhile could we come to an arrangement whereby she would pay me only eighty crowns instead of a hundred. Without saying so out loud I admitted that she didn't need all this space, something marginally bigger than a cubbyhole would be enough for her; and her pension was probably a pittance. But I couldn't capitulate immediately, as she would have felt vindicated. So I let her harp on about the same thing for a while before I agreed. Apparently, she was trying to find somewhere smaller to live.

This patrician house, formerly home to an illustrious family whose distinguished members even featured in school curricula, was now reduced to the condition of the Gypsy dwellings in the neighbourhood. And it was slowly beginning to look that way from the outside as well. The garden was untended since it would have been pointless to look after it, given its location: Gypsy children kept climbing over the fence picking the garden clean, and there was only one small patch left where my sister-in-law tried to grow some vegetables, rarely succeeding, as they usually met the same fate as the fruit and flowers. Piles of rubbish left behind by a previous tenant lay scattered by the gutter that ran along the long wall you had to pass on the way from the gate to the door of the house.

After Zora and I moved to Bratislava, the kitchen was the only part of the house that remained in its original state. The single room adjoining the kitchen, which Zora had kept for our own use, was furnished with what remained of the old furniture. Although the small desk on which she had typed at least twenty thousand pages – I, too, had typed a good few hundred on it – was still there, it hadn't seen a typewriter for ages; the last time it had been used must have been around 1969, when she was still translating and we spent a few months here in the summer. A more recent addition was a hefty wardrobe brought in from the entrance hall, out of use for ages, stuffed with old clothes left by her father, mother and brother and not worn for so long that every time we came the first thing we'd do was to carry the suits and dresses reeking of mothballs out onto the veranda and replace them in their mothball sanctuary before we left… but what had undergone the greatest change was the wall, which was once lined with tailor-made bookcases: now half the space was taken up by a wide and shapeless mattress in a tall wooden frame; the other half was piled high with duvets and pillows. It all resembled – indeed consisted of – just a dreadful heap of random stuff, the effect only exacerbated by a view of the increasingly desolate garden. At the same time, with certain features of the old room still remaining, it could have conjured up something of its cosiness of old to someone who had been here before.

That was why over the past two years, whenever we came here in the evenings, or returned late from a long walk, my

wife would turn on the lights, look around and say with a rue-
ful smile: "Our little nest".

2.

I remember when I first came here in early April 1953, some
two decades ago; actually, nineteen years and five months ago
to the day. After arriving by train I had no trouble finding the
street but I couldn't locate a house bearing the number I'd
been given. At a street turning there was an old, dilapidated building with a lower number, an entrance next to it led
into a small park that was probably out of bounds because
I couldn't see anyone there, and the next house down had
a higher number: it was a small shack with a smithy, and
in the space between the shack and the deserted park a
blacksmith was shoeing horses. At a loss, I walked to and
fro between the two houses until a woman passing by asked
"Who're you looking for?" The Jesenskýs, I replied. "Why, they
live right over there," she said, pointing to a metal gate. I went
through the gate, which had been left ajar, and only now did I
notice that my view had been obscured by some tall old trees
by the metal fence and I hadn't spotted a long, single-storey
house with small windows and a pretty glass-covered veranda; a wide path led from the gate, past a lawn and up to the
house, and behind the house you could see another lawn and
a wooden fence, and only where the wide path ended did
the actual yard begin, with an ordinary wooden table and
benches, the kind you see in taverns under tall elder trees;
and opposite the house stood another, smaller house with adjoining outbuildings, something like a barn, and an outhouse.
In the distance, beyond the yard, I could see a well-tended
garden full of trees, some tall, some less so.

A double door, its upper half made of glass, stood open
at the end of the house. I went in and found myself in a long
corridor, opposite a kitchen. I heard noises and hushed voices
coming from a door at the far end, next to the kitchen, and

so knocked and entered. The first person I saw was Zora, standing there with a small pile of books in her hands, poised to replace them on a bookshelf by the door, and next I saw a thin old woman, probably her mother, kneeling on the floor, wiping up something. I said hello and announced that I had arrived, albeit a day early.

It was only now, as I noticed the stony expression on the women's faces, that I realised I'd done something quite unconscionable. She had invited me, in my capacity as theatre critic, to come on a specific day to attend a specific event – the opening night of a new Slovak play at the Martin theatre – but here I was, having arrived in their house unannounced a day early and about to spend a couple of nights in her study, expecting food and lodging, as if I'd booked a room in a hotel or dropped by to visit old friends. I had no inkling that I would find myself in a world so utterly different from mine, one where conventions were rigidly observed, and I certainly couldn't have known that she had never before invited a stranger like me to her home. Only one of her cousins or some other family member would occasionally come and stay for a few days. With a forced smile I stammered out an explanation as to why I'd arrived a day early, something about it being a long weekend, which was why I was able to take an extra day off.

What I couldn't say was that two days earlier I'd stayed up late with Mňačko. Back then the two of us used to spend hours and hours sitting in a café, always the same one, or walking around a park, trying to figure out the political situation and compulsively sharing our speculations on the current political show trials, why they were being staged in that particular way and why the defendants were being indicted on those particular charges, and why all sorts of other things around us were happening. What I couldn't say was that we'd knocked back more than a dozen brandies and that I'd overdone it once again and as a result woken up the next

(428)

day feeling anxious, scared and trembling. What I couldn't say was that whenever I was in this sort of state I felt an urge to flee, to be somewhere completely different, except that normally this was a wish I couldn't fulfill whereas this time I had her invitation: this time I had somewhere I could flee, and so I had got on a train and here I was – a day early.

After recovering from the initial shock she introduced me to her mother and gave me her first smile, or rather, a hint of a smile, which did nevertheless validate her invitation despite the wrong date. Her mother stayed on the floor on her knees giving me a cold and aloof look and making it clear – as I realised only when my visit was over – that in this house I was a guest of her daughter's but not of the rest of the family. Eventually, after their initial surprise, they offered me a seat.

Once I was left alone I was able to relax and bask in the silence and the immensely pleasant heat emanating from the tiled stove. It was like arriving in some cosy, quiet, secluded spot after a long time wandering in the wilderness, or as if I'd been transported to a desert island on another continent, and of course at that point I had no idea that I had indeed found myself on a kind of island within the house itself, since I would spend most of the time in this room. Zora soon returned with a cup of coffee and encouraged me to look at her collection of books; she was sure I'd find something I hadn't yet read.

Profoundly impressed and awestruck I examined the books in the library, which now line the entire shorter wall of our living room in Bratislava. I discovered volumes of literary journals from the middle of the nineteenth century. Years earlier when I was at school I had to memorise all their titles and used to get them mixed up. I picked up one bound volume, then the next and was mildly surprised and slightly disappointed by turns. Yes, they did contain works by our early great poets, pioneers of literature in a language that had previously existed only in a spoken form, but the journals were mostly filled with miscellaneous material: someone had penned a piece on the fauna of a particular region, someone else was offering cookery tips... But there were also first editions of works by authors long regarded as classics, as well as a complete collection of Czech avantgarde poetry of the 1920s and 1930s. The first time I saw this vast library I was just fascinated by its enormous range: the most recent volumes had been published around the time I first started buying or borrowing books myself, and everything I saw here was a discovery for me, whether as a reader, or indeed, a bibliophile. Later I discovered that the collection covered specific periods with long gaps in between, reflecting the family's changing economic fortunes. She had bought the most recent books herself while a student at the music academy in Bratislava and in the years when she gave piano lessons to children of more affluent burghers here in the house. She stopped buying books once she started translating, in addition to editing the monthly *Živena**, when she began to receive review copies. And after the war, when she was no longer an editor at *Živena,* she would borrow books from Matica slovenská in Martin.

I took a few bound volumes of *Živena* off the shelf. I found a long essay she had written on love and being in love. Looking back it occurs to me that it was an almost phenomenological analysis of two kinds of human emotion, although in those days I wasn't familiar with the term and she certainly wasn't familiar with it either when she wrote the piece. In fact, her article was a rather dismissive review of a contemporary novel that had been highly praised and widely read. Her essay impressed me deeply, and I read certain passages of it repeatedly.

When she came in bringing a plate of cold meats for our supper and saw what I was reading, she said, as if ashamed of having written the piece: "Oh, I wouldn't bother with that, it's all out of date now." Sure enough, her essay failed to discuss whether the author had depicted the class struggle and the inevitable victory of the working classes of ancient Babylon. She had joined the communist party at the same time as hundreds of thousands of others, probably out of fear that her parents might be evicted from this house and sent to live somewhere in the countryside as former members of the bourgeoisie, but having joined the party she took everything very seriously and had it not been for me, I was thinking now, she might have believed the contemporary propaganda for longer. It might have made her life easier, although, on the other hand, I did help her become a normal human being. That night I may have tried to persuade her that this kind of thinking wasn't outdated, that it contained something of lasting value, something that had always formed part of humanity.

She commented on a book I'd chosen from the library in case I couldn't sleep that night to the effect that its author had been deluded into thinking that in this country, too, there ought to be some people living a life of luxury and decided to write short stories about them – she didn't know that the only reason I'd picked this book was that it had recently been reissued, but of course this was the period of the struggle against cosmopolitanism and in those days everything that had been published in the past, including scrap paper, was revered as part of our national heritage.

After she made my bed I stayed up a bit longer browsing the old volumes, not the ones from the previous century but those from the interwar bourgeois period, an era that now seemed just as distant, and this soon put me to sleep.

Naturally, sometimes I had to use the toilet and the bathroom, which meant leaving my room and passing through the corridor, so I must have run into the others living in the house, yet I don't recall when she introduced me to her father, her sister-in-law or her niece, who still occupied two rooms at the far end of the house at the time.

At breakfast next morning she pointed out that it was Good Friday and although her parents were not church-goers, they did fast on this day, so there would be no lunch and we could go for a longer walk. I agreed eagerly, and we took a bus to the foot of the mountain and set off. The woods were covered in snow, there was not a soul to be seen, and I felt as if transported to some imaginary country on a magic carpet. It was rare for me to find myself walking among snow-covered trees in winter, and my family outings in the summer were no more than a memory. And suddenly here I was, outside the world where I normally spent all my time going round and round in circles. I even suggested we should keep going until we reached the top of the mountain. I was wearing loafers and kept slipping and sliding, and the snow got into my shoes, but I kept going, getting slightly out of breath as we climbed because I was talking almost non-stop, the words bubbling out of me like water from a freshly-drilled spring. Even though I didn't share any intimate thoughts with her, I felt able to let myself go, to let a litany of complaints about people and the general situation come pouring out of me, particularly to do with literature or rather, with things happening on the "literary front", a particularly fitting term in those days since anyone could end up at risk of being fired at, or of having to fire at others just to be on the safe side – either way, somewhere on the frontline; I also complained about the newspaper I was working for, where the conditions were similar. Without having to recline on a shrink's couch, I could speak freely and relax, venting to my heart's delight about the whole wide world while she listened and responded with words of wisdom and understanding.

Eventually – by then it was the afternoon – we reached a mountain chalet. There we found a large group of people, Martin's crème de la crème, sitting at a table out in the sun; she did the introductions. They all knew me by name and seemed pleased to learn that I would be at the opening night;

everyone had something to say about the theatre, the author and the play, and after some witty banter they stood up one by one, put on their skis, and whizzed off home.

She invited me to tea in the restaurant. I looked out of the window at the mountains gleaming under their mantle of snow. Above the whiteness, a clear blue sky the like of which I hadn't seen for years, was slowly darkening far and wide. Enchanted by this spectacle and enthralled by the beauty of the winter landscape I suggested we stay the night and go down the following morning, otherwise we'd have to walk back in the dark. She gave a laugh and explained that all those people had already seen us arriving at the chalet together and that alone would be enough to start the rumour mill in town; I couldn't imagine the kind of gossip we would unleash if we stayed the night, even in two separate rooms. Of course; if I'd found myself here with the student who had been the object of my tragic, unrequited love some time back it would have occurred to me, too, but she seemed to me like a being from another world, a kindred intellectual spirit, who would rise above such matters and could be expected to show an extraordinary level of understanding.

We got up and hurried back down, walking faster and talking less now, but I kept slipping more and more often, tumbling into the snow and having to brush it off my coat again and again, even as she kept reassuring me that there was nothing wrong with slipping and falling over. By now it had gone dark but eventually – my shoes soaked through and through – we reached the bus terminus, caught a bus home and she made some supper for the two of us…

Saturday, 4 April 1953, arrived and she brought a copy of the newspaper with my breakfast, as on the day before, but this time I did leaf through it, before going back to the front page. There, in the top right-hand column, I spotted a brief news item: a certain Mr Beria*, who had allegedly been arrested some time ago, had now been sentenced to death as a former British spy. My first thought was that this had to be someone else, not *that* Beria, but no, I wasn't mistaken, and sure enough it was he, Lavrentiy Beria. I had to put the paper down, feeling as bewildered as if I had just received a telegram informing me that my mother had been in an accident or that some woman completely unknown to me had borne me a child, while at the same time I had the sensation of floating up there in the cleanly scrubbed blue sky above the mountain chalet, drifting like a cloud above the woods and mountains.

So maybe, just maybe, they weren't going to kill me now, was my first thought; now it was less likely that I might one day be done away with or just disappear without a trace; or that I might later end up testifying in a show trial in an apathetic monotone on a whole range of issues I had no clue about, in the manner of the testimonies I'd heard on the radio just four months earlier*. And I also had an inkling that I no longer needed to be so scared, that some ominous shadow had been lifted from me.

I wasn't a particularly prominent figure, neither in those days nor later, but I wasn't exactly a cipher either. I was a writer. Though not very important, I was somebody. People, including "the high ups", knew who I was, and I was vulnerable because I couldn't demonstrate the correct background in terms of class, race or nationality. Those in the know were aware that I was a potential target, someone who could, if necessary, be labelled a "rootless cosmopolitan". Over the past few years I'd seen a variety of people disappear. They would first be fired or demoted, but on occasion they would be arrested immediately. Who was targeted and when would be determined by the current ideological campaign: while those with certain attributes might feel safe during one particular campaign, during the next, which inevitably followed hard on its heels, these same people might be justified in feeling threatened. And maybe this would put a stop to all these campaigns in which people with certain attributes were hounded and consigned by police henchmen to the dustheap of history. Maybe...

I read the news item over and over again. Just two months ago it had been Stalin; I still remembered the jubilant pealing of the city bells, the kind we hadn't heard for a long time. Just two months ago... and now this bastard: the two events must be connected. I couldn't contain myself any longer, I had to tell her. I left my enclosure and could see through the glass door that her parents were alone in the kitchen so I walked to the other end of the corridor, to the dining room-cum-parlour-cum-living room, which was the largest room in the house, knocked on the door and entered. Zora was sitting on a long sofa with her niece, then still a schoolgirl, with her arm around the girl's shoulders, apparently in the middle of an intimate conversation. The room was in permanent semi-darkness so I didn't realise immediately that I was interrupting something. From the doorway I announced to the far end of the room the news that Beria, having been arrested some time ago, had now been executed. She said something along the lines of "oh really, you don't say," as if the information was unworthy of comment, and when I noticed that she wasn't really interested in learning why I had burst in on them, I realised that I was simply interrupting their conversation. So I returned to my enclosure and continued my raptures and daydreaming. Maybe I was wrong, maybe I was letting myself be carried away by some flight of fancy into a future that was never to be, a tomorrow when we would all emerge from this dark cave – I was being quite naïve, even although in hindsight I could see I was basically right. What was the point of prattling on to her about it; who knows, she might even have believed that this was how communism was meant to work, that whenever there was a change of government someone always had to be executed.

After lunch – no more mention was made of Beria – she suggested a walk to a grove, a place she liked to go when she just wanted a short stroll. We left the town via a drab street with dingy houses at the end of which green hills began to rise. She pointed to a hill a little further off; that was our destination. We were enveloped by a fierce, biting cold and at the top of the hill the wind whistled and howled. I was fighting the cold and the gale, and although she was wearing a fur coat she suggested generously that we might head back home.

At last I found myself safely back between the four walls of my room, next to the tall tiled stove that radiated a pleasant warmth. She reminded me that the performance started at seven and we would have a bite to eat beforehand. The play would be followed by a discussion and the best thing for me to do now would be to have a lie-down on the sofa under a couple of blankets and rest. I agreed, though I thought that one blanket would do. I lay motionless, doing my best to relax because I had known all along that the real reason she had invited me was not so that I would write a review of a new play opening in Martin for the biggest paper in Bratislava. It was to take part in the discussion afterwards, to be seen to take part, to say something that would demonstrate I was someone deserving of respect, not just some good-for-nothing upstart who was now trying to stick his nose into everything. A further reason she had asked me to come, although I had no idea of this at the time, was so that her parents could meet me and see with their own eyes that I wasn't some seedy, unshaven, uncouth tramp, or sidelocked Jew, or a permanent-ly drunk vagrant with long hair; however, if she had really wanted to present me to her parents – I thought now – she had clearly failed on that front since they had simply ignored me, but I wasn't fully aware of that at the time. The discussion would be attended by actors and directors, the crème de la crème of the local intelligentsia, presided over by František Hečko, a writer garlanded with the highest state awards. His good-humoured novel, *The Wooden Village,* depicting how a village made the transition – smoothly and wittily overcoming every obstacle – to the new collective way of life, had gone through endless reprints. As a result he saw himself as the Tolstoy of our small nation and judged others just as harshly and mercilessly as the great Russian novelist. I was one of those he had never thought particularly highly of, as I learned from Zora, who was on good terms with him and especially his wife, and his opinion of me mattered to her a great deal. Also, there would be some other luminaries from among the local writers and intelligentsia; people must have heard the gossip about her seeing this dubious character rather too often. I was supposed to make an impression on all these people and since I didn't want to disappoint her, I tried to rest and clear my head. She brought some bread and ham for supper so that we didn't go to the theatre on an empty stomach.

A great many eyes were focused on me as we entered the auditorium. Zora was a distinguished personality, the pride of the town, who typically went to the theatre alone and now here she was with this mysterious dandy whom they had probably been gossiping about. We walked in nonchalantly and took our seats in the front row.

During the only intermission I hurriedly dragged her out of the auditorium to a spot where nobody would overhear us and told her off for having invited me to see this play; now I would have to write or say something about it in the discussion and would probably end up denounced as a "rootless cosmopolitan" who looked down his nose at our national literature and new works produced by our up-and-coming writers.

She got my drift without a long explanation, including the fact that she might have made my predicament worse, more precarious, by having invited me. But she had always been good at thinking on her feet and had a ready reply. She wondered if the play really had been that bad; she didn't really mean that, of course; the play was indeed that bad; but she wondered if it was really necessary to say so out loud: after all, the author had meant well and the characters were sketched quite skilfully, albeit in a rudimentary fashion, as were the interpersonal conflicts, although in a most superficial, impersonal way; on the other hand, the play also contained an element of the tragic, except that it had been lost amidst the ballast of the schematic format. She went on making numerous rather sensible points about the play – surely something positive could be said about it, provided we assumed the author had written a play that was slightly different from the one we saw; in fact he might have written a brilliant play provided, that is, we assumed that he had written most of it just a little differently, or had just written a different play altogether. I nodded without really hearing her. It was up to me to figure out what to say and how to present it; I now knew that with an hour still to go I'd be able to come up with something. I invited her to the bar, we had a soft drink, and afterwards I didn't pay much attention to what was happening on stage – there were some gendarmes firing at striking workers – who in this play happened to be workers in a vineyard – slaughtering the most politically aware among them. I had seen endless variations on this theme before: in films, plays, in novels set in the democratic Czechoslovakia under presidents Masaryk and Beneš; this was what the wretched interwar republic had been consigned to: back then the supporters of the Sudeten German Henlein party* claimed that Czech democracy was intent on starving them to death, on decimating and even annihilating them. Later, under the wartime Slovak Republic, the ruling Catholics insisted that interwar Czechoslovakia had been determined to annihilate the Slovaks, to wipe them out as a nation; and now the communists had discovered that the interwar republic had been intent on exterminating the working proletariat. The poor author tried his best to feature in his play all the themes that had been covered by other authors before him, except that he lacked the basic skills; but surely that wasn't all that vital, surely there was a chance that he would eventually learn his craft. Now I knew what to say in the discussion.

After the show we went up one floor to a large room with a long table; gradually all the seats filled up, including those along the wall. The room (which was also used for various kinds of meetings) was far too big for the size of the theatre, just like most meeting rooms of this kind in most state enterprises and factories up and down the country, but in those days discussions and meetings of various kinds were a compulsory ceremonial, supposedly facilitating the exchange of views between intellectuals and the working masses. I didn't recognize any of the people present except for the few with whom we had chatted the day before by the mountain chalet and who acknowledged us with a nod. None of them actually intended to contribute to the discussion but people were expected to attend these events the way people in other societies and other periods were expected to attend banquets or cocktail parties. Among the last to enter was Hečko, who was middle aged and heavily built. Zora rose when she spotted him, brought him over to me and did the introductions. We both mumbled our names and he, looming high above everyone, walked over to the far end of the table and sat down. I imagined that he had come in order to stand up for the author, a "worker-writer", just in case some intellectual tried to pour scorn on him. The main purpose of the exercise was to see what impression I made on Hečko. If I scandalised him he would write all sorts of things about me in his diary, from which he would occasionally read out to his guests and Zora might have had to break off contact with him, for her own sake, too: she had brought me here as her protégé and Hečko's poor opinion of me would have reflected badly on her as well.

In those days discussions were usually slow to start. This time everyone was waiting for me to speak but if I had volunteered to take the floor first, I might have appeared to be uninterested in hearing what others had to say. Besides, custom dictated that the main discussant should not be the first to speak. Realising this, someone raised his hand and made a comment that was quite beside the point, saying that he only wanted to get the ball rolling. And so, after a moment's hesitation, I took the floor: I said the play had painted a vast social tableau, continued with some general waffle not directly related to the play, something about the young author being very ambitious, it being understandable that not everyone would master their craft in their first work, that there were a few shortcomings here and there; at this point, I became more specific – in those days whenever you were dealing with something that was a complete mess, something that was really dreadful, atrocious, total trash, you would gently suggest that there were certain shortcomings, which the author himself was sure to correct or overcome in his next work – so yes, the play had a few other shortcomings, no doubt about that, and there were a couple of other things that didn't quite work as the author had intended, but of course he had painted a vast social tableau. Next I threw in some more communist newspeak blather, which I followed by briefly listing some more shortcomings before moving on to a fortissimo finale praising our promising upcoming authors and their new works of contemporary literature.

After speaking for twenty or thirty minutes I sat down; a long silence ensued, no hand was raised, the participants were encouraged to contribute again but nobody took the floor and that was the end of the discussion; everyone stood up, there really was nothing more to be said, I had delivered such a bravura performance. I knew it as soon as I sat down, and the thought crossed my mind, with a hint of sadness, that I had shown them how these things were done, how to massage and package your message so that you did not have to spell out that it was a load of rubbish, everyone would draw their own conclusions, but all things considered, the author had received some praise.

(440)

As we left the theatre, she didn't pat me on the back as she would in later years, saying things like "See, it's all over, you did it"; we were not yet on first name terms then, but she did take my arm for the first time, she must have felt as relieved as I that it was over at last, and that my performance had exceeded all expectations. This she confirmed a few days later in a letter, whose main purpose was to inform me that she was coming to Bratislava earlier than planned, but in the very first sentence she congratulated me on the impression I had made on Hečko, who had said: "Quite a smart fellow, he knocks spots off dozens of others." His opinion meant a lot to her in those days: it was something she could share with her parents and could rest assured that word would get around Martin. It had made her almost happy that I had impressed the crème de la crème, as well as others she cared about, and I understood her relief; people could no longer speak of her with a touch of disdain in connection with me. I had passed the test.

When we got back from the theatre the two of us held an impromptu celebration. The house was dark and quiet, it seemed that nobody knew we were still up, celebrating in her room. We drank a bottle of wine and since in this house wine drinking was quite a ceremony that wasn't so much about the actual wine, we drank from cut-crystal glasses, and ate some tinned sardines and other items that were considered a delicacy in those days, chatting all the while as if this had been a run-of-the-mill theatre visit, yet we both felt carefree, elated, jubilant. And although I had much less wine than usual on such occasions, I felt as if I was sipping the finest champagne. The only thing we didn't talk about was the real reason for our celebration: the fact that it had been worth my attending the opening of the play.

Around midnight we carried the dishes back to the kitchen and she went to bed in the part of the house that was silent and totally dark, as if they weren't aware that we'd

just had a bottle of wine in her room, feasted on some deli-
cacies and had enjoyed some lively conversation. I was left
alone with my sense of elation. More wine would have been
welcome but even if that had been possible, it would have
caused a commotion in this entirely alien world I found myself
immersed in for those three days. So eventually I decided to
go to bed, on the couch in her study where she normally slept.

And on Sunday – it was Easter Sunday – I would have liked
to have just sat there resting on my laurels and thinking of
nothing in particular, but I could hear voices from the kitchen belonging to people other than her parents, so I quietly
sneaked into the bathroom, and when I was ready I opened
the kitchen door slightly and said hello. They asked what I
thought of the production: oh well, nothing to write home
about, I said, adding a couple more sentences to this effect.
She brought me some breakfast but didn't suggest that we
go for a walk, either then or later, so I went out into the yard
and found that it was by no means as cold as the day before
and it would actually have been a good day for a brisk walk
in the hills. But as I came back from my short stroll in the
yard without a coat, I could see her through the kitchen door:
the whole family was gathered in the kitchen and seemed to
be busy cooking and baking for later that day and the next. I
hung around my little enclosure; I might have taken another
look at the previous day's s paper, from which I had read
only the single brief news item the day before. I can't for the
life of me now remember how I killed a couple of hours, but
eventually I noticed fewer voices coming from the kitchen;
I could catch the odd word or two, a soup tureen and cakes
were being carried into the dining room, and that was when
Zora came in to see me – we had hardly spoken since the
morning. And suddenly, as she stood beside me, I realised
there was nothing left for me to do here. It was something
I should have realised earlier but it only dawned on me at
that point and I asked, rather awkwardly: "Do you think I

should leave now?" And although I wasn't expecting such an unequivocal answer, she said with a smile "Yes, I think you should." And she told me when my train was leaving. Clearly, it was high time I asked her.

I packed my case. She brought some lunch into my enclosure, the room I was allocated for those few days, gave directions for the shortest way to the station and apologised that she now had to go and have lunch with her family and couldn't go with me. I said goodbye to everyone, including her; there was nothing intimate about this goodbye and it was the one and only time she didn't walk me to the station.

As I went down the wide path from the house to the gate carrying my small suitcase I briefly turned towards the dining room windows; I could see a table festively laid, with the whole family assembled around it with their arms raised, holding small glasses.

(Later I, too, was initiated into this solemn Jesenský family ritual, with the festively laid lunch table, a bowl for stewed fruit and a tiny shot glass placed next to each plate. Once everyone had assembled and taken their seat, the head of the family would open a bottle of something alcoholic, everyone would get up and walk over to have their glass filled, return to their seat and stand there until all the glasses were filled, and they would all clink glasses wishing each other good health.)

That was the moment I realised that the family was now reunited, raising and clinking their glasses as if reinforcing their return to a state of affairs that had been disrupted for several days – that of a family together. Only now did it dawn on me how unnatural it had been for us all that time to take our lunch in a separate room, which was probably never used for dining, that I wasn't really wanted there, that they were glad I was gone and that their daughter could return to the bosom of the family. But even if I had not been let into their family, I knew that Zora had let me into her life.

As I reached the end of the yard and clanked the heavy metal gate shut behind me, I still felt mildly elated and walked to the station happy that I hadn't disappointed her.

That is more or less what my first visit to this house was like.

After Zora and I got married and I was accepted into the family, I would also take part in the family rituals. Over the years the number of family members dwindled until only the two of us – Zora and myself – were left, and all that we kept of the now-empty house for our visits was her room, the kitchen and part of the entrance hall. Even back then the place was run-down and deserted, and now that I was here all by myself it was almost unbearable. And much as I had looked forward to my arrival in Martin, I couldn't bear to stay very long on this desert island, and on the third day, once I had sorted out all the papers and everything that I thought had to be preserved was stowed in the trunk along with my suitcases, I said goodbye to my sister-in-law and, with a few brief stops to visit friends in Orava, I returned home, to this flat in Bratislava, back to that which is inescapable and which needs time. And time is something I now have aplenty.

3 .

As I sat down to write this account of my first brief visit to Martin some three months after Zora and I met in Bratislava and continued to see each other occasionally, I realised that what I had embarked on was literally a reconstruction, and a rather laborious one at that. Some things had stayed etched in my memory, though faded and blurred: these scraps of memories were in need of a new, clearer focus. As new details and further scraps were added, the picture began to fill out, and while it has never become complete and numerous blank spots remained, many more motifs emerged than I had anticipated.

At the same time, however, something strange happened to these memories: they have become translucent. Behind them, behind each exhibit, I can see archeological finds from much later periods. In this one, the entire Jesenský family is assembled around the dining table clinking glasses and wishing one another good health: I've found myself in the early Stone Age, in the Pleistocene, observing the scene through the window as I walk down the wide path toward the gate. More recent eras – the Aurignacian, Upper Paleolithic, and Mesolithic period – are simultaneously projected over the picture, the occasions when I was one of those standing in the dining room, with an arm raised and holding a glass between my thumb and index finger, while the number of other family members gradually dwindled. Next the even more recent Iron Age appears, with the dining room still in its original state but with just the two of us and no one else left to whose health we could have ceremonially raised our glasses; there follows the Bronze Age, when strangers had already taken possession of the dining room but the two of us still had a presence. And this, now, is the modern age, with the only one left being me, who had once witnessed this scene through the window – in those days both a welcome and unwelcome spectator.

This is the way the ground caves in beneath each memory, sometimes with a groan, as if some heavy weight had been dropped onto thick wrapping paper that has slowly begun to tear, while one may make a soft landing in later times or in the present, as if sinking deep into an eiderdown (for example, when I remember how on that fourth of April, I read the news of Beria's execution and endlessly replayed in my head the realisation that I no longer had to fear being killed for no reason). Sometimes a lone memory rises proudly above the mist surrounding it, like the tower of some tall, gleaming fortress, but more often memory takes us on a ride down in the lift of a modern highrise block, descending to the floors that lie lower, ever lower.

But no matter how blurred or how focused these memories may be, how isolated or translucent, however many different, increasingly proximate pasts lie buried as low as they can go, they don't really exist until we have articulated them; indeed, not simply articulated them, but formulated them as precisely as possible, and after careful consideration: only once precisely worded do our ideas acquire a specific contour that makes sense, not least in my case. And only once they have been transformed into semiotic signs can we wrench them from the whirling plasma of our memory, from the occasional vague phosphorescent flares, and mould them into their former image. I have a need to mould, that is, put things into words. However, what this conscious, deliberate process of articulation itself amounts to is literature. For otherwise nothing would ever acquire a distinct form, emerge from the nebula as lifelike and fresh as it had once been. I have to write literature, even if only for myself – and time is something I now have aplenty.

It wasn't until the void inside me made all the bells ring and all the drums beat again that I began to write. And writing has offered me a way of drowning out the void, something that works better than anything I've tried before: better than staring apathetically at the ceiling, than assiduously swigging brandy, or the nervous agitation that drives me out of the flat yet again.

Writing has given me something to focus on; furthermore, it is an activity that demands a certain continuity. If I happen to start the day by sorting out dirty laundry, stuffing it into a suitcase I've used for this purpose for years (it was the cheapest kind I once found in West Germany after buying masses of cheap books which I knew wouldn't fit into my luggage), then cramming empty bottles into an old and rather dirty bag (formerly used for carrying compost and plants along with their roots), hanging a suit or a pair of trousers or a coat across my arm and going out, first returning the empties, then stopping at the dry cleaner's, then going to the laundry, then to the dentist and spending an hour or two in the waiting room, then having lunch, then wandering around town for a while, window-shopping and buying groceries for the next few days, and when I finally return home feeling tired and both preoccupied and distracted, and end up collapsing on the sofa and then, driven by a sense of duty, instead of relaxing with a novel I grab the vacuum cleaner and clean two rooms (usually ending up all covered in sweat and with aching shoulder muscles), when on a day like that there is no question of sitting down and writing; or if it happens to be one of those days when I'm depressed, when I feel as though I'm at the bottom of a deep ditch, inside a huge pit and able to see only a narrow sliver of a dirty grey sky, when my thinking (I can't call it thoughts, so vague and amorphous it is) goes round in circles mulling the same few points over and over again, intensifying its own rotating motion and making me try maniacally to pull myself out of it, yet failing, when I can't bring myself to think of this other world, the world of these pages, because my brain circuits seem to have contracted in a cramp – on days like these I sometimes feel guilty about not making any headway with my work, even though nobody has commissioned it and nobody is waiting for it with bated breath.

But still, I'm finally doing something again. Writing, even. When friends ask if I've done anything lately, I can reply, with an air of mystery and a touch of flirtatiousness, but actually quite truthfully: "Yes, I've started to write something, but I don't want to talk about it yet, I haven't got very far." This has bestowed a new dignity upon me. Years ago, when I enjoyed showing off in my articles my erudition that reflected the latest fashion, I would have said that I'd discovered a space for "self-fulfilment". But in fact, what I am doing now is what I've been doing all my life: I'm writing. To be precise, I am doing what I have always done from time to time: I'm writing reportage. Except that this time I am not reporting on some distant country, having been sent there by the Writers' Union as part

of a delegation. I'm not reporting on some other subject closer to home that I used to cover. I once visited Japan and on
my way back, as I watched exotic countries and cities down
below from the small airplane window, I thought of all those
things that flashed across my retina only to fall into oblivion,
and what a shame it was for all these riches of the world to
just flash across one's retina. I hadn't forgotten this fleeting
notion, and on my return I wrote a long piece describing my
flight from Tokyo to Prague. So, as a matter of fact, what
I'm doing now is also writing reportage (I have no talent for
fiction, I'm no good at inventing things –if I tried to, it would
feel like I was lying – that is to say, wilfully manipulate some
existing, real, non-fictional material), except that this essay of
mine is not bound by a limit on length, or tied to a precisely
determined place or time, it is rather a kaleidoscopic, jerky
kind of reportage on things that have flashed across my retina, my memory, my perception and my soul.

But, of course, this is not the only truth. I used to write
essays based on my observations of exotic places as distant
as Hong Kong and Bangkok; after listening to speakers and
watching spectators in London's Hyde Park; or as I drove
through an age-old town in the hills of Wales and found
myself before the vast white ramparts of Caernarvon Castle
seeming to rise from the waters of the bay; wading through
the mud in Szarvas in southern Hungary, near the Yugoslav
border, and Nyíregyháza in the north-east, and sitting in the
cottages with peasant men and women whose fluency in
Slovak increased with their age, debating with them whether
they should move to Slovakia or not; or in Teplice-Šanov, just
after the war, as I walked down the street and passed some
Germans with white bands sewn onto their sleeves, most
likely with astonishment on my face, feeling a deep sense of
shame and wishing I could explain to everyone that this was
nothing to do with me, that this had not been done on my
orders – and at the same time as feeling shame, being aware

that only a year or two ago, when the war was still raging and I was still fearful of them, all sorts of horrendous ideas about the Germans of Bratislava had entered my head, maybe even the idea that they ought to be made to walk around the city with bands sewn on their sleeves, although that was just an idea, whereas now not only had somebody come up with that idea but they had put it into practice, and so I ended up feeling glad that I didn't share their lot, glad that it was them rather than me walking around branded with bands of white, while I could go back home and write a reportage on something that was external to me, that wasn't my fate.

But this time I'm writing only about things that involve me, in which I play a role, things that formed part of my life and that is why this isn't really a reportage. Maybe it is more of a… mini theatre production, in my own private theatre where I stage scenes from the script of my memory. A show in which I have to stand in for everyone working in a theatre, just like in the puppet theatre my father bought me for my birthday when I was a little boy. I start by putting on the hat of the stage manager who walks from one dressing room door to the next, and even though no sound can be heard from behind the doors, I knock on each one as I call out: "Five minutes!" The performers, including me (playing a number of roles, including, invariably, the protagonist) awake from their slumbers, stretch their limbs in surprise, struggle to their feet and, in response to the stage manager's repeated calls, dive into the dark hallway. Soon I see them again – this time in my role as the director standing in the stalls, in the middle of the front row – and scrambling onto the stage I explain the scene they are to perform, wave the script at them as if it was all in there, tell them to focus and jog their memories, I've seen them do the same scene many times before and all I want now is that they go through it again. The performers slowly come to life shaking off their torpor, tentatively casting about for their past gestures, muttering as if trying out their voices, but no, it's their old words that they are looking for, they have hopelessly forgotten their lines, I wish I could slip into the prompter's box but I'd make a lousy prompter, as I don't know the lines myself and am only pretending that everything is there in my script, so I have to keep playing the role of director, describing in general terms a scene I have once seen them perform as if in real life, and as I shout at the performers – mostly at myself, being one of the actors on stage – they might be under the impression that I can recall every detail of the scene, all the past words, movements and gestures, whereas in fact I have just the vaguest, haziest idea, but the least I can do is tell the actors where to stand, arrange the sets, put on the stagehand's hat and carry the props onto the stage, smooth out the backdrop against which the whole scene is supposed to be taking place, until eventually my admonitions, my shouting, my stage arrangements, my sets begin to yield results, and the actors start to move, some begin to recall fragments of their old lines, and I try to squeeze a little more out of them; but no, it's not going to get much better, I hastily climb onto the stage and look upwards, and up there in the gods see myself, this time as the lighting director, and I call out to myself: "More light!" and instruct the actors: "Let's run through it once more, and then we go live," as though I was now standing behind a video camera, filming and recording their words and movements. The results are rather pitiful, there's no comparison with the vivid performances of old, but as a director I'm aware that this is not a top-notch company, that performances like these are about as much as I can hope for, and I have to be satisfied with what I've captured now. "Lights off!", I shout to myself, the electrician up there, I send the actors back to their changing rooms where they will be all alone again, unseen by anyone, heavy-eyed, perhaps hoping that I might need them again, and I, too, leave the auditorium, I find the dramaturg's deserted office where I'll lie down to browse through my absurd script. Whole pages, entire scenes, sometimes entire acts have been left out and the remaining pages have yellowed over the months, years, decades, the letters have faded, some pages are completely blank, with just the odd isolated sentence here and there, sometimes an entire paragraph can be made out; this is my work, this wretched script of which only fragments remain. Now it's time to put on the dramaturg's hat, leaf through the script, decide which fragments to delete, how to rearrange and combine the ones that remain, perhaps add a few things; the actors might help me out; tomorrow or the day after I will be stage manager again and will summon them from their changing rooms and then, wearing the director's hat, I will pretend that I know their lines and remember exactly how they had played their roles way back when.

One day maybe I will tire of playing stage manager, director, electrician, stagehand, of performing some other key role, of filming everything in my capacity as director of photography, recording it as sound engineer, leafing through that wretched script full of blanks as author, and then as dramaturg, editing and connecting the scattered dots until it all makes sense. But meanwhile I blithely keep on directing my theatre of shadows, my one-man-show, not least because I haven't yet assumed the role I will one day, ultimately, have to perform: that of the theatre critic to whom I must demonstrate that these odds and ends amount to something, who will watch the whole performance from start to finish and will then announce his verdict to the director, the actor in the main role, the stage designer and everyone else in the crew, all waiting there, on tenterhooks.

Zora Jesenská's parents' house in Martin: view from the street

The veranda
of the house
in Martin,
31 August 1926

THE FIRST RESOLUTE SHOW OF FORCE BY THE POLICE OF THE SLOVAK SOCIALIST REPUBLIC

ZORA JESENSKÁ, 1969

It's over! yelled my husband, who had been watching. I couldn't take it and until that moment I had just been looking out on the strangely deserted streets of Bratislava. We both rushed to the TV and stood to attention as we listened to our team sing the national anthem. As soon as the final words, "they will disappear, the Slovaks will revive", faded away, we realised that the Slovaks were indeed reviving: galloping footsteps pounded down the stairs of our block of flats, the street was filled with whooping and whistling and everyone, including the two of us, ran to Slovak National Uprising Square, transformed by the swarms of cars into something resembling London's Piccadilly and the exuberant joy of a Latin American carnival. The crowds were disturbing the peace of the night by loud whistling, both oral and instrumental, by the blowing trumpets and the honking of car horns, the banging of pots and children's rattles, as well as by chanting, an activity I readily joined in: "One – two – three – four, goaaaal!", along with the popular and rhythmical Russian chant for goal: "shay-bu- boo-booboo! Shay-bu-booboobooboo!" The cars honking also picked up on the shay-boo-booboobooboo rhythm. Everyone found their own way of expressing their joy. A group of young men were dragging along something that looked like an ancient cannon. Three young lads marched down the cold street dressed only in green shorts, but holding a flag high above their heads. In fact flags, both Slovak and Czechoslovak, were also being waved from cars. One gentleman, who evidently thought that the simple waving of hands was not sufficient, pushed one leg through his car window and was waving that. A chef in a pristine chef's hat, dressed in white from head to toe apart from "4:3" drawn in black across his chest, leapt out of another car, performed a little jig in front of it, jumped back in and drove off, no doubt to return to catering for foreign-currency tourists in a hotel. People in motorcycle sidecars wielded sticks with ribbons aflutter, as if on their way to a wedding. Tram numbers 3 and 4 had been relieved of their numbers, the crowd waving them about like victory insignia. A tram and even a rubbish truck proudly sporting the sign "Reality 4:3", joined in the exuberant celebrations. A procession several thousand strong carrying torches fashioned from blazing newspapers formed spontaneously, without orders from above and without being made to stand around for hours on end. In a word, it was a demonstration of national unity and Czechoslovak patriotism as spontaneous as can be imagined. No slogans were chanted against fraternal countries.

We spent about an hour and a half in the square, smiling with others who were smiling. Then the crowd began to rush off somewhere. "Come along with us!" a boy of about twelve shouted at us from the procession, though I don't think he was aware that this was the punchline of the well-known joke about the secret police arresting people. So we went along without a care, not stopping until we found ourselves in the vicinity of a certain building housing the headquarters of a certain institution. Only in its vicinity, and not too close to it at all in fact, since the building was securely sealed off by a barricade of wagons, the kind invented by the Hussites and last used in Bratislava before Christmas when the opening of a new department store had to be protected from crowds of overenthusiastic shoppers. No one tried to break through the barricade, or posed any threat to it. Every now and then someone whistled. Then a group started chanting one of the slogans that until a few months ago adorned many walls and fences that had since been whitewashed – telling certain people to go home. I disapproved of the shouting, but only because of its lack of effectiveness. A young man, a university student by his looks, tried to nip the shouting in the bud but it was no use, the crowd took up the slogan, roaring it out into the night at the top of their voices, to the accompaniment of whistling and hooting. Because of this, and also because we started getting cold, we headed back home. On our way we found ourselves in Záhradnícka Street, at the back of the above-mentioned building, also at a relatively safe distance from it, so that we didn't catch sight of it even from a corner of our eye. We saw only the barricade of wagons on its far side. There weren't many people here and they weren't shouting anything, nor were they telling anyone to get lost. Every now and then someone whistled again. A police officer stood in the middle of the road, and quite calmly too, not shouting at anyone and no one was shouting at him either. Suddenly a lorry arrived and people in uniform started to jump off it. I didn't feel like looking at them, assuming that these were the people who worked in that above-mentioned building, on their way home; however, as it soon turned out, I was too far away to see properly and was quite wrong. So I decided to continue on my way home, especially as the people around me, completely calm up till now, suddenly began whistling and shouting at full blast and the officer who had so far been just calmly standing there turned towards them gesturing with both hands in a measured, reproving way, roughly to the effect that: "Folks, it would be wise for you to get away from here." Without hesitating I took a side street and headed for home. But after just a few steps at my usual pace, I heard shouting behind me and found myself cut off from my companions, standing in the middle of a crowd that was fleeing in panic. Despite my age I can still run if I have to, but I was brought up with a decided reluctance to run away from anything. And so I tried simply to walk. However, people in a frantic state kept bashing into me and dragging me along. The thought crossed my mind that if someone were to be knocked to the ground, they could easily be trampled to death. At that very moment I was knocked to the ground. Getting up was out of the question so I didn't even give it a thought, and just lay there trying to protect my head, hoping against hope that people would nimbly jump over me, that not all of them would stamp on me. My wish came true, the feet moved on. I opened my eyes – after closing them instinctively earlier – and saw by my head a pair of male feet in trousers obviously part of a uniform. I confess that I felt relieved: I'm safe, this is an officer of our Police who, seeing a woman well past her prime lying on the ground trampled by the crowd, has stopped to help her to her feet and offer assistance. I reached for my handbag, which had flown out of my hands, and for my hat, which had been knocked off, and slightly raised my head. That's when I was hit by something on the head. Oddly enough, although I'd never been whacked by a truncheon before, I knew immediately that it was indeed a truncheon. I realised that I was mistaken about the intentions of this truncheon-wielding officer, although I failed to understand what he was trying to achieve by this activity. Prostrate as I was, I obviously could not run away. And since the blow from the truncheon made me once again hit my head on the ground, under these circumstances I abandoned the attempt to get up. The officer pursued the activity he had begun for a while, although I cannot claim that it was a hit-or-miss affair, as he managed never to miss my head. Then he moved off, leaving me there, lying on the ground in silence, as he shouted: "One day we will teach you a lesson, you rotten rabble!" From this I understood that (a), I am rotten rabble and (b), the phrase one day we will teach you a lesson, which in Slovak unambiguously refers to the future, made me realise that he was planning to keep me, as well as others, on the straight and narrow in a much more emphatic way. At the same time as the sound of his yelling receded, I heard a girl's concerned voice: "Can I help you? I'll see you home. Are you badly hurt? Are you in pain?" I found the street completely deserted, except for the young, frail female creature bending over me. She told me that she too had been badly beaten and that she was in a great deal of pain. But she was more concerned about my condition. Only now did it dawn on me that the reason she didn't run away from the officer's assault was that she saw me fall and wanted to come to my assistance, concerned that I wouldn't be able to walk unaided. This wasn't necessary, however, as my skull is sufficiently hard and my glasses, which had been smashed to smithereens, didn't cause any injuries to my face, let alone my eyes – even though, thinking back, I know that might easily have happened.

If you think my motivation for writing up this account is in-dignation because it happened to me rather than someone else, you are wrong. After all, the officer didn't see my face, so he could not have recognised me: he wasn't beating me up specifically, he was just beating up a grey-haired sixty-year-old woman lying in a deserted street. This experience doesn't bother me either – at least it helped me imagine what lies ahead and form an opinion about it, and I needed stronger glasses anyway. It's not even the fact that the police beat people up that I find annoying: that is, unfortunately, what they are trained to do in every country. What concerns me are what might be called civilised forms of beatings up. I don't know what went on elsewhere. But here, in this street, there was no loudspeaker announcement from the lorry that brought the officers telling people to disperse, nor was anyone given time to decide whether or not they wished to disperse. No order for people to leave was given, and the speed at which everything happened made it clear to me that all of the policemen, no sooner had they jumped off the car, immediately and without any warning, pounced on people and began beating them up. And I regard that as uncivilised behaviour regardless of which country's police it is committed by, including the Police of the Slovak Socialist Republic during what I believe was its first resolute show of force.

Zora Jesenská, *Listy*, Vol II/13, 13 April 1969, p. 7.

Agneša	journalist Agneša Kalinová (1924–2014)
Albert M	film dramaturg Albert Marenčin (1922–2019)
Alma M	translator and journalist Alma Münzová (1931–2004)
Boža R	Božena Rybáriková, Zora Jesenská's cousin
Chorváth	literary and theatre critic Michal Chorváth (1910–1982)
Darka	Darka Soroková, ophthalmologist in Martin, married to Jozef Sorok, actor
Ďuro Špitzer	writer, literary critic and historian Juraj Špitzer (1919–1995)
Edo Friš	politician, journalist, historian Eduard Friš, husband of Soňa Č (1912–1978)
Ela	translator Ela Krišková (1927–)
Ferenčík	translator Ján Ferenčík (1923–1989)
Gabo Rapoš	journalist Gabriel Rapoš (1917–1994)
Guderna	painter Ladislav Guderna (1921–1999)
Gusto	Gustáv Prokeš, "his wife's cousin's" first husband (1915–1995)
Hanka	translator Hana Kostolanská (1928–2017)
Harry	Harry Racz, husband of Zora Jesenská's Tatra cousin (1924–2008)
František Hečko	writer František Hečko (1905–1960)
his wife's cousin	Sláva, née Manicová, later Prokešová, later Roznerová, (1918–2014)
Huba	actor Mikuláš Huba (1919–1986)
Jelka	Jela Jesenská (1942–1970), Zora Jesenská's niece
Jozef Bžoch	literary critic Jozef Bžoch (1926–2018)
Laco	writer Ladislav Ján Kalina (1913–1981), husband of Agneša Kalinová
Laco Mňačko	reporter and writer Ladislav Mňačko (1919–1924)

Luda Škultéty	translator Ľudmila Škultétyová (1904-1992)
Magda T	translator Magda Takáčová (1924-2018), sister of Marta Ličková
Marko	journalist Miloš Marko (1922-2008)
Marta L	translator Marta Ličková (1926-2020)
Martin R	Martin Rázus, a doctor, family friend
Matuška	literary critic Alexander Matuška (1910-1975)
Mikuláš Bakoš	literary critic and translator Mikuláš Bakoš (1914-1972)
Mináč	writer Vladimír Mináč (1922-1996)
Peter	writer and playwright Peter Karvaš (1920-1999)
Petrík	literary critic Vladimír Petrík (1929-2017)
Professor Felix	literature scholar and translator Dr Jozef Felix (1913-1977)
Roman	journalist Roman Kaliský (1922-2015)
Ružena	translator Ružena Žiaranová Dvořáková (1930-2017)
the sister-in-law	Mária Jesenská (née Masárová, 1906-2009) married to Zora's brother Fedor Jesenský
Soňa Čechová	translator Soňa Čechová, wife of Edo Friš (1930-2007)
Števček	literary critic Pavol Števček (1932-2003)
the Tatra cousin	Zora Raczová (née Manicová, 1923-2009)
Tóno R	Anton Rybárik, husband of Zora Jesenská's cousin Boža
Trachta	journalist and newspaper editor Ján Trachta (1914-1993)
Viera H	translator Viera Hegerová (1933-)
Viera M	journalist Viera Millerová (1923-1977), later married to Gustáv Husák
Viera R	Viera Rázusová (née Jesenská), cousin of Zora Jesenská, wife of Martin Rázus

p. 54: *victory of the working classes* – contemporary cliché for the communist takeover in Czechoslovakia in February 1948, also referred to at the time as The Victorious February.

p. 56: *having to disown his father during, and his mother after the war* – despite having a Jewish father, Rozner was not barred from higher education under the Nazis and escaped deportation thanks to his mother being an ethnic German, which, in turn, was to be problematic for him after the war.

p. 56: *the monetary reform of 1953* – implemented by Czechoslovakia's communist government on 1 June 1953, the reform aimed to devalue the currency, put an end to rationing and the black market, and restart the economy. Presented as a victory for the working classes and a blow to the middle classes, it effectively robbed ordinary people of their savings (which, on average, shrank to one-tenth of their original value).

p. 67: *the korzo* – in most towns and cities in the Austro-Hungarian empire a street or two in the centre where (mostly) young people would go for a stroll in the evenings to meet their peers and flirt. Bratislava's *korzo*, which survived into the early 1970s, started at Hviezdoslav Square, and comprised Rybárska Brána and Michalská Street all the way to St Michael's Tower, where the promenaders would turn around and retrace their steps.

p. 73: *First Secretary Gustáv Husák* – Gustáv Husák (1913–1991) was a Slovak politician, who joined the communist party aged 16, was one of the leaders of the Slovak National Uprising in 1944 and after the war headed the devolved administration of Slovakia. He was imprisoned in the 1950s on charges of "bourgeois nationalism", sentenced to life imprisonment and served six years. After the crushing of the Prague Spring he replaced Alexander Dubček as First Secretary of the Communist Party of Czechoslovakia, becoming the country's President in 1975. In this book, he is also referred to as "Highly-Placed" and "the man who had climbed the greasy pole to unexpected heights".

p. 140: *those who preferred democratisation to federalisation* – a split between those supporters of the Prague Spring in Slovakia who prioritised liberalising the system and increasing democratic freedoms on the one hand and on the other, the nationally oriented ones who sought a greater degree of autonomy within Czechoslovakia and promoted a change in the country's structure from being a single unit to becoming a federation. The federal system, adopted in 1968, was among the few reforms to survive the Prague Spring.

p. 149: *a Londoner* – here a person who spent the war in exile in London and supported the Czechoslovak government-in-exile based there.

p. 149: *the great show trials* – reference to the infamous Stalinist trials of the 1950s, specifically the one held in Prague in 1952 known as the Slánský Trial after the main defendant Rudolf Slánský, in which 14 top communist party officials were convicted on trumped-up charges. Eleven of them were executed.

p. 150: *your Czech mate* – Ladislav (Laco) Mňačko (1919–1994), the celebrated Slovak journalist and writer was actually born in Valašské Klobouky in Moravia, although he grew up and lived in Slovakia until he emigrated in 1968.

p. 156: *Weiner-Kráľ* – Imro Weiner-Kráľ (1901–1978) Slovak painter and graphic artist

p. 168: *Voskovec and Werich* – Jiří (George) Voskovec (1905–1981) and Jan Werich (1905–1980), outstanding figures in the Czech avantgarde theatre between the wars, founders of the legendary Osvobozené divadlo (Liberated Theatre) where they performed their plays as well as songs composed by Jaroslav Ježek (1906–1942), including *Proti větru* (Against the Wind), written in 1935 in response to the rising Nazi threat.

p. 177: *Löbl* – Eugen Löbl (1907–1987), Slovak left-wing intellectual and politician. Sentenced to life imprisonment in 1952 for "treason, espionage, and sabotage", pardoned and rehabilitated in 1963. Emigrated to the US after the Soviet-led invasion of Czechoslovakia.

p. 178: *Munich* – the Munich Agreement, a settlement reached by Germany, Great Britain, France and Italy in September 1938, which allowed the German annexation of the Sudetenland, leading ultimately to the dismantling of Czechoslovakia.

p. 179: *old Pressburgers* – Bratislava was historically known as Pressburg in German and Pozsony in Hungarian, with the current Slovak name adopted in 1919.

p. 182 – *The Jewish Centre* (Ústredňa Židov) was created in 1940 by the government of the wartime Slovak Republic, ostensibly to represent the Jewish population and look after its economic, cultural and social needs. Membership in it was compulsory and, like the Judenrate set up in countries under Nazi occupation, it served as an instrument of anti-Jewish policies and assisted with deportations.

p. 186: *arrived from Košice* – in April 1945, an agreement known as the Košice Government Programme was signed in the eastern Slovak city by the Czechoslovak Communists who had spent the war in the Soviet Union and the Czechoslovak government-in-exile based in London, setting out the principles of postwar policies.

p. 203: *series of articles about people from 1968* – a six-part series of antisemitic articles published in 1970 in the Slovak communist party daily *Pravda* and its Czech equivalent *Rudé právo,* entitled "Židovská otázka u nás neexistuje" (1970, The Jewish Question Does Not Exist in This Country), which summarised the book *Sionizmus a antisemitismus* (Zionism and Anti-Semitism) by František J. Kollár.

p. 211: *Karel Kryl record* – "Bratříčku, zavírej vrátka" (Close the Gate, Little Brother), an LP by the singer-songwriter Karel Kryl, which included several songs with lyrics opposing the Soviet-led invasion of Czechoslovakia.

p. 213: *Goldstücker* – Eduard Goldstücker (1913–2000), a Slovak literature scholar, diplomat, and representative of the 1968 reform movement, who in 1963 organised a conference on Franz Kafka regarded as a harbinger of the Prague Spring.

p. 227: *House of Mourning* – buildings in cemeteries constructed under communism for holding civic funerals in order to strip the ceremony of its religious content. Many are in use under this name to this day.

p. 242: *Matica Slovenská* – the oldest national and cultural institution in Slovakia, founded in 1863.

p. 261: *Košice, a city that epitomised Hungarianness* – Košice, the largest city in Eastern Slovakia, had for centuries been – like all of Slovakia – part of Greater Hungary, until the creation of Czechoslovakia in 1918. Ceded to Hungary in 1938, Košice was reincorporated into Czechoslovakia in 1945. The city used to be very multinational, with Hungarians representing the dominant ethnic group; it still has a sizeable ethnic Hungarian minority.

p. 268: *normalisation* – term covering the period following the suppression of the Prague Spring and the Soviet-led invasion of Czechoslovakia in August 1968 and lasting until the Velvet Revolution in November 1989.

p. 270: *the famous adage* – probably a reference to Hegel's dialectic, in the simplified form as it was interpreted under communism.

p. 283: *Dobroslav Chrobák – plagiarism* Slovak writer (1907–1951) best known for his novella *Drak sa vracia* (1943, Dragon's Return) was accused by Jozef Felix of plagiarising Jean Giono's novel *Un de Baumugnes*. Felix later softened his stance, stating that Chrobák drew heavily on Giono's work.

p. 293: *Aryanisation* – the transfer of Jewish-owned property to non-Jews from 1933 to 1945 in Nazi Germany, and later also in the countries that came under Nazi occupation.

p. 304: *study, study, study* – a quote from the 1899 article by Vladimir Lenin "A Retrograde Trend in Russian Social Democracy", widely used under communism to spur students to dilligence, though it was originally addressed to "...the workers, who, despite their wretched living conditions, despite the stultifying penal servitude of factory labour, possess so much character and will-power that they study, study, study, and turn themselves into conscious Social-Democrats—the working-class intelligentsia." (cited from the Lenin Internet Archive [2003]).

p. 314: *Štefánik* – Milan Rastislav Štefánik (1880–1919), Slovak politician, diplomat, aviator and astronomer, together with Thomas Masaryk and Eduard Beneš, one of the founding fathers of the Czechoslovak Republic.

p. 320: *the greatest show trial of them all* – reference to the Slánský Trial, see note relating to p. 112.

p. 350: *her parents' residence* – the Jesenský family home was pulled down in the mid 1970s to make way for a new four-lane road.

p. 355: *gadjos* – In Romani culture, a gadjo (masculine) or gadji (feminine) is a person who is not an ethnic Romani, or an ethnic Romani who does not live within Romani culture.

(462)

p. 360: *victory of the Czechoslovak ice hockey team against the Soviets* – in March 1969 Czechoslovakia defeated the Soviet Union, leading to spontaneous demonstrations up and down the country. Zora Jesenská's account of the police crackdown is reproduced on pp. 453–457.

p. 396: *National Committee* – the name of municipal councils between 1945 and 1990.

p. 397: *Sakharov's long memorandum* – probably a reference to the memorandum sent by the Russian dissident Academician Andrei Sakharov to the Soviet leader Leonid Brezhnev on 5 March 1971, outlining his proposed solutions to the country's urgent problems.

p. 397: *Hey Slovaks* – a hymn penned in 1834 by the Lutheran priest and poet Samuel Tomášik and, as 'Hey Slavs', later adopted by other Slavonic nations: versions exist in Croatian, Czech, Polish, Russian, Serbian, Slovene and Ukrainian. It was adopted as its national anthem by the wartime Slovak republic.

p. 398: *his wife's grandfather* – Zora Jesenská's grandfather, Ján Baltazár Jesenský-Gašparé (1825–1889), a descendant of a noble family, was a lawyer and politician who co-founded the Slovak National Party and helped to found Matica slovenská.

p. 430: *Živena* - The oldest women's organisation in Slovakia, founded in 1869 in Martin, with the aim of educating Slovak women in finance, cooking, raising children as well as culture. It published a number of periodicals, including the literary journal *Živena*, which Zora Jesenská edited from 1939 to 1949.

p. 433: *a certain Mr Beria* – Lavrentiy Pavlovich Beria (1899–1953) was a Soviet politician and head of the Soviet security and police apparatus, remembered chiefly as the executor of the final stages of Joseph Stalin's Great Purge of the 1930s, who eventually fell victim to the apparatus he created: he was arrested in July 1953 and executed.

p. 434: *testimonies heard on the radio recently* – another reference to the Slánský trial, see note relating to p. 112.

p. 438: *the Sudeten German Henlein party* – Konrad Henlein (1898-1945), founder of the Sudeten German Party of Czechoslovakia (Sudetendeutsche Partei), which campaigned for the annexation of the Sudetenland by Germany. The party later merged with the Nazi party.

The family in the reception room: father Fedor, mother Milina, grandmother Jesenská, Zora Jesenská, brother Fedor

Zora Jesenská's niece Jelka, Zora Jesenská and Ján Rozner on a hike in the Tatras, 1960

A REPORT FROM A LIFE
IN THE AFTERMATH OF A FIASCO
AFTERWORD
IVANA TARANENKOVÁ

The autobiographical novel *Seven Days to the Funeral* appeared in 2009, three years after the death of its author, Ján Rozner. The circumstances of its origin and publication themselves are reminiscent of the twists and turns of a novel – a lost manuscript that comes to light all of a sudden and achieves unexpected success. The author had spent thirty years writing his book in exile in Germany in the language of a culture from which he had gradually vanished. Only his closest friends were aware that he had been writing throughout these years. The book's publication on the cusp of the second decade of the new millenium, in a version edited by his widow Sláva Roznerová, turned out to be a major literary event. Acclaimed by the critics and the reading public alike, the book was also a commercial success in terms of Slovakia's small book market, later even spawning an award-winning theatre production. In the following years two further books from the author's archive were published.

Before his novel came out, Ján Rozner's name meant little to anyone except a handful of experts on the Slovak literature of the 1950s and 1960s, when he was known as a fierce and intellectually knowledgeable participant in the country's cultural life – as a critic and a journalist and later also a translator, though not as a writer in his own right. The few marginal references to him in literary discourse tended to reference the hardline campaigns against manifestations of "bourgeois" art (a label that was applied liberally to any work of art, from the avantgarde to existentialism) that he was actively involved in at the peak of Stalinism. Key historical events, such as the death of Stalin and of the Czechoslovak communist leader Klement Gottwald, and the exposure of the cult of personality together with the liberalisation that followed, resulted in Rozner, like many of his generation, opening his eyes and revising his views. And, like many of his peers who threw their energies into attempts to democratise the regime during the Prague Spring, Rozner fell victim to the political purges that followed the Soviet-led invasion of Czechoslovakia in August 1968: during the era known as normalisation he lost his job, was banned from working and publishing, and was banished from public life, as was his first wife, Zora Jesenská, whose political views had also made her a *persona non grata*. After her death Rozner remarried and in 1976 emigrated to West Germany with his second wife.

Finding himself excluded from public life, Rozner did not join the burgeoning dissident movement while he remained in Czechoslovakia. Nor did he actively participate in any public activities after leaving the country, except for the occasional contribution to exile periodicals, particularly the Czech-Slovak journal *Listy* published in Rome, where a few excerpts from his work-in-progress appeared. A sample published in the Slovak literary journal *Slovenské pohľady* in the early 1990s failed to attract much attention. After 1989, Rozner chose not to return to his homeland and died in 2006 in Munich, where he is buried.

Until the publication of *Seven Days to the Funeral* Ján Rozner was forgotten not once but several times. Expunged from the nation's cultural memory by the communist regime, one of the reasons why he missed out on being "rediscovered" during the hectic 1990s was that during this decade, rather than reflecting on the past, Slovak literature gave priority to exploring the new creative possibilities afforded not only by the changed political and social context but also by postmodern poetics.

While drawing on his personal life and the specific Slovak context, Rozner's novel transcends both. Its explicitly autobiographical plot is framed by the events of the seven days leading up to the funeral of the author's first wife, Zora Jesenská, who succumbed to leukaemia on 21 December 1972. This highly intimate situation – the death of his spouse, preparations for her funeral, grieving the loss of the person closest to him and reminiscing about her – forms the base to which further layers are added, enriching the narrative with a cultural, historical and social dimension.

Rozner and Jesenská were among the first cultural figures in Slovakia to be blacklisted following the suppression of the Prague Spring in 1968. Zora Jesenská was a preeminent translator, a trailblazer in the modern school of translation. A specialist in Russian literature, she also translated from German and French and, jointly with her husband, English as well. She became a household name after her translation of Boris Pasternak's *Doctor Zhivago* – one of the first in the Eastern bloc – was published as late as 1969, during the final throes of the Prague Spring.

Jesenská was the scion of a prominent and highly cultured family in Martin, a small town whose size and provincial air belied the central role it played in Slovak national life from the middle of the nineteenth century until the foundation of Czechoslovakia in 1918. Her ancestors first left their mark on the Slovak national movement back in 1848, when Europe and indeed the world was in the grip of national revolutions. Zora Jesenská's uncle was the distinguished writer Janko Jesenský (1874-1945), a classic figure in Slovak literature. Thus she was descended from a line that epitomised the national as well as the civic traditions of Slovak culture that the communist regime did not manage to challenge even in the Stalinist 1950s.

With his background, Ján Rozner was the epitome of the exact opposite of this tradition, a man of "alien", "un-Slovak" origin. The offspring of an impecunious Jewish father and German mother, he was born in Bratislava. Before it became the capital of Slovakia, Rozner's hometown, which features prominently in his writing, was a multicultural city inhabited by Germans, Hungarians and Jews and was only gradually Slovakised after the end of the First World War. It is one of the ironies of fate that this man, who was firmly embedded in the fabric of the city and epitomised its heterogeneous nature, came to be regarded an "alien element" and a constant object of suspicion.

Because of the disparity between their family backgrounds and the age difference between them – not least the fact that she was 13 years older – as well as Rozner's involvement in the vitriolic cultural campaigns of the 1950s (in fact, the couple met as a result of the tumultuous polemic triggered by Jesenská's translation of Mikhail Sholokhov's novel *And Quiet Flows the Don*), the relationship between Rozner and Jesenská ruffled many feathers in contemporary Slovakia and was regarded as a *mésalliance* by Jesenská's family. She was the one with a "pedigree", the embodiment of the "patrician tradition" of Slovak culture that evolved during its relatively short history, while he was a man of "dubious" origins, an "upstart", in the words of one of her relatives, enjoying his temporary moment in the sun thanks to the communist takeover of 1948. Nevertheless, their partnership proved to be rather satisfactory and also worked on the professional level. They cooperated on a number of translation projects, including the translation into Slovak of several plays by Shakespeare.

Being among those who in the 1960s supported the strivings for the reform and democratisation of the system, the couple were profoundly affected by, and opposed, the Soviet-led invasion. The final straw resulting in their banishment from public life was the publication of an article by Zora Jesenská in the Prague journal *Listy* (reproduced on pp. 453–457 of this volume). This article, entitled "The First Resolute Show of Force by the Police of the Slovak Socialist Republic", is an account of how she took part in a spontaneous celebration of the Czechoslovak ice hockey team's defeat of the Soviet Union in March 1969, which snowballed into a protest against the invasion and ended with the 60-year-old writer being beaten up by the police.

With the onset of normalisation, Rozner and Jesenská, like many other intellectuals who refused to conform to the regime, were gradually deprived of every opportunity to work. Publishers stopped commissioning translations from them, their names could not be uttered in public, and their books were withdrawn from circulation, including from bookshops and libraries. They also found themselves ostracised in their private lives, shunned by some of their friends and acquaintances, and found little understanding of their principled stance even among their relatives.

In the end, the communist regime even stuck its petty claws into Zora Jesenská's funeral. The secret police disrupted the actual ceremony. Jesenská's friends in her native town of Martin, where the funeral was held, were instructed to stay away, and the secret police scrutinised every aspect of the ceremony, right up to the choice of music. The distinguished translator Jozef Felix, a highly-regarded expert on classical literature (he translated Dante, for example) lost his position as professor at the university because he gave a eulogy at Jesenská's funeral. All this was part and parcel of the repressive practices of the regime that persecuted its opponents even beyond the grave, denying them a dignified funeral. The secret police's intervention at Jesenská's funeral in Martin was a tragicomic farce with distressing professional consequences for those involved. Five years later in Prague, at the funeral of the philosopher Jan Patočka, it assumed grotesque dimensions, with helicopters flying above mourners' heads and mass arrests made at the cemetery itself.

However, the novel *Seven Days to the Funeral* transcends the confines of a testimony of the period and the communist regime's authoritarian practices. It is a remarkable work of literature which makes full use of the modernist narrative toolkit, balancing on the cusp of fact and fiction (Albert Marenčin, the publisher of Rozner's novel in Slovakia, has pointed out that the author's ambition was "to write a Joycean novel, without paragraph breaks, comprised of long sentences, a continuous narrative"). It is a book of reminiscences which, at the same time, interrogates the resources of human memory and freely admits that our memories can be equally the result of intentional or unintentional creativity by the human mind.

The novel's composition is framed by the seven days that pass between the death of the author's wife and the funeral itself. The meticulously segmented chapters constitute, in fact, a countdown from one key event to the next. For the protagonist, these seven days play the role of a transit station between two periods of his life. While one life, that bound up with his wife, is coming to an end, another is undoubtedly about to begin, one which the protagonist no longer expects anything from. Beset by a personal catastrophe that has torn his life apart, he fills his time with the preparations for the funeral and reminisces about his wife, parents, friends and his native city, as well as the key social events that had determined their life.

Rozner's writing is marked by a distinct emotional distance, emphasised by the third-person narration, which is atypical of autobiographical texts. The narrator is a fastidious analyst, maniacally striving to capture every detail right down to the most minute, an endeavour that can at times feel mannered. Banal activities such as the heating up of a meal or the watering of plants alternate with methodical preparations for the funeral. The activities relating to the funeral – drafting the death notice, choosing an epigraph, drawing up a list of people to send the death notice to, as well as dealing with the official paperwork (such as handing in the deceased's ID card and applying for her death certificate) act as triggers for a stream of memories. At the same time, they enable the author to highlight aspects of the modern era that have broken down mourning and traditional funeral rites into a series of banal, mechanical and bureaucratic acts. Although neither Rozner nor Jesenská were religious, the protagonist at one point recalls, somewhat nostalgically, the ceremonial nature of church funerals, in which an individual becomes part of a ritual that transcends them and where everything is carried out within a rigid dramaturgical framework.

For this is the role the protagonist adopts in the course of the narrative, putting on the hat of a meticulous dramaturg who stages the events so that the farewell to his wife is a dignified public event. He suppresses his emotions, reviewing them rationally while trying to expunge them in order to remain focused. What makes his task more difficult is that the funeral ceases to be a private affair and assumes political and social dimensions.

There is a further dimension, public if not overtly political, to be considered. Jesenská's background, which had cast a shadow over her private life with Rozner, is also reflected in the preparations for the funeral. His private grieving is under constant scrutiny of those who see Jesenská primarily through the lens of her cultural and public role. Seeing her primarily in her capacity as a member of a distinguished family and a cultural figure, her family and relatives expect her funeral to reflect this. However, in the eyes of the protagonist, such formalities depersonalise and invalidate the intimate dimension of the event.

Just as he stages his wife's funeral, he also stages his memories, rarely lessening his emotional distance. A laconic reflection of his own psychological state, combined with the methodical and accurate accumulation of detail, is the only way Rozner is able to reminisce while remaining in control of the present, although this comes at the cost of slowing down the pace of the narrative. It is this constant striving for matter-of-factness and rational control that helps to keep the text in check, making it introspective and analytical without turning amorphous. However, this method is only superficially reliable. Although Rozner does not explicitly deal with the process of remembering and does not thematise the work of memory, he does subtly relativise it, only to admit at the end of the novel that rather than being a reliable testimony to the past, memory creates its own fictions and legends.

Despite being aware that his attempts to retrieve the past and arrive at "the truth" are a priori condemned to fail, Rozner does not give up trying to reconstruct his life after the departure of the person who had given it some kind of a meaning, which was the only thing left to him after losing the chance to do his work. On the personal level, in visualising his loved one and focusing on his loss, the novel bears a similarity to the genre known in classical literature as *consolatio*. The book turns into a memorial to their life together and a manifestation of grief, although this is not the sole narrative line. Another important aspect is Rozner's striving to unburden himself, marked by the constant stressing of his own insignificance and a continual sense of "alienness". Given Rozner's real-life involvement in the Slovak culture of the 1950s, however, the question might arise whether this attitude and the highlighting of the unreliability of memory is not being used as a sort of alibi to absolve himself of his past actions, or to avoid addressing them or to make light of them. The protagonist's basic attitude towards himself is one of putting himself down and treating himself with scorn, regarding himself as a weakling and intellectual fraud, a man lacking in internal discipline. His self-proclaimed position as an outsider can be a form of escape as well as a source of frustration and self-contempt.

The novel highlights the binary nature of the everyday. On the one hand, it represents an escape from the impact of political reality and the pressures exerted by the regime. Jesenská, who is no longer allowed to translate, tends her garden outside their apartment block, grows her collection of house plants and takes up cooking.

The state of living in inertia, impotent lethargy and stultifying banality is juxtaposed to the active public life in which both husband and wife had been involved and from which they were excluded. What they were deprived of was a life within history, in step with the times, this loss being yet another aspect of their lives' failure on which *Seven Days to the Funeral* sheds light. This is not just a record of a personal tragedy but a Slovak variation on the theme of the Central European intellectual whose life was once lived in the flow of history, only to end on its periphery and in oblivion. This dramatic relationship to history at large has been a core topos in Central European literature since the nineteenth century, sometimes predominantly utopian in nature, at other times disillusioned. It is a relationship full of twists and turns, with history becoming a force of nature. Rozner, too, understands history as an abstract force that assails human lives from the outside, absorbing them into its flux and into its events, elevating them to the stars, only to cast them into oblivion again.

The fate portrayed in Rozner's narrative – of being displaced from history – also features in works by other Central European writers, such as Dominik Tatarka, Milan Šimečka, Milan Kundera, Ludvík Vaculík, György Konrád and many others. It is exemplified by the following quote from Milan Kundera's *Žert* (1967, *The Joke*) and the fate of the novel's protagonist, Ludvík Jahn: *The elation we experienced is commonly known as the intoxication of power, but (taking a more benevolent stance) I could choose less severe words: we were bewitched by history; we were drunk with the thought of jumping on its back and feeling it beneath us; admittedly, in most cases the result was an ugly lust for power, but (as all human affairs are ambiguous) there was still (and especially, perhaps, in us, the young), an altogether idealistic illusion that we were inaugurating a human era in which man (all men) would be neither* outside *history, no longer cringe* under the heel of history, *but direct and create it. I was convinced that far from the wheel of history there was no life, only vegetation, boredom, exile, Siberia.* (Milan Kundera, *The Joke*, 1982, translated by Michael Henry Heim, p. 61).

Whereas Rozner's novel deals with the experience of being exiled – the boredom and "Siberia" of everyday life – explicitly the boredom and "Siberia" of everyday life explicitly and in great detail, the period of his life "at the steering wheel of history" is referred to only in general terms and with profound scepticism. Instead, he focuses on the disillusionment with the ideology, on life "in the aftermath of a fiasco". He characterizes the space he inhabited as a place of constant "reversals, upheavals and disasters". The essay "Potíže Střední Evropy. Anekdota a dějiny" (The Troubles of Central Europe. Anecdote and History) by the Czech writer Josef Kroutvor, published in samizdat in 1988, offers a similar characterisation of Central European existence, subject to constant ruptures as well as the specifically local role played by the everyday: *"Central Europe does not know a continuity of history, history keeps disintegrating, giving neither the times nor individuals enough time to mature. In addition to external pressures that disrupt the historical whole, another process that takes place is one of entropy on the inside, a gradual disintegration of historical awareness is also taking place, an erosion of a decelerating reality. The fabric of history succumbs to internal and external corrosion. Everyday life becomes separated from the historical framework, settling into a private shopkeeper's life for itself, for a small circle of people. [...] The life of the Central European is filled with Biedermeier-style banality, turning into ordinary life outside of history. [...] Tiny life events, episodes, replace History with a capital H."* (Josef Kroutvor, *Potíže s dějinami*. Prague, 1990, p. 63).

It is interesting to observe how Rozner portrays representatives of the regime – be they members of the secret police, state bureaucrats, or the leading politician and epitome of the era of normalisation that followed the suppression of the Prague Spring, Czechoslovakia's President Gustáv Husák: they all remain abstract figures, impersonal executors of higher powers, without a trace of humanity. We find similar depictions of such people in others writing about this period, for example in Milan Šimečka's autobiographical work *Konec nehybnosti* [The End of Inertia], written in 1988 but not published until 1992.

Rozner situates his Central European story in the reality of Slovakia. His relationship with his wife embodies the central conflict in Slovak culture, the conflict between tradition and modernisation which persists to this day. He was a creature of the city, an urban animal, while she felt at home in a small idyllic town or in the mountains. He was fascinated by avantgarde art whereas she preferred more genteel and traditional art forms.

In many ways, Rozner was shaped by his origins, which marked him out as an outsider amid the homogeneity of Slovak culture and made him approach national myths and symbols with scepticism. In a way unusually open by Slovak standards, he comments critically, offering a worm's eye view of friends and family, and particularly of well-known public figures such as the literary critic Alexander Matuška, in a state of intoxication, spouting antisemitic slurs at the top of his voice, or the communist writer Vladimír Mináč, who in 1956 wished the Russians would drop an atomic bomb on Budapest.

However, the person for whom he reserves the greatest degree of openness and scorn is undoubtedly himself. The book is also noteworthy for painting an accurate picture of Slovak society during normalisation, a picture somewhat different from the perhaps better-known Czech situation. For Slovaks, normalisation ushered in a new federal order, which they welcomed as improving their relationship with the Czechs. And although Rozner, his wife, and others in their circle suffered under normalisation, political repression in Slovakia was generally less harsh and resistance to the regime, apart from a few exceptions, not as intense as in the Czech half of the country. The figure of President Gustáv Husák is characteristic of the contradictions of this era, when the national principle was the Slovaks' primary concern. A symbol of normalisation, Husák stood for a regime which persecuted its opponents, while at the same time being the first president of Czechoslovakia who was of Slovak origin (his role is currently being explored by many Czech and Slovak historians). These paradoxes come to the fore during the funeral itself, when one of the guests angrily comments on the "Husák regime". "*If she had said the 'communist regime', everyone would have agreed with her [...]. But bringing Husák into it was a different matter; Husák was a Slovak and he had reached the highest position in the country, higher than everyone, including the Czechs; he knew what he was doing and would figure it all out, find a way of dragging the cart out of the mud; he was the only one*

*who could manage to do it. There may have been three or four people
here who didn't think so, but for everyone else criticising Husák was
crossing a line."* (pp. 403–404)

It was precisely this openness and scepticism that resonated
with the readers of Rozner's novel. It was published in the new mil-
lennium, when Slovak literature was going through the final phase
of post-modern playfulness and casualness, and writers began to
revisit and reflect on the past. And while some Slovak authors had
more wide-ranging epic works in mind, autobiographical writing
about the past was artistically more convincing, guaranteeing as
it did personal recollections and individual experiences which
helped revive and regenerate individual, family, as well as historical, memory. However, rather than limiting themselves to bearing
witness or documenting reality, authors of autobiographical works
made full use of the potential of language and literature. Depicting
the unique individual experience through the medium of literature
they created a different level of reality, a hybrid of fact and fiction.
It is this interplay and tension between the factual and the fictive,
between authentic experience and experience recreated through
the medium of language and cultural patterns, that forms the basis
of the concept of autofiction. Autofiction, a term coined by Serge
Doubrovsky when speaking of his novel *Fils,* currently represents
a dominant trend in the context of global literature. Thus without
claiming to present an objective picture of reality, this type of
autobiographical writing ensures a reflection of personal, lived
experience which lends it veracity.

In this context, Ján Rozner's novel functioned as a message in
a bottle from the previous century. Its author may not have expected to find an audience; nevertheless, his book resonates today not
only because of its message but also its artistic form. Through an
intimate account of a man coming to terms with the loss of a loved
one, it offers today's readers an insight into the specific cultural
and historical environment of a small Central European nation
during the turbulent twentieth century, one whose ramifications
are felt to this day.

Zora Jesenská in the window of her room in Martin, 1971

Ján Rozner in the window of Zora's study (the room they kept)
overlooking the garden

A PERSONAL TRANSLATOR'S NOTE
JULIA SHERWOOD

When I first read Ján Rozner's *Seven Days to the Funeral* it struck me as a remarkable memoir and a deeply moving account of personal grief. In its honest, unsparing description of a Central European intellectual succumbing to the allure of communism, of the gradual loss of illusions, the destruction of personalities and the decimation of culture that followed the Soviet-led invasion of Czechoslovakia, it reads like a follow-up to Czesław Miłosz's *The Captive Mind*. With its ruthless and caustic portraits of key figures of Slovak culture *Seven Days to the Funeral* presents a distinctive and fascinating contribution to the cultural history of Slovakia between 1945 and 1972.

But these were not the only reasons why the book resonated with me. Rozner's merciless parsing of the period of normalisation and the devastating impact of politics on people's characters echoed the experience of my own family. And there is also a personal connection: I happened to be one of the few people aware that he had even been writing the book, as my parents had known Rozner and Zora Jesenská for many years as friends and colleagues moving in the same cultural and political circles in the Slovak capital. I remember the traumatic events surrounding Zora's funeral. And we also knew Rozner's second wife Sláva – or Slávka (neé Manicová, 1918-2014), as she was known – an otolaryngologist who tended to all our throat infections and stood by Rozner after Zora's death and, indeed, until the end of his life.

This personal connection is also reflected in the novel itself: one of the mourners at the funeral, the journalist Agneša, whom Rozner asks to write the funeral speech sketching the final years of Zora Jesenská's life, was my mother, while her husband Laco, about whom Rozner is interrogated and at whose trial he is summoned to appear as a witness, was my father, Ladislav Ján Kalina. (I am also mentioned in passing as the daughter who is away with friends when Rozner comes to ask Agneša to write the speech.)

My mother Agneša Kalinová (1924–2014) was a journalist and translator while my father Ján Ladislav Kalina (1913–1981), known as Laco to friends and family, was a satirist and film historian. He is now best remembered for his collection *One Thousand and One Jokes*, published in 1969, which sold an almost unprecedented 25,000 copies before being banned a year later.

Like Rozner, my father had been drawn to the predominantly left-leaning pre-war Czech avantgarde, and both my parents, led by their commitment to social justice as well as the experience of World War II and the Holocaust, which many of their relatives did not survive, pinned their hopes on the Soviet Union and supported the communist takeover. And like Rozner and his wife, my parents would later shed their youthful illusions about the system they had helped build and throw their weight behind the reform movement of the 1960s. Their friendship was also strengthened by their shared interest in film: Rozner was one of Slovakia's first theorists of the cinema; my mother was a film critic, while my father, as a law student in Prague in the early 1930s, supplemented his income by working at Barrandov film studios and after the war was the first head of Slovakia's Koliba film studios and later taught film history. In the era of normalisation that followed the crushing of the Prague Spring, my parents, just like Ján Rozner and Zora Jesenská, found themselves banned, blacklisted, ostracised and, eventually, even imprisoned.

My parents were both arrested in late January 1972, and while my mother was released after 10 weeks in detention, my father was convicted of "incitement" and sentenced to two years' imprisonment in what was one of the first political trials of the normalisation era. We had always assumed that the reason for their arrest was our chance discovery the previous summer of a listening device hidden in the corner of my father's study in our flat in Bratislava. My father complained about this to the highest authorities (in *Seven Days to the Funeral,* Rozner mentions that he and Zora Jesenská thought my father's complaints were futile and disapproved of them), including Communist Party Secretary General Gustáv Husák, and we thought that revenge for exposing their bungling of the surveillance operation may have been a reason why my parents were singled out for arrest. I have since learned much more from secret police files relating to my parents' case, code-named "Operation OLINA". By some fluke, the entire operational file, amounting to thousands of pages, was not destroyed after 1989 and is now held by the Institute of National Memory in Bratislava.

Information in this file was used by the American political scientist Kieran Williams as a case study in a chapter on the secret police in Slovakia under normalisation[1]. In it, Williams provides an excellent analysis and summary of my father's trial and the following very plausible explanation for why my parents were targeted:

"For a Soviet-bloc security service, someone became a person of interest – either as a suspect or potential informer – if they could be embedded in a network, and the wider the better. Thanks to the multifaceted and very public nature of their careers, the Kalinas could ostensibly be linked by the ŠtB to 536 people. Then, because they were Jewish, they could be slotted into the enemy category of 'Zionists' and connected to global conspiratorial 'centres'. Furthermore, again because of their work, they had both travelled abroad frequently, to Western film festivals and theatres. And Agneša Kalinová was particularly suspect owing to her fluency in many languages, because of which she was often contacted by Western journalists and diplomats. Such ease in multiple languages would have been especially alien to the monoglot ŠtB captain, Ján Maťáš, who was overseeing their case."

Although the secret police were in possession of hours and hours of tapes, these could not be used as evidence, and so, in the months leading up to and following my parents' arrest, scores of their friends, acquaintances and even neighbours were summoned for interrogation. All of them, except for one or two, held out very well under pressure, refusing to provide incriminating information. Nevertheless, using the information from the tapes and their tried-and-tested toolkit of manipulation and psychological pressure, the secret police were able to twist some people's words and get them entangled in their own statements, as Ján Rozner vividly describes

1   Kieran Williams: "The Czechoslovak Security Service During Normalisation: The Appearance of Success", in Kevin McDermott – Matthew Stibbe (eds.), *Czechoslovakia and Eastern Europe in the Era of Normalisation, 1969*-1989. London: Palgrave Macmillan 2022, pp. 121–143

on pp. 202–203 and 211–214. Here is Kieran Williams's excellent summary and assessment of the trial:

"With the bugs out, the ŠtB resolved to salvage OLINA by targeting Ladislav primarily on material evidence that reflected and – as the ŠtB saw it – tried to influence popular opinion: the various drafts of *A Thousand and One Jokes* and of a cabaret he scripted for the Bratislava city theatre in summer 1969; the sketch of a jokes book for publication abroad; leaflets and foreign books that he had obtained and filed away in his massive collection, some of which the bug had caught him showing to a Soviet writer in January 1971; an essay he composed in summer 1970 debunking an antisemitic conspiracy theory of the 'Prague Spring' pushed by the Slovak daily *Pravda*; and recordings of protest songs by Czech singers such as Karel Kryl that had been purchased in shops or taped from the radio, before they were banned. It was the slimmest basis for sedition charges, but the ŠtB called in almost 70 of the Kalinas' acquaintances for questioning and their testimonies would be framed to make Ladislav's professional and private interests sound sinister (later, the court's judgement would rely heavily on witness statements). The ŠtB also paid six 'experts' from the Party Central Committee and the censor's office to write 'analyses' identifying the suspect writings – including *A Thousand and One Jokes* in its final, toned-down form – as anti-socialist, anti-Soviet, and Zionist.

After their arrest on 31 January 1972, the Kalinas' main defence was that the materials that they showed or played to a few like-minded friends had never been listed on a consultable index of forbidden items and were shared only in the privacy of their home, never lent out or circulated as part of a concerted effort. To the ŠtB, however, there was no innocent private space, especially once they had punctured it with their eavesdropping; Ladislav's academic, almost ethnographic methods of collecting and categorizing jokes in a card index sounded suspiciously similar to their own work, insofar as he too was tracking popular opinion. Furthermore, the law required only that a minimum of two people be exposed to objectionable material for it to count as seditious incitement. Ladislav was sentenced by the Bratislava city court to two years in

Ilava prison, primarily for composing an essay about anti-Semitism that was never submitted to any periodical, for outlining a book of jokes that was never sent to any foreign publisher, and for playing music that had been lawfully obtained. After a clinical diagnosis of severe depression, he was released under President Svoboda's amnesty on 23 February 1973, timed to commemorate the twenty-fifth anniversary of the communist seizure of power. It also happened to be Ladislav's sixtieth birthday."

Needless to say, after his release my father was never allowed to publish anything again and spent the next few years writing his memoirs "for the drawer". My mother ended up translating computer manuals at the state company Datasystém, where Marta L, one of the translator friends and former students of Zora's mentioned in the novel, was her colleague. After graduating from secondary school, I applied to study languages and over the next five years tried my luck at various universities in Bratislava, Prague and even in Kraków, only to receive one rejection after another on the grounds of "lack of places" or "not meeting all the conditions for entry". The latter was actually quite true as I didn't meet a crucial condition: I had not been born to the right parents. Meanwhile, I worked in the technical library of a cable factory and later as a secretary at the Geological Institute. By the time my eighth attempt to go to university elicited the standard reply, we had all had enough. At that point we knew that there was a route open to those the regime regarded as undesirable. Ján and Slávka Rozner had applied for and received official permission to emigrate in 1976, as had our Prague friends, the historian Vilém Prečan and his family, who went through the same process a year later. We applied in November 1977 and moved to Germany in late October 1978.

In Munich, my mother soon found employment as a political commentator with Radio Free Europe, while I enrolled at the University of Cologne, and my father proceeded to write the book of jokes that he had been convicted for at a time when it was still only an idea in his head. The collection of political jokes, *Nichts zu lachen*, was published in 1980 and he started working on another collection but, sadly, died in early 1981 before he was able to finish it, while his second book was finalised by Ján Rozner, finally appearing in 1984 as *Das lachende Lexikon*.[2]

My parents' friendship with the Rozners continued in Germany until the end of their lives. Ján Rozner was among those who delivered a eulogy at my father's funeral in January 1981, and after I moved to London, my husband (and later co-translator) Peter and I would often see the Rozners on our visits to Munich. Although, as Ivana Taranenková notes in her afterword, Rozner shunned all involvement in exile activities, he followed political and cultural developments in Germany and elsewhere avidly. He would always have recommendations on which books to read, films to see, jazz records to buy (and the latest hi-fi system to play them on), as well as plays to see at the theatre. This was when, that is, he felt up to meeting us at all, as he was often ailing or not in the mood to see people. On those occasions he would ask his wife Slávka to convey his regards. He wasn't an easy man to live with and we had the greatest admiration for Slávka and her unwavering support of him – psychological, medical and, indeed, material – always subordinating her own needs to those of her beloved husband.

I recall Rozner mentioning that he was writing a book and that, once completed, it was sure to be one of the outstanding works of Slovak literature. But since in his view it kept falling short of his own extremely high standards, he kept rewriting it for years and

2   Kalina, Ján L.: *Nichts zu lachen. Der politische Witz im Ostblock.* (Herbig, München – Berlin, 1980); Kalina, Jan: *Das lachende Lexikon. Witze und Andekdoten von A–Z.* (Wilhelm Heyne-Verlag, München, 1984). After the fall of communism, my father's by now legendary *A Thousand and One Jokes* (*Tisíc a jeden vtip*, Obzor, 1969) was republished in Bratislava (*Tisíc a jeden vtip*, Archa, 1990), and in 2020, 50 years after the original publication, I was able to have a new edition published in Slovakia, incorporating the political jokes from my father's publications in exile (*Tisíc a jeden vtip po päťdesiatich rokoch*, Slovart, 2019). In so doing I followed the example of my mother, who had dusted off the four volumes of my father's memoirs and arranged for their publication by Marenčin PT between 1999 and 2004. Her own memoirs, *My Seven Lives: Agneša Kalinová in conversation with Jana Juráňová,* was published in 2012 (Aspekt, Bratislava) and has since appeared in Czech, German, Hungarian and English editions (*My Seven Lives. Agneša Kalinová in Conversation with Jana Juráňová* (Purdue University Press, 2022).

eventually died, leaving the manuscript unfinished. And just as she had lavished all her attention on her husband, after his death Slávka focused all her energies on completing his book. She proved to be a more than competent editor, a skill that did not come as a surprise to those who knew that in her youth she had been a promising poet in her own right.[3]

At the time Rozner started writing his book, many of the people who appeared in it were still alive and may have taken offence at, or may even have suffered, as a result of being mentioned by name if the book ever appeared. This was probably the reason why, with a few exceptions, he designated many of them only by their profession. During the editing process Slávka and her editors debated whether to insert their full names and eventually settled on a compromise solution, giving only first names, which for the majority of informed Slovak readers made it easy to identify the actual persons. As I knew many of them personally, I can vouch for the accuracy of Rozner's portrayals, from the sympathetic to the satirical – his wife's cousin, the doctor (the author's future wife Slávka), infinitely kind and practical; the brash "outlaw" reporter Roman Kaliský; the sharp-tongued translator Soňa Čechová and the traditional wafer-baking translator sisters Magda Takáčová and Marta Ličková; the preening playwright Peter (Karvaš); and Rozner's "fellow-conspirator", the writer Ladislav Mňačko, and many others. And, of course, my parents – my energetic and mercurial mother who proved a loyal friend to Rozner, and my father, with his vain hope that bombarding Communist officials with his complaints would ease his predicament.

In translating the book, we grappled with the problem of names, exacerbated by the fact that English-language readers lack this background knowledge and the fact that some of the more common first names are shared by several people. An additional problem arose because the book is written in the third person, which in English translation resulted in a confusing proliferation

3 Some of her poetry, written under her maiden name Sláva Manicová, appeared posthumously in *Potopené duše* (Sunken Souls, 2017), an anthology of forgotten Slovak women poets edited by the literature scholar Andrea Bokníková.

of third-person pronouns, making it hard to tell which "he" or "she" was being referred to. To improve the reading experience, we decided on a compromise of our own: in addition to the first names, we have provided the initial letter of the characters' surnames and appended a Who Is Who: full list of names with brief biographical information (pp. 458–459).

Recently a further link between the book and my parents came to light: Ivana Taranenková drew my attention to an August 2010 interview with Albert Marenčin, the book's Slovak publisher, who mentioned a crucial role my mother played in the book's publication, so I decided to ask him about this. He confirmed that not only was it at my mother's suggestion that Slávka Roznerová sent him the manuscript, but that her role was even more instrumental: she was the one who, after Ján Rozner's death, encouraged his widow to complete the manuscript and prepare it for publication.

Seven Days to the Funeral was published at a time when the genre of autofiction was gaining popularity. I immediately thought that this example of the genre, with its engaging mix of a profoundly personal account and an insider portrayal of a piece of cultural history, would be of interest to Anglophone readers. While visiting my mother in 2011, as a budding translator I asked Slávka for permission to translate an excerpt and submit it to a literary magazine. Her instant response was: "I was hoping you would ask me that."[4]

JS London, October 2023

---

4   The excerpt (the opening pages of the book) appeared in 2012 in the journal *Passageways*, published in the US by Two Lines Press, and a further excerpt appeared in the Prague-based journal *BODY* in 2015.

Julia Sherwood is a translator from Slovak, Czech, Polish, Russian and German into English (with Peter Sherwood), as well as into Slovak. She was born and grew up in Bratislava, Czechoslovakia (now the Slovak Republic), but studied English and Slavonic languages and literature in Cologne, London and Munich. She was editor-at-large for Slovakia for *Asymptote* from 2013 to 2023, administers the group Slovak Literature in English Translation, is the editor of Seagull Books' Slovak list and co-curates the website SlovakLiterature.com. She lives in London. Her joint translations with Peter Sherwood include Daniela Kapitáňová's *Samko Tále's Cemetery Book,* Pavel Vilikovský's *Fleeting Snow*, as well as books by Uršuľa Kovalyk, Balla and Ivana Dobrakovová, and from the Czech, *Freshta* by Petra Procházková and *Hana* by Alena Mornštajnová.

Ján and Sláva Rozner with Julia and Peter Sherwood, Munich, 1987

Peter Sherwood is a translator and critic. He was a lecturer n Hungarian at the School of Slavonic and East European Studies from 1972 to 2007. From 2008 until his retirement in 2014 he was László Birinyi, Sr., Distinguished Professor of Hungarian Language and Culture at the University of North Carolina at Chapel Hill. In 2020 he won the Árpád Tóth Prize for Translation. He has reviewed regularly for The Times Literary Supplement. He lives in London. His translations from the Hungarian include collections of essays by Béla Hamvas and Antal Szerb, most recently, Ádám Bodor's novel *The Birds of Verhovina* and Krisztina Tóth's short-story collection *Barcode*.

MODERN CZECH CLASSICS

Published titles
Zdeněk Jirotka: *Saturnin* (2003, 2005, 2009, 2013; pb 2016)
Vladislav Vančura: *Summer of Caprice* (2006; pb 2016)
Karel Poláček: *We Were a Handful* (2007; pb 2016)
Bohumil Hrabal: *Pirouettes on a Postage Stamp* (2008)
Karel Michal: *Everyday Spooks* (2008)
Eduard Bass: *The Chattertooth Eleven* (2009)
Jaroslav Hašek: *Behind the Lines: Bugulma and Other Stories* (2012; pb 2016)
Bohumil Hrabal: *Rambling On* (2014; pb 2016)
Ladislav Fuks: *Of Mice and Mooshaber* (2014)
Josef Jedlička: *Midway upon the Journey of Our Life* (2016)
Jaroslav Durych: *God's Rainbow* (2016)
Ladislav Fuks: *The Cremator* (2016)
Bohuslav Reynek: *The Well at Morning* (2017)
Viktor Dyk: *The Pied Piper* (2017)
Jiří R. Pick: *Society for the Prevention of Cruelty to Animals* (2018)
*Views from the Inside: Czech Underground Literature and Culture
(1948–1989)*, ed. M. Machovec (2018)
Ladislav Grosman: *The Shop on Main Street* (2019)
Bohumil Hrabal: *Why I Write? The Early Prose from 1945 to 1952* (2019)
*Jiří Pelán: *Bohumil Hrabal: A Full-length Portrait* (2019)
*Martin Machovec: *Writing Underground* (2019)
Ludvík Vaculík: *A Czech Dreambook* (2019)
Jaroslav Kvapil: *Rusalka* (2020)
Jiří Weil: *Lamentation for 77,297 Victims* (2021)
Vladislav Vančura: *Ploughshares into Swords* (2021)
Siegfried Kapper: *Tales from the Prague Ghetto* (2022)
Jan Zábrana: *The Lesser Histories* (2022)
Jan Procházka: *Ear* (2022)
A World Apart and Other Stories: Czech Women Writers at the Fin de Siècle,
trans. and ed. by Kathleen Hayes (2022)
Libuše Moníková: *Transfigured Night* (2023)

Forthcoming
Beyond the World of Men: Women's Fiction at the Czech Fin de Siècle,
trans. and ed. Geoffrey Chew
Jiří Weil: *Moscow – Border*
Ivan M. Jirous: *End of the World. Poetry and Prose*
Jan Čep: *Common Rue*
Egon Bondy: *Invalidní sourozenci*
Jaroslav Hašek: *The Good Soldier Schweik*

*Scholarship

MODERN SLOVAK CLASSICS

Published titles
Ján Johanides: *But Crime Does Punish* (2022)
Ján Rozner: *Seven Days to the Funeral*

Forthcoming
Alfons Bednár: *Hodiny a minúty*
Leopold Lahola: *Posledná vec*
František Švantner: *Nevesta hôľ*
Gejza Vámoš: *Atómy Boha*